Paul Hughes was born in South Wales and, as a professional squash player, represented both Wales and England. He also played Subbuteo for Great Britain and won more than 100 caps representing Wales.

He now lives happily in the sunny south of France with his wife and two cats.

THE PROPHECY

THE PROPHECY

Paul Hughes

ATHENA PRESS
LONDON

THE PROPHECY
Copyright © Paul Hughes 2008

All Rights Reserved

No part of this book may be reproduced in any form
by photocopying or by any electronic or mechanical means,
including information storage or retrieval systems,
without permission in writing from both the copyright
owner and the publisher of this book.

ISBN: 978 1 84748 360 7

First published 2008 by
ATHENA PRESS
Queen's House, 2 Holly Road
Twickenham TW1 4EG
United Kingdom

Printed for Athena Press

To my wife Karen, who convinced me to use a laptop instead of writing the entire book by hand, and everyone at Athena who brought the project to fruition.

Prologue

The link between the powerful minds of the Spellweavers had been formed.

The ether tingled with their presence. These mighty creatures of almost pure energy occupied, at this moment, an area of space and time that no human had seen or ever would.

Once contact had been made, The First initiated communication.

THE FIRST: The girl and the man have moved.

THE SECOND: A power surge caused an opening.

THE THIRD: It is as I said. They are breaking down.

THE SECOND: The energy leaks into the land.

THE FIRST: It is as foretold.

THE THIRD: But it is too early.

THE FOURTH: It is as I have said before. The loss of the book has caused this.

THE SECOND: The book cannot be read by any but the Weavers.

THE FOURTH: So you say, but they are opening.

THE THIRD: Until then we continue to watch and keep records.

The link was severed but the air still tingled with the power that had been generated. The Spellweavers had returned once more to do what they did best: record and manipulate until the gods returned once more to their children.

Chapter One

Yorda could see the bird tapping out his name on the door with its beak. After each third tap it would stop, turn its head stare at the young man, and then say in a voice that he certainly never expected from a woodpecker, 'Why don't you answer?'

What mystified Yorda about this was not so much the question but the voice. I know woodpeckers think, but I've never heard one talk! he thought to himself. Three more taps – tap... tap... tap – and again the tilt of the head, followed by the same question, 'Why don't you answer?' The only difference was that this time the bird was speaking even louder. Once more the woodpecker pulled back his head to deliver another set of taps, but before the beak touched the wood the whole scene disappeared, only to be replaced by sunlight flooding through a small window at the side of Yorda's bed.

The bird might have gone, but the tapping was still there, as was the voice. Yorda realised that he had been dreaming and the noise that had woken him was his old friend Martin, hammering at the door. He had no idea how long Martin had been there. In his dream the woodpecker had tapped out his name on the door and called him five times, but he had no way of knowing whether that meant that Martin had called him five times, twenty-five times or only the once.

'Why don't you answer, Yorda?' came the cry again, followed by a much louder rapping on the door. Finally Yorda was fully awake and called back, 'I'm coming, Martin.' At least that was what he had intended to say, but all that he managed was a slight gurgle and a little gasp of air.

Waking up had always been a problem for Yorda. As a young child he had loved staying up late, talking to his father about the stars in the sky, asking his mother about the trees and plants that surrounded their little hut or about the animals that always seemed to be nearby. The problem with being allowed to stay up late was that he just couldn't get up in the morning.

As he grew up, Yorda found that his waking and sleeping hours stayed constant so even now, at the age of nineteen, he still had problems getting out of bed. Today was no exception.

'I'm coming, Martin,' he repeated as he stumbled to the door. This time his voice sounded stronger. The door opened, revealing a middle-aged man clothed in a long woollen cape, which shielded him against the morning frost. It was strange to see a man so obviously worried about being cold, covering himself with this warm cape and yet leaving his head completely devoid of any hair or covering. This seemed to be the fashion at the moment, although it was one that Yorda, who was very proud of his long flowing locks, refused to follow.

'What's the problem, Martin?' Yorda asked. His voice was still not completely awake yet and sounded croaky even to his own ears.

'Another two cases,' stated Martin even before the door was fully opened.

'Oh no!' Yorda breathed. 'Both children?'

'Yes, two sisters,' Martin answered.

Yorda turned away. 'Come in and you can tell me who they are while I get my pouch.'

Yorda walked back inside. He opened a few more shutters to let in some more light. Martin followed close behind him. This wasn't the first time Martin had been inside, but he was still amazed at how a home could be so clean and yet so incredibly untidy. Martin could see the door to Yorda's bedroom open on the other side of the room. This room contained a small stove close to the door with a table and four small chairs next to it. A couple of lower-level tables were in the opposite corner, small pouches covering their surface. Martin noticed that each pouch was fastened with a different-coloured ribbon.

And a different smell, he thought, as he passed the first small table. His nose screwed up involuntarily, but almost instantly a much more pleasant smell filled his nostrils as he turned his head towards another pouch. There were several mortars and pestles in evidence, some perfectly clean, others with powders, nuts or other indistinguishable, partially crushed objects inside. Many books, all of which seemed to be open, were strewn about the room. The most amazing thing he noticed, though, was that there was not a speck of dust to be seen.

Martin lifted his head and saw Yorda looking at him. 'As I said, they are sisters, aged about six and nine. Symptoms started last night but, as with the other cases, they took a turn for the worse in the early hours of this morning.'

Yorda started towards the door. 'And I suppose they had both been to the city yesterday?'

Martin followed him out. The sun was now showing through the trees and the morning frost was already starting to disappear. It promised to be a lovely day. 'Yes, they went into the market early and arrived home late in the afternoon. I really cannot understand it. We've had five cases in less than a week. You say it's nothing to be concerned about but I don't think it's natural!'

Martin stopped talking as he hoisted himself up onto his horse. Yorda remained standing next to Martin's horse. He usually preferred to walk or run everywhere. He looked up at Martin while stroking the stallion's ears. 'Yes and yes! There is nothing to be concerned about because with treatment the girls will be fine by tonight. You are right, though: it certainly isn't natural. This is a new illness that we have never seen before.' Yorda hesitated, looked up at Martin, and carried on. 'At least not here.'

Martin took the reins of his horse and they set off towards the village, Yorda jogging alongside Martin but still managing to talk without breathing hard.

Yorda was thinking. Everyone was calling this illness 'voice-kill'. Only pre-pubescent children would contract it. The symptoms were very simple: a temperature followed by a sore throat and then loss of voice. Nothing serious. Normally if the child was kept warm then the fever would pass after three or four days and the voice would return in about two or three weeks – very annoying and not very pleasant, but hardly life threatening. With the correct treatment the child could recover completely in a matter of hours.

The first case had been discovered in the village a couple of weeks ago but Yorda had heard of cases in the city over the past two months. Yorda had been in the town having a quiet ale with

Ron and Jel, two local farmers. Jel had told him how his daughter had just recovered from a fever but could no longer talk other than in a slight whisper. He had not been overly concerned about the fever. He had kept her warm and given her plenty of hot soups and broths and she had soon started to recover, but he was at a loss to explain the disappearance of her voice. He'd asked Yorda to have a look at her. Later that afternoon, Yorda went to Jel's home and examined his daughter, Julonne. There was no inflammation in her throat; she had no pain or discomfort when eating or swallowing. She had lost a little weight but nothing to be overly concerned about. The only signs of any problem still existing were some small white spots at the back of her throat. Yorda could dimly remember reading in one of his medical books about a similar complaint but he had never seen an actual case. An infusion of burrowroot was suggested and within two days Julonne was in full voice.

Since then, Yorda had treated eight children, all successfully. All of the children in the village who had contracted voicekill had been in the city either the same or the previous day, and none of the infected children had passed their symptoms on. As a healer he felt it his duty not only to cure but also to find the source of the illness, so he had determined to go to the city today – if he could wake up in time. Martin's insistent knocking on the door had saved him the trouble of waking himself up.

Martin and Yorda chatted intermittently on the way to Darren's home. Most of the talk was Martin playfully ribbing Yorda about the baker's daughter's interest in the young healer. Yorda blushed. He had noticed Ivaine a lot more recently. She no longer seemed to be the childish little crybaby he remembered. She had, almost overnight – at least in Yorda's eyes – blossomed, and become much less of a little girl and more of an exciting young woman. In fact now that he was reminded of her, most unsuitably by Martin, he would try to get a little present for her while in the city.

They had arrived at Darren's little cottage and were welcomed inside. Yorda went straight to the bedroom where the girls were in bed. Both had a high temperature but had not yet lost their voices or developed the little white spots in their throats.

'Good, you called me early enough to nip the problem in the bud.' Yorda turned and smiled at Darren. 'If you could leave me now, just for two minutes.'

He turned back towards the girls and unclipped his pouch. Reaching inside, he pulled out a little vial of blue liquid. He turned towards the girls and unstopped the vial. Very carefully he put two drops on the forehead of each girl. As he did so he whispered a couple of words. For an instant the liquid in the vial and on the girls' heads glowed slightly and then returned to the pale blue it had been before. At the same moment, the girls' breathing became softer as they gently relaxed and fell into a peaceful sleep.

Yorda touched their foreheads with the back of his hand. 'Good, the fever's gone.' He rose and went back into the living room. 'They will be as right as rain and very hungry when they wake tonight.'

Darren asked him how much he owed, at which Yorda smiled. 'A few of those ripe apples I saw hanging on your tree would do nicely and, as usual, a promise that you treat all your animals well. Three apples will keep my stomach full while I walk into the city. I think it's about time I found out what is causing all our children to become sick.'

Darren thanked Yorda and plucked six apples off the first tree they came to.

'If you need three to go into the city, you will need another three for the return journey.'

Yorda thanked Darren and bade his leave. The young healer took a bite from one of the apples, relishing the sweet juicy taste, and started to jog towards Parkent. He was so involved in his own thoughts that he didn't notice his jog becoming a slow run, then a fast run, and finally a sprint which would have left even the swiftest horse in his wake.

Chapter Two

Parkent was not a large city. It had grown up along the banks of the River Solne. Traders would come to the city from far and near to sell and buy almost any type of goods imaginable. In the past fifty years, what had been a few small villages had gradually grown and merged to form this small city.

Yorda had not been to the city very often. Anything he needed could be found back in the forest and his own village, so he had no real need to come here. Sometimes, if there was a passing troupe of musicians or actors, he would make an effort to see them. He had always loved music and wished he had learnt to play an instrument when he was younger. His mother had sung to him as a child and he seemed to remember her voice being like the water flowing gently down the mountainside. She would sing lullabies that made him think of a breeze blowing through the flowers in the meadows. His father would hum along and, although he seldom did more than hum, words would always form in Yorda's mind that seemed to emanate from his father – words that came from a language he didn't understand but which seemed important to him. When the songs were finished, sometimes he would ask his parents where the words came from. They would just smile and say that the words were memories that were not yet awakened.

A small crowd was gathered on the southern road into the city. They were watching a man who was obviously in great difficulty with his horse. It appeared that the horse had reared up, throwing his rider, who had managed to keep control of the reins and was now frantically trying to keep himself from being hit by the hooves. The horse was bucking and kicking and obviously in great distress. Yorda moved nearer and gently leaned towards the horse's mind.

'Ah... the horse has been frightened by a snake,' Yorda said quietly to himself. Yorda stayed with the animal. 'No... several snakes… on the road… still there in front.' Yorda could see no snakes but the horse obviously still could. Gently he reached out and showed the horse the road through his eyes. 'There are no snakes. No snakes.'

The horse started to relax and the image of the snakes disappeared. Yorda pulled back and looked around. There were no snakes anywhere, but the horse had seen them. By now the rider had control of his mount and was talking to him and cajoling him. Yorda was pleased. The man obviously knew his animal and was giving him plenty of time before trying to remount him. A lot of bad horsemen would have been taking the whip to their steed for throwing them for no apparent reason.

The crowd disappeared and Yorda walked on into the city. Two eyes followed his motion. The owner of the two eyes turned away, a smile upon his lips, and looked once more at the horse. 'No more snakes. No more snakes.' He turned and followed Yorda into the city.

Yorda much preferred the company of animals to people, which was the main reason he lived in the village and came to the city infrequently, but when he did make the effort to come he was always pleasantly surprised at the smells that seemed to assail his senses. To Yorda there was no such thing as a nasty smell or a nice smell – just a smell. In fact, not just a smell; every smell had to have a source. For instance, the man who had just passed him: his sweat was two, maybe three days old. He was dressed in fine quality clothes, walked with an air of confidence and had fairly new riding boots on. Yorda assumed that he was someone from out of town – maybe three days' ride away – who had just arrived and was looking for an inn to get some warm food and a hot tub of water to wash himself. The next smell was of cooking meat. Pork. The smell was not quite right, however; a slight undercurrent suggested that whoever ate this pork had better not be far from a quiet spot because it would not stay too long in the stomach. Another scent wafted over from his right – A particularly fine ale if I am not mistaken, thought Yorda. He turned towards the Lantern, a small inn that he would drink at on his rare excursions to Parkent. The landlord knew Yorda, not because he was a regular but because he only ever ate fruit with his drink.

'Hello, young fellow. Some ale and a fine vintage apple?'

'Good to see you, Josh. Just a drink today. This ale you are selling: it's the first time you have had this one.'

Josh lifted his head to look at Yorda.

'That nose of yours! You haven't even tasted it, yet you know it's a different brew. Came in yesterday. A new brewery has started up downriver in the fen district. It's good stuff.'

'You never serve bad ale, Josh, which is more than can be said of some of the taverns here.'

'Anyway, Yorda, what brings you to Parkent?'

Yorda knew Josh well enough not to take offence at his direct question. Josh was interested in everyone and everything. There wasn't much that went on in the city that Josh didn't know about.

'Voicekill. Wow, that ale is really good. If I'm not mistaken there is a tiny bit of cardws salt in there. Have you heard of many cases?'

'You know your ale, young fellow. Yes, nasty little bug. Most of the children have had it. Never seen the likes before. I said to a few folks that you were the guy to see to get their children well quickly, but the local physician seemed to get the kids back to form in a couple of weeks. People seem to be moving away from the more natural ways of healing and drifting towards these new physicians. I think if it was more serious, however, you would have had some people turning up on your doorstep.'

'You know that they are all welcome, Josh. If I can help, man or animal, I will.'

'I know that, son. Anyway, enjoy your ale. I have some customers with empty pots over there.'

Yorda looked around the inn. He spotted an empty table in the corner, went over and sat down, facing away from most of the clients. He had not been seated long when a voice just behind him said, 'It's not natural – voicekill.'

Yorda turned his head towards the voice and saw a tall man with long blond hair standing beside him. The voice seemed to be as light and happy as a young child's and yet as strong and old as a seasoned warrior's. He smiled and added, 'Do you not agree?'

Yorda nodded. 'I've never seen anything like it before.'

'Oh, but I think you have.' The stranger looked straight at Yorda, still smiling.

Yorda stood slightly and motioned to the stool in front of the stranger. 'Take a seat, Mr…?'

'Mertok, just Mertok,' the stranger replied.

'Take a seat, Mertok. Why do you think I've seen it before?'

Mertok sat and looked at Yorda. 'Let me rephrase that. You know of its existence elsewhere but not here and not now.'

Yorda looked into his tankard and inhaled slowly through his nose. He lifted his head and looked at Mertok, a puzzled expression on his face.

'Nothing?' said the stranger.

'I'm sorry, Mertok?' replied Yorda.

'I said, "nothing",' replied Mertok. 'You smelt nothing. Am I right? You get information by sight, touch and smell. You can see me, touch me, but you cannot smell me.'

Yorda was completely unprepared for this.

'I'm sorry?' Yorda said again.

Mertok laughed. His laugh was like bells tinkling in the wind. Yorda could not help but smile also.

'I believe that your name is Yorda. The innkeeper mentioned it earlier today. I've been looking for you.'

'Josh never mentioned anyone asking for me.'

'Of course not. He wouldn't remember me asking. It wasn't important to him.'

Yorda was becoming more puzzled. It was true, Mertok had no smell. He had never met any human or animal without a smell. Whether it was sweat, soap, bad breath, unclean clothes, wet fur, anything, he could always smell something. But Mertok was different: not even his clothes had a smell.

Mertok smiled again. This time his eyes were set like steel.

'I've had a little fun with you, Yorda. I know you are very puzzled by me but there is a serious side to all of this. A very serious side.' Mertok looked past Yorda's head. The tavern was filling up.

'Now if you will excuse me, I have some work to do. Please meet me here tonight at 10 p.m. If you intend doing any shopping, please do not enter any more animals' minds, or imaginary snakes may be the least of your problems. If I don't get to see you again, send my regards to Toreal and Melisse.'

Before Yorda could ask him how he knew his parents, Mertok had turned and left the tavern. Three large men followed him almost immediately.

Chapter Three

Mertok left the inn and walked to the side of the street. He hadn't had enough time to give Yorda his message before the trackers had found him. Once a tracker had picked up your scent it was only a matter of time before they found you. Mertok smiled ruefully. All creatures had some sort of odour about them. At least, all creatures except the ones that made up Mertok's race. Mertok was not an ordinary creature: he was an elf. To all other creatures, elves had no scent, but to another elf it was as though you had a sign on top of your head with your name in large letters.

OK, now they had found him there were three options. He could try to escape and elude them until the mission was finished, but there was no telling how long that would be, and to avoid a confrontation with a tracker for any length of time was incredibly difficult. So far he had managed four months, which must be a record. Option two: he could kill the trackers. Not so easy with three of them. They always travelled in threes. This was not because they needed each others' help in the search – one could find the target as easily as ten could – but three was the most efficient. More than three could rouse suspicions if stopped by any army or sheriffs' patrols. Only one or two would give the prey an easier chance of killing them.

Option three: he could let the trackers kill him. It would be quick and efficient and probably painless. Not that this mattered much to an elf. Even though they were a long-lived species, death held no fear for any elf. Their souls would be released and sent to the Floating Islands where they could join in the Endless Song with their ancestors. Even now, if he listened carefully, Mertok could hear the distant sweet music that all of the White Elves could hear.

Now that he had actually located Yorda, option three would solve nothing. No, option three was not a valid choice until his message had been passed on to Yorda. He must somehow engage the trackers in battle. Killing the trackers without forfeiting his own life was really the only option open to him and would gain more time for Yorda.

He looked around and decided to move away from the busy street. Even if he succeeded in vanquishing his opponents, too many people might spot the bloodshed and, if he was taken into custody by the authorities within the city, his mission might fail.

By now the trackers had left the inn and the eyes of all three were in contact with Mertok. They made no attempt to split up. Casually they crossed the street towards their prey. Mertok turned and headed down a narrow alley just to his right. He exited into a large yard, on one side of which was a smithy. The blacksmith was not around, nor were there any other people present. To his left was what looked to be a deserted building. The windows were boarded up but the door was hanging open by one hinge. Mertok picked up a long metal rod that was leaning against the unlit forge and quickly crossed over the yard and entered the house. He climbed the stairs and looked around. There were three bedrooms off the corridor at the top of the stairs. All three doors were open. He quickly looked inside each. The first room was empty with the window boarded up. He closed the door and left.

The second room was also empty but the third one had a few pieces of furniture inside and the window was open. He closed the door of bedroom three then turned back into bedroom two, closing the door behind him. Except for a small table and a couple of chairs, the only things in the room were about a dozen slates of wood, some nails and a hammer on the floor next to the window. Mertok hoped that if he could take out the first tracker, then leap out of the window before the other two entered the room, it would even the odds somewhat. Two against one was a much better position to be in and would probably turn the tide in his favour.

A creak on the stairs told him that he was not alone. They must be confident, thought Mertok. Elves normally made little or no noise, especially when close to their target. Mertok lifted his bar and stood back. His breathing was slow and rhythmical. With a final prayer to his Mistress to take his soul, he bared his teeth.

The door burst open and one of the trackers flew through the doorway, but his dive was misjudged because he landed face down on the floor before reaching his target. The back of his head was missing and the tracker was very dead. Mertok heard a thud and a loud gurgling noise outside in the corridor. He moved slowly towards the door and could see a second tracker lying there, obviously dead, with a poker through his neck. The third tracker was making the gurgling sound because he was being held at arm's length around the throat about a foot off the floor by one of the largest men the elf had ever seen.

The gurgling stopped and the thick fingers of the hand opened and let the body slump to the floor. The man turned. He had a hammer dripping blood in his other hand.

Mertok quickly summed up the situation. What must have happened became clear. The trackers had entered the building and followed him upstairs. At this stage of the kill, all of their senses were devoted to their prey in front of them. This huge man had obviously followed them up the stairs and it was he who had caused the slight creaking. A poker through the neck had surprised the first tracker as he turned, the second had been throttled and the third had had a hammer across the back of his head, the impact of which had thrown him through the door. Mertok again lifted the bar in readiness against this man-mountain.

'Put down the bar, laddie. If ye bend it on my 'ead 'ow do you think I can make my 'orseshoes with it?' A smile lifted the corners of the big man's mouth. Mertok held firm.

'Stand your ground, mister. You may have surprised three unarmed thieves but I will prove a much more worthy adversary.'

At this, the man's smile turned into a chuckle and then an explosion of laughter.

'Three *unarmed*,' and he emphasised the word, 'thieves? Laddie, ye must think I was born yesterday. Let me tell you what I see.'

He bent down next to the tracker he had killed first and pulled the poker out of his neck. 'OK. My name is Dawson. I'm the blacksmith. I've just packed up work for the day when I see you through my window rushing into the yard. You pick up a metal bar and 'ead for my 'ouse. I'm just about to come out of the forge to call after you when these three geezers enter the yard and follow you up into the 'ouse. They obviously ain't soldiers or sheriff's men so I pick up my 'ammer and poker and follow them in. As I get to the front door, I see the three of them going upstairs, but they are making no sounds at all. Nothing.'

Dawson stood up and glanced at the poker, still wet with the tracker's blood.

'This confirms what I was thinking, laddie. Green blood. Now, I know of only one race that 'as green blood – elves.'

Mertok raised his eyebrows.

'Don't look so surprised, laddie. I'm not the only man to know that elves exist.'

Dawson looked once again at the poker.

'To my way of thinking I see three men that make no sound, following a fourth. The only men I know that make no sound at all when they move are trackers. They must be trackers from the Dark Elves, so I'm a-figuring that you could do with a bit of 'elp. I thought perhaps they might 'ave 'eard me behind them on the stairs but they were too intent on getting you. You must be a pretty important elf. I 'ave never 'eard of trackers being sent this far south to locate a prey.'

Mertok relaxed a little. This man had just saved his life but he had a few questions himself.

'Well, Dawson, you say your name is. I guess I owe you my life and for that I am indebted to you, but you seem to know an awful lot about elves for a blacksmith. And that brings me to another point. If you are a blacksmith and you live here, then why is there no furniture in your house? And also, why has your forge been unused for days? There seem to be no clients and, from the smell of the place, there have been no horses here for a while.'

Dawson chuckled again, a deep rumbling sound which seemed to come almost from the earth itself.

'Even when being pursued by trackers you don't miss much, laddie. This 'ouse is empty except for the last couple of chairs because I'm leaving the city. And you are quite correct: I 'aven't used the forge for about a week. There is no action around 'ere. I think I retired from soldiering too early.'

For a moment the big man's eyes lost their focus and stared straight past Mertok. Old memories flooded back into his head. The smile faded from his lips to be left with a look of sadness. As quickly as it appeared, it left. Dawson tilted his head to the side, almost as if puzzling over something, and then he said, '*Eliathil rhôn maieril. Yrn aygar hirrin cherail.*'

Mertok's jaw dropped and at the same time he put down the metal bar.

'The pledge of friendship in my language.'

All wariness left the elf as he stepped forward and crossed his arms in the elven form of acceptance.

Chapter Four

Yorda sipped his ale and mused over his encounter with the stranger. He got up and walked over to the bar where Josh was cleaning some pots. He looked up as Yorda approached.

'No need to come to the bar for another ale, Yorda; I would have brought it over to you.' He smiled brightly and put his cloth down while reaching for a tankard.

'No thanks, Josh. I've had enough for the time being. It really is a fine ale.'

Josh smiled again. He took great pride in his inn. His food was always freshly bought and of the finest quality. So too were his beers. It was true that you paid a little extra in the Lantern Inn, but nobody ever complained. He kept his guest rooms clean and had fresh linen every day. Even though he knew that everything was of the best quality, he appreciated each and every compliment. 'Why thank you, Yorda.'

'Tell me, Josh, what do you know of the man I was just sitting with?'

Josh returned the tankard to its rack and carried on cleaning his pots. 'Sorry, Yorda, I've been busy and didn't really notice you with anyone.'

'He said that his name was Mertok and he says you told him earlier today who I was.'

Josh stopped his polishing and tried to remember. 'Can't say I recall anyone asking about you.'

'He said you wouldn't remember,' Yorda muttered to himself.

'What's that?' asked Josh. 'I couldn't hear you.'

'Nothing, nothing. Thanks anyway. Tell me, Josh, could I take a room for tonight? I have a little business in the city and I am not sure how long it will take.'

'Sure, Yorda, you can have room number three. I'll get some sheets put on the bed for you.'

'Thanks, Josh. I'll see you later.'

Yorda turned and walked out of the inn. The afternoon was moving on and Yorda reckoned he had a good five hours before his meeting with Mertok. Even though he was intrigued he didn't ponder overlong on this mystery man. He would find out everything soon enough.

His thoughts turned to Ivaine. He had known the baker's daughter for as long as he could remember. As children they had played together constantly. Being a typical boy, he had done all the things young boys did to young girls: pulling her hair, hiding dolls, teasing her and of course making her cry. Ivaine would be continually running to her mother complaining of the things that Yorda did to her, but she would always come back to play with him.

As they got older, Yorda found that he teased her less and less and actually became more of a protector to her and would stop other boys from playing tricks on her. Recently he had started to think of her differently again. He was finding it more and more difficult to be in her company. They no longer shared childhood games, as they had outgrown these. He enjoyed being with her but found that he became tongue-tied for no apparent reason when in her presence. He noticed little things about her that he couldn't recall seeing before: the way one side of her mouth lifted higher than the other when she smiled; the slight tilt of her head when she was thinking. Most of all, though, he noticed her eyes: pale green but bright and always sparkling. Her eyes seemed to stir a memory in him but of what he couldn't tell. Almost all of the young boys and girls in the village seemed to be seeing somebody, but Ivaine had never shown any interest in any of the boys who tried to court her. Similarly the girls who flirted openly with Yorda, of whom there were many, received no reciprocation.

Yorda stopped walking and looked around. His daydreaming about Ivaine had caused him to walk without really looking where he was going and he had arrived at an area of the city he didn't recognise. He looked around him to try to get his bearings. He could see in the distance the spire of the church and realised that he must have been walking at least half an hour to be so far north of it. The only thoughts in his mind for thirty minutes had been of Ivaine. He smiled: he knew of worse things to be thinking of.

He noticed near the end of the street a few shops and walked towards them. The first store had a small selection of clothes and fabrics at very reasonable prices. The second was much smaller than the first and seemed to be far more interesting. An old lady sat outside in a rocking chair, smoking a clay pipe. A couple of small tables were set up next to her and an assortment of rings, brooches, talismans and suchlike were arranged upon them. He walked over and bade the owner a good afternoon. The old lady looked up at him and nodded. Yorda lifted a few rings to get a closer look at them.

'Is she very beautiful?' the old lady asked.

Yorda smiled and turned to her. 'Yes, she is. Is it so obvious to you what I am seeking?'

The old lady gave a laugh, which turned into a fit of coughing. When she had recovered she replied, 'Young man, when you reach my age you see things far more clearly. You were walking down the street with a huge smile on your face, quite oblivious to what was going on around you. Then you walk over to look at old jewellery and you ask me if it is obvious to me that you are looking for a present for a lady. What colour eyes does she have?'

'Green.'

'And her hair?'

'Long and black. Straight.'

The old lady stood up and walked over to one of the tables. She picked up something and turned to Yorda.

'I think she would like this.'

Yorda took the object. It was a leather hairgrip, beautifully made. Around the outside were inlaid some yellow and green jewels. He looked at the old lady.

'It is exquisite but I cannot afford this.'

'The jewels are not real; they are malachite, inexpensive but none the less delightful to behold. You don't seriously think I could afford real gems.'

Yorda looked sheepish. The old lady started to laugh.

'I am teasing you, young man.'

Yorda started to laugh too but stopped almost immediately as the old lady's laugh turned into another fit of coughing, much more violent than the last.

'Your hand,' she managed to say in between coughs. Yorda gave her his arm, which she held on to to stop herself from falling. He gently took her back to her chair.

'How long have you had this cough?' he asked with some concern, after she had recovered slightly.

'Oh, don't look so worried, young man. At my age you get these sorts of problems!'

'What does your doctor say about it? Has he given you anything to help?'

'Doctors, physicians, healers, hah! They can do nothing. They all look at me as you do, with concern in their eyes, but they know that my time here is coming to an end. Don't look shocked, young man. I have lived a full life. I am more than ninety years old and have lived more and longer than most people. And believe it or not I look forward to walking the Halls of the Dead and meeting once more my friends who have left this world already.'

While she was talking, Yorda was holding her hand. He never knew why, but he found that being in physical contact with someone who was ill seemed to give him the ability to diagnose illnesses. When he had been six years old, he had found a rabbit lying outside on the floor. He had picked it up and brought it to his parents.

'Mummy, the bunny has darkness all around him and he wants to sleep.'

His mother had taken the rabbit from him, and as he had passed it over it had died.

'He was very old, darling,' his mother had said, and then she had given a worried glance at her husband. As Yorda grew, he found this ability grew with him. He found that not only could he get some form of mental contact with animals when he touched them, but he could also do it when they were a short distance away. This talent was more limited with people. He could not get a mental bond with them, but he found that by touching them he could feel where their pain was and more often than not accurately diagnose their problems.

Yorda looked into the old lady's eyes.

'I am a healer too and it saddens me to say that they are right.'

He reached into his pouch and pulled out a couple of small

bottles. He took a small cup and poured a little from each bottle into the cup. 'Drink this. I cannot heal you but your cough need not be there to trouble you.'

As the old lady drank, Yorda muttered a few words. Instantly the liquid started to warm slightly.

'I don't know what you gave me but my chest has cleared and my whole body seems warmer. How often do I need to take that?'

Yorda smiled. 'Just the once. It's a mixture of herbs and water. It works quickly and is permanent. Quinill and tarron leaf.'

'I have been given quinill and tarron leaf before but never have I experienced this effect.'

'The herbs must be ground up within minutes of picking and the quantities have to be correct or they lose their power,' replied Yorda.

The old lady looked up at Yorda and handed the cup back. But as Yorda took it she held on for a couple of seconds. 'You know, I'm not so sure it is just the herbs that have done this, young man.' She released the cup. 'I've been around and I have seen a lot of things. I don't know what else you did to that drink but herbs don't give that result in so short a time. Thank you nonetheless. Please take the hairgrip. It is my gift to you. I know your young lady will love it.'

Yorda thanked her and they parted company. He headed towards the city centre. After looking at the quickly lowering sun he felt sure he had time to make one more call before heading back to this mysterious meeting with Mertok. He wanted to talk with a well-known physician who might be able to give him some more information about voicekill. Yorda knew that this illness was from another region but he didn't know where.

What was more confusing was that he had no idea how he knew it was from somewhere else. Perhaps his parents had mentioned it when he was younger. It worried him a little that recently he seemed to be having ghosts of memories that seemed to be familiar to him and yet were just tantalisingly too far away for him to grab them before they had left his mind. It was like this for voicekill. He had no frame of reference for the illness but he recognised it almost as if it was something he saw every day. He was very proud of his memory; it was almost infallible. And he didn't like these fringe memories.

He soon arrived at the physician's house. A plaque inscribed 'Dr Jason Darrish – Enter and be healed' was on the door. Yorda smiled. He knew Dr Darrish was indeed an excellent physician but perhaps he was a little over-theatrical about his abilities. He knocked on the door and entered. There were some chairs lined up next to each other in a passageway to the right of the main hallway. Yorda took a seat. The waiting area was empty except for him, so when a young lady called for the next patient he walked straight in.

Dr Darrish sat at a large oak table. There were about seven or eight books on the table and many, many more on bookshelves around the room. In fact, Yorda couldn't remember ever having seen so many books in his life. He noticed the titles of several of the books: *Blood Letting and Its Many Benefits*; *The A to Z of Herbs*; *Medicinal Benefits of Salt Water*. The gentleman in front of him, who was still unaware of Yorda, had written all of these tomes.

A slight cough from Yorda got the doctor's attention. He looked up. Dr Darrish was in his late fifties, with wispy grey hair, a thin face and an enormously long nose upon which perched a pince-nez. Yorda introduced himself.

'Ah yes, you must be the young gentleman healer from the village just at the edge of the forest. So good to meet you.' The doctor rose and extended his hand. His handshake was firm and vigorous. 'Please sit down. What may I do for you? You certainly don't look ill!'

Yorda asked him what he knew of voicekill. It seemed to be coming from the city, as only the village children who had travelled to Parkent had become infected.

'No, no, no, young fellow, I fear it is much worse than you think. Messages have arrived in Parkent telling of the same illness in every city in the land. There have been no fatalities, thank goodness, but also there have been no effective treatments to shorten the duration of the illness, unless I am to believe what some of my patients say.' He paused a little here and then leaned forward. 'I understand that when you treat this illness early on, the recovery rate is a matter of hours?' He hesitated a little and then said, 'I hope that I am not being too presumptuous, but could you tell me what you are using?'

'Anything to help,' replied Yorda. 'If the child has already lost its voice I would suggest a hot tea of barrowroot, but if I see the child early enough when the temperature starts, I just dab a few spots of oil of liturnam on the forehead. Normally the child will sleep and the fever breaks before the infection takes hold.'

The doctor smiled slightly and gently shook his head. He removed his pince-nez and rubbed his nose.

'I realise that you village healers have your secret remedies and I understand totally that you don't wish to reveal them. I use the same herbs as you but my results are not even one tenth as effective as yours seem to be. You must be adding something else to them.'

'Honestly, no. If my results are more effective I can only think it must be because I crush my herbs within minutes of picking them, which may make them more potent.'

The doctor looked unconvinced.

'I will take your word for it. Anyway, I am glad you are here because I have something to ask of you. Most physicians are proud men and, like you village healers, guard their secrets rigorously. However, I am not most physicians. I have a lot of knowledge which I readily impart to others.' He pointed to the books that bore his name. 'True, I receive some recompense from their sale but I am not a man who uses his money to extravagance. I hope and believe that I return most of it to my patients with good, low-cost medicine that all can afford – and those that cannot will have their treatment for free. Nevertheless, there are times,' and here he winked at Yorda, 'but not many, when I am at a loss to help some of my patients. I am not too proud to ask for help and, from what I a hear recently, you seem to be a remarkable healer. Tell me, Yorda, may I recommend you to some of my more unusual and tricky cases? I will obviously pay you for your help. You see, I believe that physicians should be open to all avenues of healing, even to recommending secret cures.' Here he winked again.

'Like you,' Yorda replied, 'I try to make sick people well. I would be only too happy to give what aid I am able, but I will take no money. There is little I need that I do not already have.'

'Splendid, splendid!' said the doctor.

'So there is nothing more that you know about voicekill?' asked Yorda.

'As I say, it appears to be in all the land. Only one thing is baffling me, however. It always seems to start in the cities and works its way out to the surrounding villages. Also, as far as I can fathom, almost every city reported its first cases at the same time, so I don't think it can be a carrier of the illness distributing it. I am working on the theory that it must be something to do with it being a seasonal thing, but that doesn't explain why it always starts in the city. In any case, if I come up with anything I will send word to you.'

Yorda and the doctor stood and shook hands and promised further meetings; then Yorda left. As the door closed, Yorda turned and made his way back to the Lantern Inn to meet Mertok once again.

Mertok helped Dawson load the last of his furniture onto the wagon. He tied the ropes tightly as Dawson accepted some coins from an old man wearing a long black cloak. The man nodded at Mertok, then climbed up into the wagon.

'Pleasure doing business with you,' he said as he took the reins and started the wagon.

'I'm sure it was – for you!' Dawson looked at the coins the man had given him for a few moments and then tipped them into his money pouch and tucked it away inside his jacket. He turned and picked up his bags. 'Guess I'll drop these off at Brooks's stables until I go.'

Mertok watched the big man look wistfully around the yard. 'You going to miss this place?' he asked.

'Nay, laddie. Four years is quite long enough. Smithying is a good life but it's too quiet for me.'

Mertok nodded.

'You promised to tell me how you know my language. I know of no human who can speak it.'

Dawson pulled his bags over his shoulders. The two men walked to the far end of the yard and closed the gates as they left.

'I come from a land called Dunroon. You 'eard of it?'

The elf shook his head.

'Didn't think so. No one seems to 'ave. I sometimes wonder if I dreamt of it. I was a soldier in King Pardol's army. We were a peace-loving people. Sure, we 'ad the occasional border skirmish but nothing serious. King Pardol was a great diplomat as well as king and would always find a peaceful solution to any problem with our neighbours. Then we 'eard of terrible fighting in the lands to our south. An army led by a ruthless general was sweeping north, brushing all opposition aside. When our king 'eard of the atrocities that were being committed on the defeated, he went to see our neighbours to form an alliance. We sent envoys to meet with this general to discuss our situation; the envoys returned on their 'orses minus arms and 'eads. "General Balok does not talk, General Balok destroys" was carved on a placard 'anging from the lead 'orse's neck.

'We sent our armies out to meet this general. When we engaged in battle it was as if the world was tearing apart. 'is men gave no mercy and asked for none in return. I will never forget the look of fear in their faces. Our men thought they were scared of us. We were very, very wrong. They kept advancing onto our spears and lances. For every one of our men that fell, they lost five. As they fell some of them cried out in thanks for our saving them. We didn't understand. After three days we 'ad pushed them back to the edge of our borders and then… it came.'

Dawson's face had turned white with the memory of the battle. Before he could continue, they arrived at Brooks's stables. A young stablehand ran out, took the big man's bags and received a coin for his trouble.

'Look after my 'orse or you'll get a clip across the back of your 'ead. I'll be back for 'im tomorrow.'

They left the stables and turned back towards the Lantern Inn. The two men walked without talking. Mertok was prepared to wait, as he could see that the big man was deep in thought, so he steered him into the inn and ordered two large mugs of ale. They sat and sipped at their drinks; then Dawson looked deep into Mertok's eyes.

'To this day I am unsure if it was all a dream or if it was real. We 'ad pushed them back over a small 'ill. As we got near the top, the enemy fought with a fervour I could not believe. Some of them threw themselves onto their own swords rather than be pushed over the brow of that damned 'ill. Then we 'eard the drums start. A slow thudding beat. At the very moment the drums started, all of the enemy dropped their weapons and turned towards the top of the 'ill. We too 'alted. We could not kill unarmed men who faced away from us. So we also looked in the same direction.

'Just cresting the 'ill we saw a white charger with a tall man dressed all in red astride it. 'e was holding a long rope which trailed be'ind him. As 'e got closer we realised that 'e was leading something along on this rope. The first thing we noticed was the smell. Rotten flesh it reminded me of. Then a dark form started to rise up and up and up. It must 'ave been twenty-five feet 'igh and black as night. Its eyes glowed like red 'ot coals. It stopped and stared at us. The battlefield went silent as the drums ceased. All we could 'ear was the breathing of this thing that seemed to 'ave no shape or form. It was just… there. I 'ave no other way of describing it.

'Then a voice burst forth over the battlefield. It was the man in red. "General Balok bids you welcome. Please meet my pet, the Vortak. He wishes to make your acquaintance." With that 'e flicked the rope that 'e 'eld and it became parted from the collar that was around the beast's neck. At this point all of the enemy's men dropped to the floor, covering their faces. We could 'ear them praying to their gods to spare them. The beast lifted its arms and the sky grew dark. It moved forward. Any man near it that it touched started smoking and then burst into flames.

'And then the beast was among us. It ripped and gouged and burned anything that came near it. Nothing could 'arm it. Looking back on it I don't think General Balok needed an army. 'is men were just prisoners from other conflicts that 'e sent into battle for 'is fun.

'The beast pushed us back. We tried to lure it towards the woods to make it more difficult for it to pursue us but it kept coming forward. I climbed a tree and took my battleaxe out. As it passed under my branch I leapt onto its back. The moment I touched it my body burned as if acid had been poured on it. I remember lifting my axe and bringing it down on its skull. As it made contact with its flesh the beast screamed and I was thrown away, although by what I don't know.

'The next thing I remember was waking up in the company of elves. They told me that I'd been found almost three weeks earlier, lying in the forest. Most of my skin 'ad been burnt away. I was still 'olding my battleaxe. For all of the time I was unconscious they 'ad treated my skin with 'ealing salves. I know of the magic in your forests and lands. This magic made my skin 'eal with almost no scars.

'The elves 'ad not 'eard of either my people or lands, nor of the beast or General Balok. At first I could not understand your language, nor your people mine. They taught me the elven tongue and the tongue of the men of this land. It was nearly three years before I was completely well again. I was taught 'unting and tracking skills, archery, fighting and many things that men do not know. Many times we returned to the spot where I was found, where the elves searched for clues as to where I 'ad come from and, more importantly, 'ow I got there. As you know, Mertok, no man can enter the elven forests unnoticed and yet I was many days' walk from the outside.

'I learnt too of the Black Elf. We were left largely untouched by 'im as he was much further west, but we were aware that 'e was building 'is army and that someday 'e would come. When I was well I was told that I should leave the elven lands to be with fellow men. I would always be made welcome if I came again to their borders. My battleaxe they charged with some elven magic so that it will never chip or go blunt. When I left the forest I wandered from village to village for many months, trying to find information on my people, with no luck. Eventually I came 'ere and for four years I became a blacksmith.

'You know, laddie, it's been nearly ten years since I was found by your kin but I still want to return to my people. The memory of the war stays with me as if it was but yesterday.'

Mertok listened as the story unfolded and when Dawson seemed to have finished he asked, 'So what do you intend to do now?'

'As I said before, it's too quiet around 'ere. My life was the army before I came 'ere. Maybe I can go back to 'elp the elves against the Black Elf.'

'Perhaps I have something that will interest you. I am meeting someone here in a short while whose life has some similarities to yours. Will you take another ale with me and hear me out when he arrives?'

Dawson sat back with a grin on his face. He brushed his short black hair backwards with his fingers.

'Well, laddie, I've nothing else planned at the moment. As I don't intend to leave until tomorrow morning, you 'ave a few hours to tempt me with something. One thing though' – Mertok cocked an eyebrow – 'the next ales are on me, my elf friend.'

Dawson ordered two more ales and the two settled back until Yorda arrived.

Chapter Five

Yorda sat next to Mertok and Dawson. 'Nice to see you again, Yorda my lad.'

'You too, Dawson. How goes the pony?'

'Right as rain thanks to you.'

Mertok looked from one to the other.

'You know each other?

'Some more ale, Josh!' the big smith roared. 'Sure, this young man saved a pony's life a few weeks ago. It had been bitten by a stagfly and the bite became infected. There's not much can be done normally except to put the animal down, but young Yorda 'ere 'appened to be in Parkent and came to see me.' He turned to Yorda. 'I don't know what you put in that poultice but two days later 'e was champing at the bit to get outside and run around. Thanks, laddie. I never like to see a good animal put down.'

Josh turned up and put three large tankards of ale on the table. Dawson paid and the innkeeper passed on to the next customer.

Mertok turned to Yorda. 'I think I caught you by surprise this afternoon. I'm sorry I had to rush off but I had a little unfinished business to take care of.'

Dawson tried to stifle a laugh but only succeeded in almost choking on his beer. 'Unfinished business, laddie? Aye, that's an understatement.'

Yorda put his ale down on the table.

'Tell me, Mertok, how do you know my parents and how do they know you? I have never heard them talk of you.'

'Before I answer that,' Mertok replied, 'I assume you have booked a room to stay tonight?' Yorda nodded. 'Good. Then I propose that the three of us take our ales to your room now so that we can be undisturbed and, more importantly, not be overheard. What I must tell you is of great importance.'

Yorda glanced slowly from Mertok to Dawson. Mertok stared intently at the young healer while Dawson just shrugged his shoulders to signify that he too had no idea what this important message could be.

'OK. I'm in room three. I'll just get the key from Josh. I'll meet you at the door to the room.'

Yorda went over to the innkeeper and asked for his key.

'There's a nice fire in the hearth for you and the bed is aired and ready.'

'Can you send up some more ale and also some food? I'll stick with bread, cheese and fruit, but you'd better put out some hot food for the other two. Just give me a selection of whatever you have.'

He joined Mertok and Dawson outside his room and unlocked the door. As Josh had said, the fire was burning brightly and the room was warm. A fresh lavender smell pervaded the air. Yorda looked over to the window and could see the remains of several candles; they had burnt down, but they were undoubtedly the source of the aroma. Good old Josh, he thought to himself.

The three men sat down at the table in the corner of the room. Before they got a chance to talk, a tap at the door alerted Yorda to the fact that the food had arrived. As usual, Josh had outdone himself. Goats', sheep's and cows' cheeses, ryebread, malt and whootberry loaves; a tureen of stew with potatoes and various legumes, as well as a bowl of apples; a jug of milk and two large pitchers of ale. Josh winked as he ushered one of the serving girls out.

'I know when you lads get together for an evening's card session, you get very hungry,' he said.

He winked again and left. Dawson chuckled.

'I had no idea that's what goes on in Josh's rooms in the evenings. I should come here more often.'

The three men realised just how hungry they were when the food was set down in front of them. Yorda and Mertok tucked into the cheese and bread while Dawson took large mouthfuls of everything he could see. Some of Josh's wife's legendary home-made carrot cake finished the meal off nicely.

'Now,' Mertok said, 'my message to you, Yorda.' He took a deep breath and leaned forward. 'When you were growing up, did your mother or father ever mention my name?'

Yorda shook his head. 'Not that I can remember.'

'OK. Did they ever talk about elves?'

Again Yorda shook his head. 'I have sometimes heard stories in the village about elves and goblins and fairies and suchlike. They are told to the children along with stories of brave warriors, princesses and the like.'

'I can see that this is not going to be as easy or as quick as I had hoped. Have some more ale.' Mertok took the pitcher and refilled Yorda's tankard. 'If I were to tell you that I was an elf, what would you say?'

Yorda stopped drinking and lowered his tankard. He started to chuckle and then, seeing that neither Mertok nor Dawson were joining him, he stopped. 'I'd say you were either playing a joke on me or you have taken a knock to the head.'

'Would that it were but only that,' Mertok muttered. 'Let me show you something.' Mertok took a small knife from his belt and drew the blade down against his palm.

Yorda jumped up from his seat. 'What are you doing? You could cut—' He stopped in mid-sentence and a gasp escaped his lips as he saw green blood oozing out of the wound.

'If I was joking or if I had been the victim of a knock on the head, then my blood would be the same colour as everyone else's. But it's not, as you can see, so I am not human. If I'm not human I must be something else, so why not an elf?'

Dawson turned to Yorda. 'It's true, laddie. I've seen elves, even lived with them for a while. They exist.'

Yorda stood and backed away from the table. 'This is some sort of a trick. I wouldn't expect this of you, Dawson, saying you have lived with them. Everyone knows that they exist only in stories.'

Mertok carried on as if he hadn't heard Yorda, 'And what's more, you are an elf too. Or at least a half-elf. Please, Yorda, hear me out, no matter how bizarre this may seem.'

Yorda sat back down. 'OK, I'll listen, if only to find out how you have green blood oozing out of your hand. Carry on.'

'I want to give you a few things to think on before I give you the message. First of all, you have seen my blood is different. Next, when you saw me today for the first time you could not smell me. Have you ever known anyone else, man or beast, to have no scent? Next, the horse earlier today – you calmed it when you saw it frightened by the imaginary snake. You touched its mind, Yorda. Humans cannot enter the minds of animals; even elves have limited ability where that is concerned. But you calmed it almost instantly by taking away the image of the snake. Next, we have been drinking this very strong ale since we came in this evening but you are as fresh as a daisy. Even Dawson here has started to get a little glassy-eyed, but you and I could drink this all night and it will have no more effect than water.'

Dawson interrupted. 'Then why the 'ell are you drinking it then? It's a waste of good ale if you don't feel good after a drink.'

Mertok smiled briefly, then carried on. 'I'll wager that you have never been drunk. What's more, I'll wager that you've never been sick or even had a fever.' The elf could see that his words were giving Yorda some food for thought.

'Yorda, do you not hear the songs of our people in your head? They are with me always, even this far from home. You must hear them.'

The young healer had to admit to himself that music and voices seemed to always be in the back of his mind.

'*Analla com aya. Mas haiey*,' Mertok spoke gently.

'*Tor jaya reith aya. Mas borsiya*,' Yorda joined in. 'I had always assumed that I made up the words. They mean nothing to me.'

'You hear the words but do not understand them.' Mertok hung his head slightly. 'That is not good news. We had hoped that this would not happen.'

'Am I missing something 'ere?' Dawson interrupted. 'From my time with your people I was told the music and words that you 'ear were a racial memory that is known and understood by all elves.'

'It is – or at least it always has been until now. But Yorda here is a little different from other elves. He doesn't know it but he is a very special being.' Mertok turned back to Yorda. He measured his words carefully as he spoke. 'You need to know where you, and most of all, your parents came from.' He turned slightly towards Dawson. 'I think this will interest you more than you realise. There is an interesting parallel to your story.' The elf reached forward and lifted one of the pitchers of ale. He topped up the tankards and set the pitcher back down. He was gathering his thoughts.

'As I have said before, I am an elf. My people live many days' ride from here to the north-west. As with your people,' and here he nodded to Dawson, 'there are many different communities, many bloodlines and indeed different races of elves. Our legends tell us that elves were one of the first creatures to walk this planet. We were "born" many hundreds of years before humans. As with humans, elves do not always agree with each other, but differences are seldom, if ever, resolved with violence. Elves grow to a very great age. With age comes wisdom, so the oldest and wisest of elves enter into the Council of Elders, who officiate and give decisions on these differences. The resulting decision is nearly always accepted without question.

'On rare occasions, however, the decision is not accepted, so the elf would be assigned to another area where the problem would not be encountered again. On very rare occasions this either does not work or the elf does not wish to do so and the elf will be asked to go into voluntary exile. As I say, it is very rare. In my people, only a handful of elves have left in the last 500 years. This is true of other elven groups. Of the elves that go into exile, many eventually return and are reintegrated upon acceptance of the elders' decision. Of course, some never return and are never heard of again.

'About 200 years ago an elf named Marosham was exiled. He was many years in exile and not heard from. Then we heard tales of an elf recruiting exiles and of them forming their own people. They were a hostile people who took what they wanted from other elves. We called them the Dark Elves because they followed the way that our legends call the Dark Path. Over the years Marosham, or, as he now calls himself, the Black Elf, has built up an army and, as Dawson here knows, there are wars among his elves and the elves who follow the Path of Light.'

Mertok stopped talking and stood up. He walked over to the fire, placed a couple of logs on it and then returned to the table. He didn't reseat himself but instead walked around the table as he continued.

'Twenty-two years ago your father, Yorda, was in a patrol of elves on our border, as we had heard that a raiding party of Dark Elves was in the area. The patrol was brought on alert when we heard the sound of crying. Your father moved forward towards the sound and found a young woman staggering through the woods, sobbing to herself. She was hardly able to walk and in fact collapsed a few seconds later. Your father signalled for the patrol to search the area while he went to the young woman's aid. Like yourself, Dawson' – Mertok laid a hand on the big man's shoulder as he passed him – 'she had entered the forest without being detected by any elves, which is unheard of in our history, but nevertheless there she was.

'Your father lifted the girl and took her back to his village. She had been injured and had many wounds on her body, but fortunately none were life threatening. Your father and the elven healers tended her wounds. It was several days before she woke and, like you also, Dawson, she had no knowledge of my language. She was tended to, and over the coming months she gradually started to understand us and learnt our language. When she could communicate sufficiently with us she told us she had no memory of anything before waking up in the village. We taught her the language of man because, again like you, Dawson, she would eventually have to return to her own kind. She learned at an amazing rate and quested for knowledge continually.

'Over the time she was with us, she and your father became very close and something happened that has never happened before in elven history: an elf fell in love with a human. Your father went before the Council of Elders to ask permission to marry her. The elders conferred for many hours. Eventually they called for your father and told him that they would not refuse his request but asked him to be mindful that an elf lives many times the lifespan of a human and that he would outlive his bride. It was then that your father told the elders that the human was with child. You, Yorda, to be exact. The elders immediately asked him to leave the council as they wished to confer some more.'

Mertok sat down again. 'There is a prophecy that has been spoken of in our race since the start of our history which says:

> There shall come a time when the Black Elf shall drink of the magic of the land.
> He will rise in power and challenge the council of elves.
> A champion will return to the kingdom of elves to defeat him.
> The power of the Half-Elf and the Black Elf will pass to the survivor.

'When the Council of Elders found that your mother was carrying the child of an elf, they believed that you were come to fulfil the prophecy. Your father had also believed this as soon as he found that your mother was carrying you. He knew as an elf he would outlive your mother and quite possibly you, as he was unsure if you would live the lifespan of a full elf. He asked the council to grant him the *Manneith*, a ceremony where he would lose his elven longevity and powers and to all intents and purposes become human. He would live the same length of time as a human, suffer the same illnesses as a human, take on a human smell but still retain his elven memories. Even his blood would become the same colour as a human's blood.

'The council agreed that to fulfil the prophecy you had to leave the kingdom and live with mankind, and therefore your father's wish to receive the *Manneith* was granted. Eventually Marosham would hear of your existence and if you still lived in the land of elves he would come to kill you. By living with men you would be far away from him, and the council believed you would be hidden and unknown to him.'

'Would it not have been better and safer to 'ave kept Yorda with the elves?' interrupted Dawson. 'It would be almost impossible to lay siege to an 'eavily protected elf city.'

Mertok nodded towards Yorda while looking at Dawson. 'The boy is here so the decision was right. Also, the prophecy must be fulfilled. If he had never left my people I have no doubts that Marosham would have found a way to get to him. As it was, not even our own people knew where he was.

'However, things have changed. Your father, Yorda, was an elf-lord, and as you are of his line so too are you. The elf-lords are of the oldest lines of elves. They have certain attributes that other elves do not. An elf-lord cannot be hidden unnoticed among other elves as they emit a force that can be felt by other elves. When an elf-lord child passes from his first to second stage of life, his force is ignited. It is similar to puberty in humans. Yours, Yorda, started about three years ago. It was then you became an adult. It was not known for sure if you would have the same attributes as a full elf, Yorda. In fact we had hoped that your force would not manifest itself, so that you could remain hidden until it was time for you to return to us. But two things happened which were unexpected.

'The first was that your force upon ignition hit the elven lands like a strong wind passing over fields of long grass. If someone had shouted from the highest tree that an elf-lord was among us it would not have been more noticeable. The second thing that happened was that the force that all elf-lords carry is identical, but your signature is unique. You may as well have written a letter to Marosham telling him that you had reached adulthood. Your signature was all around us but outside of us, so we knew you hadn't yet returned to the forests.

'The Council of Elders knew that Marosham would send trackers after you to kill you, so it was decided that we too would send elves to you to offer protection while you return. Many elves were sent singly to find you. When they left the forest something very strange happened. Your signature was different. It was still strong but now it was no different from the signature of any elf-lord. We believe this to be because much elf magic ceases to work outside of our lands. The second change was we no longer had any idea of direction as to where you might be. These changes worked for us and against us, as it also did for Marosham. We knew it would be harder for you to be found. It would take thousands of elves to search all the human lands. My people re-entered the forests and returned to their homes.

'The Council of Elders decided after much debate to send into the lands of man as many elf-lords as could be spared. This was agreed by other elven councils. We believed that, as your signature was no different outside the forest from that of any other elf-lord, we could confuse the Black Elf's trackers that were being sent for you. Their orders were to bring you back dead to Marosham. We knew that our elf-lords could confuse, slow down and maybe even kill the trackers. Even if some of us were killed, the time taken to return to Marosham to confirm if the body was yours was extra time for you to live.

'We have continued to confuse his trackers over the past three years, but Marosham has recently devised a plan to flush you out. He had learnt much about men in the time that his trackers walked among them. Most of all he learnt how poor and ineffective were their healing arts. So he sent forth his trackers again, but this time they were armed with an elf illness that he knew could affect humans.'

Yorda sat bolt upright. 'Voicekill?'

Mertok nodded.

'So when we met earlier today and you told me that I knew of its existence, it was part of my racial memory?'

Mertok nodded again. 'Exactly. His trackers were sent to all the major cities and ordered to spread the illness. He knew that if either you or us were to treat and cure this illness much quicker than human medicine did, we would be discovered. He also knows that elf-lords have limited ability to sense the thoughts of animals, so his trackers were given a similar power. His magic endowed them with the ability to scare animals, and by doing this they were to note any signs of the animals being calmed much faster than expected. You remember earlier today the horse that saw the snakes?'

Yorda responded. 'I wondered how the horse had seen snakes when there were none there. I took the image away from it.'

'And you were almost dead within minutes. Luckily I was there too. As soon as you had finished calming the beast I stepped into the animal's mind also and let the trackers sense my signature. I knew then that I had found you but so had they. I had to make them believe that I was you. If they killed me, at least you were alive. My signature was the last one on the horse, so when they felt it they had my "scent" as surely as if I had been rolling in pigs' muck.

'I evaded them without too much trouble. Luckily they had left the scene a few minutes earlier or I would be dead now. I could now find you but they could now find me. I led them away from you and then doubled back and followed you here. I thought I could warn you, but they entered the inn before I had a chance to talk to you. I left and they followed. If they had killed me they would have returned with my body to their master. When they found out it was not you they would have returned in force and killed you, for now they know you are here.'

Dawson stopped the elf at that point. 'I don't understand something. 'ow would they know this laddie was 'ere if yours was the signature they picked up from the 'orse?'

Mertok stood again and walked to the window.

'Somehow, Marosham knows you are a healer, Yorda. I don't know how he knows, but he does. That is why he sent an illness that could affect humans, but when treated by an elf healer the patient would recover very quickly. We have tried to heal these people to divert his trackers but, as I mentioned before, some of our magic doesn't work outside our lands. For some reason which we don't understand, you can heal outside our forests as fast as our best healers can within them. It was Josh who told me this morning of a healer in your village who could cure voicekill in a matter of hours or even less sometimes. I was on the way to your village hoping I was not too late when you calmed the horse. You must have passed the trackers on the road in.'

'What happened to them, the trackers?' Yorda enquired, although he guessed the answer even before it was verified.

'Thanks to Dawson they are no longer a threat to you or to me, but when they fail to contact Marosham more will be sent. He may already know you are here and for that reason we must leave. We will have a couple of weeks' start on them but they will now come in many groups of three if they already know.'

Yorda looked very unsettled. 'A few hours ago I was a villager who had a measure of success with healing animals and people. And now I am the son of an elf-lord who is being sought by assassins because I may be the person who will end the reign of some evil, magic-using elf according to a prophecy that was written thousands of years ago. It's almost like a fairy story.'

Mertok lifted an eyebrow and gave a half-smile. 'Now, fairies are another story. Believe me: you really don't want to meet them.'

Yorda spluttered. 'Don't tell me they exist too!'

'There are many things in this world that are believed to be only stories told to children, but all of those creatures and many more besides either exist or are based on truth. Dawson himself has been face to face with a demon of awesome power and size that would not be out of place in a nightmare.'

Yorda turned towards the big man. 'Is that true, Dawson?'

'Aye, laddie, it's true enough, but it's not an experience I would care to repeat.'

Dawson repeated the story he had told Mertok earlier of his encounter with General Balok and his awesome creature.

Yorda sat back at the end of Dawson's tale and gave a big sigh. He looked from Mertok to Dawson and back again. He seemed to come to a decision. 'When do we leave?'

'After we have slept, breakfasted and stocked up on provisions for the journey. Tomorrow at noon should be the latest. We travel light and we travel fast.'

'And when we reach the elven forests,' Yorda asked, 'what happens then?'

Mertok bent towards Yorda and looked him straight in the eyes.

'We defeat Marosham.'

Chapter Six

The three soon-to-be travellers woke after a few hours' sleep. Dawson had a thumping headache but Yorda and Mertok were on fine form. The cold mornings of early spring were giving way to a much brighter, warmer start to the day. The trio went downstairs to break their fast and found Josh singing to himself and serving the other residents.

'Good morning, gentlemen! I'll be with you in a minute,' he shouted cheerily, disappearing into the kitchen.

'Doesn't 'e ever sleep or stop smiling?' grumbled Dawson.

'When you enjoy your work as much as he does you don't need that much sleep,' smiled Yorda.

'Well, from what I 'ear you must 'ate your work with the amount of time you sleep.'

'Don't get confused with liking your work and liking your bed,' answered Yorda. 'I could quite happily lie in bed all day but quite equally, if needed, I can survive on very little sleep. I see that is not the case with you,' he teased.

'Hrumph!' growled the big smith.

Mertok was enjoying the exchange between his two companions. 'Here, eat this, Dawson.' He broke a small piece off a dark-brown wafer that he took from his pouch. 'It will take away your headache.'

'Have you got anything for his grumpiness?' joked Yorda.

'You're still not too old to get a clip behind the ear, laddie,' retorted Dawson.

Josh came over with some hot rolls, butter and honey, milk, sliced fruit and mugs of steaming tea.

'Hope your game went well,' he said jovially. 'No need to ask who lost,' he added, looking straight at Dawson.

''eaven preserve me!' said Dawson. 'Even the bloody innkeeper 'as a go at me.'

Mertok and Yorda both burst out laughing but Josh, not

understanding the joke, hurried off and busied himself with his other customers. By the end of the meal, Dawson seemed more like his usual self and even paid Yorda's bill for the room, muttering, 'Money's no use in the elf forests so might as well use it 'ere.'

The trio went down to the local market and stocked up on provisions for the trip. Yorda and Mertok bought a selection of dried fruit as well as fresh, whereas Dawson opted for dried meats. Some loaves of black bread, which Dawson assured them would last for weeks without going mouldy, were also purchased. Some hard cheese and a few tubs of honey joined the list. All three knew of different herbs and types of bean that would give them plenty of energy as well as filling their stomachs, and quite a selection eventually found its way into their travel bags. Dawson hurried off to get his horse from Brooks's stables, saying he'd meet them back at the inn. Mertok, too, said he had to get his horse and hurried off in the direction of the city walls.

'Where are you going?' Yorda shouted after the elf when he saw the direction he was taking. 'There are no stables that way.'

Without turning, Mertok shouted back, 'Who said I left my mount in a stable?'

Intrigued, Yorda followed him.

'You have a lot to learn, I see, about my people's horses,' Mertok said when Yorda drew alongside him. 'From the moment it enters this world, an elven horse is wild. Only elves may befriend and ride one. Only elves may befriend and ride one. They cannot be broken by any of the short-lived races of this world. Elven horses have a lifespan many times over that of a normal horse and, when they are chosen as a mount for an elf, they form a bond that lasts the entire life of the horse, or, in rare cases, the life of the elf.'

'What happens when one or the other dies?' enquired Yorda.

Mertok slowed and looked at Yorda. 'The one remaining alive mourns the other for a while. If it is the horse that dies, the elf will choose another mount and the process starts again. However, if the elf has died, then the horse refuses to let another ride it. It will be used to breed other stock or just reintroduced to the wild horses in the elven forests. Either way its life continues to be good and healthy. Ah! We are here now.'

The two had reached the city limits and passed through one of the large entry gates that were periodically found around the city's perimeter. Mertok walked a few metres and lifted his hands, cupping them around his mouth. Yorda looked ahead and saw a few people either entering or leaving the city, but as far as the eye could see there were no horses.

'You don't honestly expect me to believe that your horse will hear you shouting. You could roar like a mountain cat and he won't hear.'

Mertok dropped his hands and chuckled. 'Even a child would realise that I couldn't shout that loud.' With a twinkle in his eye he lifted his hands and cupped them around his mouth again. Soft as a whisper, Yorda heard the words '*Meryat, darimbar*'. As the words left Mertok's mouth, Yorda could almost see a ripple in the air moving outwards from Mertok's hands, fast as an arrow. The movement in the air spread just as does pond water after a stone is dropped in it.

Within seconds, at the limit of his vision, Yorda could see a horse, as white as snow, galloping towards them. It was fast, very fast, and was soon with them. As it slowed to a stop, Mertok held its head and breathed gently into its nose. 'Meryat, my friend, it is good to see you.' The horse snickered and flicked its ears. The white stallion stood proud and erect. Yorda could see no other colour other than white in its coat. The horse turned its head and looked at Yorda and snickered again. 'It's OK, Meryat; he's a friend.' Meryat moved closer to Yorda, who reached out and rubbed the horse's nose.

They walked back to the inn and met up with Dawson, who was busying himself with an enormous black stallion that was as large in horse terms as Dawson was in human terms. The man's love of horses was evident. He talked continually and gently to the big black while adjusting his bags. Several times he reached into his jacket and brought out a sugar lump, which the animal gratefully took.

'I'll just get my bags,' said Yorda as he went into the inn, leaving Mertok and Dawson to admire each other's horse.

Two minutes later Yorda emerged with a bag containing all his provisions, which he fastened to his back. 'OK, I'm ready. Let's go.'

Dawson looked around. 'Where's your 'orse, Yorda?' he asked.

Yorda smiled. 'I don't have one. I normally walk or run when travelling. If I have a heavy load I sometimes use a mule and cart to carry it; otherwise it goes on my back.'

Mertok looked at Yorda. 'You can't be serious, Yorda. Even a full elf needs a horse for distances or speed when travelling. We may have to do both on our journey.'

'Believe me,' said Yorda, 'you have no need to worry about that. All my life I have been banned from any games of speed or endurance with the children from my village because I win too easily, so I normally run with the wild horses or wolves, or even the big cats in the mountains. I haven't lost yet,' he added with a smile.

'At least give me your pack. Ted 'ere can carry it,' said Dawson.

'Ted? What sort of a name is that for a horse?' asked Mertok,

Dawson looked affronted. 'Where I come from there is a legend that the first 'orse who befriended a man was a big black stallion. A famous warrior was drowning in a river and the 'orse waded in towards 'im. The warrior clung to 'is mane and was pulled to safety. When the 'orse exited the water the warrior was sitting astride 'im, exhausted. The 'orse carried 'im to the nearest village where the inhabitants took care of 'im. They became lifelong companions. The warrior named the 'orse Tedaris.' So saying, he affectionately slapped the horse's neck and then fastened Yorda's pack to his own. 'Obviously when I met this big fellow 'ere, 'e reminded me of the legend so I 'ad to name 'im after the famous Tedaris.'

'No offence meant, Dawson; it is a fine name,' said Mertok as he leapt into his saddle in one movement. 'We head north to the Bantus Mountains. Once we have crossed those we circle round to the forest of the Elänthoi, then west to the elven forests.' Mertok lifted his reins. 'We try to avoid the villages. I don't want to leave any clues as to who we are or where we are going. I don't want the trackers' work made any easier. We sleep under whatever cover we find. We go as fast as the slowest horse, or,' and here he glanced at Yorda, 'Yorda can manage. Neither horse nor rider should become overly tired. We never know when we may need extra speed or strength. Is everything clear?'

Dawson and Yorda nodded. Yorda thought he glimpsed Meryat nodding as well. Dawson mounted Ted with rather less ease than the elf had managed and the group moved towards the north gate of Parkent.

The three companions moved forward slowly, with Yorda almost seeming as if he were just a normal city-dweller chatting to parting visitors. Several jokes were passed from one to the other with some mirth being shared by Yorda wanting to bet with Mertok over which of the horses would be the last to tire before Yorda did.

Although Mertok used no saddle – he merely sat astride the horse on a blanket – he did have several saddlebags containing all his provisions. These he placed on his horse with no noticeable means of fastening, but they seemed to stick like glue. Dawson glanced over at one point.

'I see you two don't 'ave any bed rolls or blankets.'

'I have several folded neatly away,' answered Mertok.

Dawson nodded. 'I forgot.' He turned towards Yorda. 'During my time with the elves I learnt a lot about their arts and crafts. They make the most amazing materials, which are like silk but much finer and stronger. It 'as the ability to keep you warm when you are cold, cool when it is 'ot, and dry when it is raining. It is so fine you can fold it many times without it appearing much thicker than it was at first.'

Dawson stopped talking and reined his horse around. Mertok had stopped several seconds earlier and was now dismounting.

Yorda turned. 'Where's he going?'

The big man got off his horse. 'I've no idea,' he answered. 'Only one way to find out.'

So saying he led his horse over to where Mertok was now standing talking to a young woman. She was no older than sixteen or seventeen and was leading a bay mare behind her. Mertok had noticed her a little earlier. She was stopping and talking to some of the men who had just entered or were leaving Parkent. He could hear them laughing at her and walking off. As the three of them got closer and passed her, he caught a little of what she was saying. She was trying to sell the horse complete with saddle, bags, bridle and halter. It was this that had made him stop and circle back.

'Why are you selling her?' asked Mertok.

The young girl turned towards the voice and saw Mertok looking at her. She was very teary-eyed as she answered. 'I came here three days ago with my husband and baby. We were on our way south to Mertown. My husband is' – she gulped back a sob – 'was a cooper. He had a job with the brewery in Mertown. Two nights ago he went for a drink. On the way back to our lodgings a pickpocket robbed him. He gave chase but was too drunk and fell. He hit his head and… and… and died.' This time the sobs turned into tears.

Mertok sat her down on a small wall and signalled for Dawson to give her horse the once-over.

'What will you do now?' Mertok asked the girl.

'I will go back to my parents' farm, but I have no money to bury my husband. If I sell the horse I can pay.'

Dawson walked over to them and nodded at Mertok. 'She's a fine mare all right.'

'How much are you asking?' Mertok asked, turning back to the girl.

'I'm not being greedy, sir,' she said to the elf. 'Thirteen crowns is a fair price but nobody will pay because they think I have stolen the horse.'

Mertok reached into his pocket and pulled out two small gold coins. 'Take these. I will buy the horse.'

The girl's jaw dropped. 'But that is far more than the horse is worth, sir.'

'And far less than your husband was worth, I should wager. I am sorry for your loss. It is no way for a fine man to die and from what you say he was a fine man. The extra money will help you get his body prepared and dressed if you wish to take him back with you to have him buried at your home.'

'Why do you believe me, sir, when no one else has?'

Mertok took her hand as she got up. 'It is quite simple. If you had been lying I would not have stopped.'

The girl's mouth opened in a silent 'Oh!' She thanked him and rushed off. Dawson watched her go and took the reins of the horse.

'Two questions, Mertok. One: why do you want another 'orse? And two: 'ow did you really know she wasn't lying?'

Mertok examined the horse while he answered. 'Number one. I know young Yorda here says he does not need a horse, but two travellers on horseback and one on foot will be at the very least noticeable and more than likely suspicious, whereas three horses is not unusual. So, Yorda, I am afraid that much as you wish to run all the way to the elven forests to win your wager with me, it would be better for all concerned if you ride with us. As for question two, I think you know the answer, Yorda.'

'There were several signs which told me she was telling the truth,' answered Yorda. He jumped up onto the mare and the three moved on. 'When she said she had a baby with her I knew that was true because I could smell her breast milk. She had fed the child only a short while ago. Also her tummy has not yet regained its normal size. Thirdly, there is a small insignia on the saddlebags. It is the mark of the coopers' guild. Fourthly, her accent is not local so she has obviously travelled here from another area. Fifthly, her horse still has the images of her and her husband travelling together. Finally, I suspect it was none of those reasons, Mertok.'

The elf laughed. 'All of those and none of those. They merely confirmed what I knew as soon as I talked to her. Some people, in fact most people, are easy to read just by their mannerisms. Also, elf-lords "feel" some emotions. She was telling the truth; I could feel it.'

'You can do this with anyone?' Yorda enquired.

'No, not everyone. Like I say, most people are just down-to-earth, straightforward people. They have nothing hidden. These I can read. Sometimes, however, there are people who have powerful auras around them. They may just have very disciplined minds. Magic-users I cannot read. I'm not saying these people are trying to hide anything: it is just that they are better shielded, for lack of a better word, than others are. You and Dawson for instance: you two are unreadable. I get no "feelings" whatsoever from Dawson, and you are half-elf so I suppose it is not surprising I get nothing from you. Josh at the Lantern, however, was very easy. With him I could even "suggest" things.'

'Such as?' Dawson seemed intrigued.

'For instance, he will not remember us staying at the inn last night. Sure, he knows that there were people in residence, but he will not remember our descriptions. It may give us a little more time if any trackers are following us. Hopefully it will delay them a little.'

The three passed through the north gate. While there were other people around, Mertok suggested that they should stay on the road.

The weather was warm and the horses were content to trot along at a brisk pace. A lot of work had been done on the road since the new coaches had been introduced to the area in the past few years. Communication with other cities was becoming more common. Parkent had grown rapidly in recent times and traders from all over the country were making regular journeys to see this new city and find out what wares they had to sell there. To this end, the city planners had made a concerted effort to make the roads more passable for fast-moving, horse-drawn coaches as opposed to the old carts that would be pulled along at walking pace by oxen.

In the warm air the three travellers spent most of their time chatting and learning about each other, or at least as much as they wished to reveal at the time. Occasionally, when there was nobody in sight, Yorda would dismount and jog alongside the others, quickly remounting when somebody came into view. Mertok was quite impressed with this as, even seated on his horse and having the excellent eyesight that is always attributed to elves, he was unable to spot travellers on the road as early as Yorda did. He started to believe that perhaps this half-elf really was as special as the prophecy seemed to suggest he was.

They made good time the first day. Towards evening, as the light started to fail, Mertok noticed that they were the only ones on the road, so he signalled the others to follow him and rode into the trees a short way off.

'It will be more difficult for anyone to spot us now and far easier for us to hide if we see any trackers on our trail.'

'Wouldn't the trackers be trying to hide in the trees as well?' asked Yorda.

'They have no reason to. Any trackers travelling north would need to move quickly if they were behind us. The road is the quickest route. Any trackers catching our signature may leave the road, true, but that is a chance we have to take.'

A few hundred paces off the road they came to an old, disused trail, probably used before the road came into existence. Yorda dismounted and sniffed the air.

'It looks as if only animals use this path now. There is no smell of men here, at least not for quite a while.'

The path seemed to move nearly parallel with the road so they followed it until night closed in around them. Mertok let Yorda take the lead. As an elf, his night vision was excellent and he could see the trail almost as well in the dark as he could during daylight. The speed with which Yorda moved ahead suggested to Mertok that the young man was equally at home in these dim conditions. He made a mental note of this and added it to the other abilities that Yorda had shown. He needed to learn as much about Yorda as Yorda needed to learn about the elves and Marosham.

Dawson was another matter. Mertok looked around at the smith. He had no doubt that the big man, having lived with the elves, would have no trouble moving through the forest at night, but he would have to use all of his senses to their limits, listening to the sounds of the woods around him, the smells that wafted in front of his nose, the movements of shadows around him. To a normal human travelling in these conditions it would be very difficult, if not impossible, without a lamp or burning torch, but Dawson seemed more than able to cope without any apparent difficulty. Mertok knew that the training given Dawson by the elves would make him a worthy ally – as if he didn't know it already after he had dispatched the three trackers back in Parkent. No, Dawson had no real surprises in him; Yorda was the unknown factor here.

After an hour or so, Yorda stopped and told Mertok that he could see a hut up ahead. Mertok dismounted and told the others that this was the same hut that he had stayed in on his way to

Parkent. Even though Yorda had believed he was leading the way, it seemed that Mertok had known of this route all the time and was in fact testing the young man. Yorda wasn't the least bit upset at this; after all, he would have done the same to Mertok if the positions had been reversed.

As they sat down to eat some of their provisions, Yorda asked if they should take turns on watch in case the trackers came.

Dawson took the chance to answer before Mertok had finished his mouthful of cheese. 'We 'ave the finest watcher possible, laddie: Meryat. Elven 'orses seldom sleep. From what I could make out in my time with them, once an 'orse 'as bonded with an elf it no longer needs sleep. As long as 'is partner sleeps, the 'orse seems to draw whatever rest it needs from this.'

Mertok had finished his cheese by now. 'As long as we are near to each other, only one of us needs to sleep. If we are separated, the bond grows weaker. Meryat will let us know if anything untoward happens. Tell me about your parents, Yorda. It has been a long time since I knew them.'

'I don't really know what to say,' replied Yorda. 'They were... my parents.' Mertok gestured for him to continue.

'My earliest memories were of growing up in the village where I live. They always told me that I was a special child and that I would do great deeds when I grew up. I think all parents say that to their children. My mother was a healer. She knew and taught me a lot about the healing properties of plants and herbs. She said that she had vague memories from another life of sick and injured people near her, so it was a natural progression to go from healer in one life to a healer in another. I suppose, now that I know a little more history about my mother, she wasn't talking about another life but about memories that came from her time before she lost her memory. My father did anything and everything. He was very good at growing things. He took great pleasure in growing plants side by side that everyone else said could not be done.'

Mertok lifted an eyebrow. 'It seems that not all of his elven powers have left him then.'

When Yorda looked a little confused by this statement, Dawson added, 'The elven gardens are incredibly beautiful. Just about all known plants are grown there next to each other with ease.'

Yorda continued. 'My favourite garden of my father's was the dwarf trees. By careful pruning of the roots and training of the trunk and branches, my father would reproduce the huge trees of the forests in perfect detail but they would not be much larger than my hand. The tiny trees would even produce fruit just like their larger cousins.'

'Are they still in the village?' asked Dawson.

'No. About six months ago they decided that another village might benefit from my mother's healing powers. They thought I was old enough to continue on my own here.'

'Where did they go?'

'They headed west and said that they would send a message when they had settled somewhere.'

'You haven't seen them since?' demanded Mertok.

Yorda started to laugh. 'About once a week. They are in a village about twenty miles away.'

He stopped laughing suddenly and turned to Mertok. 'You don't think that they are in danger from the trackers, do you?'

'I very much doubt it, Yorda. You can relax. Your father no longer gives off a signature so he cannot draw the trackers towards him. They will have no reason to visit their village. Even if they do, your parents know enough about trackers to stay out of their way.'

Yorda looked unconvinced but agreed with Mertok's reasoning.

At that moment a loud whinny from Meryat brought the three companions to attention. Before they had time to move they heard a loud howl, followed by a second, and a little further off a third. Mertok rushed for his sword but Yorda beat him to the door.

'Wait!' shouted Mertok.

'It's OK,' replied Yorda. 'Don't leave the cabin. I'll be back in two minutes.'

Mertok nodded to Dawson, who had lifted his axe.

Once outside the cabin, Yorda moved quickly to the horses and sent out messages and pictures of calm to them. Then he turned and walked towards the howls that were still in the distance but moving towards him. Wolves. And judging from their howling, quite a lot of them. He hadn't gone very far when he stopped, listened and sniffed the air. Without making a sound he climbed a tree and waited. Soon he could see them: eight large wolves padding softly forward, ears pricked and noses twitching, picking up the sounds and smells of the forest around them. Yorda smiled. He knew that the wolves could not smell him or hear him and they would only see him if he wanted them to. He had played this game – and to Yorda it was a game – many times with the wolves and even mountain lions over the years.

He saw the leader, an old, large, black wolf. The animal had seen many fights judging from the scars he carried. Just before the old wolf passed under the tree, Yorda let himself drop from the branch. He landed several feet in front of the wolf. The old wolf jumped back and snarled. His hackles were raised, making him look even larger and more menacing. He crouched, ready to jump. Yorda stared at the leader and probed mentally.

'Grerrak, how are you?'

The wolf froze. His name had been called, but not from any of his pack. Also he had heard nothing. He turned his head from side to side, indicating to his pack that he was ready to attack. He snarled again and crouched ready to leap.

'Grerrak, no! Sniff the air. What do you smell of me?'

Grerrak stopped and sniffed. Nothing. The creature in front of him had no smell. No smell of food, no smell of disease, and most of all no smell of fear. No smell of fear! This was new to the wolf. His prey was always afraid, if not of him, of his whole pack.

'Come, Grerrak!' Yorda knelt down and beckoned to the wolf. 'Come, or I will come to you.'

The voice held no menace in it and Grerrak inched forward slowly. Yorda reached out and touched the wolf on its nose.

'There is no hunting here tonight, my big fellow. But if you meet a group of three who have no smell like me, you may play with them, but beware: they are dangerous. Only play. You may turn them around so they cannot pass, but they are not good hunting.'

The wolf growled quietly.

'Now go with your pack and hunt elsewhere.' Yorda leaned

forward and touched noses with the big wolf. The wolf gave him one big lick and then turned and padded off. He gave a deep, low growl and the others followed. Yorda turned and made his way back to the cabin. A pity, he thought. I would have enjoyed joining in their hunt this evening.

'Wolves?' Mertok asked as Yorda entered the cabin. Yorda nodded.

'And?' Dawson continued.

'I asked them if they would hunt elsewhere tonight. They agreed.'

Dawson looked at Mertok, who shrugged his shoulders.

'Enough excitement for one evening,' said the elf. 'I think we should rest now and make an early start tomorrow.'

No one disagreed.

Chapter Seven

The next few days the companions made good progress. They kept themselves far enough from the road to avoid being seen but close enough to spot anybody that might have been following them. They were about a day's ride from Mattol, the most northerly city before the Bantus Mountains. Yorda had never been this far north, except as a baby, and was fascinated by the different types of plant growing here. The land had been rising slowly but steadily and the air seemed much fresher but a little thinner. He sniffed the air and a smile spread across his face.

'What is it, Yorda?' asked the elf.

'If I'm not mistaken I can smell fertlan.'

'No, you are not mistaken. It grows here briefly during the year. How do you know of it?'

'My mother used it on me when I was a baby. I don't know how she used it but I can vividly remember the aroma it gives out. I never forget a smell.'

'We use it on our children too,' Mertok said. 'If it is crushed and held under the child's nose, it acts as a stimulant. Very useful for recovery from illness. If it is taken as a drink it has the opposite effect and can help children sleep. When I get to know you better I may be able to work out how it was used on you.'

Dawson burst out laughing. 'Aye, laddie, my money is on the latter. What with your running faster than anyone else and out playing with wolves and the like, I reckon your parents must 'ave used up their supply in a very short time.'

Mertok too started to laugh.

Yorda looked at Dawson, who boomed out his laugh, and then across to Mertok, whose laughter was light and melodic, and then he too couldn't help but join in with them. The three companions were fast becoming friends. Even Meryat started to shake his head and snort as if he wanted to join in the fun.

Finally, when Mertok had stopped laughing, he turned to

Yorda. 'When you return you should gather some.'

Yorda stopped laughing. 'You think that I shall? Return, I mean?'

'We believe the prophecy predicts that you will triumph. If we did not, there would be no point in us trying to find you. Marosham must believe the same thing or he wouldn't be trying to find and kill you.' Mertok gave an encouraging smile to Yorda, who gave a shrug of his shoulders.

'I'm not sure how your logic works to make a statement like that, but thanks anyway.'

As they drew closer to Mattol they could see the twin towers of the duke's mansion. It was situated on the southern side of the city just inside the city walls. Mattol was much better protected than Parkent. Although war was rare in these parts it was not unknown for the mountain men to descend from time to time to raid the city. The duke had had to raise taxes to pay for extra fortifications in the north of the city and to increase patrols on the outlying farms. The lands here were incredibly fertile and the companions passed by many small fields, well cultivated and well maintained. Even though the local people weren't happy with the extra taxes, they all appreciated the extra safety. Dawson relayed all this information to the others. He had spent some time here after leaving the elves. He explained that the mountain men were fierce warriors. Many believed that they were the descendants of the first settlers here, driven into the mountains by the duke's ancestors, who took the land by force many years ago.

'Do you feel anything, Yorda?' asked Mertok.

'In what way?'

'You wouldn't need to ask if you could feel it. It is a signature from an elf-lord. There must be one in the city. We can make contact if we get a chance.'

The three dropped down onto the road and made their way to the city gates.

As they approached the wall, a voice from above shouted down. 'State your business.'

'We are just travellers looking for food and rest,' answered Mertok.

'And what do you hence?' the voice continued.

Yorda whispered to his companions, stifling a laugh, 'And what do you hence?'

Mertok ignored him. 'We go to the mountains. I hear there is gold in the streams that flow down from them.'

'You must be mad. There is no gold there, but it is not of my concern. If that is your want, so be it. Advance and enter.'

The gates drew open and the three travellers moved into the city.

'I cannot believe the way that sentry speaks,' said Yorda. 'He would make a fine addition to the travelling plays that pass through Parkent during the summer months.'

'It's an old tradition,' said Dawson. 'The sentry 'as to adhere to the old ways for entry and departure of visitors. I think it is quaint.'

The three dismounted and led the horses to a water trough. Dawson looked around. 'Nothing much 'as changed. I know a good inn near 'ere where we can take a room and get some good food.'

'We can replenish our supplies and leave tomorrow,' added Mertok.

They soon found the inn and got their horses stabled. Mertok went up to the room while Yorda and Dawson went to the local market to fill up on supplies.

'So what exactly is Mertok going to do?' asked Yorda.

' 'e 'opes to be able to contact the elf-lord that is 'ere. When elf-lords are close enough together, if they are receptive to each other, they can sometimes form a link. From what I understand, once a link 'as been created they can almost guide each other to make a physical contact.'

'All these different powers I am supposed to have and yet I have no knowledge of them,' said Yorda.

'Elves don't consider it a power any more than I consider 'earing to be a power. It's just something they 'ave and use. I am sure that you too, laddie, can do the same thing but you 'aven't been trained yet. It seems to me that you can do things that elves can't.'

At that moment a deep growl grabbed their attention. Both men turned. Just across the square where they were standing, they could see a group of people gathered around a cage that contained an animal. Yorda and Dawson moved across to see what was going on. As they got closer, Yorda could see a beautiful white mountain lion pacing back and forth in the cage. Two rough-looking men were standing just in front of the animal's prison.

'C'mon, c'mon. This fine animal is worth more than that. Where else will you get a pure white skin at this price?' said one of the men.

He was dressed in black leather trousers and shirt. Around his waist he had a belt with strings of teeth and small strips of animal fur, possibly tails, and animal feet. He had greasy long black hair and a sharp pointed face. The other man was muscular and seemed to defer to his much smaller and leaner companion. He stood back a little way behind the other man and carefully scrutinised the spectators and passers-by. Yorda recognised the animal. A pure white shorthaired mountain lion. He had seen one or two over the years but never this close. They were very rare. He knew hunting took place, but most true hunters would kill an animal for food and then use the skin after. A reputable hunter would also leave rare animals alone. The killing of animals solely for their skins was becoming more prevalent. It sickened Yorda, and from the look on Dawson's face he wasn't too happy about it either.

Yorda took a step forward but Dawson grabbed his wrist in a grip of steel.

'Steady, laddie,' he said quietly. 'Don't make a scene. We don't want too much attention drawn to us.'

Yorda halted but nodded slowly.

'I know, Dawson, but why do people do this? Any skin would do if someone wanted a warm coat. Why take such a rare and beautiful animal?'

'For that very reason,' answered the big man. 'Times are changing, and not for the better. People want things because they can't 'ave 'em. It used to be they wanted things because they needed them. It 'appened where I came from and now it's 'appening 'ere.'

Yorda knelt down and looked at the big cat. It stopped its pacing and looked back at Yorda.

'Don't do it, laddie,' Dawson said quietly, but Yorda ignored him and probed gently forward. The cat responded instantly.

'Home, want home. Cubs hungry.'

'Calm yourself. I will help. Can you find your way home?'

'Near. Half-day running.'

Yorda felt a nudge in his side. Dawson had stuck an elbow into him.

'You are being talked to,' he said, and nodded to the man in leather.

'You look like you know animals, sir,' said the man. 'How much would he be worth to you?'

'What are you asking for *her*?' answered Yorda, emphasising the 'her'.

Dawson groaned. The quiet shopping trip seemed to be taking an unexpected and unwanted turn.

The man in leather turned to his partner, who nodded. 'Three Mattol silvers for the skin.'

Most of the onlookers gasped. It was obviously much more than the animal was worth, even though it was very rare.

'I don't want the skin; I want the whole animal. I can do the butchering myself,' answered Yorda, who glanced back at the cat: 'Soon, soon, calm, calm.'

The big cat sat down and started cleaning itself.

'Don't do it, laddie,' whispered Dawson, trying to look away.

The man in leather looked at the cat.

'You have a way with animals, sir. Normally I would charge more if you wanted the animal alive, but I feel generous today. You can have the live animal for the same price.'

'I would have thought that as you don't have to do the skinning it would be less,' said Yorda, standing up and staring straight at him.

'Do you want – her – or not?'

'Yes, but not now. I'll take her tomorrow. I need to get a cage.'

'What is this?' said the man in leather. 'Are you trying to pull my stirrups?'

'Believe me, I have no intention of pulling anything of yours,' answered Yorda. 'I know you are asking me more than the animal's worth but I have my reasons for accepting the price. No one else would pay this price so I suggest you wait until tomorrow morning. I want food and water for her, at no extra charge, and I will see you here tomorrow at ten.'

The man in leather seemed taken aback at the more forceful tone that Yorda now had.

'Right, you have a deal,' he stammered. 'Now you must pay me.'

'Tomorrow, when I collect her,' replied Yorda. And before the hunter had a chance to reply, Yorda turned sharply and marched off.

Dawson caught up with him.

'One: you 'ave a lot to learn about bargaining, laddie. Two: what are you going to do with a mountain lion? And three: 'ow on earth do you expect to pay for 'er?'

Yorda smiled.

'One: I didn't need to bargain. Two: I'm going to release her. And three: I have no intention of paying one single copper coin for the beautiful animal.'

Dawson stopped in his tracks.

'What?' he hissed. He moved forward quickly and caught Yorda up again.

'What do you mean, not pay 'im? 'ow do you intend to get the lion if you don't pay 'im? Oh no, oh no... you are going to steal 'er, aren't you?'

'You got it in one, my dear friend,' answered Yorda, continuing to walk on.

'Look, laddie. What them men 'ave done is wrong, and I will be the first to admit it, but it is not illegal. You start breaking the law and you'll end up in the cells.'

'Only if I get caught,' smiled Yorda again. He turned and hurried off, with Dawson following, shaking his head.

When they got back to the inn, Yorda and Dawson were still arguing. Dawson told Mertok what had happened and was amazed when the tall elf immediately burst out laughing. Dawson couldn't believe it.

'Why on earth are you laughing? You told us not to draw attention to ourselves and this young scamp goes and scuppers it all.'

'I know, I know,' answered the elf, calming down slightly. 'It's just that your grandfather, Yorda, would have done exactly the same thing in your position. I know I should be angry but I can't help it. Anyway, you know you can't do it, Yorda.'

'Oh, I can't, eh? And why not?'

'We cannot jeopardise this mission just for a lion.' Mertok took on a serious tone.

'Listen, Mertok. This is my land, my people, my way of life. Even if I have elven ancestry my whole life has been spent here. You have wrongs to right in your land. It is the same in mine. Someone has to do this and it looks as if I am the only one who can at the moment. Sure, I can't right every wrong but I can't ignore it either. There are lots of things going on that I don't know about and therefore cannot get involved in, but something is happening here and now, something that I can prevent. If I ignore this when I could have done something, I will regret it for a long time. I am in a position to do something.'

Mertok looked at Yorda for a moment. 'Very well. If it must be done, it must.'

'OK,' said Yorda, turning to Dawson. 'How are you at opening locks, my blacksmith friend?'

'Whoa there. Slow down, laddie! 'oo said anything about me 'elping?'

'I seem to remember you saying back in Parkent that life was a little too quiet for you nowadays. I felt sure that you would enjoy a little bit of fun.'

'OK, OK, I'll 'elp you, but I really can't see that this is going to be fun. As a matter of fact there isn't a lock around that I can't open.' He reached inside his belt buckle and pulled out a couple of wires and winked. 'These little babies will get me in anywhere.'

Mertok added, 'I assume you two gentleman will be doing this tonight, so I suggest you get a little rest. I will stay here while you are out because if you get caught you will need a little help to get you released from jail.'

Chapter Eight

Yorda and Dawson left the inn when everyone else was asleep. They retraced their way to the square where the lion was being held. As they got close to the cage they could hear a low growling coming from inside. The lion was pacing its small prison. Yorda sent out calming signals to the animal. A few bones were strewn on the floor of the cage and a bowl of water was just inside the bars. At least they had given her food and water.

Dawson moved to the cage door and looked at the lock. He whispered over to Yorda. 'You sure the lion won't come for me the moment this door is open?'

'You look after the lock and I'll make sure she stays with me.'

The lock was a simple device, so Dawson took his picks out of his belt buckle.

Yorda, meanwhile, extended his arm towards the big cat. The lioness moved forward and rubbed the side of her head against his outstretched fingers. Once she had made contact, Yorda had a much clearer link with her. The lioness told him that she had been hunting for her mate and cubs when she had got caught in the hunters' trap. White lions mated for life and stayed in small family groups. Yorda knew if she didn't return to her cubs there was a chance that they would starve, as her mate wouldn't leave them to hunt for food himself. He knew that sometimes this happened in the wild, which was part of the reason the white lion was so rare. But what happened naturally was one thing; this was another.

Dawson had picked the lock and was gingerly opening the cage door. Yorda told the lioness to follow him and instructed Dawson to go on back to the inn. His job was done, and Yorda and the lioness would move much more quietly and swiftly alone.

The two of them moved silently and quickly towards the city wall, Yorda always slightly in front of the big animal. They soon arrived at the steps leading up to the ramparts. Yorda knew that there was no way they could get out through the city gates but there were always other ways. The two shadows mounted the steps and, with a silent 'thank you', the lioness leapt off the top and landed without a sound on the ground outside the city. She turned once to look back up at Yorda and then quickly disappeared into the darkness. Yorda turned and made his way back to his companions. When he got into the room, Dawson was sitting down with Mertok.

'Everything passed off OK?' asked the elf.

'Well, the lioness is free and is probably halfway home now,' answered Yorda, 'but I was followed back to the inn.'

Dawson leapt up and reached for his axe. 'Trackers?'

'No, there was only one and he followed me into the inn. If it were a tracker he would have gone to get the rest of his group for support when he knew where I was staying. Anyway, the lioness told me that this man has been watching her alone all day long. I think we have found your fellow elf-lord.'

Mertok looked at Yorda. 'You are learning fast, but you play a dangerous game. How can you be so sure?'

'The lioness could sense no evil from him. She sensed the same feelings from him as from me. That was a good enough recommendation for me. I think he is about to reach the door.'

As soon as Yorda had finished speaking they heard a tap at the door, followed by a low warbling whistle. Mertok picked up his sword and Dawson took stance with his axe. Yorda sat cross-legged on the table.

'Enter and identify yourself,' said Mertok as he slipped the bolt on the door. The door opened and a tall, blond-haired man not unlike Mertok stood in the doorway.

'Thalién!' shouted Mertok, and he stepped forward to greet the newcomer.

'Mertok, it is good to see you,' replied the stranger.

Mertok invited him in. As he entered, Yorda noticed that with one sweep of his head Thalién took in every detail of the room. His bearing was very similar to Mertok's.

'Yorda said that it was an elf-lord that was following him tonight and not a tracker, Thalién.'

'Did he indeed?' said the elf with surprise in his voice. He looked over to where Yorda was sitting on the table. 'You knew I was following you?'

Yorda nodded. 'You were sitting behind the crates by the weaver's shop.'

Thalién turned back to Mertok. 'This must be the one that we seek. Not even you, Mertok, could have noticed me tonight.'

Mertok glanced at Yorda with a slight grin on his face.

'Yes, this is he, but he has no knowledge of his heritage and is unschooled in our ways.'

'There appears to be no need for schooling in some of them,' said Thalién.

He extended his arm to Yorda. Yorda accepted the offer and they grasped forearms.

'Greetings, my friend. It is good to meet you.'

Yorda returned the greeting.

Thalién turned to Dawson.

'Greetings to you also.'

'*Eliathil rhôn maieril. Yrn aygar hirrim cherail*,' answered Dawson.

'A second surprise, Mertok,' said the elf as he crossed his arms in acceptance of Dawson's greeting.

'This is the human who lived among our people a while ago. It is he who appeared in our forests injured.'

'I have heard the stories. It is good that you have companions. It will make your return easier.'

'Do you not mean *our* return?' said Mertok.

'No. There are already trackers in the city. I must lead them away or at least stay here until you have passed far enough away that they cannot sense you. I will follow on later.'

'As you must,' answered Mertok.

'Can't we just get rid of them?' asked Dawson. 'The four of us could handle three trackers easily enough.'

'That is true,' said Thalién, 'but there is still the risk of Yorda getting killed. The most important thing is to get Yorda safely to the elven forests. I am going to take watch outside the inn. If the trackers show, I will lead them away. If they do not, I will stay close to you until you leave the city and then move back in to keep my signature strong for them.'

With that, Thalién bade them farewell, turned and left the room.

'He looks a lot like you,' said Yorda to Mertok.

'Don't let that fool ye, laddie. All elves 'ave similar features.'

Yorda smiled at Dawson. 'That's as may be, but he looked a *lot* like our friend here. My guess is that they are related. Also, they weren't pleased to see each other: they were relieved.'

'You are perceptive once again, Yorda. We are indeed related, but there again, most elf-lords are. Anyway, if we are to awaken refreshed we should get some sleep.'

Yorda noticed the way Mertok had neatly evaded his observation by answering without giving any real information, but that was Mertok's business, and out of respect for the elf he pursued it no further.

When they awoke the next morning, Mertok went outside to talk to Thalién but returned quickly.

'We must leave now,' he said.

'Thalién?'

'Yes, Yorda. He is nowhere to be seen. He would only have left here if the trackers had spotted him.'

'Or if he had spotted them,' added Yorda.

'Either way,' continued the elf, 'he would have taken them in the opposite direction. We must use his diversion to our advantage while we can.'

They gathered all their belongings, paid the innkeeper and went to the stables to saddle up quickly.

'I would liked to 'ave stayed to see the faces of them 'unters this morning,' Dawson said to Yorda as he put Ted's saddle on. 'I don't think they will be too 'appy when they find their prize skin 'as disappeared.'

'Serves them right,' answered Yorda. 'She will probably be back with her mate and cubs now.'

They made their way to the northernmost exit of the city in relative silence. Mertok looked troubled and constantly glanced from side to side, looking and listening.

When they left the city, Yorda looked around him. 'Where's the road?'

'No more roads for us, laddie.'

'Dawson's correct. From here on until we get to my home we

pick whatever route we can. At the moment, the fastest route is due north. I think we should ride hard to put as much distance between Mattol and us as possible. I want our signatures to disappear from here.'

Yorda leaned forward, stroked his mount's head and then dismounted.

'I think I need to stretch my legs. You two think you can keep up?' So saying, he bounded forward and shouted, 'Come on, Bettine!' His horse shook her head, lifted her tail and galloped off after him.

'Bettine?' Dawson sniggered. 'And he made fun of my Ted?'

With one glance back over his shoulder, Mertok followed after Yorda, and Dawson joined in the chase after a little chuckle.

Two hours later a group of four men left the city and headed due north.

Two hours after that, another six riders in two groups of three took the same route.

Chapter Nine

The companions made good time. Both Mertok and Dawson had travelled this way before. After leaving Mattol, they moved swiftly north. There were no signs of habitation this side of the city but somewhere up in the hills lived the mountain men. Yorda asked Mertok if they could be a problem in their passage north.

'They are a strange people,' the elf informed him. 'They will watch us but we have no reason to fear them. They are basically peaceful. The only grievance that they have is against the city. Mattol is theirs, or so they contend, and it is sure that someday they will make a bid to reclaim it, but it is rare that they bother travellers.

'The mountains just up ahead are called the Bantus Mountains. The mountain people live somewhere in there. When winter arrives, they move down to these hills just off to the west. That is the time that they make any attacks on the city. They are used to the harsh conditions and they have bred horses that are used to deep snow and mud, so they can attack and withdraw without much worry that the city guard will follow them. In fact, they hope that they will be followed. That way they can cut off the guard easily and attack the city again. The guard knows this so the city concentrates only on repelling attacks and not trying to follow and capture the mountain men.

'At the moment, neither side gets an advantage, but both are hoping the others will overextend themselves. Either the duke will say enough is enough and send a large force into the mountains to seek out the mountain people, or the mountain men will try to send everyone they have to attack the city in a desperate bid to take it. If either happens, then the aggressor will surely lose the outcome. At the moment, both leaders are sensible enough to realise that the small skirmishes are typical of two communities living side by side in a harsh environment. I know that is an oversimplification of the situation, but it is the way of men.

'What always amazes me is that even in this tense situation both sides trade with the other, although the duke would not admit it openly. It is for this reason that travellers are seldom harmed, because, if it were so, then trade from the city would most certainly be stopped and the north gate sealed.'

The friends stopped by the side of a stream where its rushing waters had made a hollow in the ground and a small pool had been formed.

Mertok led his horse straight to the stream. Yorda and Dawson knew better and waited until their mounts had cooled a little before allowing them to drink.

'The cold water doesn't affect Meryat?' Yorda enquired.

In answer Mertok simply said, 'Are you hot and panting from running Yorda? I thought not. It is the same with elven horses. The work he has done today is no more than a short canter to the horses of men. The cold water will not affect him.'

When the horses had rested and were fed and watered, Mertok looked north.

'We must make for the base of that first mountain. We should reach there by nightfall. If we make camp tonight at the start of the pass, we can make good inroads into the climb tomorrow.'

They mounted up and headed towards the pass.

After they had been riding for about an hour Yorda moved forward to Mertok's shoulder.

'You know we are being watched, don't you?'

'It is the mountain people. They miss little of what is going on here. As long as we do not inadvertently stroll into one of their camps they will not bother us.'

'It doesn't make me feel any easier knowing that,' said Yorda, dropping back.

They travelled on in silence, each of the friends aware that many eyes were watching them. The evening drew in as they reached their proposed camp. Dawson spoke first.

'I think they stopped watching us about an hour ago.'

Mertok nodded. 'We must have been fairly near to one of their camps. As soon as we were heading away from it they left us alone.'

Once the horses had been taken care of and the camp set up, Mertok outlined their next steps. Going east and round the base of the mountains would take longer, but the terrain was generally easier. It would also offer less chance of being spotted in the open by any of Marosham's trackers. Going through the mountain passes would obviously be a lot quicker but more hazardous, with plenty of places to fall into traps.

Yorda pointed out that, because the pass was the ideal place to lay traps, it would also be the very route that the enemy would least expect them to take. Mertok also pointed out that the resources of the enemy weren't limitless, and it would be unlikely that enough trackers could be left indefinitely in the passes just on the off chance that Yorda would head in precisely this direction. Dawson thought that the mountain people would not take too kindly to the trackers making their own camps in this area. Passing through was acceptable, but setting down roots, albeit temporarily, was viewed very suspiciously by the real inhabitants of this area.

The company bedded down for the night after agreeing to take the mountain pass. They hadn't been asleep very long when a soft neighing by Meryat woke them. Mertok went to his horse and returned almost instantly.

'We have company. Three, maybe four humans. It appears that they are trying to surround us. We have a couple of minutes before they arrive.'

Less than two minutes later, four men rushed into the small clearing where only moments before the three friends had been sleeping. All four had swords at the ready and eagerly plunged them into the sleeping rolls that lay on the floor. Hearing no sounds from the sleeping forms, one of the men pulled back one of the blankets on the ground. Underneath was some pushed-up soil, which gave the impression that there was a body under the roll.

'Drop your swords or never lift them again!'

The four men turned as one to see Mertok with his bow raised and an arrow notched ready to shoot. One of the men lifted his sword and moved towards Mertok. The arrow took the sword from his hand and another was notched even before the sword hit the floor.

'That was just a warning. The next arrow will meet flesh.'

The four men looked at each other.

'I know what you are thinking,' said Mertok. 'There are four of us and one of him. Even if you are correct, I could kill two of you before you got near me. However, I have some friends myself.'

Dawson walked out of the shadows, hefting his big axe. 'Aye, and I'm sure I could crack a few skulls with my little pet here.' He patted the head of his axe as he talked.

'It looks as though my friend the lion trapper has been following us.'

Yorda walked out of the shadows and looked straight at one of the men, who was dressed all in black leather.

'You took my lion and you will pay for that,' he hissed at Yorda.

'Number one: she was not your lion, nor was she mine,' he replied. 'Number two: if you had asked a fair price then maybe I would have paid you.'

'I have done nothing illegal in capturing the lion and we agreed a price. I demand my money.'

Mertok moved forward. 'So, trying to murder us all in our beds is doing nothing wrong. I think not, my friend. I believe a fair exchange is your lives for the price of the lion. You can walk out of here minus your weapons or you stay and become plant food. The choice is quite simple.'

The man in leather signalled for his men to drop their weapons.

Dawson stepped forward. 'I will see these gentlemen out,' he said to Mertok, and he indicated for the four attackers to lead on.

Mertok looked at Yorda, who had gone quite pale. 'Are you OK, Yorda?'

'Would you have killed them?'

'If I had to, yes, but it rarely comes to that.'

Yorda dropped his eyes. 'How am I supposed to kill Marosham? I cannot kill an animal, let alone a man.'

'That is for you to decide and not for me to say. The prophecy is the prophecy. For whatever reason, you will try to kill Marosham.'

'What is it like?'
'To take another's life?'
'Yes.'
Mertok thought for a moment.

'It is something I have had to do very rarely. To an elf, life is very sacred. We live a long time and give birth much less frequently than do humans, so for us a taking of a life is the greatest crime we can imagine. The elven history has little of war, unlike the history of humans. Dawson was a soldier and he has taken lives in the defence of his land and ruler, but I think it is no easier for him than for me to end a life. No matter the reason, it is always hard to know that your actions can cease the existence of another being. Sometimes there is no other route and we must follow the path that we are given. You cannot imagine killing Marosham, but believe me, if you do not then he shall surely kill you and then he shall do the same to every other elf in my kingdom.'

'I have thought long about this prophecy,' said Yorda. 'Is there no way that we can capture Marosham and put him in prison? I cannot believe that his death will avert the war that is brewing in your land.'

Dawson had returned and was listening to the conversation.

'Laddie, you may be right, but in my experience I 'ave seldom seen men with the sort of power that Marosham 'as being kept prisoner long. When you 'ave the sort of fanatical following that these people 'ave, then to break them you 'ave to destroy the leaders. Sometimes, war is the only solution.'

'Do not think overlong on this, Yorda. It is the gods that decide our fate. What shall be, shall be. I think the best thing that we can all do for the moment is to catch up on our sleep and let tomorrow determine what happens.' Mertok turned and went over to his sleeping roll. 'Remind me to repair the holes that those men made with their swords. It is much easier to repair holes in material than in flesh.' With that Mertok turned over and closed his eyes.

They awoke the next morning to a grey, cold-looking sky signifying the coming of a storm. The companions broke their fast with hardly a word passing between them. They saddled up and headed towards the mountain pass ahead.

They had not been riding long when Yorda called to them to stop. He pointed behind them the way they had just come. A single lone horse was galloping quickly towards them. There was no rider on it. The horse was travelling much too fast for a normal horse; it was quite obviously an elven mount.

As it got closer, Mertok stifled a gasp. 'Lëoram! It cannot be!'

Dawson and Yorda looked at Mertok.

'You know the horse?' asked Yorda.

'Yes. It is the mount of Thalién. This can mean only one thing: he has been taken by the trackers. Lëoram is making his way home but at that speed he will surely fall and kill himself going through these passes. Even an elven horse cannot stay sure-footed at that speed.'

'I will stop him,' said Yorda, and he set off at a run towards the frightened animal.

Mertok shouted after him. 'He will be much too fast for you, Yorda!' He quietly added for Dawson to hear, 'Even if he does catch him, Lëoram will stop for no one except Thalién until he gets home.'

Yorda quickly dropped down through the tree level until he could spot the horse. As the animal drew level with his position, Yorda leapt out and raced after him. The horse, seeing him, accelerated. Yorda stepped up his pace until he was drawing level. Mertok and Dawson watched this from above.

'It is not possible!' gasped Mertok. 'No elf can run at that speed. He is outpacing the horse.'

As he said it he noticed Yorda taking a huge leap and landing astride Lëoram. Within seconds the horse had slowed to a canter and then Yorda was turning him about and heading towards his two companions. When he reached them he dismounted and led the animal over to Mertok.

'Not even an elf could mount another's horse, Yorda, let alone one that is returning after the death of its bonded partner.'

'After what you had said earlier I didn't know if it was possible myself, but I had to try. I couldn't let him charge up through the pass. It would be certain death even for a sure-footed elf horse. When I got near him I sent out calming thoughts. I sensed that he wasn't afraid so I risked mounting him. As soon as I could touch him he relaxed. He told me that he lost Thalién's signature a few days ago and became frightened, so he could think only of coming home. He also told me something else. I am really sorry for your loss, Mertok. Thalién was your brother, wasn't he?'

Mertok turned away and inhaled deeply. 'Yes. His death will be a shock for the Council of Elders and for the kingdom of elves. He will be greatly missed. I will grieve for him but not until we defeat Marosham. Thalién knew the risks of taking this mission and entered into it wholeheartedly. It is good that you could save his mount. That in itself is truly remarkable. We shall take him home with us.'

'About going home,' said Yorda. 'I think we should make a move as soon as possible. When I was waiting for Lëoram to pass me I saw six riders in two groups of three coming from the direction we were yesterday. They were moving fast.'

'Trackers?' asked Dawson.

'There can be no doubt,' said Mertok. 'I can see no other reason why six mounted men should be following our tracks at speed, and for it to be two groups of three makes it almost certain. How far away are they, Yorda?'

'I think they will be here in two hours at the earliest, maybe three at most. They could not see me because they disappeared behind a small hill before I caught Lëoram. It is possible that they saw the horse.'

Mertok paused a moment. 'It appears that Thalién could not buy us enough time to get completely out of signature range before they killed him. It is strange, but when we left the city I thought that his signature had passed out of range too quickly. I assumed that he had taken them south of the city. We must take advantage of his sacrifice. We have to assume that we only have two hours' lead.'

'Can we not ambush them, Mertok?' suggested Yorda.

'I have been wondering about that myself, but I do not think it would work. It would be difficult to ambush experienced trackers. Anywhere that would be a suitable spot, they would approach with caution. I also do not think that we could effectively eliminate all six of them without incurring some casualties ourselves. I think the best thing we can do is to try to outdistance them.'

'I 'ave a suggestion, Mertok,' Dawson said, moving towards the elf, who nodded for him to continue. 'I spent a little time in this area when I passed 'ere after leaving the elven forests. Not far ahead of us this trail becomes a stone track for a while. Once we get on that, if we move carefully we will not leave any tracks for them to follow. That will slow them down a little.' Dawson looked up to the sky. 'I am sure that we are going to get a storm. Before it arrives, the mist you see at the top of the pass will descend quickly.' Dawson nodded in the direction of the pass where thick mist was forming. 'Once they get into that they will slow even further to avoid being ambushed. It will take them quite a while to catch up to us – if we were going that way.'

Mertok turned his head quickly towards the smith. 'What are you saying?'

'A short way up the track, there is a very small stone trail that tracks back down the mountainside to the east and eventually drops down into the woods and leads around the mountains. If we take that I know it means it will take us a lot longer than going through the passes, but we may well shake the trackers off. At the very least it will buy us a few hours.'

'I have to agree with you. It is the best option. We should dismount. It will be easier to mask any tracks we leave. You and Yorda will lead and I will follow a short distance behind to make sure we leave no trail. If they do not get misled, then I will try to hold them up to give you a little time. If you hear me shout I want both of you to go on without me as fast as you can and *not* to come back. Do you understand? It is not open to discussion.'

Yorda and Dawson nodded slowly.

Dawson found the side path after a little searching. Mertok carefully held aside the small bushes that concealed the track, making sure that he didn't break or damage any of the plants. He pushed them back into position carefully after passing so that no disturbance could be seen.

Sure enough it was not long before the mist dropped right down around them and it soon started to rain, not heavily but incessantly. The rest of the day was spent moving as quickly as they could. They soon left the stone trail as they dropped back down towards the woods on the eastern side of the pass. Once they mounted up they made good time. They stopped only briefly to feed the horses and eat a little themselves. As the day wore on they started feeling a little more confident about things. Mertok knew that the trackers would eventually turn back from their false trail but it would not be easy to pick up their new direction, although he was equally sure that they would after a while.

The three companions rode through the night with their cloaks wrapped tightly around them. Mertok had a light cloak that not only repelled any water but seemed to take on the colour of his surroundings as he passed, giving him perfect camouflage from any would-be enemies. Yorda didn't mind the rain but equally preferred to be dry and warm rather than cold and wet. Dawson grumbled but continued as any former soldier would.

The next morning the sun broke through the mist and the rain stopped. The sight of the steam coming off Yorda and Dawson made Mertok smile. Yorda dismounted and decided to jog for a while to loosen up his tight limbs. Their whole demeanour seemed to have lightened quite a bit from the previous night and they were starting to feel quite pleased with themselves when they walked straight into the trap.

Chapter Ten

The sound of running water diverted them from the course they were on and they headed towards a small creek to the side of the wood. A fast-running stream was coursing down the creek, which was empty save for some fallen trees and a lot of smallish boulders. Mertok and Dawson dismounted and filled their water skins and let the horses drink.

Yorda stopped after a moment and looked around. 'Do you hear anything?' he said to the others.

Mertok immediately lifted his head and looked around. 'No. You are right, Yorda: there is no sound of birds or animals here.'

Dawson moved closer to his friends. 'Do you think the trackers are 'ere?'

'No,' answered Mertok. 'If they were I am sure we would be dead already.' He looked at Meryat and Lëoram, who were quite happily drinking from the stream. 'The horses sense nothing; I sense nothing either.'

Yorda looked around. 'I feel a tingling in the air. There is something not natural in this creek.'

As he finished speaking, the boulders around them started to move and shimmer in the light. In a matter of moments they had transformed themselves into the forms of about twenty men, all holding crossbows pointed at the friends.

'By all the gods, a spell of concealment!' said Mertok. 'No wonder the horses sensed nothing. This is strong magic.'

Dawson reached for his sword and one of the men released a bolt. It sped towards the big smith, who only had time to see it heading straight for his chest. Time slowed for the big man. In the fraction of a second he had before the bolt hit, everything became crystal clear. He remembered fallen comrades telling him that the arrow or axe that hit them seemed to take an age to arrive. He was in the same position here. He could see the bolt heading towards him, the feathers on the flight turning in the air as it headed for its target. It neared and he tried to keep his eyes focused on this small piece of metal and wood that would surely end his life. It closed to within six feet. He could see the gleaming tip that looked so very sharp. Five feet, and a small movement to his left. Four feet, and a hand appeared. Three feet, and fingers closed around the weapon of his death. Time returned to normal speed and there was Yorda, holding the bolt. He had plucked it out of the air as easily as you would catch a ball being thrown.

'I told you not to shoot unless ordered,' barked a voice. 'Fool.'

A large, dark-skinned man cloaked in a large cape moved towards the man who had released the bolt. He struck him with the side of his hand and the man fell to the floor.

'The next time you disobey an order you will join these three in chains.' He turned back towards Yorda, Mertok and Dawson. 'That is a neat trick, boy. Now that I know you can do it I will make sure that there are always five aimed at your head. I am sure you cannot catch them all.'

He turned to another of his men. 'Get the horses.'

Yorda turned his head and sent out a 'Flee but stay near' message to the animals, who immediately took flight before they could be approached.

'Never mind,' said the man, who was obviously the leader. 'Chain them!'

'Who are you and what do you want?' asked Mertok, taking in the position of all the men around him.

'That is the first and last question you will ask me. You speak when spoken to or you will regret it. Pain is a great persuader. It is enough to know that you are my prisoners and you are now in the employ of His Imperial Majesty Karfal of the Frisian Empire.' He turned to several of his men who were waiting behind him. 'Put the manacles on them and place them with the others.'

While they were still being covered by the archers, three men stepped forward and manacled the three friends and quickly led them away.

They left the creek and made their way to a small basin, formed in the land a little way off. A further twenty or so mercenaries were gathered around a group of twelve men, all manacled. The leader ordered the companions over to the others sitting on the ground. Mertok noticed that all the weapons confiscated from them were being loaded onto a small cart containing what were obviously the items taken from the other prisoners.

After a short while the leader walked over to Dawson. 'You are obviously the leader here. Who are you and what are doing in this area?'

Dawson looked straight at him and said, 'I am leading these two men 'ere through the mountains. We got caught in the bad weather and 'ad to drop down 'ere until it cleared. They are 'unters and are trying to get to the eagles' nests 'igh in the mountains. The feathers are fetching an 'igh price in Parkent.'

The dark man looked at him dubiously.

'Perhaps you tell the truth and perhaps not. Anyway, it is not important. Your hunting days are over. When we return, you will enter His Imperial Majesty's army and will fight against our enemies to keep our empire safe. Until then, you walk when I say walk, you run when I say run, and you eat when I say eat. You will obey instantly or you will receive pain just as instantly. When we march, you keep up or you die.'

He looked at the three of them and at the rest of the prisoners and leered, showing a set of rotten, uneven teeth. 'You see, it is a very simple, easy life in His Imperial Majesty's army.'

He turned to another of his men. 'Give them some food along with the others.' He walked off, leaving them with the other prisoners.

Mertok looked around them. Most of the prisoners looked very like mountain men. They were not normally caught in traps. A concealment spell must have been used against them as well. At the edge of the group was an elderly man with his head bowed forward. The guards seemed to take particular pleasure in goading him and giving him an occasional poke with a spear or sword tip. The old man just ignored them and made no movement, nor did he rise to their baiting. He just sat there and ignored them.

Mertok turned to the nearest prisoner. 'What has happened here?' As he spoke he pushed towards him mentally to get him to answer. As he did so, the old man turned his head slightly in the direction of Mertok.

The prisoner whispered his answer. He confirmed that most of the prisoners were from the tribes of mountain men from the hills and that they had been captured in similar circumstances to Mertok's company. Of the old man he had no idea. He had already been here when they were captured. He talked to no one, but the leader of the mercenaries obviously had some grudge against him because the guards constantly taunted him.

Mertok leaned towards Dawson. 'Have you still got your lock picks in your belt?'

'Yes. I can get us out of these manacles no problem when I need to.'

He looked over to Yorda, who gave a slight smile and nodded towards his hands. Mertok followed his gaze and was amazed to find Yorda quickly slipping the manacle off his hand and back on again before any guard noticed. How he did it he had no idea because they were very firmly manacled. Yorda showed that he could do the same with his foot too. He looked back to the old man, who was still sitting with his head bowed.

'I suppose the upside is that the trackers will not come anywhere near this group with so many soldiers here.'

Yorda answered. 'Or perhaps they will get captured as well. That would make life interesting, wouldn't it?'

One of the guards started to hand out some dried bread and water to the prisoners, who all ate greedily. The three companions also finished the food they were given.

The leader of the mercenaries soon had them all on the move. They were still headed in the direction the friends wanted to go.

When evening came they made camp. The prisoners were pushed roughly into a small circle in the middle of the camp and half a dozen guards watched over them. They were relieved every four hours. Mertok was intrigued by the old man and managed to move next to him. He had noticed that during the march all of the other prisoners stayed away from the old man. Even though he appeared old he kept up with the pace set by their captors.

They were offered a little food again and one of the guards threw the old man's at him. When he walked off, Mertok leaned forward and picked it up, then passed it to the old man, who reached out and took it from Mertok without looking at him.

'You don't want to befriend him, my fine soldier-to-be.'

Mertok looked up and saw the leader of the mercenaries walking over to them.

'This is a very dangerous man, aren't you, old man? Or at least you were. Are you missing your staff, old man? Drashak, throw me the staff.'

One of the mercenaries sitting near the fire got up and walked over to where some swords and axes had been stacked up on the ground. He reached in and extracted a short staff, rather like a walking cane but a little longer. It appeared to be made of wood, intricately carved with what looked like dragons winding themselves round the cane from the base to the head, which itself was shaped like a dragon's head. Its eyes were inlaid with jewels, possibly sapphires, which glared balefully out, away from the person who held it.

Drashak brought the cane over and gave it to his leader, who held it in front of the old man but just out of his reach.

'Have you decided to tell me how this is used yet, or do you need some more convincing?'

The old man lifted his eyes to the mercenary chief but said nothing.

'Very well. Drashak.'

The mercenary who had brought the staff walked over to the old man, bent down and punched him hard in the face. The old man fell sideways but didn't make a sound. Mertok started to move but the mercenary leader turned to him. 'If you want to live I advise you very strongly not to interfere.'

Mertok stopped as several of the mercenaries moved towards him. The old man struggled to get up, blood oozing from his nose.

'Your bully boys need to train a little more. My mother could hit harder than that.'

It was the first time Mertok had heard the old man talk. His voice belied his age: it was full and resonant.

Drashak lifted his hand to strike again and the old man lifted his chin to accept the blow, staring directly into his tormentor's eyes.

'Hold,' said the leader.

'You heard him answer back, Sharnak,' the mercenary said.

The leader, whose name Mertok now knew was Sharnak, simply smiled. 'He has plenty of time to learn respect, and more than enough time to tell me the secrets of his staff.' He turned back to the old man. 'I saw you using the staff to make your fire the evening we captured you. His Imperial Majesty has told me of these staffs that magic-users employ. If I return with the knowledge of how this staff works I will let you live. But believe me, old man, if His Imperial Majesty receives a useless piece of wood your death will be slow and painful. Now talk.'

The old man looked up at Sharnak. 'Pass it to me, boy, and I will show you how it works. Perhaps it can be used to turn you into a toad, but there again why should I improve on what the gods have given you?'

'Damn you, old man,' said Sharnak, and he kicked out at the old man, knocking him over once again.

'Believe me, you will talk,' he said as he walked back to join his men.

Mertok moved towards the old man. 'Are you all right, sir?' he said.

The old man turned towards Mertok. 'It would be better for you, elf, if you leave me alone.'

Mertok was shocked.

The old man smiled slightly and continued. 'Surprised, eh? I can read your signature as easily as if you had "elf" written all across your face.' At this the old man turned away and ignored any further attempts at conversation by Mertok.

The next morning, Sharnak moved everybody out early and forced them along at a fast pace. They continued to skirt around the base of the mountains heading north-east. Mertok managed to talk occasionally with Yorda and Dawson but they kept their voices down so that the mercenaries could not hear them above the sound of the horses.

'These mercenaries seem to me to be veterans of many wars,' said Dawson. 'They are cruel but are obviously under orders to bring us back alive in as good a condition as possible.'

'I concur,' said Mertok. 'Until we can find a time to make our escape I would like us to stay close to the old man. He is not what he seems. He could tell I was an elf from my signature. This is new to me. Humans cannot read elf signatures. There is something strange here. Our captors believe him to be some sort of magic-user, or at least a magic manipulator with that staff of his.'

All the while they marched, their captors took it in turns to goad the old man, who kept his head bent to the ground and ignored their comments. Occasionally, an extended foot would cause him to trip, which was greeted with hoots of laughter from the mercenaries, but the old man would lift himself back up and continue as if nothing had happened.

It seemed to Mertok that the old man would only talk to his captors when their leader was present. The elf gathered as much information as he could from the other prisoners. It appeared that a group of mountain men had been watching the mercenaries as they travelled south. When they had lost track of them they had moved to where they were last seen to try to pick up some trail, and suddenly they had appeared right in front of their eyes. They had been quickly overpowered, and even though no one was killed, one of their group had sustained a bad sword wound to his side. Mertok's attention was directed to one of the prisoners who was walking as quickly as the rest but obviously trying to hide his pain. Mertok had noticed him earlier and suspected he was carrying some sort of injury. The man was obviously in pain but would not show it to his captors, but Mertok could see that it was taking him a lot of effort to hide it. He would try to get to the man later if he got the chance, to see what he could do to help.

The day drew on and Sharnak called them to a halt, telling his men that they would rest for a while. The prisoners drew together and one of the mercenaries passed some water round, not missing a chance to accidentally catch the old man a sharp swipe to the head as he passed.

Mertok asked another of the mountain men why the old man was being treated so badly.

'Beats me,' the man answered. 'He was captured before they took us. They take great pleasure in causing him as much pain as they can. He just takes it and does nothing. When they are not looking at him I sometimes see him lift his eyes to look at them. He is always careful not to move his head too much so that they do not notice him, but his eyes give me the creeps when I see that stare. It is pure hatred. If looks could kill, our captors would be dying horrible deaths at this moment. There is one thing that is strange. His manacles are different from ours.' Mertok had noticed that the old man's manacles were a dull golden colour whereas everyone else had black. He made a note to see if Dawson recognised the metal. As to why only this man had different restraints he had no idea, but it might prove important to find out.

A sudden fit of coughing caused Mertok to turn. The prisoner who had been wounded had started to cough quite violently after drinking his water and a mixture of blood and water was being brought up. One of the mercenaries had come over to see what the matter was. Mertok noticed that he was the same one who had shot at Dawson when they were captured.

'What is the problem here?' he demanded.

One of the other mountain men started to speak.

'Quiet! I am asking him,' he said.

The prisoner was still coughing, though not as violently. But as he held his hand over his mouth, the mercenary could see a patch of red on the man's shirt near his stomach. He reached over and tore open the shirt. Under the material a pus-seeping, bleeding, black wound was evident. There was the smell of dead flesh. Whether the wound had been caused by a dirty sword or whether it had become infected afterwards was difficult to tell, but it was bad enough to be the death knell for the prisoner. If they were in the elven forests a skilled healer might have saved him, but here the infection, coupled with the severity of the wound, was too serious. The man was going to die and in a lot of pain too.

The mercenary realised this and drew his sword. He lifted it high and started the downward arc that would remove the man's head, but before the metal of the sword could strike flesh, Yorda had thrown himself at the mercenary and knocked him clean off his feet.

The soldier got up and turned to Yorda, who had gone back to the sick man. 'You will die for that, dog,' he said, and he picked up his sword again before moving towards Yorda.

'Stay your hand, Lareem,' boomed the voice of Sharnak. 'What is going on here?'

Lareem took great pleasure in telling his leader that Yorda had attacked him. Sharnak looked long and hard at his man before turning to Yorda.

'What do you have to say about this? I remind you that if I think you are lying I will kill you myself.'

Mertok inched forward and he could see Dawson was doing the same. If they had to die trying to save Yorda, then so be it. From the corner of his eye he could see the old man watching what was going on, but not with the same fear that the rest of the prisoners were displaying.

Yorda casually glanced up at Sharnak. 'Your man here was just about to kill one of your prisoners for no reason.'

Sharnak moved towards the injured man. He took one look at the wound and drew his sword. Yorda looked up at him. This time he could not stop the blow, as there were too many of the mercenaries gathered round. Sharnak lifted the blade and with amazing speed turned and took off the head of his man who had only moments before tried to kill the prisoner.

'That was just one time too many that you took a decision contrary to mine, Lareem. I am the commander here.' He looked around at his men. 'It would be wise for all of you to learn from this.' He turned back to Yorda. 'I think a lesson shall be made of you for this, but first I must put this poor sod out of his misery.'

'Wait,' said Yorda. 'This man is much more use to you alive than dead. Let me treat him. I am a healer.'

Sharnak looked at Yorda and then at the prisoner, who was still coughing up blood. He turned to his men and shouted. 'We camp here for the night! Set up the sentries and get some food cooking.' As his men dashed around to do his bidding he turned back to Yorda and moved forward until his face was only inches from the young man. 'I haven't yet worked out how you managed to catch that crossbow bolt, but maybe there is something special about you.' He looked over at the old man, who was no longer watching the exchange. He turned back to Yorda. 'Perhaps you need special attention as well.' He stood up. 'If the prisoner can walk tomorrow, he lives. If he cannot travel, then he dies, and you will pay for striking one of my men.' With that he marched off.

Mertok and Dawson shuffled over to Yorda. 'Laddie, don't ye ever do something stupid like that again. These men would kill you as soon as look at you.'

Yorda smiled a grim smile. 'I tried a little trick of Mertok's. When I was talking to him I tried to project thoughts of letting me live. It seems to have worked. By the way, Mertok, if it hadn't worked, then I would have killed him before his men had got to me. You were right in that little chat we had the other day: sometimes you have to kill or be killed, and it took this situation to make me realise it.' With that he turned to the injured prisoner.

When they had been captured, all of their weapons had been confiscated, but they had left Yorda's pouch containing his herbs. He examined the man's wound. Gangrene had set in but he thought that it would not be this that killed him – yet. He suspected that the entry wound from the sword had punctured his lung and he was bleeding internally. All the walking was not giving the man's body any chance to recover. The man needed rest and the wound to be cleaned.

Yorda asked one of the guards for some hot water and some dressings. The guard gave him some cold water and the shirt from the dead mercenary.

Yorda took some herbs from his pouch and crushed them in his hands, mixing them with the water until the potion had achieved the texture of a rough paste. When this was done he spread a little over the wound and got the man to drink down the rest with some more water. As he did so he whispered a few words under his breath. Almost instantly the old man, who had been lying down facing the other way, turned and sat bolt upright, staring straight at Yorda.

'What manner of creature are you?' he hissed at Yorda.

Both Mertok and Dawson noticed this and moved closer to their friend.

The old man looked at all three of them. 'An elf, a human and this... this thing,' he said, staring straight at Yorda.

Yorda looked at his friends and then back at the old man, completely speechless.

'What are you talking about, old man?' said Mertok.

The old man's eyes were firmly fixed on Yorda. 'What are you?' he said again.

Mertok was as confused as Yorda at this outburst. Perhaps the old man was getting special attention from the mercenaries because he was quite mad. Whatever the reason, he didn't seem particularly sane at the moment.

Mertok asked the old man again what he was talking about. This time the old man turned to Mertok. 'You know as well as I do that the injured prisoner is a dead man. You know it, I know it and Sharnak knows it. Yet for some reason this creature thinks he can do something for him. Look at the prisoner now.'

Mertok and Dawson turned to the injured man. He was no longer coughing up blood and there was a tinge of pink entering the gangrenous part of his wound.

'There is no form of healing that should do that in only a matter of minutes. Even your elven healers, using all of their magic, could not do this in this short a time; yet this creature does it using a few useless herbs.'

Mertok looked at the old man. 'It obviously worked. The herbs must have been the correct ones.'

He was standing up for his friend but he knew that there was no way that the man should be recovering as quickly as he was.

The old man leaned towards Yorda again. 'Tell me, creature, where did you learn the words of power?'

Yorda looked even more bemused. 'What words of power?'

'The words you said after you gave the man his treatment.'

Yorda looked uncomfortable. 'I didn't say anything.'

Mertok nodded to his friend. 'I think he means when you whispered to your patient.'

'Whispered?' said the old man. 'What he said I could hear louder than if you shouted at me. You are a fool too, elf, if you did not hear the words.'

'What did you say to your patient, Yorda?' asked Dawson.

Yorda stammered. 'Just the same things I say whenever I treat any patient. Whenever I perform any healing I always seem to hear a voice telling me to say the words. I don't even know what they mean. After talking to you I assumed they were part of my elven heritage.'

The old man moved closer and stared at him. 'Believe this: you may be part elf, but the words you just uttered come not from this world.'

Mertok moved closer to the prisoner. 'What are you saying, old man?'

The old man looked deep into Mertok's eyes. He said nothing for a few seconds.

'You really have no idea who this travelling companion of yours is, do you, elf?'

Dawson decided to add his viewpoint.

'Mertok, Yorda, come away. This old man is obviously quite mad.'

Without taking his eyes from Mertok, the old man responded.

'Do not assume someone is insane because they have knowledge that you cannot even begin to comprehend.'

So saying, the old man took one more look at Yorda, then moved away and refused to speak again.

Chapter Eleven

The next morning the sick man was well enough to walk, much to the amazement of the mercenary commander. He was still very weak but his wound was now a bright pink colour and the skin was closing nicely. Sharnak ordered Yorda to be brought to him, and two of his men quickly obeyed, pulling the young man up unceremoniously and almost dragging him to their leader.

'It appears that you are skilled in the healing arts. You may prove useful to his Imperial Highness as a court physician.'

'I have no intention of doing anything for you under duress,' Yorda almost spat back at him.

Sharnak laughed and then leant closer to Yorda's face.

'If his Imperial Majesty orders you to bark like a dog you will do it, because his second order will be very unpleasant for you. And,' he added, looking over at Mertok and Dawson, who were keeping their eyes on the exchange, 'especially painful for your comrades, if you know what I mean.' His sneer showed Yorda that this was no idle threat. 'Before we move out I want you to look at some of my men who are suffering from infected sores.'

'Only if I can do the same for the prisoners. Their manacles are chafing and they need treatment also.'

Sharnak barked a nasty laugh. 'You make no demands of me, you filthy cur. You do it or I kill your friends.'

Yorda looked over at his two comrades; he had no doubt that Sharnok would do as he said.

'Very well, but healthy men march faster and arrive in better condition.'

Sharnak glared at Yorda. Yorda wondered if he had overstepped the line. The commander of the mercenaries walked around Yorda and stopped behind him. 'You have got spunk. Normally anyone who answers me back is dead very soon afterwards.' He continued walking until he could face Yorda again. 'However, what you say is correct and so you shall tend to your fellow prisoners, *after* you have seen to my men.' Sharnak continued walking until he was behind Yorda, then delivered a heavy punch into Yorda's kidneys. Yorda fell to the floor in agony and stars swam around his head for a moment.

The commander walked back into Yorda's line of sight.

'You are still alive, but don't think about answering me back again or next time I will remove your kidneys.'

Sharnak ordered his men to give Yorda what he needed to treat his men and the prisoners.

When they left their camp, the prisoners and captors alike seemed in better humour than at the start of the day. Mertok suspected that Yorda had done more than just treat any wounds. After having seen the recovery of the first man that Yorda had treated, the elf was wondering what powers Yorda had exactly.

They travelled quickly that day. The weather was fine and, even though winter was approaching, the air was not too cold. All traces of the bad weather from the previous days had completely disappeared.

They continued to move north-east and were soon into lands that Dawson had never visited before. As they marched, the soldiers continued their baiting of the old man, who carried on marching and ignored them. Several times he was tripped but just got up and carried on as if nothing had happened. Mertok noticed that the old man's staff was always guarded by four men, and he wondered exactly what was so special about it that it needed constant attention.

Most of their route was still largely in woodland with few open spaces, but at one point Yorda noticed off to his right, a couple of hundred yards away, their horses, led by Meryat. He mentioned it to the others that evening. Mertok had noticed them too and said that when they got their chance to break he would call the animals in so they could make their escape.

The next evening, after the soldiers had given them their rations, the old man moved over to the three friends. 'I suggest if you are going to escape then you had better do it soon. I overheard our friends,' he nodded towards the mercenaries, 'saying that they would be meeting up with the other raiding parties in a few days.'

Mertok had been thinking about the route they had been taking and this bit of information fitted in. About a week's walk from here, if they changed direction and headed north, they would get to the Great Sea. It made sense that this land of Frisia that he had never heard of would be somewhere across this sea. The other raiding parties would be joining them from the east and south-east. None could be coming from the west, as this was where the elven forests lay, and any raiding party headed in that direction would not be returning any time soon.

During his time as a captive, Mertok had got to know the other prisoners and now felt that he should do something to help them escape. But he also realised that his mission with Yorda was too important for him to waste time on saving others. He also realised that Yorda would almost certainly insist on saving the others, so he had to think of a plan to take this into account.

The next day they changed direction and headed directly north. They were soon passing a large forest to the west and Yorda noticed the old man was getting visibly agitated and kept glancing towards the forest. He noticed too that Mertok kept looking over to his left.

'What is it, Mertok?' Yorda asked, after seeing him glance in the direction of the forest for about the twentieth time in under an hour.

'That is the forest of the Elänthoi, Yorda. It is said that anyone who enters there will roam the endless paths for the rest of their lives. Our captors have obviously never been this way before because if they had they would not venture so close.'

'Who are the Elänthoi?' Yorda enquired.

'The children of humans would know them as fairies,' said Mertok.

'You mentioned them once before, back at the inn,' said Yorda.

'Yes. And as I said there, the Elänthoi are not the happy, mischievous people that your stories make them out to be. Their forests are close to ours and many hundreds of years ago we sent elves there to explore. Elves have a great love for trees and forests. They are our home, so it was only natural that we should explore, wondering if these forests were home to other elves.

'Few elves returned and those that did were deeply shocked. They spoke of a little people who possessed great and awful magics. They were very ferocious and deeply possessive of their lands. The elves that returned were told to inform us that we were not welcome in their lands.

'Since then we have tried several times to make contact in peace, but our people have never returned. We have now placed their forests out of limits to our people.'

Just as Mertok was saying this they heard the whinnying of Lëoram and Meryat. Mertok was instantly alert. 'It appears our chance to escape has not only arrived but it is imperative we do so now.'

Yorda had heard the horses and turned to Dawson. 'Trackers are here. It appears that the two groups we sent in the wrong direction have caught up with us. They have a third group with them.'

'You are fools, you vermin of the Frisian dung heaps!' shouted the old man. 'You will never live to see your homes again! You will die like the dogs you are!'

Sharnak turned his horse and rode back to where the old man was spitting out oaths at his captors. 'You foolish old man, you must enjoy the feel of my boot in your back – you keep asking for more of it.'

The old man looked up at Sharnak and smiled. 'Your mother lies with the pigs and your father could be any of a hundred men.'

Sharnak shook with anger. 'You have gone too far, old man.' He drew his sword from its scabbard. The other mercenaries looked on at this outburst. Dawson quickly got his picks out and opened his and Mertok's manacles as Yorda neatly slipped his off. There was another whinny from Meryat, and Mertok shouted, 'Down on the floor!' A second later a hail of arrows flew towards the mercenaries. Several of them fell without knowing what had happened. Sharnak turned and shouted, 'Ambush!'

His men were well trained and, at any other time, Dawson would have been impressed with the way they responded. They broke quickly to make their targets smaller for the attackers while four of them kept guard around their prisoners. Rather than trying to find shelter to defend themselves, Sharnak had his men immediately on the attack and taking the battle to the attackers. The leader turned and said to the men guarding the prisoners, 'Kill them all. They have some friends who look to free them. We shall show them that they have attacked us in vain.' With that he rode off in pursuit of the attackers.

One of the guards moved towards the old man and lifted his axe. Before he could bring it down, Mertok was on him and had quickly rendered him helpless. He looked around. Dawson had taken out another guard and Yorda had disarmed a third. The fourth, seeing he was outnumbered, quickly turned and headed off to join his comrades.

Dawson released the prisoners while Mertok called to Meryat and the other horses. The last prisoner to be released was the old man, who looked at Mertok. 'It appears I owe you my life, elf. That debt must be repaid some day.' With that he held up his hands and the staff that had previously been guarded by four mercenaries flew to his hand. The moment it arrived he slammed it onto the floor and instantly all was quiet. The sound of the battle in the trees ceased. 'His Imperial Highness of Frisia shall live to regret the day that Grandmaster Wiltor was captured and tormented by these animals.' He raised his hands again, but before he could bring the staff down a second time Yorda had grabbed his hands.

'Release me or you will die,' said the old man.

Yorda held firm. 'I don't know why, but I suspect you cannot kill me. You are frightened of me for a reason I have yet to work out. Whatever you intend to do with that staff I beg you to reconsider. You are free now. Be grateful and use whatever power you have to escape. Let these people fight among themselves.'

Meryat and the other horses had arrived and Mertok and Dawson were mounting up.

The old man looked at Mertok. 'You will discover what form of creature you have here,' he said, turning his eyes back to Yorda, 'and you may regret your course of action. But it is your path, which you must take, as I must take mine. I hope our paths do not cross again, elf.' With that he stamped his staff once more on the floor and he disappeared.

Mertok shouted to Yorda, 'We have no time! We must go while both our enemies are busy.'

Yorda jumped up onto Lëoram and the three comrades galloped off. Within seconds they could see that some of the trackers were following them and were closing the distance quickly because Dawson's horse could not maintain a high speed.

Mertok shouted, 'Head west into the forest. We will take our chances there. At least the trackers will not follow us in.'

All three turned and headed towards the closely packed trees that bordered the forest. Less than 400 yards further and they rode full speed into the forest of Elänthoi. The trackers pulled up short and one of them was heard to say, 'Our work will be done for us. Let us return to King Marosham; he will be pleased at this result. The half-elf is no more.'

Chapter Twelve

The three friends continued at full speed when they entered the forest. After about 400 yards, Mertok signalled for them to stop. 'It is as I thought. The trackers would not dare to enter here.'

Dawson moved up beside Mertok. 'Begging your pardon, my dear friend, but if the trackers will not enter the forest, then why did we?'

Mertok turned to his friend. 'If we did not have to then I too would have preferred a different option. Unfortunately they were too fast for us and would surely have caught us in a very few minutes.'

'I could 'ave kept them occupied to give you some time.'

'No, dear friend. In an open space they would have just ridden around you to get to Yorda. This was the better of two bad scenarios.'

Yorda had dismounted and was studying the trees and plants around him. 'These trees must be of a vast age. Look at the size of these trunks.' He looked upwards. 'This is not possible. They must be several hundred feet high, but when we entered the forest I could swear that they were nowhere near as tall as I now see them.'

Mertok looked around slowly. 'Yorda, you are in the realm of the Elänthoi. Nothing within this forest is truly as it seems. The Elänthoi are great magic-users, more so than my race. Magic is strong within the elven forests but here we believe it has no match on earth.'

'So what do we do now?' asked Dawson.

'We head west and hope that we find our way out of this place before we are discovered.'

Yorda nodded slowly to his right and left and quietly said, 'I think it is already too late for that.'

Dawson and Mertok followed Yorda's head movements but

could see nothing. Sensing their confusion, Yorda moved towards his friends. Looking back the way they had come he said, 'Do you not see them moving between the trees? They are circling around us. I see at least forty of them.'

'I see nothing, Yorda.' Mertok squinted in the direction Yorda was looking.

Just as Mertok had finished speaking, a slight movement ahead of them caused Mertok and Dawson to turn. A smallish man, about the size of a ten-year-old boy, had moved into view. He lifted his hand and lots of other creatures like him seemed to spring into existence around them. In a high-pitched voice the man said, 'Why have you entered this forest, elf? Your people know that you are not welcome here.'

Mertok moved slowly towards the man. 'I offer you my humble apologies. We were being chased by elven trackers who wished to kill us. They would surely have caught us if we had not entered the forest. We have no wish to trespass; we only wish to return to my lands and people.'

The little man signalled to another, who quickly approached him. The two conferred for several seconds in a language unknown to Mertok and the others before the little man turned to them again.

'The trackers of whom you speak have left. It appears that they understand we do not permit trespassers.'

'We do not wish to disturb you,' Mertok continued. 'We will leave your forest as soon as we can. We ask your permission to head west a little way before leaving your borders. If you have someone to show us the way we would be most grateful.'

The little man sighed. 'Alas, that is not possible. We do not wish to have contact with the outside world. Unlike you elves and humans, we the Elänthoi do not crave the company of other species. We learnt many, many years ago that creatures like you want only to invade, occupy and expand. This we do not tolerate and so anybody who enters our lands is forbidden to leave. Thus it must be with you.' Another signal from the little man and the surrounding fairies moved in towards the three friends.

Dawson reached for his axe and Mertok drew his sword. The little man spoke again. 'You do not really think your weapons will help you here, do you? Even if you could use them you are heavily outnumbered.'

Before Mertok could answer, the little man lifted his hand and the axe and sword disappeared from their grasps and reappeared by his feet. At another signal, three of the fairies stepped forward. Each of them carried a small dart in his hands, which, with a quick snap of the wrists, they threw at the three friends. Mertok and Dawson were hit instantly before they had time to move. Yorda lifted his hand almost quicker than the eye could see to catch the dart. To his surprise the dart moved in the air and dipped around his hand before finding its target in his neck. He felt no pain but was aware of everything going black around him before his legs gave way and he dropped to the forest floor where his companions already lay.

Light appeared around the outside of Yorda's vision. Slowly he started to focus on the world around him. He could hear frightened, high-pitched shouts close by where he lay. He struggled to sit up but his hands and feet were bound with… nothing! There was nothing holding him but he could not move. Slowly he turned his head to seek out his companions. He could make no sense of what was going on around him. Ah yes! The fairies.

He started to remember what had happened. How had the dart moved in the air? Darts travelled in straight lines, not in curves. He shook his head. Why couldn't he concentrate on what was going on around him? What was that deep howling that seemed to be coming from all sides as well as above and… yes, and below? The fairies were darting to and fro; some were shooting arrows into the trees, while others were standing frozen with fear. Their leader was trying to restore calm, the only figure who seemed to be in control. Where were Dawson and Mertok? He was sure they were with him when… when what?

Yorda could see the horses; they were grazing off to the side as if it was the most natural thing to do when the whole world was falling apart around them. The trees were moving. The damn trees were moving – now that *was* strange. Yorda seemed strangely detached from the surrounding world. Could someone stop that howling and make the trees stand still! Where had those pesky fairies gone? They seemed so cute and small. No, not cute and not that small.

Yorda again shook his head and tried to gather his thoughts. Mertok? Was that him on the floor near the horses? Dawson? He was lying face down in the grass. So green and lush. It would be so nice to be a horse. He could eat the grass all day until he was tired, and then he could lie down in it and sleep until it was time to eat again. Trackers? Why did that word keep springing into his head? Trackers! Were they here?

At last Yorda's head cleared. He had to free himself and get to the others. If only that howling would go away. It was almost unbearable now. He crawled towards his friends. When he got to Dawson he could see that the big smith was breathing deeply but was unconscious. Yorda lifted his head and looked around. All the fairies had now gone. He could see their leader bringing up the rear as his men fled into the forest. The howling was getting louder and Yorda wondered at the creature that could scare the Elänthoi from within their own forest.

'Hello, Yorda. It is good to meet you at last.'

Yorda turned his head towards the voice. The howling had stopped and it had been replaced by this mellow, unbelievably ancient voice. Just ahead of him stood a man; at least he thought it was a man. It didn't really have a solid quality to its body. But, yes, Yorda believed that this creature could be called a man of sorts.

'My name is Rimanathon among the Elänthoi. Come, stand up.'

'I am sorry, sir,' Yorda answered with awe in his voice, although he didn't quite know why. 'I am afraid that I cannot. I have been bound by the fairies.'

Rimanathon smiled. 'No longer. Please stand.'

Yorda found that he could move and stood up.

'My friends?'

Rimanathon turned to Dawson and Mertok. He lifted his hand and both of his friends started to stir. Mertok got up slowly and looked around before fastening his gaze on the man. To Mertok this man looked just like an elf. To Dawson, who had turned to face their rescuer, he looked like one of his own people, tall and strong. To Yorda he looked transparent.

'Do not be afraid,' said Rimanathon. 'You are safe now. The Elänthoi have departed. Their job is done. You have been brought to me. All is as I wished and planned. The rest is up to you. Follow me!' With that he turned and walked into the forest. Mertok and Dawson rose and strode after him. Yorda stood his ground.

'Why?' he shouted with a lot more courage in his voice than he felt in his body.

Without looking back, Rimanathon answered, 'Because you must.'

Yorda nodded. Not really understanding why, he followed his friends and the horses, which trotted along behind this strange man.

Chapter Thirteen

All of the friends and horses calmly walked behind the man without saying anything. They had been walking for about a hundred yards when the man stopped. He raised his hand and a haze appeared in front of him.

'Follow me,' he said quietly, and he walked straight into the haze and promptly disappeared.

Mertok, Dawson and the four horses followed, but Yorda stopped.

'Now, if you please, Yorda. We don't have as much time as you may imagine,' said a voice from beyond the haze.

Yorda followed.

He emerged in a clearing. It reminded him of the clearing around his hut back in his other life that seemed so far away now.

Dawson approached him.

' 'ere, laddie. This is just like my land. 'ow could we be in a forest one minute and in fields with lakes all around the next?'

'You are mistaken, my friend,' said Mertok. 'We are back in the elven forests. I can smell the Silverdene River and the bark of the alianth trees. Look over there, my friends: can you not see the golden-horned unicorns?'

Rimanathon approached them. 'You see what you want to see. Where we are now cannot be understood or accepted by your minds and to try to do so would surely damage you. Please come and sit. There is food and drink for you. Whatever you require is here.'

'Are we your prisoners?' asked Yorda. 'Because I cannot stay. I have important business elsewhere with my friends.'

Rimanathon looked surprised. 'That is the second time that you have questioned me, Yorda. Most strange.' To the others he continued. 'When you have eaten, I shall speak to you. And you, Yorda, do not worry about time. In this place there is no time unless I allow it. Please, I have no intention of keeping you prisoner, but I have important news for you and your quest to meet Marosham.'

Mertok and Dawson calmly walked over to the food, but Yorda just stared at this strange creature. 'How do you know of our mission?'

'Yorda, I know nearly everything. It is a price I have to pay for being who I am. Please, come and eat. I will explain everything presently.'

Yorda joined the others and saw to his delight that the table in the middle of the clearing was laden with all of his favourite foods: the most luscious fruits you could imagine; cakes and sweets; soft and hard cheeses; many types of bread; freshly made butter; cream and milk; nuts. Everything he could dream of was there.

'This is the best roast lamb I 'ave ever tasted,' said Dawson, filling his mouth with a handful of raisins.

'And these strawberries are the best I have ever tasted,' said Mertok, munching away on some cake.

Yorda kept quiet until he had finished eating and then turned to Rimanathon. Before he had a chance to say anything, Rimanathon clicked his fingers and the tables were gone and the friends were sitting in a log cabin in front of a roaring log fire.

'What is going on here?' asked Yorda, jumping up.

'Relax, Yorda,' said Mertok. 'This gentleman has invited us into his home to share his food. The least we can do is be polite.'

Rimanathon stood up and walked in front of the fire, turned and looked at the three companions. He lifted his hand and said,

'Now you are all alert and aware.'

Instantly Dawson and Mertok got to their feet.

'Please, sit down. I mean you no harm but I have something important that you should hear. Your mission to fulfil the prophecy is in danger.'

'What do you know of the prophecy?' demanded Mertok.

'Please, sit down I beg of you.'

Yorda noticed that Rimanathon's voice had lost the tone that he had used to get the others to obey earlier. Now he talked as any friend would in front of a big fire before bedtime.

'I ask you only to listen to me. What you do after is up to you.'

He paused and waited until all three friends had nodded; then he continued.

'There are things that I am about to tell you that no living creature should ever know, but certain circumstances have occurred which require me to impart this knowledge to you. First, however, you should learn a little about me.

'As I have said, my name is Rimanathon. This is the name that you will know me by. My true name among my kind is The Third. The Elänthoi call me Rimanathon, which means "bringer of death". They believe that my coming into their forest will cause the destruction of their race. They cannot harm me, which they find difficult to accept, as they are the most powerful creatures that come from this earth. They do not understand how someone can walk among them with impunity. However, that does not concern you here and now.

'Mertok, you come from a race that has been on this earth for many millennia. You pride yourselves as being perhaps the oldest race. It is true that you and the Elänthoi were created as the first living beings on this planet. The Elänthoi were before you, which is why their magic is greater, but before them was darkness.

'Your world was created by a group of gods known as the Helanth, beings with virtually unlimited power. Their magic was used to create all the worlds in the sky. When you look up to the sky at night and you see the twin moons of this land, you perhaps cannot believe that there are other worlds like this one, worlds as alike and as different as the foods that you ate earlier. All of the worlds in the night sky were created by the Helanth. Each of the gods decided the form of the creatures that should walk the earth. The first was the Elänthoi. Next came the elves. Hundreds of years passed between the birth of the Elänthoi and the elves but to the gods it was but a blink of the eye. Many other creatures, most of which you have not met, and some of which you are never meant to meet, were also created. Last of all was man.

'At first there were no barriers between the creatures, but then the Helanth realised that their creations were not meant to mix so they gathered up many of the races and took them to other worlds, which they also created. To the gods it was just a game. They wanted to see what would happen when their creations were given life and the power to make their own decisions. To them, all life was at the same time meaningless and precious. Who can question the gods? Your values and beliefs are as insignificant as those of the insects that crawl on the ground. What is important to you has no significance in the great scheme of things.

'When all the worlds were created and populated, the gods decided to leave and create another universe with different values and concepts that you could not even begin to imagine let alone understand, but they needed to know what was going on in their first experiment. To this end they created me and others like me. We are known as the Spellweavers. Our existence is solely to record everything that happens on this planet and eventually give it to the gods when they return.

'After we were created the gods took us back in time to before the birth of all creatures, so in some ways you could say we were the first, even though we were the last. We were given the power to travel to any world through portals that only we could access. My kind were given the Great Books of Knowledge and Magic to help us continue the experiment. We were also given the power to shape the future by indirect means: a subtle nudge here, a push there when needed kept the balance of the planet. Each planet created by the magic of the gods contains a little extra of their magic that can be used by the creatures on the planet. How they use it is for the Spellweavers to monitor and record. The most powerful magic on each planet is contained within the portals and this magic was designed not to be used by any but the Spellweavers for many thousands of years.

'Unfortunately, one of the Great Books has disappeared. For beings with our powers this is unimaginable; for beings like you this is catastrophic. The Book is being used to weaken the portals. When this happens, the power within goes back to the land and makes the magic available to any who can use it. This is not the plan of the gods but we can do nothing to change it as we are only allowed minimum intervention. As the portals weaken they begin to open and can be used by any creature. You can imagine the problems that would arise should all the creatures the gods have created suddenly find themselves face to face with creatures they were not meant to meet for thousands of years. Many of your races on this planet will fight over the smallest excuse. When you see something you don't understand you are afraid.'

Rimanathon turned to his side and clicked his fingers. In the corner of the room a dark, oily mass rose from the floor. Over eight feet tall, it had razor-shaped claws at the end of each of its four arms. No discernible features could be seen in the area where the head should have been. Mertok and Dawson rose as one. On the table that had appeared in front of them were Dawson's battleaxe and Mertok's bow and quiver of arrows. They quickly seized their weapons and prepared to repel this monstrous creature that bore down on them. Rimanathon clicked his fingers again and the creature disappeared.

'There, you see? That was a creature that you should not meet until you have developed further. Even you, Mertok, as one of the oldest race of creatures who walk this earth, would have killed it without question. True, the creature would have killed you too, which proves my point that your races are not ready to meet, but meet they will if the portals continue to break down.

'Since the loss of the Book, other things have started to happen of which I cannot speak at this time. What I can say is that whoever has the Book is trying to influence the future of the worlds created by the gods and maybe even ultimately challenge the gods themselves. Who can tell? We can shape the future but we cannot foretell it. The three of you were chosen and were guided here to meet me because it is you upon whom the futures of the worlds rest. Yorda, there is something special about you that you will hopefully live to fulfil. Dawson too, you are a vital cog in a mighty wheel. Neither of you should be here, but here you are. Of that I will speak no more, other than to say, make your existence count. Mertok, it is you who was chosen to find the others and take them back to face Marosham. He too has been given a part in all of this, a part that he should not have had.

'I can give you no more information. We may meet again. Of that I am not certain, but, as I have engineered our meeting here through your adventures, then I will try to help you in the limited way that I am allowed.

'Mertok, I have some good news for you. To get you here I was obliged to allow the trackers to pick up your trail before you got into the mountains. Had that not happened you would all be dead now. To do that I needed you to spot the trackers. Yorda did that when catching Lëoram. You think that Thalién is dead. He is not. I cancelled his signature so that the trackers would fasten onto yours and follow you. He is making his way back to your people. When he enters the forests he will regain his signature and with luck he will meet once again with Lëoram.

'Yorda, I want you to take this. It is an amulet that will let you enter any portal once. On the other side will be a place of no magic, a world that is dead. This place may be of help to you in the future. I can tell you no more because I know no more. Your people would call this a feeling or a premonition, but to me it is something that must be done for no other reason than that it must. I too will understand why only after it has been used.

'Dawson, I must tell you to remember the lesson today with the creature that I brought from another world. It is a lesson that is especially important to you but I am not permitted to say more. Remember that all is not as it first appears. Gather information before you commit yourself to a course of action that cannot be reversed.

'I see that you have questions to ask, but I am afraid that cannot be allowed. Maybe if we meet again I shall allow you that courtesy, but for now your place is only to listen and try to understand what little has been imparted to you.

'When you leave, you will not be troubled by the Elänthoi. They will be occupied with other things until you are out of their lands. Now you must follow me to the portal where we shall take our leave.'

All of the comrades followed Rimanathon and walked through the portal where they found themselves back in the fairy forest. Yorda turned to thank the Spellweaver but he had gone. He heard a voice in his head say, 'Yorda, you are not like the others. Many things will come your way. You are the future. Make wise decisions, for you are as dangerous as you are ignorant.'

With that strange message echoing in his head, the three friends were alone.

Chapter Fourteen

The companions found themselves back in the forest of the Elänthoi. It was as Rimanathon had said: the fairies did not trouble them. A few times they heard the sweet, high-pitched singing that was typical of the Elänthoi, but, as they approached, the singing stopped, only to start up much further away. It was almost as if the Elänthoi were hiding from them.

The variety of flora and fauna that they saw was truly remarkable. It was again as Rimanathon had said: this part of their world had been designed to be separate from the rest of it.

Mertok had been watching Yorda ever since they had left the Spellweaver. 'Speak to me, Yorda. I do not know why, but there is something different about you.' Yorda looked over at Mertok, who continued, 'I sense a difference in you. Your signature has become stronger since we entered the forest.'

'That is not the only thing I see, laddie.' Dawson joined in the conversation. 'You appear to be taller to me.'

Mertok moved over to Yorda and found himself actually looking up to meet the young healer's eyes. 'You are correct, Dawson. Yorda must be three inches taller than when we entered the forest. Do you feel anything, Yorda?'

Yorda looked back at his friends. 'I am not sure. One thing I have noticed is that the voices that I sometimes hear in my head, such as the words I always say when I am healing someone, are louder and clearer here. I can hear clear words – or at least I think they are words – and sounds that were just outside my hearing before are now just audible, although I have no idea what they mean. Perhaps the magic of this forest has something to do with it; I just don't know.'

'Whatever it is, laddie, if you keep growing you will be larger than me,' laughed the big smith.

They rode on, all the while noticing that, even though they had been en route for many hours now, the forest was not getting any darker or lighter. The other thing they noticed was that the light seemed to be coming from around them and not from above them.

Mertok decided to make camp and rest, as they had now been travelling, according to his calculations, for at least twenty hours. No one seemed hungry, not even the horses, and they all put this down to the feast they had had with Rimanathon.

'I see no point in even asking the horses to keep watch,' said Mertok. 'I believe our Spellweaver friend has arranged safe passage for us until the borders of this land.'

Upon saying that, the elf turned over and closed his eyes and immediately fell asleep. Dawson did likewise. Yorda stood and walked around a little. He could not understand what was happening to him. In his head he could hear the voices – voices that were not of the race of humans and he was sure were not of the voice of elves. He could feel the earth living beneath him and with every step he took a tingle passed up his body as his feet made contact with the earth. He felt stronger, older and wiser. He had indeed grown several inches. Was it Rimanathon's doing or something else? Some power older that Rimanathon even? The voices in his head seemed to come from a time before time, but why he should think that he could not tell.

The young healer walked over to the horses, who seemed pleased to have his attention. Lëoram seemed to understand when Yorda explained that Thalién was alive and well and would be reunited with his horse in the elven forests. Even though he longed to be with his bonded master, Lëoram was also content to stay with Yorda. He moved over to Bettine. Although the horse was not of elven stock Yorda could sense great intelligence and also loyalty. This too was something new for the young man. He felt as if all his senses were heightened – not too surprising really, he told himself, after all that he had been through. He said a brief goodnight to Meryat and Ted and then went back to where his friends lay down. As he drifted off to sleep, night descended around them in the forest.

While they slept they were visited by the creatures of the forest. Animals unlike any they had seen before came and lay next to them. Insects the size of a man's hand flitted about them before dropping down and alighting on Yorda and his friends. Some deer with black antlers and very long ears came to stand with the horses, who just looked at the newcomers and then lay themselves down to sleep. The burrowing animals moved towards the friends and just lay and watched without moving. The high-pitched singing of the fairies moved slowly towards the sleeping comrades. Closer, closer... Suddenly many eyes were upon the sleeping forms. The Elänthoi formed a ring around them and softly sang, songs that had not been sung for generations. Songs of the creation of the earth, songs of heroes of old, songs of heroes of present and songs of heroes to be. None of the company awoke even when their names were mentioned in the songs.

The next morning, Yorda was the first to open his eyes. It was light again, the same strange light that came from all around them and not from above. Mertok and Dawson awoke a few minutes after Yorda.

After the friends had breakfasted they prepared the horses and continued west. Yorda noticed that both Dawson and Mertok seemed very subdued and found it difficult to get much in the way of conversation out of them. They had travelled for most of the day when Yorda suggested that they stop to give the horses a rest.

'Yorda?' said Mertok. 'Are you all right?'

'Yes, I am fine. Why do you ask?'

Mertok looked strangely towards Dawson.

'We have only been riding about an hour. There is no need to rest the horses.'

Yorda couldn't believe what he was hearing. He knew Mertok had seemed lost in thought, but to totally lose track of time like that was very strange.

'I think perhaps it is you that is not well,' answered Yorda. 'We have been travelling all day. I know that you and Dawson have been deep in thought but surely you have not lost track of time?'

Dawson gave Mertok a strange look.

'Laddie, Mertok is correct. We 'ave not been long in the saddle. I would put it at about twenty minutes rather than the hour that Mertok thinks.'

Yorda touched Lëoram's neck and then looked back towards his friends.

'It seems that Lëoram and the other horses all have different perceptions of our time en route today. Which of us is correct?'

Mertok looked around him, at the trees, the plants, the small animals toing-and-froing, and then looked up to the sky. 'Things are not as they seem here. The lands of the Elänthoi do not exist as do other lands. It is said in the stories of my people that the fairies live outside time. A week here may be a year or but a second in the lands outside. So it must be in our perception of the passage of time. We have no way of telling time. This light that surrounds us is not light from the sun so we cannot calculate true time. It appears that we cannot trust our senses so we must believe Rimanathon and just continue west until we exit from the forest.'

The comrades continued on their way. Yorda made a mental note of the distances between the objects they were passing and tried to calculate the speed they were travelling and the distance they were travelling to come up with some sort of time scale. No matter what their perception of time was, they could only travel at a certain speed. After several hours he reported his findings back to his friends with a certain degree of smugness, as it appeared that his calculations coincided with his perceptions of the passage of time. He was very surprised when both Mertok and Dawson told him that they had been doing almost exactly the same thing but their observations led them to believe that they were correct.

'It appears that the only things we can be sure of is that we are all together,' said Mertok. 'The magic of these lands is strong. Have you also noticed that we leave no tracks behind us?'

His two companions nodded. They too had noticed this but had not mentioned it in case it was only each of them that had seen it.

'Something that worries me,' continued Mertok, 'is how can we be sure that we are actually going west and not in a big circle.'

'Of that I am sure,' said Yorda.

' 'ow are you so positive, my young friend?' said Dawson.

Yorda pointed in the direction they were headed.

'I hear a voice in my head. It has been there since we entered the forest. I don't know if the magic here has been some sort of conduit for it but it is getting stronger as we head in this direction.'

Mertok stopped his horse.

'And why does that mean we are heading west, Yorda?'

'Because it is Marosham that is talking to me. He knows now that I am on the way home. He tells me that his trackers have failed and he has recalled them all to await my arrival. He tells me this and many other things. His voice is in my head all the time.'

'Do you reply, Yorda?' asked Mertok.

'No. There is no need. He knows that I hear him. He also knows that I do not fear him any longer. Now that I have heard his voice I have heard his fear, his pain, his anger, but most of all I have felt, rather than heard, his hate. He despises the rest of the elves. He wants to destroy every last one of them, and what better way to do it than to start with us, Mertok.'

Yorda spurred his horse forward and headed in the direction he had just pointed. Mertok and Dawson followed in silence, each deep in his own thoughts.

Later that day they decided to make camp again to eat and sleep. They could no longer distinguish between night and day. The same all-surrounding light covered the passing of the hours and days and nights. They had no idea now if they had been travelling only hours or weeks.

Mertok and Dawson were again asleep in an instant when their heads touched the ground. Yorda sat up and thought about what was going to happen to him and his friends. His life had completely changed in the past few weeks. Everything that he had believed in seemed to have changed in such a short time. Before he had entered the fairy realm he had thought that he had come to terms with what was going to happen, but since he had been in this land things had changed. He had grown in size almost in a matter of minutes. He could feel this tingling every time his feet touched the ground. Marosham's voice in his head was now a constant companion that was trying to eat away at him and undermine his determination.

He was sure that Marosham was also trying to get information about Yorda's position. For some reason that he didn't understand, Yorda realised that if Marosham had been in contact with him before they had entered the forest he probably would have told him everything he wanted, but now his mind was strong and he was determined not to let Marosham carry out his threat.

The Black Elf was powerful. He alternated his contacts with Yorda. First he would speak softly and promise Yorda untold wealth and power if he joined him and his army in the assault on the rest of the elves. He would then threaten Yorda, telling him what he would do to his companions when they had been captured, because captured they surely would be. Sometimes he would just send images into Yorda's head – pictures of death and destruction – all the while telling Yorda that with him at his side all the death would be quick and painless, but if he didn't join him then Marosham would make sure that the most suffering conceivable would be inflicted on the elves.

Yorda knew that the fairy forest had done something to him. Of course, it altered everybody's perception of things, but this was different. Other voices were in his head, not only that of Marosham. He could hear the voice that had always given him the words he used while healing. Other words were being told to him now. What they meant he did not know... yet. But he was sure that they were important and he had no doubt that as he got closer to the elven forests all would become clear.

His thoughts were interrupted by a soft rustling to his left. He turned and saw what was undoubtedly the most beautiful creature he had ever beheld. It was a pure white horse. The animal was grazing just at the edge of the clearing where the friends had made camp. As the animal lifted its head and turned, Yorda could see why it was so magnificent. At the top of its head, in between the ears, there was a golden horn. It was a unicorn. Yorda had read stories of this animal and Mertok had mentioned seeing one when they were with Rimanathon.

The young man got up and moved towards the animal, all the while sending out soothing signals. The animal looked at him and said, 'Your coming here, Yorda, spells doom for us all, but is as it must be. You live, we die; you die, we live.'

'I don't understand. Of whom do you speak?' Yorda asked.

'To ask a question of a unicorn is allowed but to get an answer is as a wish. You must capture me to obtain this information. Come, Yorda, let us see how fast you really are.'

With that the unicorn turned and without a backwards glance galloped off.

Yorda took one quick look at his sleeping companions and hurtled off in pursuit of the animal.

At first it was the usual game that Yorda used to play with the wolves, the mountain lions and the forest lions. He would gain on them and then let them get away. With this magnificent animal, however, it was different. The unicorn ran as if its life were at stake. Trees and bushes seemed to pass almost in a blur. Yorda ran faster and faster towards the great creature but could not gain ground. Sometimes the beast would stop and drink from a stream or burrow into the earth with its nose as if looking for something. Yorda would creep up slowly and try to move around behind it so that he could not be seen, but always at the last moment the animal would leap away from him before he got close enough to reach out and touch it.

The faster that Yorda ran, the further ahead of him was the unicorn. Occasionally the great animal would almost issue a challenge to him.

'Yorda, where is this amazing speed that you possess? Is it all a myth or is it just that you have met your match?' This spurred Yorda on even more. He ran even faster. For the first time in his life he could feel his heart thumping in his chest. His breathing became laboured and sweat started to run down his back, arms and chest. Still the unicorn ran.

Yorda completely lost track of time. He seemed to remember hills, valleys, giant trees, rocks the size of houses that the unicorn leapt in one bound and Yorda followed in similar fashion. Other animals came to watch. There was a constant line of creatures staring out at these two beings tearing through the forest. Yorda even caught a glimpse, or so he thought, of fairies lining their route: small people all singing in joy at the sight of two magnificent creatures vying for the right to be called the swiftest in their land.

Yorda could feel his legs starting to tire. This was a new experience to him. He looked ahead towards the fleeing unicorn. The animal no longer seemed to be jumping as effortlessly as before. Before. What did that mean? How long had they been running? Yorda looked at his hands. His nails were long. He looked at his shoes. They had been worn away and he was now running barefoot. His clothes were in tatters, dirty, ripped and old looking. His hair had grown and was flailing wildly behind him in the wind. Had it been days, or weeks? No matter. The only thing that was important in the world was the unicorn. He put all his efforts into following the creature.

'You are fast, Yorda, but alas I see you tire. Soon I shall take my leave of you. It has been fun but you are no match for one such as me.'

'No!' shouted Yorda. This could not be. He remembered times when he had run underneath the eagles and swallows and had matched them without effort. Lëoram the elf horse had been slow and clumsy compared to the unicorn. Why could he not gain on the animal? He knew it was getting tired. If only he could call it to stop. Yorda stopped in his tracks. The voices in his head had stopped. There was no Marosham. No whispering. No songs. Nothing. Except…

Yorda cupped his hands to his mouth. He took a deep breath and let his head clear. He could feel the tingling in his feet as they touched the soft earth upon which he stood. The words must come to him. He waited, and waited. The unicorn was getting further away. Everything was becoming clearer to Yorda. He waited and still the unicorn got further away. He was almost out of sight now. The words started to come to Yorda. As his heart slowed and his breathing relaxed, the voices came back. There was Marosham, mocking and beckoning to him at one-and-the-same time, but there was also the voice that had been with him since childhood, except now it was clearer. One word was being said over and over again: 'Cherolin.'

That was it. Yorda took one deep breath and lifted his tongue to the roof of his mouth and let out the finest word he had ever said.

'CHEROLIN.'

The unicorn stopped, frozen to the spot. It turned and jogged back to Yorda.

'It appears that I have met my match. You have my name and with that you bind me. Speak, Yorda, for you have little time. I must answer you, but it is for you to interpret. I speak only the truth. You may ask three questions and then I am released from you with a new name.'

Yorda thought for a moment.

'How will I be the doom of you all?'

The unicorn looked directly at Yorda. The animal's eyes were totally black, but as Yorda looked into them he could see images forming. The answer to his question was in image form. First, he saw himself standing over the dead body of an elf: it was Marosham. Then the image shifted and he could see huge creatures appearing out of thin air marching towards a line of fairies. The fairies were unleashing their darts and arrows but the creatures continued. As they moved forward the very trees of the forest burst into flame. The first line of fairies stood their ground as the creatures drove through them. All the animals of the forest joined in the battle to save their land. They too were trampled. The image changed, and now Marosham was standing over the body of Yorda. This time when the fairy forest reappeared, all was peaceful.

'Your second question?' asked the unicorn.

Yorda was still trying to make sense of the first set of images. He thought a little while and then said, 'I have changed since entering the forest. What is happening to me?'

He looked once more into the unicorn's deep, bottomless eyes.

'You are the sum of your parts, Yorda. You have been created by great magic, not only of this world but of others. Magic is what you must master. Do not let it master you. This land is the most magical of this world – perhaps of all worlds – and when you set foot in it, it has been seeping into you and awakening within you some of what you are. You are much, much more, but it is unclear if you will be able to use it.'

The great creature lifted its head and said, 'Your final question? Think well on this because it is your last.'

Yorda stood for what seemed an eternity. Things seemed no clearer now than before. Finally he looked once more into the eyes of this beautiful animal in front of him. 'I hear voices in my head. One I know to be that of Marosham. The other voice gives me information. It helps me to heal and is now giving me other words that I do not understand and sometimes cannot quite hear. It gave me your name. Tell me of this voice.'

The unicorn gave a little laugh.

'You have given me the easiest question of all. The answer is at the same time useless to you and of great importance. The voice tells you that which you know but don't know; that which you want but can't have, yet already have. It is a voice that you don't know but yet should not fail to recognise. It is you, Yorda. The voice is yours. What you hear in your mind is what you are saying, have said, or will say. You must listen to yourself, but most of all you must hear yourself.

'I have answered your questions. You should feel proud that you have bettered me. Remember, however, that had you not known my name then you would be lost in this forest for ever. Return to your companions, they are waking.'

With that the unicorn shook his head, turned and trotted off. Yorda shouted after it.

'Cherolin, wait!'

The unicorn continued on its way. A voice in Yorda's head whispered, 'It no longer has the same name. Once used, the unicorn's name becomes useless and it takes its next name.' The voice was then silent.

Yorda turned around and saw he was back in the clearing with his sleeping companions. Mertok was starting to stir and opened his eyes. On seeing Yorda he leapt up from his lying position and called to Dawson, who upon looking at Yorda leapt to his feet also.

'Yorda, what has happened?' said the elf.

Yorda looked at himself and realised that he had almost completely changed from when they had last seen him. His hair was almost down to his waist, he had a long beard and moustache and his clothes were in rags.

He explained to his friends what had happened. Mertok examined the young man and worked out from the length of his hair and beard that he must have been chasing the unicorn for several months.

'That is not possible,' said Yorda. 'If it were true I would have needed to eat and drink and rest in that period.'

'Normally I would agree with you,' said Mertok, 'but we are not in a normal situation. To Dawson and myself we have been asleep for several hours. We are in the same condition as when we lay down. The horses have not changed. Yet you have travelled many miles, seen many things and have grown older; and you have finished in the same spot from where you started. This is not a normal situation. Come, we must get you more clothes and cut your hair before we continue. I have a feeling that time to us is relative and everything outside this forest must wait for us, but we cannot wait for it. We must continue.'

Chapter Fifteen

The three friends journeyed for a short while before Dawson spoke.

'Is it me, or is it getting darker?'

Mertok had noticed it too. He looked over at Yorda, who seemed unaware of it. 'Yorda? What do you think?'

Yorda snapped out of his daydreaming and looked blankly at his friends.

'I am sorry,' he said. 'I am so tired after my encounter with the unicorn, I can hardly keep my eyes open.'

Mertok reined in Meryat. 'I am so sorry, my friend. I have never seen you tired until today. Dawson and I have slept while you have not. We shall stop a while for you to rest.'

Mertok and Dawson sat and talked while Yorda made himself comfortable on the floor. Within seconds he was asleep. His dreams were troubled. He was in a great forest and was hunting Marosham, who was always ahead of him. He was in turn being followed, by what or whom he did not know. All that he knew was that he could hear the sound of the forest being destroyed behind him and he knew for sure that if he stopped then he would be destroyed as well. The voices in his head were shouting at him, giving him instructions, but he could not grasp the words and so he continued onwards towards Marosham. The Black Elf was laughing as he ran and beckoning to Yorda to follow him.

'Come towards me, Yorda. You can die at my hands or you can stay where you are and die at the hands of your pursuer. You make the choice.'

Yorda could not make the choice. Whatever was behind him frightened him so he did not want to stop, but also he was frightened of what would happen if he caught Marosham. He just kept running, but now he could feel heat behind him, and the sounds of the forest dying got closer. He could feel lives passing out of existence behind him, and in front of him he could feel the numbness of life not being allowed to exist. In his head the voices continued, the endless chatter of many sounds all intertwined and intermixed, and then he could hear one voice breaking through. 'Yorda, it is you who decide. It is not what is in front of you or what is behind you that drives you. You are free to make the choice, but make it you must.'

Yorda awoke bathed in sweat, with Dawson and Mertok looking confused.

'Yorda,' said Mertok. 'Something very strange has happened while you slept.'

Yorda sat up. Even though his dreams were strange and disturbing he felt much fresher after his sleep.

Mertok continued. 'The moment you fell asleep, the forest became dark. The moment you woke up this strange light that comes from all around us was back. I suspect that it is you that is the cause of the light. When you were tired earlier, Dawson and I noticed that the light was much more subdued than normal. I have no idea why, but it is you that is controlling this light.'

Yorda stood up, not quite knowing what to say.

'When it was dark,' continued Mertok, 'I could see some of the stars through the canopy of the forest. I recognised them. We are going in the correct direction. I believe it is not far now before we exit this place.'

'I feel it too,' said Yorda. 'I feel the magic of this place seeping up from the earth into my body. I think this is why I have grown during our time here. For some reason I am using the magic of this forest, but I have no control over it.'

'Yet,' said Dawson.

Mertok turned to the big smith, who continued without being prompted. 'Since we met Yorda, 'e 'as shown us different abilities that neither elves nor 'umans 'ave. You 'ave said yourself, Mertok, that we are in a magical place. Per'aps Yorda is right and the magic 'ere is starting to cause other abilities, which we 'ave not seen yet, to awaken. If 'e can control these powers it must surely be an aid to fight Marosham, which is why 'e is afraid of Yorda.'

'You may be correct, Dawson,' said Mertok, 'but it may also be that if the magic of the forest is aiding Yorda, then when we exit the land of the Elänthoi he may also lose what he has gained here. We must wait and see.'

'Until then,' Yorda said with a slight smile, 'we must continue in that direction.' He pointed west and moved towards Lëoram and started to load up.

When they eventually neared the borders of the fairy lands they felt many eyes upon them. Soft singing came from all directions.

'I wish I knew what they were saying,' Dawson muttered to himself.

'I am starting to understand some of their language,' said Yorda. 'They wish us well on our journey.'

'They seem to 'ave changed their tune since we entered the forest, laddie.'

'I think Rimanathon may have had a hand in this,' added Mertok.

'And maybe the unicorn,' Yorda said with a smile.

Daylight started to break through the trees and the three friends exited to a damp chilly morning rain. They quickly cloaked up and continued west. They had not gone too far when Mertok announced that he knew where they were and changed course to a more south-westerly direction. The land beneath the horses' hooves was a lush green grass. The companions allowed their steeds to graze whenever they wished. It seemed strange, but they all believed that they were safe until they got to the elven forests. The atmosphere became much more relaxed and when the sun eventually burned through the mist and drizzle, and when they had warmed up a bit, they even started to joke a little.

Mertok started to sing softly, his voice a mellow tenor. The others listened without interrupting. The magic of the elves was within the song. Dawson and Yorda were completely captivated by the strange yet beautiful music that came from the elf. Meryat and Lëoram, also, seemed uplifted by the song and trotted forward with their heads held high and their ears pricked up. When he had finished, Dawson asked him what the song was about.

'It is a song that is sung by the elves when they have been away and are nearing home. It is a song of welcome to the trees, the earth, the plants and all the living creatures that walk, swim and fly. It is a song that asks for permission to re-enter the golden lands where we have been blessed with virtual immortality, where everything we ever need is all around us and all we have to do is look and it is there for us. It is a song that asks our departed brethren who are now in the Blessed Isles to wait for us, for we shall return to them when our time here is done.'

'Amen to that,' said Dawson, who rode on solemn faced.

When they stopped to eat and take care of the horses, Yorda dismounted and exclaimed, 'Hey, I can still feel the tingling in my feet when I touch the ground. It is not as strong as in the fairy kingdom, but it is there nevertheless.'

'And the voices?' asked Mertok.

The grin that was on Yorda's face disappeared.

'I still hear Marosham, but he is a lot weaker. The other voices, however, are slowly getting stronger. I can still make out only a few words here and there but the language is not known to me. I feel that it is only a matter of time before I start to understand more of what is being said.'

As evening descended Mertok pulled his horse around. 'You see that hill in the distance? Beyond there we will see the borders of my country. It is still a day's ride so it would be better if we camped here tonight and rode in tomorrow.'

Dawson and Yorda agreed. Dawson pointed to his right where a little way off they could see a flat area of land with a small copse that would make a good shelter for the night.

It seemed strange to sleep so near to their destination and yet still feel safe. They were sure that Rimanathon had something to do with this, but Yorda also believed that Marosham had resigned himself to the prophecy running its course and that the final conflict between them would take place after Yorda had returned to the forest.

Their evening meal was taken in almost complete silence. Each of the group seemed lost in his own thoughts, thoughts that only he would know. Yorda kept standing up and walking to the edge of the copse. There he would stare towards the elven forests as if expecting something to happen. After several minutes he would return and sit once more with the others. After he had returned for the fifth time, Mertok reached over and put his hand on Yorda's shoulder.

'What do you see when you look yonder, my friend?' he softly asked while nodding in the direction from which Yorda had just returned.

'My eyes see nothing,' Yorda replied, 'but my mind sees many things. I see death. Perhaps mine, perhaps Marosham's, and perhaps yours too, my friend. I am looking for something different, something that perhaps can stop the killing. I am a healer, not a warrior. There must be some way to solve this conflict other than by war.'

'You speak as a healer and you have the heart and conscience of a healer. However, there have been wars before and there will be wars again where the only thing a healer can do is to help the injured and dying. Wheels have been set in motion here, Yorda – wheels that were started many, many hundreds of years ago. You are but a part of this wheel that must turn along with the rest of the wheel, but perhaps you are the strongest part of the wheel. Even though you must follow the path of the wheel, perhaps it is your part that will stop the wheel turning. I believe Rimanathon to be correct when he says that we all have our parts to play. Yours is the bigger of the parts that we three are playing. It is your part that is necessary to stop the death of many elves.'

'How many other deaths will be caused by my success?' Yorda said quietly, almost to himself.

Mertok looked at the despair that was on Yorda's face. 'I do not understand. What deaths will be caused if you are successful?'

Yorda told him of his encounter with the unicorn and the images that the unicorn had shown him. He described the deaths of the fairies as they valiantly tried to protect their land from the invading creatures.

Mertok listened and when Yorda had finished he spoke softly.

'What the unicorn has shown you, I take to be similar to the prophecies we have in the elven kingdom. Everything is symbolic. Remember, Yorda, the future is the future. It has not happened yet. No matter what happens tomorrow, it cannot decide what happens the next day. True, it can influence it, but it cannot decide it. Rimanathon himself said that if he had not intervened in his own way, then we would have been killed back in the Bantus Mountains. This would have stopped our prophecy from being fulfilled. If we have a storm tonight, you may be killed by lightning. I say this merely to demonstrate that what little we see of the future is only a projection. The future is what we make of it. Anything we see of the future must only be used as a guide that can help us.'

'I know what you say is correct, Mertok, but the images that he gave me were so real and so strong.'

'Come, my friend. Think on it. The unicorn gave you two scenarios. The first was of you being killed and the second was of you being victorious. What does that tell you?'

Yorda thought a while upon this and then, sounding a little more relieved, answered. 'It tells me that if the unicorn could tell the future then there would not be two choices for me. There would only be one possibility, so therefore he cannot have the power to foretell what will happen.'

'Exactly,' said Mertok. 'Come, I think you should sleep a little. You have still not fully recovered from your time in the forest of the Elänthoi.'

Yorda agreed and lay out his sleeping roll. He pulled his blanket over him and turned away from his comrades and closed his eyes. Even though Mertok seemed to make a lot of sense, Yorda could not help feeling that the unicorn had access to knowledge of the future that was accurate and unchangeable. He hoped it wasn't so, but he couldn't shake the feeling of unease.

The next morning when they got up, Yorda was feeling back to top form. He still felt a slight tingling from the ground, but other than that he seemed to be completely recovered from his experience of chasing the unicorn.

Yorda decided to walk into the elven forests and just led Bettine and Lëoram. Mertok and Dawson were both excited as they approached the outskirts of the forest. For Mertok he was returning home. When he had left on his quest to aid Yorda's return, he had been one of many elf-lords sent out to seek the young healer. He knew then that many would not return. He believed himself to be one of those, so he counted himself to be very fortunate to return home. He said a silent prayer to those who had not made it back, giving thanks for their sacrifice which had made it possible for Yorda to return alive.

Dawson considered himself lucky for a different reason. When he had left the elf kingdom years before, he had set out to find his home and people. He had not succeeded in that aim. He had never thought that he would end up back here again, but to do so was something that made him happy. These people were the most magnificent creatures that he had ever encountered. His time with them was one of wonder, enlightenment and learning. He hoped that his time again with them would be as good.

Yorda approached the line of trees that marked the border of the kingdom with trepidation. He knew that there was no turning back. Whatever must be, must be. He was the catalyst to the events that were taking place. He hoped that whatever happened he would act according to all he had learnt as a child and make his parents proud of him.

So thinking, he stepped past the first tree and entered the forest, lifted his hands to his head, screamed and fell senseless to the ground.

Chapter Sixteen

Mertok and Dawson rushed to Yorda's side. He lay unmoving on the ground. Mertok immediately touched the side of Yorda's neck.

'He is alive, Dawson, but I have no idea why this has happened.' Mertok rose and looked around him carefully.

'I 'ave checked too,' said the big man. 'I am sure there is no one 'ere to 'ave attacked the lad. We are alone.'

'Not for long,' answered Mertok. 'Do you hear that?'

'My ears are not as good as yours, my friend. No, wait. I do 'ear something.'

Mertok raised himself up and turned towards the sound.

'It is a welcome call. I think some of my people are here to greet us.'

A short while later a company of elves broke through the trees. The lead elf moved towards Mertok.

'*Shorienil Mertok ahll*,' the elf said, raising his fist to his chest momentarily.

'Greetings to you also,' answered Mertok.

Immediately several of the elves went over to Yorda.

'What has happened here?' said the lead elf.

'I do not know,' answered Mertok. 'The moment Yorda set foot in the forest this happened.'

'We felt you and, to a much greater extent, Yorda, you say?' Mertok nodded. 'We felt Yorda very strongly as you all entered the realm. It is sure that Marosham knows that he is here. We must leave now before the Dark Elves come to meet us. They have increased in great numbers since you have been away. But enough talk, my lord. I am sure the council will explain everything when you return. We must get Yorda to a healer to find out what is wrong. We have orders to go to the Eternal City.'

'Lead on,' said Mertok. 'I will stay close to Yorda and my friend Dawson.'

As they travelled, the elves examined Yorda but could find no sign of physical attack on his body.

'It is most strange, my lord,' said the lead elf after one of his healers had reported on Yorda's condition. 'We can find no physical signs of illness or injury.'

Mertok thought for a moment. 'He told Dawson and me that he kept hearing voices in his head that were gradually getting stronger. One of the voices was that of Marosham. Perhaps he has launched some kind of mental attack on Yorda.'

'Anything is possible, I suppose, my lord,' said the healer who had been tending Yorda. 'I believe we must wait until we get to the Eternal City and our best healers can use their magic to try to find the problem.'

Mertok turned to the healer elf. 'Unfortunately *try* is not good enough in this case. To fulfil the prophecy Yorda must stand against Marosham.'

The healer elf nodded and returned to Yorda.

The lead elf, whose name Mertok discovered was Sulan, kept receiving news from the scouts he was sending out to check their route. Once or twice he changed direction.

Mertok moved up to him. 'Has Marosham become that strong in my time away that you are sending scouts out in this part of the forest?'

Sulan looked grave as he replied. 'You will hear all when you talk to the council. All I may say is that the elves of the western forests have joined with him and as we talk they are fashioning plans to attack us.'

Sulan added no more as another scout joined them and passed on information, which caused another change in direction.

Soon they heard a challenge ahead. Sulan seemed relieved. 'It is my brother, Rhiân. His patrol was sent further north when we knew you were near. It is good that he is here. We are many now and it is extremely unlikely that Marosham will test us here.'

Mertok noticed that the whole group was visibly relieved. It had seemed inconceivable that an elf would be disturbed by anything within his own lands. Times were changing.

The group journeyed for two days, in which time there was no change in Yorda's condition. He was breathing and seemed in no discomfort, but other than that they could not rouse him. It was almost as if he were in a deep sleep. The elves were joined by several other groups and were now more than a hundred strong. To Mertok this constituted an army. This worried the elf. It had been many years since there had been any wars in the elf forest, and to see this many elves all armed was indeed worrying.

The tension seemed to diminish greatly within the group on the third day. Dawson noticed that the light was becoming distinctly golden. The colours of the plants and trees were more vivid. The air that he breathed had a purity that he did not believe could exist. It almost seemed as if he were arriving in the Halls of the Dead. His people often talked of the place where all would go after giving their lives in battle. It was a place of perfection where all wounds were healed, all wrongdoings forgiven; a place where the battle-weary would be given rest and allowed peace and tranquillity for the rest of eternity. To find a place like it while he was alive was truly marvellous; yet here it was: the Eternal City.

Huge trees sprung up around them. Steps carved from the trunks of the trees rose up from the ground into the vast heights where they arrived at a network of platforms that interlinked all of the trees of the forest. High above them Dawson could see people moving along these platforms, some of which were no more than shoulder width. The elves were the most sure-footed creatures Dawson had ever seen and they had no fear of heights, so walking on these narrow walkways posed no problem. As the group moved forward, Dawson could see tree houses built in the huge trees, vast constructions built out of the living wood. Massive conduits carried water up to these houses, the water pumped up by magic, Dawson assumed. The leaves of these sumptuous trees became more and more golden as they ventured towards the heart of this magnificent place. The only thing that unsettled Dawson was the number of elves dressed in battle armour and carrying weapons. Even in this place, the heart of the kingdom of elves, they were preparing for a possible invasion.

The Eternal City was huge and it took almost a day's ride to get from one side to the other. In the last few miles, they were greeted by a small group of elves who dismissed all but Dawson, Mertok, Yorda and the elves caring for him, and bade them follow. They explained that the council was being convened and it was important that Mertok should impart all the information he had gathered.

They soon arrived at a large pool, which was formed by a conjunction of several small streams. Standing in front of the pool were two elves, who dismissed all but the three companions.

One of the elves was dressed in long, flowing robes. He moved forward and gave the customary elven greeting, which both Mertok and Dawson returned. The elf smiled and nodded at Dawson.

'You do not remember me, young man,' he said. 'I came to see you when you first entered the forest. It is good to see you so well. We will talk about your journeys later, but first I must talk to Mertok.'

Dawson had noticed the difference in the way this man talked compared with all the other elves they had met. Everybody had called Mertok 'my lord', but this man not only referred to him as Mertok but even spoke to Dawson before addressing the elf. He looked at his friend, who didn't seem the least put out.

He took Mertok to one side while the other elf, a female, went over to Yorda. She held a crystal above his head and said a few words. She regarded the crystal for a few moments after this and then got up and gestured to several elves that had been waiting at the base of one of the large trees that was at the edge of the pool.

'Take him to the infirmary.'

She turned to Dawson.

'Would you like to stay with your friend? He will have the best treatment we can give. If you wish I can show you to your rooms. We will all meet for our evening meal shortly and you can freshen up if you like.'

Dawson realised that his smell must be quite strong to the elves and her very subtle suggestion to freshen up was the polite way of saying, 'Go and get washed, man.'

'I would really appreciate the chance to clean up and get some fresh clothes, my lady,' he tactfully conceded.

The elf smiled. 'Please, my name is Salurian. I am the chief healer in the city. Come, I will show you to your quarters.'

They walked a short way and then ascended one of the many sets of steps cut into the trees. Dawson wasn't too happy about climbing up to the tops of the steps and walking across the narrow walkways that linked the trees. Seeing his discomfort, Salurian said, 'Do not worry; you cannot fall. There are invisible guard rails protecting the sides of the walkways. We have installed them wherever you walk. We know that those who are not of the elves often have problems with heights so we have taken this precaution for you and also for Yorda, as we are not yet sure of his elven powers.'

Even with this safeguard, Dawson was still a little hesitant as he crossed his first walkway. Salurian continued to talk as they walked.

'I have made my first examination of Yorda. It is most strange. He has no physical injuries. My attempt to examine his mind was met with a barrier of some sort. I have never seen the like of this before. It is strong. The only thing I am sure of is that the barrier is of Yorda's making. Whether it is a barrier to stop something from entering, such as Marosham, I do not know. Perhaps it is a barrier to stop something from leaving.'

She stopped outside a small tree house and opened the door. Inside was a room with a bed, some chairs, a table and a huge tub of steaming water. On one of the chairs were some robes, which were obviously intended for Dawson to put on instead of his travelling clothes when he was finished washing.

'If you require anything, just ring the bell on the table and someone will come. If you wish to see Yorda then they will take you to the infirmary. You will soon find your way around. Please feel free to explore the city. We are safe here, for the moment. You cannot get lost. You will be summoned for the meal presently. Until then, enjoy your bath.' With that she gave a big smile, turned and left.

Mertok had gone with the other elf. The elf in the long robes turned to Mertok. 'My son, it is good to see you again.'

'As it is you too, father,' answered Mertok.

'I have a surprise for you, Mertok,' the elf said as they climbed one of the trees.

Neither elf said anything further. They soon reached a large hall built in the converging branches of several trees. Mertok let his father lead their way in. The room was immense. Mertok remembered this as the meeting hall for the Council of Elders. It was here that they would soon congregate to hear Mertok's news and discuss the conflict with Marosham.

Mertok's eyes adjusted quickly to the change in light as they entered and he saw, standing in the centre of the hall, Thalién.

'Brother!' Mertok shouted, and he rushed to embrace Thalién. 'I believed you dead when Lëoram came to us.'

'It is good to see you too, brother,' said Thalién. 'You say you have seen Lëoram?'

'Yes, he has travelled here with us. Yorda spotted him racing into the Bantus Mountains. He gave chase and caught him before he could injure himself. He brought him here with us.'

Both Thalién and their father were amazed at this news.

'How did he catch him?' asked Mertok's brother.

Mertok took his chance to tease his family. 'He chased him on foot and then leapt up on him before he rode him to where Dawson and I were waiting.'

'You cannot be serious – this is an elf steed,' said his father.

'He would not let any but me ride him,' added Thalién.

'I know that normally this is true, but this young man has powers that are quite extraordinary. He has tremendous speed and endurance. He once chased and caught a unicorn during our time with the Elänthoi.'

'You entered the forest of the Elänthoi and are still here?' The older elf seemed completely amazed. 'I think that the whole of this story should be told to the council when we convene after eating.'

'Yes, father,' Mertok said, and bowed his head.

At that moment a female elf entered the hall. 'The meal is being served, Your Majesty. We await your attendance.'

The older elf nodded and turned to his boys.

'Even the king of the elves gets hungry. We shall eat and meet with the council afterwards.'

Before they descended to their meal, the King sent for Salurian to enquire as to the condition of Yorda.

'There is no change, my king,' said the healer. 'I can find no reason why he does not respond. We have tried many of our stimulants to no avail. Even the magic-users get no reaction from him. The barrier that has been put up is completely impenetrable. I think that rest is the only treatment we can give him for the moment.'

'And if that does not work?' asked the King.

'At this time I am afraid I have no other answers.' Salurian bowed her head.

'Do what you can and keep me informed. By the way, has your mother descended yet?'

'Yes, the Queen is awaiting you, and, Father, how is Mertok after his journey?'

The King smiled and placed his hand on Salurian's shoulder.

'He is fine, my daughter. You shall see him after the meeting of the elders.'

The King descended and made his way to where the meal was to be served. A large clearing under the canopy of some of the largest trees had been prepared as an outdoor kitchen. There were a dozen tables lined up in two rows with a large table at the head. Gathered at the tables were the highest-ranked elves in the city along with visiting elf-lords. At the top table were Mïælla, the king's wife, Mertok, Thalién, Salurian, and Dawson, who was looking a little overawed by all this.

As the King approached, an elf stepped from close by the head table and announced.

'All rise for King Tramulan.' The sound of trumpets blowing filled the air. The assembled guests and dignitaries stood and waited until the King had seated himself before they retook their seats.

When everybody was seated, King Tramulan stood and spoke.

'My friends, my family, my subjects. Today we feast a special occasion. My eldest son has returned from the land of the humans. He brings with him he who is spoken of in the prophecies. His name is Yorda. Alas, he cannot make the feast; he is being treated in the infirmary, but we hope to see him soon. The mood for this meal shall be one of happiness. A coming together of friends and family. Let us give thanks for the food before us. Eat and be happy.'

With that, the King sat down and elves carrying platters of

assorted foods, cooked and raw, approached the tables and served all that were seated.

Dawson knew that when elves ate together like this, it was a very special occasion and, as with this meal, a theme was always agreed upon before eating. As the King had decided this was to be a meal of joy and happiness, it was forbidden to talk of other things, so the questions he wanted to ask Mertok of Yorda's health would have to wait until the meal was finished.

He looked over occasionally at the king and queen of the elves, sitting at the same table as him. This was indeed a great honour, one that a mere soldier/blacksmith would normally never expect to happen in his lifetime. He started to realise the gravity of the whole mission that he was upon. The big man tried to put these thoughts aside, in respect of the pre-meal wishes of the King.

He glanced briefly again at the King. It was hard to believe that he was the father of Thalién and Mertok. The family resemblance was there for all to see, but they all looked so young. He could have mistaken them for brothers. Elves lived for such a long time that it was quite possible that the age difference between the brothers and the King was many hundreds of years. Because of their longevity, children were not born often to this wonderful race of people. His attention was brought back to the meal when one of the serving elves asked him if he would like some more mead. He accepted the offer and joined in the conversation that was going on around him.

Miëlla, the queen of the elves, entered the infirmary and was shown to the bed where Yorda lay. She reached out and placed a hand on his forehead. She too could feel the barriers that had been set up in Yorda's mind. Sighing gently she sat down next to him. The other elves left the two together. The Queen reached forward and took Yorda's limp hand in her own. A slight increase in the colouring of his hand spread swiftly to the rest of his body and she could see the distraught look on his face ease a little. She knew that there was little else she could do to help him, but the energy she passed into his body would give the young man some extra strength.

Miëlla had no idea how long Yorda would stay in this condition but she was determined that he would recover. Sitting back on her chair the Queen took a deep breath and started to talk to Yorda. Even though she could not tell if he heard anything she knew that any soothing sounds would help, if only a little. Unsure of exactly what to say, she described the Eternal City to him and the day-to-day life of the people that lived within. The first day she sat and talked for about two hours, and when Salurian came to wash and turn him, the Queen bade him goodbye with a slight kiss on his forehead.

Over the following days the Queen was a frequent visitor to Yorda's bedside. Some days she would just sit and hold his hand, each time putting a little energy into the young man, and others she would talk. Stories of his father and mother while they were in the forest would be passed on to the unconscious patient. The Queen even talked about Yorda's father when he was a young boy himself. She was very careful about what she said when talking about his parents. Nothing that could be a shock to him was mentioned, as this could cause problems in his present state. There was something she would really like to have told him but she knew that it must wait for when or if he recovered. Miælla put the thought of 'if' out of her mind. She knew that it was vital to the future of her race and her subjects that the young man lying in front of her should recover and fulfil the prophecy. Occasionally Yorda would stir as if he were starting to awaken and the Queen would call for the healers to come immediately, but each time he would sigh and gently drift back to wherever it was that his mind was at that time.

On one of the days that the Queen visited she brought some personal items that had belonged to his mother and father. It was well known among the elves that any object that belonged to an elf, or human come to that, would retain memories of the person that it belonged to. By holding the object an elf could gain a lot of information about any former owners. It was true that this information was sketchy, but sometimes you could get images of the people that had used it, and occasionally images of places and events could be recalled.

The first item she held out for Yorda was a hairbrush that his mother had used. She took his hand and slid the handle of the brush into his fingers, then, using her own hand, placed it over his so that he had a firm grasp of the handle. She spoke of how his mother loved to have her hair brushed. When she had first come to the elves she had had a nasty injury to her head and the elves had to cut a lot of her hair away to tend to the wound. As it grew back she would spend a great deal of time arranging her hair to cover the scar until the hair around the spot grew back. Mïælla had often sat with his mother in the days before she left the city and talked with her while brushing her hair. Yorda's mother loved it when she was pampered in this fashion.

The next object she brought belonged to his father. It was a little wooden whistle which his father used to play when he was a child. She placed this too in Yorda's hand and told him of how his father loved to be alone when he was a young boy. Playing with his brothers had no interest for him; he only wanted to go and tease the animals in the forest and to play little tunes on his whistle. Mïælla laughed a little as she told Yorda that he had never managed to learn how to play the whistle very well but could be seen regularly walking down the main street in the city, blowing it with his head held high. He would imagine that he was leading a large band and his job was to keep everybody in line. He would become very angry if any of the other boys teased him about it. The other children soon learnt not to tease him too often as he had quite a temper on him and was very quick to get into fights with the other boys, more often than not coming out on top and forcing the boy involved to listen to him play some more of his whistle while sitting on top of the poor child.

The Queen sometimes told Yorda stories of when she was a child. Even though it was many hundreds of years ago she could remember quite vividly events that had happened. Elves had excellent memories and in fact were very proud of their abilities to recall events that had happened long ago. When an elf is born a lot of the racial memories get passed down from their parents, which makes schooling in history almost obsolete. Age, unlike in a lot of humans, causes no deterioration of memory; in fact it seems that as an elf gets older his memory becomes sharper.

She told him stories of her parents and grandparents. They were dead now. Even though elves live for many hundreds of years, they too eventually pass from this earth. Except for rare cases when they are killed in an accident or in battle, an elf decides when it is his or her time to pass on. She explained to Yorda that the Song of the Elves, which is present in the mind of every elf, is always calling them to the Floating Islands. Eventually, when an elf reaches a great age, they feel the call of the Song is too strong to resist and they invite all their family around them to tell them that it is now their time. Miëlla impressed upon Yorda that it was not a time of sadness. To be called to the Floating Islands where all the elves joined in the Endless Song was a time of great happiness. The family would gather together and join hands. All the memories of the leaving elf would then be passed on to that elf's following generations. In this way it could be seen that the old elf was happy to be going to meet with his own ancestors but would live on in his living descendants.

She turned to Yorda and smiled. 'Even so, I do miss my mother and father, as I am sure do you.'

Miëlla took a handkerchief from her sleeve and wiped her eyes. Leaning forward she kissed Yorda on the head and left him to the ministrations of the other healers.

Chapter Seventeen

Yorda had entered the forest and immediately clutched his head. As his legs buckled beneath him he heard the voice that had been slowly getting stronger in his head scream out, 'NOW IS THE TIME TO UNDERSTAND.' The force of the voice set every nerve end screaming. He was aware of only one thing – pain. He blacked out and dropped to the floor.

When he opened his eyes he was in a classroom. At the front of the classroom was a large figure. Yorda tried to make out who he was but he could get no clear picture of the teacher's features.

'Good,' said the figure. 'Now is the time to understand.'

Yorda looked down. He was sitting at a child's desk. In fact, as he looked down, he noticed that he was actually a child. He assessed that he was about six years old. He lifted his head and looked back towards the front of the class. Slowly he lifted his hand.

'I don't understand,' he said in what seemed a very small and squeaky voice.

'That is why you are here,' said the teacher.

'Where am I?' asked Yorda.

'At this precise moment you are lying on the floor at the border of the elven forest.'

Yorda looked around again. There were drawings on the walls, obviously drawn by young children. He could see about a dozen or so small desks identical to the one he was sitting at. As he looked toward the front of the room again, he saw that next to the teacher was an elf, very similar in size and appearance to Mertok.

'Mertok, you are here!' he shouted, and he leapt to his feet.

The teacher slapped a wooden cane he was carrying hard on the desk in front of him. Yorda froze. There was something about this faceless creature that scared him.

'This,' the teacher said, 'is not Mertok. This is an elf. It is just an example of an elf. What do you know about elves, young

Yorda? I want you to write everything you know about elves on the board in front of you. You have ten minutes.'

Yorda sat down again at his desk. In front of him was a slate board, which he hadn't noticed earlier. Next to it was a piece of chalk. He lifted the chalk and thought for a moment. He tried to remember all he knew about elves, all that he had heard as a child and everything that he had picked up from Dawson and Mertok. When he had gathered his thoughts he moved the chalk towards the slate board and found to his amazement that everything he had been thinking about was now written on the board.

'Very good, young Yorda. You have remembered everything that you have been told since you were born and have recalled all you have seen in the past few weeks.'

Yorda looked up. The classroom had changed slightly. The drawings on the walls were more detailed, obviously done by older children. There were fewer desks around him. When he looked down he noticed that he was taller. He was now about nine years old. He still could not make out any features on his tutor's face, but he recognised the voice. It was the same one that had been in his head, whispering alien words to him.

'Who are you?' Yorda shouted. He got up and ran to the door. The handle would not turn. Yorda turned and looked towards the windows. He was sure there were windows in the room earlier, but now there were none.

'I want to leave! You have no right to keep me here!' he shouted at his tutor.

'You cannot leave, and no one can enter, my child,' said his teacher in a gentle tone. 'Come, Yorda, you have told me what you know of the elves. It is my turn to tell you what I know. Listen well, for I can impart this information to you once and only once.'

Yorda turned and came back to his desk. He looked at his teacher, who lifted his cane and pointed to the chalkboard on the wall at the front of the classroom. Yorda stared at the board and thought he could see a slight shimmering running over its surface. It seemed but a moment that he had been looking at the board when his teacher said, 'You have done well, my star pupil. You learn quickly, Yorda.'

Yorda was very confused. 'I don't understand.'

'Oh, but you do,' said his teacher. 'Look around.'

Yorda looked once more at his surroundings. They had changed yet again. Now there were only six other desks in the classroom. There were still many drawings on the wall but now he could see other sheets of paper on the walls with strange characters on them. He felt sure he should know what they were but he could not quite grasp their meanings. When he looked down at himself he could see that he had grown again and was about eleven years old. He looked up again and saw his teacher standing next to him.

'Now that you have learnt the history of your father's people, you must learn their language.'

Yorda saw lips on the faceless features of his instructor. The lips were moving but they didn't match with what he heard being said. Yorda watched in fascination. Occasionally he managed to match the lips with the sounds that were coming from his teacher. After a while he could see the lips moving in time with the sounds that he was hearing, but the language was different. It seemed older almost than time itself, yet it was also new and fresh. Each word seemed to have a richness that he hadn't noticed before. There also seemed to be a depth and power to it that transcended any speech he had ever heard. Yorda realised that the words he was hearing were the words that were often in his head when he healed, but now he understood them and, more than that, he could even speak them.

'I don't understand,' Yorda said once again, but this time the voice that came from his throat was no longer the little squeaky voice he had heard before. It was the breaking voice of a teenager. Yorda looked down again and saw that he was now about thirteen years of age. He looked up and saw that there were now only three other desks in the room with him.

'You have done well, my young pupil,' said his teacher, faceless as always. 'You have learnt in seven years what would take most of my pupils at least ten. However, we do not have the time to stop now. Look to the front of the classroom.'

Yorda turned towards the teacher's desk. On the desk he could see a large book. It was almost the size of the desktop. He estimated that it was about twelve inches thick. Yorda stood up and walked to the front of the class. He reached out and touched the bindings of the book. As his fingers ran down the book's spine he felt a tingle – the same tingle that he had felt in his feet every time he touched the earth in the forest of the Elänthoi.

'Yes, that was a lucky advantage you gained there,' said his teacher. 'Even I did not anticipate that. That may prove important later on.'

Yorda looked back at his teacher and noticed he was not alone again. The classroom had changed once more. There were now only two desks in the room. His desk was empty but the desk next to it contained an elf. This elf, however, was different from most of the elves he had learnt about. This elf was Marosham. Yorda and Marosham regarded each other.

'Hello, Yorda. I understand you are coming to see me,' said Marosham.

Yorda looked around him, and then looked down. He was now about fifteen years old.

The teacher turned to Marosham. 'Now, now, young Marosham. No talking in class unless I say. You know the rules.'

'Yes, sir. Sorry, sir,' answered the elf.

The teacher walked to the front of the classroom. He leaned over and opened the book. Yorda noticed that all the pages were blank.

'Come, Yorda; come, Marosham. It is time to read of the Great Book of Knowledge and Magic.'

Marosham stood and approached the book. Yorda noticed that Marosham was no older than he was and a little shorter.

The teacher stood behind them and put one hand on each of their heads. He gently turned Yorda's head to look at the left-hand page and did the same with Marosham, but instead guided his gaze to the right-hand page.

'Here you will drink of the magic that exists in all lands. You will each take half of the knowledge. When the time comes, that knowledge will be joined. Now read.'

Yorda looked at the page but saw nothing. He tried to turn his head to see what Marosham was doing but the teacher held him firm. He looked again at the book. When he at last blinked, he found himself seated at his desk once more. His was the only desk in the classroom. He looked down and saw that he was fully grown. His gaze lifted and he sought his teacher. He was alone in the room. Slowly he got up and walked to the door. His hand reached forward and held the handle. He slowly turned it and felt the latch move. The door opened and he looked outside. It was blackness that greeted his gaze. He looked once more upon his classroom, then stepped out into the dark.

Chapter Eighteen

Dawson looked about him. He was seated at a large round table. They were in the massive hall that Mertok had been in earlier when he had met his brother Thalién. Both Mertok and Thalién were seated at the table, both slightly to the left of Dawson. Arranged around the table were the elders of not only the Eternal City, but also elders from elsewhere in the elven forests. Tramulan, the king, and his wife, Miælla, were seated next to each other.

Tramulan rose from his seat and called the meeting to order.

'My lords and honoured guests. We are gathered here today to discuss and hopefully form a solution to the problems that confront us in our lands. It is long since there have been any wars between the elves, and not since the beginnings of our history have we faced such a war that is descending on us. I have heard but three days ago that Marosham has formed an alliance with the Western Elves. This is grave news. The Solhantille have always believed that they are the oldest of the elves. Although this has been and continues to be an area of conflict between them and the other three tribes of the elves, it has never until now caused more than heated debate at the councils held between us.

'It appears that Marosham has used his silver tongue to poison our kin against us. Even now our scouts return telling us of large gatherings of elf armies in the west. It is becoming more and more difficult to defend our outlying villages from the attacks by Marosham here in the east and south of the realm. When he raids he arrives as if from nowhere and leaves the same way. Our best trackers cannot follow his trail for more than a short distance and then it disappears completely. If we knew where he was to attack, maybe we could surprise him, but it seems that he travels vast distances in a matter of hours to strike where we least expect.

'I have asked the elders of the Sharnadille and the Merhantille to meet with us, the Lohadrille. My request is simple: I seek an alliance between the remaining three races of elves to defeat the threat that is almost upon us.'

Tramulan took his seat and waited for a response. One of the permanent members of the council rose from his seat and addressed the assembly.

'It is with great sadness that I hear the King of All Elves speak in this fashion. To my understanding, he is asking the three remaining races of elves to declare war upon the Solhantille. I do not believe that war with our brethren is an option. Marosham and his invaders may be considered an enemy, but the Western Elves are our brethren. There must be another answer to this.'

The elder sat down and was replaced by an elf resplendent in flowing, brightly coloured robes. His eyes flashed green and his finely sculpted features showed great strength and intelligence.

'May I introduce myself to those whom I have not yet had the pleasure to meet. My name is Rhônel. I have been sent on behalf of the Sharnadille. We live in peace to the south of the lands of the Solhantille. The words of His Majesty are very true. A large army is being prepared to come east to these lands. We of the Sharnadille have no wish to see elves killing elves. We have sent our emissaries to the Solhantille, asking them to reconsider their actions. They see you as the aggressors, Your Majesty, and have no wish to cause any rift between themselves and my people. The elders of the Sharnadille have convened a meeting of their council. It has been decided that as neither Marosham nor the Solhantille have shown any aggression towards my people, then we cannot show favour to either side in this conflict.'

Rhônel sat back down to be replaced by another elf who had been sitting further round the table. This elf was much smaller and older than Rhônel. When he stood he showed great presence. Dawson had the feeling that he was listening to an elf of very great age and wisdom.

When the elf spoke, his voice was much deeper than he expected. He spoke slowly and clearly, making every letter of every word audible to all present.

'My friends. My fellow elves. Your Royal Highness, Tramulan. As king of the Merhantille, I am most alarmed to hear that there is the likelihood of war between our peoples. This saddens me and deeply shocks me. As is the case with my brothers of the south, the Sharnadille, we have no quarrel with either Marosham or the Solhantille. Equally we have no quarrel with the Lohadrille. I have spent much time consulting with the elders of my people and do not wish to see either side cause casualties among the other. I propose to ask the Solhantille to send a delegation of their Council of Elders to meet with us and discuss the situation. It has always been the way with our peoples to decide matters in open debate at the Council of Elders. To this end I have already sent envoys to the Solhantille and have put forward my suggestion. They have received it favourably and are at this moment sending some of their most senior council members to a neutral venue within my boundaries. I trust this meets with the approval of those present here this evening.' At this he sat down.

Dawson leaned towards Mertok and whispered, 'Everybody seems to be taking this very calmly. Does no one realise what Marosham 'as done? 'e 'as killed many of your people and sent trackers into the lands of my people, causing illness. Why does nobody mention this?'

Mertok tilted his head towards Dawson. 'It is the way of all council meetings. Nothing has ever been so urgent to necessitate rushed decisions and heated arguments. So it is here. Each of the visiting dignitaries will have a chance to speak, as will you and I and Thalién. After we have all said our piece, the council will dismiss us and they will come to a binding decision.'

'I do not understand this at all,' returned Dawson. 'What about the prophecy that says there will be a war? Does nobody 'ere listen to that?'

'The prophecy cannot influence the decision,' answered Mertok. 'The prophecy is something that was written down thousands of years ago and is something that may or may not happen. Even though all of us here may believe the prophecy, it is not something that should influence our decision. Our decisions here should create the future. We should not let the future be determined by something outside of our influence.'

Each of the people around the table got their chance to give their views without interruption. When Dawson received his opportunity to speak, he told them of the trackers that he had met back in Parkent and of the illness, 'voicekill', that they had been spreading among the children in the lands outside of the elven forests. He told them of the attempts to kill Yorda by Marosham's men. He gave them his viewpoint as a soldier, telling them of the wars he had been in, in all of which a peaceful solution had at first been tried, and then eventually of the blood that had been spilled in the attempt to regain peace. The gathering listened without interruption as he told them how he believed that some people, whether it be elves or men, enjoy killing and would disguise the reasons for doing so to make it seem acceptable to others. This was so with Marosham as far as he could see.

Dawson spoke for much longer than he thought he could. When he eventually sat down, Thalién leaned towards him and whispered, 'You must have been a great leader of men when you were a soldier. Your wisdom shows through in your words. I am honoured that you were with my brother and Yorda on your trip here.'

One by one the guests at the table stood and gave their viewpoints. It was noticeable that the elf-lords of communities in the lands of the Lohadrille all wanted to stop Marosham and the Solhantille with force as soon as possible, each giving examples of atrocities that had been done to their people. Visitors from other regions mostly seemed to want further talks with all concerned.

Finally Mertok rose and looked around the gathered elves.

'I have listened to all that has been said here this evening, and no one has yet mentioned the prophecy.'

At this, one of the Council of Elders stood and said, 'This is out of order, Mertok. You know well that in open debate it is not allowed to discuss the prophecies handed down by our ancestors. That is the prerogative of the Council of Elders when we meet after this meeting has been adjourned.'

'Forgive me,' said Mertok. 'I am not going to talk directly about the prophecy but about the people mentioned within it. We have within our city a young man whom we have brought here from the land of the humans. This man was born of a human woman and an elf. He is the first mixed-race birth between these two peoples since our history began. This person has come here willingly even though he knows nothing of our people or of their ways. He has shown remarkable powers that neither elf nor human has shown before; therefore there is something very special about him.

'As a race, we elves believe in, shall we say, omens. We look to the skies, to the colour of the leaves on the trees, the smell in the air. We believe that everything upon our earth is there for a reason, and within our boundaries we always search for that reason. Our Councils of Elders,' and here he bowed towards the elders seated around the table, 'make many decisions for the good of our people based on these omens and signs. We have among us someone who is so very different and yet at the same time alike to each of us here. This person cannot go unnoticed. He is here for a reason and I believe it is a very special reason. The fact that Marosham has tried to kill this person many times, and, I would like to add, has failed many times, must be some sort of omen.

'Every person here felt the power of Yorda's signature hit the kingdom when he came of age. We have never felt a signature such as his. That too is surely an omen that must be considered by the council. The moment Yorda entered our lands he fell to the earth and has not moved since, yet he lives. That is something that is surely significant to us. We have travelled through the lands of the Elänthoi and are here to tell the tale. That is an omen. All the time we have travelled with this young man it has been on the basis that there is to be a war with Marosham. I see nothing to have changed that premise.

'We have met with this human here, Dawson, who has lived among us after being found in our forests. That too is something that is not an everyday occurrence. And think also of the chances of us meeting up with Dawson in the same city where Yorda comes from. That is also something that I am sure you will realise has a greater meaning.

'All of these coincidences and occurrences have not come to pass by luck alone. There is a greater meaning here that perhaps we are missing, and I believe that we all shall suffer the consequences if we do not act upon what we see. There is only one person who seems to understand what is at stake here and that person is gathering a large army at the west of our borders, ready to invade and destroy anything and everything that gets in his way. If you believe that once he has accomplished his mission he will stop there, you are all very much mistaken. There is one thing that none of you have heard yet and it is that of which I shall now tell.'

Mertok spoke of their meeting with Rimanathon. All gathered round the table listened as Mertok told them of the information given by this mysterious Spellweaver. The elves knew many, if not all, of the creatures that roamed the earth, but Rimanathon was by far the most exotic being that any of the gathered assembly had heard of.

When Mertok had finished, the gathering sat quietly, mulling over his words. After a short space, Tramulan stood.

'We have heard from all gathered here this evening. Is there anything that anyone wishes to add before the Council of Elders sit to make their decision?'

'I have something to say,' came a voice from the entrance of the room.

Everyone turned and saw Yorda standing in the doorway, framed by the golden light behind him. Salurian, the head healer, accompanied him.

'Yorda!' said Mertok as he rushed to embrace his friend.

' 'ow are ye, laddie?' added Dawson as he joined him.

'I am sorry to break into the meeting,' Yorda said, 'but I have to tell you all about what has happened to me while I was unconscious.'

Tramulan held up his hand. 'I think we should take a short break and continue the meeting in an hour. Yorda should be told of what has happened in his absence.'

Everyone agreed and one by one they left the meeting room, leaving the King and Queen with Mertok, Dawson, Thalién, Salurian and Yorda.

When they were alone, Mertok introduced Yorda to the King.

'This is the young man whom we believe will fulfil the prophecy, Father.'

'I am pleased to meet you, Yorda,' said the King. 'I am surprised to see you here. The last time I saw you, you were unconscious.'

Salurian stepped forward. 'I am sorry, my father. When last I looked in on my patient, there was no change. He was still unconscious and none of our healers could penetrate the barrier surrounding his mind. Bethol called me but a few minutes ago to say that Yorda was awake and had insisted on talking to his friends. I am sorry, but he would not take no for an answer and so I brought him here.'

'Do not worry, my daughter, you have done no wrong,' said the King. 'And you, Yorda: I trust you are feeling well?'

'Perfectly well, sir,' answered Yorda, completely unaware of the protocol involved in talking to the King.

Tramulan could see the others' surprise at the way Yorda talked to their father, but he smiled and continued. 'Walk with us, Yorda, and give me your version of the events that have brought you to us.'

They descended from the great hall and walked through the forest. All the while Yorda explained what had transpired since he had met with Mertok. The King listened without interrupting, even though most of what Yorda said had been told to him by Mertok and Dawson. When Yorda told them of his experience while unconscious, they all paid close attention, as this was something new to all of them.

'How much of what you saw when you were in this state do you believe, Yorda?' asked the King.

Yorda looked at the others around him and then answered the King in the elven tongue. Both Mertok and Dawson were amazed.

'But you can't speak this language, laddie,' said Dawson.

'It appears that this is yet another of his remarkable abilities which you have mentioned before,' said the King with an amused smile on his lips.

Dawson immediately moved to the back of the group, realising that he had committed a faux pas in talking without being addressed while in the presence of the King. This made Tramulan smile even more. 'Come, Dawson, you saved the life of my son, Mertok, and that makes you as close to family as can be. Do not be afraid to speak whenever you wish while you are in the company of my immediate family. Protocols are only meant to be upheld outside of a group such as this one.'

This made Dawson feel a little better, although to be considered part of a royal family such as the one he was now with was a little daunting for the big smith.

'So tell me, Yorda,' continued the King, 'this person who was teaching you, do you have any idea who he was?'

'Not at all, sir,' answered Yorda. 'I am not even sure if it was a man or a woman. When the teacher spoke I heard the words but they had no quality that distinguished them in any way, other than to say the voice was like all voices that I have ever heard and yet also unlike any voice that I have ever heard. I never got to see my tutor's face. It always seemed to me to be blurred.'

'How do you explain Marosham being in the same room and being taught at the same time as you?' asked Thalién.

'I do not believe we were in the same time. Or at least I feel we were taught at the same time in the place that the schoolroom existed. It is difficult to explain, but the teacher said that I had been there many years and yet to me it seemed but a few minutes. I believe we were taken to another time, which was the same time to both Marosham and me while we were there, but was a different time from the one we are in now. Maybe it was a little like the way time moved differently to Dawson, Mertok and me while we were with the Elänthoi. I cannot explain it yet, but I think it is significant that we were there together. Other than that I do not know. What I am sure of, however, is that whatever is to happen between Marosham and me has been engineered by someone. For whatever reason, again I do not know – yet – but I must continue on this mission. Of that much I am sure.'

The group had stopped by a small stream where silver-coloured fish leapt and swam against the current. The King dipped his hand into the waters and a glow spread from his fingers until all the fish were bathed in the light. When he took his hand away it seemed that each of the little fish had more energy, and their silver colour was more vibrant, almost as if they had been feeding, which Dawson guessed they had.

'The mission,' said the King with a sigh. 'I am not sure if our other elven brothers will see it as we do. I hope the Council of Elders will accede to our wishes to fight against Marosham. I believe, as do all of us here, that Marosham not only means to kill you, Yorda, but also wishes to control all the elven nations. He is very clever and so must we be.'

They walked a little further and the King asked Yorda about his encounter with the unicorn.

'The unicorn believes that your coming here will spread doom among his kind. Do you have any idea why he would say that, Yorda?'

'No, sir. It appears to me that the Elänthoi have their own prophecies, such as those of the elves. In the elven prophecy I appear to be the saviour; whereas my success here will spell the destruction of the Elänthoi. However, if I fail here, then all in the lands of the Elänthoi will continue as was.'

'This is strange to me,' said the King. 'I always believe that a force for good will do good everywhere. I cannot understand how your good work here can cause so many problems elsewhere. If – and it is a big if – we are successful here against Marosham, then I will pledge any help we can give the Elänthoi should they need it. Perhaps we may yet be able to forge a close existence among our peoples. Come, Yorda; we should return to the others so that you may talk in front of the council. After that, I suggest that you and your travelling companions should rest for a few days. You have had a difficult journey here and soon it may prove to be even more difficult. You will all need your strength, as will I and the rest of my people.'

They all returned to the Great Hall where everybody was assembling. The King entered last and took his seat, whereupon everyone else sat. Tramulan raised his hand and stood once more.

'My friends, we have discussed the upcoming crisis that I believe concerns all our peoples. I know that some of you here may not as yet share that view, which is why this meeting has been called. We have all given our viewpoints and suggestions upon which the Council of Elders will decide shortly, but there is one other person who wishes to speak. This young man, as you have heard, is a very special person because he is the first ever offspring of a human and an elf. I believe his birth was more than an accident but was meant to be for a very particular reason, and that reason is to rid us of the threat of Marosham. Yorda, I ask you to address the meeting.'

Yorda stood and looked around at all those gathered.

'A few brief weeks ago I lived in the forest a short distance from a city called Parkent. I had a quiet life there as a healer of people and animals. I used the skills that had been passed down to me from my mother and father whom I knew only as gentle, peaceful humans. All of that was changed suddenly when I met Mertok and Dawson. A mysterious illness was striking at the children of my world, an illness that, although not fatal, caused a lot of misery and discomfort to young, innocent children. It is an illness that I believe comes from the very people that I am addressing now: elves. I had some measure of success in treating this illness, more so than other physicians and healers. I was to find out that this was no accident. The illness had been spread by Marosham, with the intention of finding me and killing me.

'At first, when I met Mertok and he told me of this, I thought it far-fetched, but in the time I have spent travelling here I have found all that he has told me to be true. During my trip here I have learnt that everyday things that I have taken for granted all my life are feats that other people cannot do. I have even done things that neither elves nor humans are apparently capable of. I have met and talked to a unicorn. I have caught and ridden an elven horse that was returning home in the belief that his bonded partner had been killed. And when entering the elven border my mind was taken from my body to a place and time unknown to me, where I met and went to school with Marosham.'

At this there were quite a few mutterings around the table, whereupon Tramulan stood and said aloud, 'Within these meetings the speaker has the ears of all present. Interruptions are not tolerated. I must ask you all to hear this young man.' The King sat down and all was quiet again. Yorda continued.

'You may not believe what I have just said but hopefully in the time that you are here I will be able to show you that I am speaking the truth. When I was with Marosham in my school-room we were each asked to read a separate page of a book. When we looked at the book the pages were blank, but since that time I have learnt to do things that I could not before.' Yorda walked over to the trunk of one of the trees growing up through the Great Hall. He reached out and gently touched the bark. Within seconds a small protuberance was seen pushing through the bark. A few seconds later a bud appeared and leaves quickly sprouted from it. A further few seconds saw a small beginning of a branch start to appear. Yorda took his hand away. A sprinkling of gasps sprung up around the table. Yorda returned.

'You have all seen what I have just done. I have never done anything like that before and I believe there are many other things that I can do just as amazing as that. I believe this power was given to me by my faceless teacher, for whatever reason I cannot tell. But as surely as I was given this power I know that Marosham was given some other power from the part of the book that he read. Every time I take a step forward I feel a tingling sensation in my feet. I believe that this new power I have is being taken from the life in the land beneath me. It is as if I am sucking energy from the very ground we stand on. Marosham must be doing the same thing.

'Why? Why should two creatures be taken from the land where they were born to be schooled in things that no other living being has knowledge of, and furthermore schooled by a teacher that does not want to be recognised? Also, we have been schooled in different things. I have not had much time to ponder this, and I hope the Council of Elders, who are much wiser than me, may shed some light on this, but the only thing I can think of is that we have been given our various powers so that we may be pitted against each other.

'I cannot believe that these powers we have been given are solely for our own use; they must be for a greater purpose involving all living things. For this reason I ask you to stand against Marosham, not against other elves, for he will not use his power for good. He has never shown any sign of doing deeds that would benefit any other living creature, so if he does attack and vanquish the Lohadrille then I see no reason to believe that he would stop there.

'My part in this is now clear to me. I must go against Marosham, but your part must be to stop the war that is brewing. War is never correct, but we must show strength and join together to stop Marosham invading this land. What will happen when Marosham and I meet I do not know, but there must be only one survivor. Of that I am sure. What the role of the survivor will be, again I am not sure, but I think that the separate information we were given in the schoolroom is to be taken by the victor. I have nothing else to add to what I have already said, so it leaves me to say only to the Council of Elders to think on what has been said, and I pray that their decision will stop this war from happening.'

Yorda sat down and he saw from the corner of his eye Mertok giving him a slight smile and nod of his head. The King rose again and addressed the gathering.

'I thank you all for coming here and giving your views on the situation that is upon us. We shall now close the meeting and ask the Council of Elders to convene and make a decision on what has passed at this table.'

With that, Tramulan left the Great Hall, followed by all but the Council of Elders.

Chapter Nineteen

While the council were in session most of the guests retired to their quarters to think over what had transpired at the meeting. King Tramulan asked Yorda to accompany him and Queen Mïǽlla. Yorda's friends took their leave and went off in various directions. Even with all the pressure of what had happened to them, Yorda could see that Dawson was laughing with Mertok and Thalién and quite obviously enjoying himself. That was good, Yorda thought, because he was sure that the sound of laughter would soon disappear for a long time in this part of the world.

The royal couple and Yorda walked through a section of the forest that was quite obviously a part of the royal estate. Here and there he could see what he considered to be guards to the King and Queen. The elves he spotted were all dressed in the same colours: green tunics with golden braids on the shoulders and a flash of red across the breast, just underneath a small unicorn figure in silver. The guards were not openly armed but Yorda was sure that they had some sort of weapon concealed on their person. It seemed very unlikely that the King or Queen would be attacked in their own city, especially as war had not yet begun; but perhaps the guards were not just for the royal family. As they walked, King Tramulan pointed out different herbs that perhaps Yorda would be interested in. He said this with a smile and Yorda realised that the King was teasing him.

'Yorda, my child, let me tell you a little about your family. Your mother was found not far from this city. You know the story of this?' Yorda nodded and the King continued. 'She spent some time with us as she recovered from her injuries. She was a remarkable woman.' Tramulan stared off into the distance and stopped speaking. Yorda waited but the King did not continue. He looked towards the Queen, who simply smiled and gently shook her head. Yorda felt that this was perhaps something the King did quite often and waited quietly with Miǽlla until the King continued.

'Ah! Where was I? Oh yes, your mother, Yorda. Even though she was a human she had an amazing knowledge of herb lore. She very quickly learnt all we could tell her about the herbs we grow in the forest and then told us of herbs that she believed she had used before she lost her memory. These herbs just in front of us...' The King bent down and picked a few leaves off a small plant growing at the foot of a bushy plant. 'Do you know what this is, Yorda?'

Yorda took the leaves and lifted them to his nose, taking a deep sniff. He then rubbed them between his thumb and forefinger, breaking them up to release the smell from within. He took another long sniff, then shook his head. 'No. I have no idea.'

Tramulan took a few more leaves and put one in his mouth and started to chew it. 'Neither have I, nor does any other elf. Your mother asked for a small garden to grow herbs. She used a lot of the herbs that we use on a regular basis and started to cross them to create new species. A lot of them failed and never grew but some were more successful. You will see some of them during your stay here. This herb started to grow just after she left us. We have no idea what it is for, and despite all our herbalists' attempts we have yet to find out a use for it. Myself, I find it tastes very pleasant and whenever I need to think deeply about things I come out here and just chew on a few pieces. I have no idea if I am using it correctly but it seems to help me organise my thoughts. I asked you if you knew what it was because I understand that your mother taught you about herbs and lotions and suchlike.'

'That is true, sir, but like you I have no idea what this is for. I would, however, with your permission, like to study this and other herbs that you have here.'

'That is something you may do even without asking, Yorda. Your parents, Yorda: how are they?'

'I saw them not too long before I left and they were both well. I suppose by now they will have realised that I have made my way here.'

'Your father was a very clever man and I have no doubt that he knows where you are, or at least knows where you are trying to go. He gave up a lot for the love of your mother. It is no small thing to give up your chance of being king.'

Yorda gasped. 'My father was your son?'

Tramulan smiled gently and looked towards Mïælla. 'Our eldest. Thalién and Mertok were after him.'

'Then you are my... my grandfather?'

'Yes, Yorda. And this is your grandmother.'

Yorda was speechless and just looked open-mouthed at first his newfound grandfather and then his grandmother. Mïælla moved forward and put her arms around him.

'Welcome home, Yorda,' she said, giving him a big hug. 'I wanted so much to tell you this when I came to see you in the infirmary but was scared that the shock might have harmed you. I don't know if I did any good but I could not bear to leave my grandson, whom I had never seen before, just lying there with no family around him. It is so good to see you recovered, my child.'

When she had finished, Tramulan held his arms out and embraced his never-before-seen grandson. 'It was a difficult decision for me to send my only other sons out to look for you. I might have lost all my heirs in this confrontation with Marosham. But I always knew that Mertok and Thalién were more likely to find you than anyone else.'

'They are my uncles, then,' said Yorda, more in a statement to himself than to Tramulan and Mïælla.

'You have family here, Yorda,' said the Queen, 'and you are welcome to stay among them as long as you wish.'

'I thank you for the offer,' said Yorda, 'but when I am finished here with Marosham, I must return home, for the villages around Parkent are where my life is. I will visit the elven forests when I can, but I have work to do there. I have been brought up as human and, even with the powers and knowledge that have been given to me, I still believe myself to be human.'

The Queen looked at Yorda.

'Do you have someone special waiting for you, Yorda?'

Yorda smiled at the perceptiveness of his grandmother.

'I really don't know, my lady. There is someone of whom I am very fond. I have only come to realise my feelings for her recently.

I believe she feels the same way about me but I am not sure. She will have no idea of where I am now, and if I am away for too long she may even forget about me.'

Mïélla moved towards Yorda and put her hand on his shoulder.

'There is no way she will forget you, Yorda. You are a very special being, whether you are elf or human or a mixture of both. You will not be forgotten. I understand why you must return but while you are here you must take the opportunity of seeing as much of our lands as you can. By the way, when we are alone I would love it if you called me Grandmother or even Mïélla. "My lady" is too formal except on official occasions. Will you promise me at least that?'

'Of course, Grandmother,' answered Yorda.

They walked on further into the gardens with Yorda constantly asking questions about the plants that they passed. It seemed to him that his grandmother knew more about the flora here than his grandfather, but perhaps it was because he had a lot on his mind that Tramulan answered less frequently than the Queen.

When they got back, it was late evening. There was still a golden glow in the air but Yorda could tell that the light was coming from within the forest rather than from the sun above it. He joined Dawson, Mertok and Thalién in supper. A small meal of wafers covered in the best honey he had ever tasted was served to them in Mertok's rooms, which were situated in, as far as Yorda could see, the tallest tree in the forest. Thalién wanted Yorda to go over how he had managed to capture and befriend Lëoram. This seemed to Thalién to be the most remarkable power that Yorda had yet shown, and he asked Yorda if he could possibly try to achieve the same success with the mounts that had returned riderless over the past few months. Yorda said he would be only too pleased to try to relieve the mourning that these animals were going through.

A few of the elf-lords that were in the outside world had returned today, saying that they had felt Yorda when he had entered the boundaries of the kingdom and knew that their work in the outside world was finished. Mertok believed that all of the remaining elf-lords would start their journey home and hopefully all that were abroad would return safely. If a war was to be the outcome of Marosham's plotting, they would need all the warriors they could get.

After they had eaten, Dawson went down to look in on Ted, his horse. He knew that the elves were the finest horsemen he had ever seen and that the elven ostlers would take care of his horse better than anyone. Anyone except the big man himself. While he made his way to the stables he couldn't help wondering if fate had brought him back to the forests where he had been found years ago. Perhaps he could retrace his steps and find out how he had got here and if there was a way back to his home. Even now he believed his people might still be waging war against General Balok. Perhaps it was too late for him to make a difference but if he could help, even if it meant his death, he had to try.

When he got to the stables he found Ted lying down in his stall, fast asleep. One of the elves taking care of him came over.

'He is a fine animal, worthy almost of elven stock. He is very tired after his trip. We believe his time in the forest of the Elänthoi has weakened him. He is not used to having that sort of magic around him all the time. I must admit we were amazed that a horse of human breeding could survive there. Animals are much more perceptive than humans are and it must have been a great shock to him to have so many strange things going on around him. We have given him something to make him sleep while nourishing him and soothing his mind. He will sleep for two or three days and when he awakes he will be as strong as he ever was. In fact, we believe that he will be much closer to elven horses than before. He is an intelligent animal and I think he will understand much of what has gone on before.'

Dawson thanked the elf, then knelt down by Ted. The elf stayed no longer than he needed, realising that Dawson wanted a little time alone with the big black stallion.

'Well, my friend, you 'ave served me well. These last days could not 'ave been easy for you. You deserve to rest. I will come and see you as soon as you wake up.' The smith gently rubbed his horse's nose, then got up. He ran a cursory eye over the animal, nodding to himself. The elves certainly knew how to take care of their animals. He had learnt much from them when he had been here before. He smiled, turned, left the stables and made his way to the quarters allocated to him.

The next morning Yorda and Dawson met up at breakfast.

'What do ye think of your 'omeland, laddie?' asked the big smith.

'I'm not too sure if I can call it that,' answered Yorda. 'I have only been here a couple of days. There is so much here that is strange to see, and yet in my mind it seems as if I have lived here all my life. My time spent with the teacher has taught me a lot. I find it difficult to distinguish whether what I now know has been given to me by the teacher or whether I knew it before.'

Dawson seemed a little confused by this, so Yorda continued. 'You know sometimes when you have a very vivid dream? Perhaps you dream about someone you have seen in Parkent. It may be someone you don't actually know but have seen passing by on the street. During the dream this person becomes someone you know very well, like a close friend. The next time you see that person after you wake up, for a few seconds it really seems as if you know that person until you realise it was the dream that caused it. That is how I feel at the moment, but I am not sure if the knowledge I have has always been there or if it has recently been given to me.'

Dawson nodded, although Yorda was not too sure if the big man had actually understood. He was not sure if he had really understood it himself.

'I hope when this is all over I will have some time to myself to try to make sense of what has happened to me, and in fact all of us. What do you intend to do after all this has passed?'

Dawson never even stopped to think before answering Yorda. 'I want to try to find my way back to my 'omeland again. I really think the answer lies in this forest. After our encounter with Rimanathon I think per'aps that I came 'ere through one of those portals.'

'I too think that, Dawson. Rimanathon said that you had a part to play in all of this and I feel that it is not an insignificant part. Neither of us should be here, he said, but we are, so we must play out our part.'

Dawson thought for a moment, then said, 'Do ye still 'ear the voices?'

Yorda looked at his friend for a moment. 'Yes, I do. Marosham has gone quiet for the moment but he is still there. We have some sort of contact between us. He is far away at the moment. I can feel that much. The other voice is still there. Sometimes I can understand what it says and sometimes it speaks in a different language. I wonder if it is the teacher.'

'What makes you say that?'

'Before I met the teacher, I could hear the voice in my head. It spoke in a language unknown to me. Since meeting the teacher I can understand the language and can even remember what was said to me before. However, now that voice speaks in a language that it has not used before. It is the same voice but different words. Does that make sense?'

Dawson chuckled a little. 'Very little of what 'as 'appened to you makes sense, laddie. I just accept it and act on it. Remember, I am a soldier by trade. We don't try to make sense of things. We just act on orders and try to correct wrongs.'

'You deserve far more credit than you give yourself, my friend,' said Yorda. 'Nevertheless, I believe I still have more training to undergo. How I will get that training I do not know, but I am being led somewhere, and between you and me I am getting a little fed up of being pulled along like a puppet by this voice or teacher or whatever you like to call it.'

Mertok joined them at that moment. 'We believe the Council of Elders is ready to give us its decision. We are to go to the Great Hall.'

The friends rose and went off to hear the decision.

Chapter Twenty

When they reached the Great Hall there were already several elves seated around the large table. Mertok told Yorda that the elders were waiting in one of the side chambers until everybody was seated. When all were seated the King made an entrance, whereupon everyone stood once more until Tramulan had taken his seat. As soon as he sat down, an elf who was waiting by the room where the elders were opened the door. As the Council of Elders walked into the room, everyone, including the King, bowed their heads until all were seated. When all was quiet Tramulan stood.

'My lords, friends, family and guests. We have been summoned here to hear and accept the decision made by the Council of Elders. It has always been our way to ask the most wise among us to arbitrate on certain matters. The council has always served us wisely and well. I have no doubt that they will continue to do so. As always, I must remind all of us here that their decision will be binding upon all.'

Tramulan sat back down and an old grey elf, dressed completely in white robes, stood and addressed the table. His voice resonated with age and wisdom as he started to speak.

'I, Marianth, elected Speaker of the Council of Elders, wish to inform all present of the decision we have taken. Our decision has not been an easy one to make. In my lifetime, which stretches back many hundreds of years, too many for me to count nowadays...' Yorda smiled slightly as he realised that even within a formal meeting such as this some humour was being injected by Marianth. He judged the old elf to be quite a character under different circumstances. The elf stopped talking just for an instant and looked across at Yorda. Had he caught Yorda's thoughts?

'...much too many for me to count nowadays,' he continued while looking at Yorda, 'the council has never had to decide on something as far-reaching as this. We have been told of the possibility of war between our peoples. This cannot be. Disputes we have had before, and even minor wars, but this seems to be a war to completely destroy one of our peoples. To ask the Merhantille and Sharnadille to become embroiled in this problem is unfair, as of yet we have no positive information to lead us to believe that Marosham has any aggressive tendencies towards you. However, if he does, then we cannot wait until it is too late for you to defend yourselves against him.

'It is disappointing that no one of the Solhantille came here to speak, for we could then have understood what drives them to attack us, but it is not without precedent. The Solhantille have not attended council meetings for many years now and we have come to accept that they wish to live their lives apart from other elves.

'We have listened to a most remarkable young man, Yorda, who has come back into the fold of his people, willingly, even though he believes that it may cost him his life. He had no knowledge of us some weeks ago and yet he is prepared to die for us. This shows great strength and courage, something his father was renowned for. We of the council have discussed the prophecy and believe it to be true and also believe it to be upon us. Whether there is a war or not, what will be will be. The confrontation between Yorda and Marosham will take place, of that we are sure, and we can do nothing to stop that, for whatever we do will surely force the prophecy to be fulfilled. What we can do is to try to stop the war.

'A decision has been reached. There will be no take-up of arms against the Solhantille yet. The Merhantille and the Sharnadille are to secure their borders until the Lohadrille and Solhantille have decided their fates. To this end, we of the Council of Elders will go to the Solhantille to tell them of our decision and to discuss the matter with their elders to stop the war from escalating.

'I see from your faces that some of you do not agree with this decision, but I also know that you will accept it. If nothing else, after meeting with our fellow elves of the west we shall have a much better understanding of the reasons behind their proposed invasion. If we need to reconsider then we shall do so. I ask my king to await our return. It may be that, in the long run, war cannot be stopped, so I suggest to the Lohadrille that they too should secure their borders and prepare for war should we return unsuccessful.'

Marianth nodded to his fellow elders, who stood and followed him out as they re-entered the chamber they had been in earlier.

Yorda turned to Mertok. 'Is it me, or have they basically done nothing?'

'Sometimes doing nothing is what achieves the most. I have not the wisdom to question the decisions made by the elders. I am but one elf with a short life experience; they are many with many thousands of years of life experience. Our entire history has been created by elves such as these. How can I question anything they do when our society has lived peacefully and flourished because of their decisions?'

Yorda looked at his friend. 'I am sorry but I cannot agree with you. I feel that wisdom in this instance has been replaced with slowness to react. Marosham has read of one of the Great Books. So have I. Nothing like this has happened before. I am talking of knowledge never before being given to a living being. No matter how much wisdom the council has, they are dealing with something that nobody can understand.'

Mertok smiled at his friend. 'Perhaps that is why they are doing nothing. Can anyone make a good and faithful decision on something when they do not have all necessary information and furthermore actually know that they do not have all the information? The only information they have is that of the prophecy. They believe that it will come to pass. They hope that in the meantime there will be little bloodshed. Actively pursuing war will cause many deaths.'

'And letting Marosham invade will also cause many deaths,' Yorda replied quickly.

'This is why we have the Council of Elders to give all of us a clear course of action. I agree with you, my dear friend, but our system of solving disputes has worked for many thousands of years.'

'I hope that it works now,' answered Yorda.

The next day, five of the Council of Elders, including Marianth, rode out to meet with the Solhantille. They were escorted by a small band of elves, which King Tramulan insisted upon, even though Marianth requested no support riders.

Many elves lined the streets of the Eternal City to bid goodbye to the riders. Dawson stood and watched with Thalién.

'I 'ave seen this situation many times over the years. Seldom 'as it resulted in a peaceful conclusion.'

'You speak as a soldier, my friend. I do not have your experience in these matters. All I can hope is that elves will not wish to kill other elves. If that is the case then we shall have peace.'

'And if not?' asked the big man.

'If not? Then that is something we must prepare for,' answered Thalién as he strode off towards his rooms.

Dawson decided to find Yorda. After enquiring of several elves he found him working with some of the elven horses that had returned home without their riders. He watched his friend as he moved between the horses. Each of the steeds kept wary eyes on Yorda as he moved among them. Some of them simply galloped off until they were a short distance away. One or two of the horses allowed him to approach; these the young man simply touched on the forehead with his hand; then he leapt up onto their backs and carefully took them through a few paces before dismounting and passing to the next animal.

After a minute or two, Yorda noticed his friend watching and walked over to him.

'How goes it, Dawson?' he asked.

'Not so bad, laddie,' the big smith replied. ' 'ow are things coming on with the big fellas over there?' Dawson nodded in the direction of the horses Yorda had just been working with.

Yorda pointed to the grey mare that had run off a couple of times when Yorda had approached earlier. 'She wandered in this morning. Apparently her rider disappeared a few years ago when Marosham was starting his messing around. I have found that I can call animals from a distance now, rather than having to be near to them. I sent out a call for all horses that have lost their bonded partner to come back to this place. Some of them, like the white you saw me riding a few moments ago, are quite happy for me to go straight up to them. The moment I can get a physical contact with them I am able to soothe their minds and help them to deal with their grief. It is a little like when I caught Lëoram. As soon as I was on his back, I managed to calm him.

'With most of these horses they are quite happy letting me walk up to them and touch them. A few, however, like the grey over there, are still a little unsure. I could run after her to catch her, but I believe it is better if she comes over of her own free will.

'The horses I have tended can now be bonded again. From what I understand from them, they all want to have a bonded partner but the pain of the loss from their previous one is so strong that they are afraid of it happening again. I just remove that fear and try to leave them with the good memories and the thought that it could be almost as good once more.'

'In that respect they are very much like you and me, don't you think?' said Dawson.

'How so?' asked Yorda, taking his eyes away from the horses.

'Per'aps you are too young, but when a man and a woman share a deep love for each other, when the relationship breaks up one or other quite often finds it very difficult to try it again, because they do not wish to experience the pain of breaking up once more. I see no reason why animals shouldn't feel the same way as us, per'aps to a smaller degree. These 'orses are far more intelligent than any other I 'ave ever seen, so it seems reasonable to me that they should feel the same or at least similar emotions as us.'

'I suppose you are correct as usual, my friend,' mused Yorda. 'I have never had a relationship break up like these creatures here, but having been in touch with their feelings I can understand their pain and their reticence at trying once more.'

'You miss 'er, don't you, Yorda?' Dawson said softly.

Yorda looked at Dawson's strong features. 'For a soldier and a blacksmith you seem to notice far more than you should. Yes, Ivaine is in my thoughts more than I thought she would be. The longer I am away from her the more I want to be with her.' Yorda fell silent and looked away.

'We 'ave a saying where I come from,' said Dawson, breaking the awkward silence. He waited until Yorda turned back to him. 'We always say "The longer apart, the closer to 'eart."'

' "The longer apart, the closer to heart." Yes, I think that is very true, my big friend. I hope that Ivaine finds it true also.'

Dawson laughed and slapped his friend on the back, trying to lighten the mood. 'Of that I am certain, Yorda.'

Yorda smiled. 'Thank you, my friend. You have helped more than you imagine. Once this business with Marosham is over I will go back to her.'

'Glad I could 'elp a little,' replied Dawson.

Yorda looked out towards the horses. 'I think my work is done here today. I will return tomorrow. I think the grey mare will be a little more relaxed with me tomorrow.'

The two friends walked back without talking much. Yorda collected a few herbs on the way, explaining to Dawson how they could be used. Dawson had been given a good education on herb lore while he was with the elves before, but he let Yorda continue and nodded or looked interested as and when it was required. He knew that Yorda must be thinking almost constantly about the upcoming encounter with Marosham, and wondered if the Black Elf had been in his friend's head lately. He decided to ask him.

'Yorda?' he began slowly. 'Have you ever tried to contact Marosham?'

Yorda stopped and realised what his friend was suggesting. 'You know, I never even thought about it. If he can get into my head, then I must be able to get to him. We are linked somehow.'

'What I was thinking,' said Dawson, 'is that per'aps you could somehow find out what 'is plans are.'

Yorda continued walking. 'I will talk to the elven healers when we get back. They may have some way they can help me. I have no idea how to do it, and even if I can I am not sure how it will work out.'

Now that he was lost in thought, Dawson couldn't get another word out of his friend until they got back.

After they had eaten, Yorda went to see Salurian and explained what Dawson had suggested.

'We have some healers here who have a little experience with entering the minds of others. It is only done when we have a patient who is unconscious, but if they explain their techniques it may be of help,' the head healer suggested.

'I don't know what I hope to achieve with this, but even if I shock him by showing that I also have the same powers as him, then it may help in the long run.'

Salurian called a meeting with her healers. By this time Mertok and Thalién had heard about the attempt at contact with Marosham and they turned up too.

Élonel was introduced to Yorda as the elf who had the most experience in mind contact. Yorda asked him to explain his procedures. The elf gathered his thoughts. 'It is something I have never been asked to explain before. When I need to enter another's thoughts I just do it.'

Salurian leant towards her fellow healer. 'Try to remember exactly what goes through your head as you are doing it.'

Élonel closed his eyes for a moment. 'The procedure that I use may be of no help at all in the task that you wish to attempt. My patients are always unconscious and I have direct contact with them, not only in mind but also in body. However, if what little information I give you can be of help in stopping this war, then I am only to pleased to assist.

'Before entering my patients' minds I try to get as much information as I can about their character, such as whether they are mild-mannered or of strong will. Do they get frequent illnesses? What work do they do? And so on.'

'How does this help you?' asked Yorda.

'With this information I try to adopt a similar outlook within my own mind, as I feel a similar mind can much more easily enter another's,' answered Élonel.

'That makes sense,' mused Yorda. 'Please carry on.'

'The next stage for me is to make contact with the patient physically. Normally I hold their hand or touch their forehead. It doesn't really matter, but for me contact is imperative. This is a big difference in what I do and what you are intending to do.' He looked towards Salurian as if expecting her to say something, but she only nodded for him to continue.

'After physical contact I try to narrow my thoughts down to a small tube that joins my head to the head of the patient.'

'How do you feel as you are doing this?' interrupted Yorda.

Élonel thought for a minute. 'It is strange but I have never really paid much attention to it before because I am too involved in the procedure. I suppose that it feels as if we are one and the same person, but I am looking down on myself from another's eyes. As I enter the mind it almost feels as if I am entering my own. I feel as the patient feels, I hear as the patient hears, but because I am not the patient I have the ability to be apart as well as joined. This helps me to locate physical as well as mental imbalances.'

'Do you ever talk to the patient during this time?' asked Yorda.

'Physically, yes, but I don't recall ever trying to make contact non-verbally,' the healer answered.

Yorda thought for a second, then said, 'OK, that is how you get in. What about leaving the patient?'

'That is more difficult. Sometimes I almost have to fight to leave. In this case, when I talk to the patient afterwards, they tell me that they had such a feeling of support from my mind entering theirs that they didn't wish it to stop. I always try to retrace my steps that I have taken inside their brain and when I reach the "tube" I concentrate on closing it as I leave.'

Élonel paused and looked at Yorda. 'I don't think there is anything else that I can add to help you.'

'You have given me as much information as you can and I thank you for that,' replied Yorda. 'I hope that it will be enough to contact Marosham.'

Chapter Twenty-One

Yorda insisted that his attempt to contact Marosham be taken inside the paddock where the elven horses he had been working with were kept. His friends, although not sure why he had asked this, agreed to his demand. They had set aside the following morning for this task and, although Yorda wanted to do this alone, the King had decreed that Mertok and Élonel were to be there also. Dawson insisted that, as it was his idea, he wanted to be in the group. Yorda smiled at his friend and, giving him a slap on the back, said that he would be only too glad to have the big man along.

The group that were to go along to the paddock broke their fast together and discussed what was to be done. Yorda said that he only wanted to see if he could instigate a contact with Marosham – all that was happening at the moment was that Marosham could contact Yorda whenever he wanted.

'What are your intentions should you be able to contact him?' Mertok enquired.

'I want to show him that his little trick of tormenting my thoughts and taunting me can be reversed if I require it. This may stop him from doing it. He obviously knows that I cannot stop him from doing it, but a little of his own medicine may make him think twice about continuing.'

Mertok looked gravely at Yorda. 'Why didn't you tell us that he was doing this to you? I realised that he could sometimes enter your thoughts, but from what you are now saying it appears that he is doing it on a regular basis.'

Yorda sighed. 'Mertok, my friend, there is nothing anyone here can do, so it seemed pointless to burden you with it. I have to deal with this myself. It is irritating more than anything else. His touch on my mind is superficial. He can only annoy me by name-calling and threats and suchlike, but if he likes playing those games then I shall indulge him by playing along with him.

Maybe by taunting him I can learn something of his plans. At the very least if I make contact he will know that I am learning my abilities, and perhaps it will make him advance his plans too quickly and make some mistakes. To be totally honest, I am not quite sure what I hope to achieve here today but I just have this feeling that I need to do something rather than just sit here and wait for him to come.'

Yorda looked around the paddock. He could never understand why the elves called this field a paddock, because there was no fence or gate. It was just a clearing in the forest, as far as Yorda could see, where the horses seemed to congregate. It was, however, his favourite place. Now that he had learned more about himself, Yorda felt that he was not too dissimilar to the horses that returned here after losing their bonded partners. As well as missing Ivaine more than he thought he would, he believed himself to be alone in the world. He was half-elf, half-human, the only one ever to have existed. Even though he had his friends around him at this very moment, he felt that everything he had been for the past nineteen years had been pulled away from him and he was now learning a new life.

In a bizarre way he felt that the only person to have anything in common with him was Marosham. They were interlinked in some unknown way. The prophecy dictated that they were destined to meet but he had also shared a schoolroom with the Black Elf when the mysterious teacher had made them read the Book of Knowledge together. He was now trying to reinforce that bond between them. Was this meant to be? Was he doing the right thing? Yorda had no way of knowing, but he believed it was something he had to try.

As he continued his gaze around the paddock he saw a few of the horses looking interestedly at the group of elves who were intruding on their space. Most of the horses were quite happy just grazing or standing still in that peculiar fashion common to all horses, with one of their back hooves casually draped forward so that only the tip of the hoof touches the ground.

He continued his scan of the paddock and could see just on the border of the field and the forest the grey mare that he had been trying to befriend. She was a beautiful beast but Yorda found her more difficult to form a bond with than any animal he had ever known. She was moving slowly from tree to tree, sniffing the floor, looking for something that would only interest a horse, or maybe following a smell that lingered on the ground – Yorda had no idea from this distance. He sent out a few soothing thoughts. 'Good day, my fine lady. Have you found something interesting there? I will come to see you later today and maybe we will talk a little.' Yorda pushed his thoughts towards the mare, who lifted her head and looked straight towards him. He was sure he detected a slight nod of her head before she carried on sniffing at the ground in front of her.

Mertok noticed the direction that Yorda was looking and turned to follow his gaze. When he saw the mare he tapped Élonel on his shoulder. The healer turned to Mertok and saw a frown on his face and followed his gaze. Élonel, too, frowned when he saw the grey mare.

'Right, I think now is as good a time as any to start,' said Yorda, sitting cross-legged on the ground in front of him. Élonel turned back towards Yorda and sat in the same fashion, directly in front of him. Mertok sat to Yorda's right, all the time looking in the direction of the horse on the outskirts of the paddock. Dawson, not quite sure what he should do, decided to sit on Yorda's left. He had noticed the two elves glancing at the mare but was unsure why they frowned. If they felt that he was to be included in their thoughts they would no doubt tell him. For the moment he occupied himself with Yorda.

Yorda closed his eyes and started to breathe slowly and evenly. Élonel spoke softly and slowly to him. 'Yorda? Try to remember the sensations you felt when Marosham was in your head talking to you. Recreate the same feelings. It may give you a link to him.' Yorda nodded and did as Élonel suggested. He tried to remember the sound of Marosham's voice in his head. As he concentrated he felt that he could remember that each time Marosham came to him it was almost as if the Black Elf's voice was attached to a long cord which stretched back away from him. Yorda imagined his thoughts were at the end of a similar line and cast out around him. All the while he kept the name of Marosham firmly at the front of his thoughts.

Yorda was aware of the sounds of his friends around him. In fact he seemed to be more aware than usual. He could almost hear their heartbeats around him and also the heartbeats of the horses in the paddock. Perhaps it was his own heart he could hear. The only thing he was sure of at this moment was that he had to find Marosham.

Yorda concentrated even more. Was that Marosham's voice he could hear in the distance talking to other elves? Yes. He was sure that he was getting closer. Even though he could not make out the actual words he knew that he was homing in on his target. He could feel his thoughts accelerate towards the Black Elf. Faster and faster they went until they crashed into a wall. He had reached Marosham but his mind was still outside of his target.

Yorda focused himself and waited for a little while. Marosham didn't seem to know that he was just outside of his head. Yorda probed gently around the outside of his enemy's head and was surprised when he sensed a small opening just in the centre of Marosham's skull. He moved forward and pushed gently into the opening. He knew that there was no actual opening in the skull but in his heightened state of awareness he believed that he had found some sort of psychic entrance. He moved through the opening and, for a fleeting instant, he was sure he got the sensation of surprise and even fear hitting him, but then it was gone.

'Why, Yorda, you do surprise me!' said Marosham. 'You have been practising, haven't you? Congratulations, my dear friend. What can I do for you?'

Yorda did not want to show any reciprocal feelings to Marosham and merely ignored the question.

'You are not the only one who can invade others' private thoughts, Marosham.' Yorda felt that a certain amount of bravado was needed here.

Mertok had turned his head once again in the direction of the grey mare, which was now looking at the group seated on the ground. The horse had now entered the paddock and was standing still, staring intently towards them. He looked back towards Élonel, who was still speaking softly to Yorda, reminding him of the procedure he felt he should follow.

'I am glad you paid me a visit,' said Marosham, 'It saves me the trouble of contacting you.'

Yorda tried to feign total disinterest in what Marosham was saying and instead concentrated on his own thoughts. 'I am in your head now, Marosham. You cannot influence me here. I am the invading force and you will listen to me now.' Yorda tried to sound as confident as he could. He had no idea if he was correct or not. Whenever Marosham had entered Yorda's head, even though he could do no damage to Yorda, Yorda could find no way to stop the Black Elf from delivering whatever message he wished. He hoped that this would be equally true now that the tables had been turned.

'I have no wish to influence you, my dear friend, but now that you are here I can maybe prove to you things that you do not wish to believe. I will leave myself open to you to probe as you wish.'

Although Yorda was intrigued by this invitation he had no wish to let Marosham guide him. It was he who would take charge of this situation.

'You know that you will lose if you declare war on the other elves. There is only a certain amount of patience that even elves have before they decide to hit you hard,' said Yorda.

Marosham's reply was almost melodic. 'Yorda, Yorda, Yorda. What have they been telling you? I have no wish to declare war on anybody. All I ask, and all I have ever asked, is that I receive a fair hearing for my ideas.' Marosham deliberately failed to give any more information to Yorda but held back and waited.

'OK, I will play your game, Marosham, as long as it pleases me,' answered Yorda, trying to maintain control of the conversation.

'Now that you are in my head, Yorda, you can tell if I am lying. We are joined, you and I, in more ways than you can imagine, but for the moment I will open myself up to you. Come follow me.'

Yorda could feel Marosham's voice trailing away, so he followed it. He had the sensation of entering a large, open hall as he once again joined with Marosham.

'Here, my young friend, is the centre of my knowledge.

Anything you ask me will be answered in picture form as it exists within my mind. You will know that I speak the truth here.'

Yorda interrupted. 'You say you do not want to declare war on anybody but you enter my thoughts and tell me that you wish to kill me and every last elf that stands against you.'

Marosham gave the sensation of smiling. 'What I must do and what I want to do are totally different things. Let me explain. To kill you is something that I must do, but I have no wish to do it. We are brothers, Yorda.'

'Never,' said Yorda, breaking into Marosham's words.

'No, no, no. Of course we are not blood brothers, but we are linked. Linked inextricably. The prophecy has placed us as opposites. We must fight and one of us must die. Even if you ignore everything else that is happening in the world, our meeting must happen. I do not wish to die and I am sure you do not; therefore we both must kill the other. Our relationship with each other is irrelevant in this situation. So you see, Yorda, I *must* kill you but I do not wish to.

'We are very special people, Yorda. For thousands of years, probably from the start of time in fact, we have been talked about as the prophecy was passed down through the generations. Finally we have arrived, and what happens? We get taken to a special school – together – not at the same time in the time zone we exist in at this moment, but at a time when we were the same age, which as you know has never been.

'We have had knowledge imparted to us that no other elf has ever been given, but knowledge that is different from the knowledge received by the other. Do you not see it now, Yorda? Each of us has been given this different knowledge by some godlike creature for a reason. If I were so evil and you were so good, then surely you alone would have been given this information. Neither of us is right or wrong, good or evil. We are just tools of the gods. This is all a test. Whoever comes out alive from our test will take the power of the other and use it to rule, justly and fairly, but until we meet and decide our fate I cannot be threatened or attacked so I have created my own army for defence.

'Why has this all happened? That is the question I ask myself. I was thrown out of the company of the other elves because I asked questions. I said "why?" when the elders made rules and I said "why?" when the elders made decisions. When I suggested ideas to help run the community and advance our people I was continually refused because I would be "changing the way things have been done for centuries". So what? If the change is for the better then it is necessary, otherwise we stagnate.

'You have seen yourself. We are the oldest civilisation on the planet and yet we are backward compared with man. You have lived with man and seen their wars and killing. They advance all the time whereas we stay stagnant. Do you seriously believe that man will not eventually come and take from us what we have? They cannot do it yet because they have not yet the resources, but the advances they are making will soon give them the power they need to take what they want. You have seen yourself how man now hunts just for pleasure. They kill what they consider to be inferior or what they consider to be a threat. It is only a short time before they look to our borders. We too must be as strong as, in fact stronger than, them. If they look to us and see someone who does not wish to expand but someone who is more advanced and stronger then them, then they will leave us alone. That is all I ask. I can see this happening, and I know that you can see it also.'

Marosham stopped and let Yorda absorb what he was saying. Yorda thought about it and probed around Marosham's thoughts to try to find any deception, but could not find any.

'You are just trying to confuse me, Marosham. I believe that you believe what you are saying, but it is distorted. It is true that there are some evil humans, but the vast majority are good people who would live in friendship with the elves or any other creature. Of that I am quite sure. I believe that it is you who wish to take and destroy other creatures and usurp their land for your own use. I have learnt a lot about elves and I know that any ideas that would help their race would be seriously considered and not dismissed out of hand. I have made new friends within the elves. Friends who have free speech but rely on the wisdom of others whom they trust.

'You are just twisting words, Marosham, and you are scared because you know I will triumph. I felt your fear when I entered your head. My strength is growing and, by the time we meet, you will know that it is I who will win. The power that goes to me will not be used to rule but will be used to help all living creatures: man, elf, fairy, animal, every species. It is what I do best and what I will continue to do.

'I must bid you farewell now that I understand a little more of what you intend. Never fear, I will come to you again to worry you as you tried to worry me. Goodbye, Marosham.'

Yorda started to pull back but suddenly found a blockage.

'I am sorry, my friend, but I cannot let you go,' came the voice of Marosham. 'You let me lead you to the centre of my mind and now it is here that it ends. The prophecy must be fulfilled, but not in the way that you had hoped.'

Yorda felt himself being mentally bound up. His exit route had somehow been blocked.

'I did not believe that it would be this easy,' came the gloating voice of the Black Elf.

Yorda tried to search around for a way out but Marosham blocked every move he made. Tighter and tighter wound the mental bands. Yorda could feel his breath being squeezed out of him. Slowly but surely the young healer was being crushed to death.

Yorda's friends noticed the difference in his breathing almost instantly. It was plain that their friend was uncomfortable. At first, Élonel said that for a short while at least Yorda should not be disturbed. He himself had had similar symptoms when treating patients who were in a lot of pain. It could be that the twisted mind of Marosham was causing some discomfort to him. Within seconds of saying this, Élonel realised this was more than mere discomfort.

'I must go in for him,' said the elf. 'He is in trouble.'

Mertok took a quick glimpse towards the grey mare, who was now walking slowly towards them. He turned back to Élonel.

'Are you sure you can help?' he said.

'I have no idea,' answered the healer, 'but I cannot sit here and do nothing.'

He reached out and touched Yorda's head. Breath was coming in staggered gulps from the young man. Élonel linked into

Yorda's mind and followed the direction of thoughts towards Marosham.

Pain wracked Yorda's body. Marosham didn't just want to kill Yorda: he wanted to enjoy it. Marosham knew that he was defenceless. He had him completely pinned down, unable to move. Tighter and tighter wound the invisible bands; then suddenly they lessened a little. A roar broke out from Marosham. '*Get out!*' Yorda tried to move in this temporary respite but his bindings were too tight and starting to get tighter again.

Élonel felt an explosion in his head as Marosham hurled him out of his mind. The elf was thrown backwards onto the ground with pain screaming through his temples. He welcomed the blackness that descended around him.

Mertok was at Élonel's side in an instant. Dawson got there a fraction of a second later. The tall elf put his head down to the healer's chest.

'He is still alive, but barely. We must get him back to the healers' hall.'

'What about Yorda?' asked the big smith.

Mertok hesitated. 'There is nothing we can do. He must fight this battle by himself.'

The sound of hoofs made Mertok turn his head. The grey mare was now galloping straight for them. Mertok stood and moved towards the horse to intercept her.

Stars were dancing in Yorda's brain. He could see the Black Elf standing in front of him. He was obviously in some discomfort himself. Perhaps things weren't so hopeless after all. Yorda tried to concentrate and focused all his energy on sending out aggressive thoughts of his own.

Marosham rocked slightly as he was assaulted by Yorda's attack.

'You are learning quickly, my brother, but it is too little too late.'

The bands tightened even further. Little by little Yorda was dying. His attacks were only slowing the inevitable.

Mertok stood his ground as the horse headed straight for him. Three seconds, two seconds, one second and the horse was upon him. The elf tried to leap onto the mare's back but she sensed what he was about to do and turned slightly, hitting him squarely in the chest as she galloped straight over him.

Dawson watched this and rose himself. He walked forward and crouched low. He had stopped runaway horses before, or at least diverted them. The mare's eyes were wide and mad. Dawson could sense that this animal was going to get to Yorda whatever the cost. So be it.

Man and horse collided. The big smith got his arms around the mare's neck but the power of this horse was unlike any he had experienced before. His grip started to loosen and the animal trampled straight over the big man. Forward she ran until she got to Yorda. The horse skidded to a stop and then opened her mouth wide, showing her teeth. The large mouth descended towards Yorda, who had fallen to his side, his breath coming in short, agonised bursts. His lips had turned blue and his eyes were now open, staring blankly with his pupils wide open.

The mouth got closer and closer. Mertok stirred and lifted his head. He turned and first saw Dawson bleeding and unconscious on the ground and then, as he shook his head to clear his vision, his blood froze. The animal had fastened its teeth into Yorda's leg and was ripping the flesh off it. 'No!' he cried and then tried to lift himself. His legs turned to rubber and he collapsed back onto the ground, powerless to help even himself.

Yorda was gasping his last breaths. Marosham was getting stronger while his feeble efforts were getting weaker. He tried to launch one last attack, which the Black Elf brushed aside. He moved towards Yorda and the young man watched as Marosham lifted both arms. The Black Elf moved behind him. 'You will not see the final blow, my brother, but it will be quick.'

Pain the like of which he had never before felt coursed through his body. Yorda screamed, and as he felt his life leave him he heard another scream. 'NOOOOOOO! You cannot do this to me! Not you!'

Chapter Twenty-Two

Mertok was the first to rise. Bodies were scattered around him. He stumbled towards Yorda. On his left lay Élonel and Dawson. Next to Yorda lay the grey mare with the flesh from Yorda's leg still hanging from her mouth. He could not tell if she lived or not. He bent down to Yorda. Blood was streaming from his leg but he was still breathing. Mertok lifted his young friend's head.

'Yorda?' he whispered softly. 'Are you still with us?'

Yorda's eyes opened slowly. His glazed look slowly cleared and focused in on the elf.

'Mertok? What happened?' His breath was still laboured and he was obviously in a lot of pain.

'Marosham's horse attacked you,' said the elf. 'We tried to stop her but she was too strong. I think she may have killed Dawson.'

'No, Mertok,' said Yorda. 'She rescued me.'

Yorda struggled to sit up. He took a deep breath and surveyed the carnage that surrounded him.

'I feel life here, Mertok. They all live, but only just. Take me to Élonel.'

Mertok lifted his friend and carried him to where Élonel lay. Yorda put his hand on the healer's head and muttered a few words. The elf's eyes opened slightly and a small smile played on his lips. 'Yorda, you live, thank the gods.'

'Sleep now, my friend,' said Yorda, and the elf instantly closed his eyes.

'He will be OK. Take me to Dawson.'

When Yorda looked at his friend he almost laughed. 'It will take more than this to kill him. He will have a fine set of hoofprints running down his chest tomorrow but other than that he has only been knocked unconscious and will wake shortly. Please, I must see Shirrin. Take me to her.'

By this point elves were rushing into the paddock. The noise had been heard and help was summoned.

Yorda put his hands on the neck of the mare. 'She bit me to cause me physical pain. It was so intense it ripped me from the grip Marosham had on me. He tried to force her out as he did Élonel. She was unprepared for any attack on her as she was only trying to save me. She has been badly injured.'

Yorda closed his eyes and concentrated. He started whispering slowly at first and then faster and louder until it was almost a loud chant. The grass around them slowly started to fade from green to brown and then dried and shrivelled. Mertok saw a shimmer of air around both the horse and Yorda. The other elves who had entered the field stopped and watched with amazement.

Almost as soon as it had started it had finished. The mare lifted her head slightly and turned towards Yorda. 'You are still with us? I am glad I could help.' With that she lay her head back down on the floor and her breathing became more relaxed and regular.

Yorda looked up towards Mertok. 'I think she will be all right. It will take time for her to recover completely but I have healed the scars that were in her mind after the onslaught from Marosham. She tells me her name is Shirrin. She was bonded to Marosham. I suppose I should be surprised, but surprises seem to be normal for me recently.'

'You must now treat yourself, Yorda,' said Mertok.

Yorda gave a wry grin. 'I cannot use my power on myself. I must trust to your good people here. I will heal quickly though.'

Mertok called for help to take his friends back to the healing halls and for an elven ostler to look after the mare. He then accepted assistance for himself.

Although Yorda healed faster than any of the elves could believe, he needed to use crutches as the mare had bitten a large chunk of flesh and muscle from his left leg. For two days, bed rest was prescribed by Salurian, which Yorda at first was too weak to refuse. His journey back to the healing halls immediately after the incident in the paddock was just a blur to him. After his ordeal in Marosham's mind and then helping to heal Élonel and Shirrin, Yorda had drifted into and out of consciousness several times on the way back.

He had woken in bed with several healers around him. The first face he had seen was that of Salurian. She was applying a salve on his injured leg and when she realised that he was awake she looked up and smiled. 'That will teach you to fool around with dis-bonded horses. They are not all as easy to tame as you have done up to now.'

Yorda tried to speak but found that even the action of opening his mouth took more energy than he could muster.

Salurian ordered one of the other healers to bring a drink, which she held to Yorda's lips. The cup was tilted back just enough for the golden liquid within it to trickle slowly into his mouth. Immediately Yorda felt a warm tingling feeling pass down his throat into his stomach and then it seemed to radiate outwards through his body. He almost instantly felt a lot stronger and looked up quizzically towards the healer who had given him the liquid. She was, as far as Yorda could make out, a young, female elf. Her hair was long and golden, as with most of the elves here, but seemed almost to glow. She lifted her head and smiled at him. Her grey eyes held large, dark pupils that seemed to engulf him as he looked at her. Salurian saw the way he looked at the healer.

'You won't be the first patient to fall in love with his nurse,' she said, suppressing a giggle.

Both Yorda and the young elf blushed.

'Forgive me,' said Yorda to the elf. 'I didn't mean to stare.'

'The liquid you have just drunk sometimes has that effect for a few minutes. It will soon wear off,' said the young elf.

Salurian agreed with her and said so to Yorda, but she had noticed that the look her nurse had returned to her patient had nothing to do with the medicine she had dispensed.

'Miõla? I think you can look in on the other patients now,' she said, dismissing the girl.

Yorda watched her leave and then asked Salurian about the others in the paddock.

'Your healing powers are quite remarkable, young man. Élonel is progressing well but has one mighty headache. Apart from that, he seems totally recovered. I don't think he will be doing any mental healing for a little while, but you never know – the experience may have taught him something that can aid his talents. Your friend Dawson is a very tough man. He is fine but keeps complaining that no horse has ever knocked him down before and insists he has gone soft. If he has gone soft,' she said with a wicked smile 'then I would have loved to have seen him before. Mertok has no injuries. He has some mixed feelings, however. Because he failed to stop the mare from reaching you he thinks he has failed in his duty, but, as it turned out, if he had succeeded in stopping the horse then we dread to think what might have happened to you.'

'Oh, I know exactly what would have happened to me,' said Yorda. 'Right about now you would be cremating me. And Shirrin, what of her?'

Salurian stopped dressing his wound and scowled.

'What did you do to her, Yorda?'

'What do you mean? Is she all right?'

The head healer paused for a moment to gather her thoughts.

'The horse is fine. She lay where she fell for several hours after you had seen to her. She was very tired after her ordeal, but once she rose she went back into the forest. She has returned once to eat some food that had been left out but seems none the worse for wear, which is more than I can say for the patch of the paddock where you did your healing.'

Yorda looked confused.

'Do you not remember what happened when you did your healing on the animal?'

'No. I remember placing my hands on her and whispering some words that came into my head.'

'Some words that came into your head?' interrupted Salurian in astonishment. 'Did you not know what you were saying?'

Yorda struggled to sit up in his bed a little bit. Salurian gestured to two nurses to help him. When he was comfortable he continued. 'Ever since I was young I have heard voices in my head, whispering words that I do not understand. I notice this more so when I am healing. The voice is much more powerful and I have the feeling that it is commanding me to repeat what it says. The same thing happened with Shirrin. When I put my hand out to touch her I could feel her pain. She was close to death and passing away very quickly. The voice started to whisper to me at first. As always I repeated the words exactly as they came to me. At first they were slow but then they came quicker. I could feel energy leaving me and going into Shirrin. The poor creature was confused. I think she had accepted that she was to die. When the words stopped coming to me I removed my hands.'

Salurian sat by the edge of the bed and let one of her nurses finish dressing his leg. 'Mertok and Dawson have both told me of your healing powers. I believe that the potions and herbs you mix are no more potent than the same ingredients mixed by another. Your power comes from elsewhere. The patch of land where you healed the horse is now completely dead.'

'Dead?' answered Yorda.

'Yes. It seems that all the life from the grass and the soil itself, for an area of about two paces around you and half that deep, was sucked dry of its life force and given into the animal you were treating. Has anything like that ever happened to you before?'

Yorda shook his head. 'No, nothing like that has ever happened. You said earlier that Shirrin had lain down for several hours before leaving and then came back to eat later?'

Salurian nodded, noticing that Yorda had sidestepped her question.

'Then in that case how long have I been here?' he asked.

The healer stood up and walked over to a nearby table where two crutches were lying. She picked them up and came back.

'When you were brought here you were in a lot of pain and barely conscious. I helped you to sleep so that we could treat your wound without you being in too much discomfort. You have slept for two days. Your powers of recovery are quite amazing. The wound that was inflicted on you would leave most elves permanently maimed. Some of the muscles in your thigh were completely severed and a good deal of tissue had been torn from the leg. The skin can regenerate with our help but I didn't think we could do anything for the loss of muscle.

'However, in the time you have been sleeping, your leg has grown new tissue to replace the muscle. It is still very fine and I do not recommend putting any weight on the leg yet. I am sure that telling you to stay in bed for several more days is no use.' She lifted an eyebrow slightly, and when Yorda looked a little sheepish she knew that she was correct. 'So if you insist on moving around I would like you to use these.' She placed the crutches on the side of the bed.

'Thank you, Salurian, I appreciate it. I would like to go to see the patch of dead earth. First, however, I have a question. I seem to remember that when I was in the paddock, Mertok said that Shirrin was Marosham's horse. Is that right?'

Salurian hesitated for a moment and then sat once more by the side of the bed.

'You heard correctly, Yorda.'

'I know when she bit me and I was being torn out of Marosham's mind that he called Shirrin's name. When I was healing her she told me her name and I realised that Marosham knew her, but if she was Marosham's horse they must have been bonded.'

Salurian nodded and Yorda continued.

'But why is she not with him now? She is wandering around with the other horses that have had their bonds broken through the death of their elves. He is alive.'

Salurian looked at Yorda. 'Shirrin has been here for quite a while now. When Marosham left us 200 years ago, she went with him. She had always been considered one of the best elven horses ever bred, and when they bonded it seemed only right and correct. Marosham was one of the cleverest elves in the realm. He showed great potential in many areas. He could have been a great healer, a great warrior or eventually even a great elder, but he was too selfish, and his ideas, although at first appearing to benefit all, were ultimately only to his advantage.

'When he was banished, Shirrin went with him, but as I said she returned to us. At first we thought that Marosham must have died and it was true that for a few years nothing was heard of the Black Elf. But when we got reports of his ill doings once more, we were all completely in the dark as to how the two of them were parted. She stays clear of all elves and does not generally even bother with the other horses. When your signature hit the forest was about the time she started coming to the paddock on a regular basis. This was not significant at the time but maybe after the events of a few days ago we should have paid more attention to her.'

Yorda lifted himself a little more in the bed. The liquid that he had drunk earlier had definitely made him feel a lot better.

'I must see her as soon as possible in that case.' Yorda looked around him.

'What is it, Yorda?' asked Salurian.

'My stomach has just started telling me that I am hungry. Do you have any food here?'

Salurian laughed. 'That is a very good sign, young man. I will get food brought to you immediately and then after you have eaten' – she patted the crutches on the bed beside him – 'you can practise with these. If you feel well enough after that, I will arrange for you to go to the paddock to look for Shirrin.'

With that, Salurian stood and walked to the door. Before she left she turned her head and said, 'Mertok and Dawson will be pleased to see their friend is back to normal.' She emphasised the word 'normal' and gave a little smile before leaving.

Chapter Twenty-Three

Mertok and Dawson entered the room almost at the same time. Behind them were several elves carrying trays of food and wine. Yorda stopped eating and tried to stand.

'What do you think you are doing, laddie?' said the big smith. 'Sit yourself down.'

Yorda gratefully did as he was told. The sudden attempt to stand and turn had brought stars to his eyes and a fresh wave of pain from his leg. Mertok smiled and sat at the table along with Dawson. The serving elves laid out the food on the table.

'You didn't think we would let you have a feast all by yourself, did you?' asked Mertok.

'I have managed to get a bottle of fine elven wine to toast your 'ealth, laddie,' said Dawson, filling two large goblets from the flask he was now holding.

'Why only two glasses? Who isn't drinking?' asked Yorda.

'Unfortunately, you,' answered Mertok. 'Salurian said we could come and join you but under the strict instructions that we weren't to give you any wine.'

Dawson pushed the flask towards Yorda.

'But if you were to take the wine yourself, laddie, then strictly speaking we 'aven't given you any.'

The three comrades burst out laughing. Yorda poured himself a small amount and lifted his goblet. 'To friendship.'

'To friendship,' echoed Mertok and Dawson. They drained their glasses and tucked into their food.

Yorda was sure he had never eaten as well or as much as this in his entire life. Even Dawson was hard pressed to out-eat the young man, but he forced a few extra mouthfuls in before pushing his plate away from him and leaning back on his chair. He opened the front of his shirt and Yorda saw two perfect horseshoe shapes on his chest. The blues and blacks of the bruise had a yellow tinge around the outside of the shapes, making them seem as if they were lifting out of his chest.

'You weren't the only one with a memento of that damned 'orse. She was strong all right. I ain't 'ad an 'orse run through me like that before.'

'Lucky for me she did,' said Yorda. 'I don't think I would be here enjoying good company and a wonderful meal if you had stopped her.'

Mertok looked at Dawson. He knew the big man had mixed feelings over his failure to stop Shirrin, but he was coming to terms with it.

'In fact,' continued Yorda, 'by showing a human quality of fallibility you helped to save my life, so I propose a toast to fallibility.'

The three friends filled their glasses. 'Fallibility,' they all announced, and downed the contents. Toasts for hospitality, long life, good health, tall trees, blue skies, and many other subjects were offered and accepted until Salurian broke the revelry. When she saw that Yorda had been drinking, she ushered Mertok and Dawson out of the room, Dawson commenting, 'My, she's gorgeous when she's angry.' This promptly got a well-timed kick in the rump from the old healer. 'And strong too,' continued Dawson as he hurried out.

Although Salurian appeared angry she knew that no real harm had been done, but she insisted that Yorda take a short nap if he intended to go out to the paddock before nightfall. Yorda accepted without complaint. He had to admit to himself that he was feeling a little tired and he wanted to be as fresh as possible to see Shirrin.

When he awoke after his sleep, Yorda tried out his crutches. Any attempt at putting weight on his injured leg sent waves of pain through his body. He soon realised that the strength he had felt earlier on in the day was solely due to the drink given him by Miõla. Now that the effects were wearing off he could see that he was much weaker than he had thought. Nevertheless, Yorda persevered until he could handle his crutches quite well. Then he decided that perhaps it would be better to wait until the morning before making what would now be quite a trek to the paddock to see Shirrin.

The following day Yorda felt a lot better. He realised that there had been no voices in his head since the paddock and secretly hoped that perhaps Marosham had received some sort of injuries during their meeting and could no longer force his way into his mind. Perhaps, he thought, this was too much to hope for, but the temporary respite brought no complaints from him. A nurse came to change the dressings on his leg and Yorda was quite surprised himself to see how well he was healing. The skin had almost closed over the wound. Gentle prodding, at which the nurse scowled at him, showed that the bulk of the muscle in the thigh was growing back very quickly. Yorda tentatively tried to put a little weight on his leg when the nurse had turned away and found far less pain than the day before, but was not foolish enough to believe he could use it without his crutches.

Yorda took breakfast in the main hall where he was joined by Thalién and Dawson. He noticed that Mertok was nowhere to be seen. He was told by Thalién that there was news of a raiding party not too far from here and Mertok had ridden out with some others to see if they could catch any of the raiders. They had had very little success in the past, the raiders seeming to strike and then disappear without leaving any tracks. Yorda remembered the time they had been captured by Sharnak's mercenaries. The spell of concealment had hidden the mercenaries from them. He mentioned this to Thalién, who shook his head.

'Such a spell would not work here. The magic of the kingdom would not accept this sort of spell.'

'But do you not have a similar spell to conceal the barriers that have stopped us falling from the walkways high above us?'

'That is a different thing, Yorda,' Thalién replied. 'The magic you speak of conceals living creatures. In the kingdom we can hide objects to a certain extent, but even so we know they are there. We may not see them but we are aware of them. You may not see the wind but you feel it. Our best trackers can not only feel these things but they "see" them almost as well as you and I see each other now. No, a concealment spell would not work here.'

'And yet they seem to disappear almost before your very eyes. I suggest that Marosham has indeed perfected some form of spell that cannot be detected. Just because it hasn't been done before does not mean that it cannot be done now. The world around you is changing, Thalién, and you need to change with it or be left behind.'

With that Yorda got up and hobbled off on his crutches, leaving a startled Thalién.

Dawson put his hand on the elf's shoulder.

' 'e means nothing, Thalién. That is not Yorda speaking. 'e as been through a lot these past weeks and the last three days in particular. I think 'e is probably in a lot of pain at the moment and it must be playing on 'is mind that 'e 'as to face Marosham once more. For a young man 'oo 'as never faced war or violence 'e 'as been thrown into a world completely alien to 'im. Give 'im a little space, eh?'

Thalién sighed. 'Perhaps you are right, my big friend.' He too got up and went off. As he walked, Thalién remembered the last thing Yorda had said: 'The world around you is changing, Thalién, and you need to change with it or be left behind.' It was a sentence he had heard before over 200 years ago, but then it was said by another elf who was now threatening to destroy the kingdom.

Yorda finally got to the paddock and was feeling quite tired but much better than he had thought he was going to be. One of the nurses had given him a small flask of the golden liquid, which he was told was called lirrip juice.

Yorda looked around the paddock but could not see any sign of Shirrin. Some of the other horses that had lost their bonded mates came up to him. He could feel them saying that they had missed him over the past few days. Yorda took time to spend a few minutes with each of them, comforting them and trying to convince them that the other elves could also be company for them. He sensed that some of the horses were starting to believe him and hoped that maybe one day soon some of them might once again find another partner to replace the one they had lost.

He walked over to the blackened patch of earth where he had helped heal Shirrin. As he moved into the circle of dead soil he felt the now familiar tingle from the ground disappear. He stopped and turned around and walked out of the small patch of bare earth. As soon as he stood on the untouched grass the tingle returned. Once more he put his foot onto the blackened patch. Nothing.

Yorda knelt down at the edge of the ring. He reached out with one hand and closed his eyes. His fingers traced around the edge of the circle. He could feel the same tingle with his hands as he felt with his feet, and whenever his finger moved into the darkened area the tingle disappeared. Yorda opened his eyes and concentrated on the soil just outside the ring. He placed his finger on the floor and a small flower started to grow. His finger moved slowly towards the blackened soil. Keeping the same thoughts in his head his finger touched the black earth. A jolt passed through his body, not violent but as if a wind had hit him. It was just enough to make him draw breath. He felt as if he were carrying a heavy weight but he kept his finger in contact with the ground. He could see a few stalks of grass slowly starting to rise out of the soil. He moved his finger slowly around the edge of the circle and, wherever it stopped, a few blades of grass would appear. He had moved a few handwidths when fatigue overcame him and he sat back on the grass. The tingling from the ground was more noticeable for a short while, and then it subsided into the usual feeling that he was now accustomed to.

Yorda sat at the edge of the circle for a few minutes while he regained a little strength. He tried to make sense of what had happened. It started to dawn on him that all of his healing power had come from the very land he walked upon. It was obvious when he thought about it. The energy used to heal must come from somewhere and the energy within his body was not limitless, so it couldn't have come from him. Sure, the herbs that he used helped but, after all, was it not the energy contained within the herbs that caused the curing process? There was no magic involved. The life energy in the herbs was in effect given to the patient.

It was the same with Shirrin. The life energy within the ground around him had been used to heal her. Because she had been badly injured, it naturally took more than usual, so it had to come from somewhere: the earth around him and the life within it. Since he had felt this strange tingling from the earth into his feet, Yorda had noticed that his healing powers seemed to be far stronger and faster than before, noticeably since he had been in the lands of the Elänthoi. Both the elves and the Elänthoi had great magic within their lands. Yorda mused that it must be contained within the ground they walked on.

He realised he must be some sort of conduit for this magic and when he heard the strange voice in his head, speaking words he had not heard before, this seemed to be the link that enabled him to use this conduit and let the magic flow through him. He remembered the words of the old man who had been one of his fellow prisoners captured by the mercenaries, Grandmaster Wiltor. He had called it the Words of Power. Even the elves, with their great and ancient knowledge, didn't know what it was that Yorda was doing with his healing, but that old man had recognised what Yorda was saying.

Yorda sat up. The old man knew what Yorda was saying; he had knowledge and understanding of this mysterious language that came into his head. How he wished he could have talked to Wiltor. What else did he say? Yorda thought back to their time together. He remembered the old man asking Mertok what kind of creature Yorda was. What did he mean by that? He had recognised Mertok as an elf and he obviously knew the humans, but he didn't recognise Yorda. The more Yorda started to understand his powers, the less he seemed to know about everything.

His musing was interrupted by a gentle nudge in his back. Yorda looked around and to his surprise and great delight Shirrin was standing behind him.

'You are recovered, Yorda?'

'Thank you, Shirrin, yes. I am much better. I owe you my life but I wish you could have found a less painful way to save it.'

If a horse could have laughed, then Shirrin would have done so. The shake of her head and the way she looked at Yorda showed him that she saw the irony in his remark.

'If I could have found a less painful way for me to save your life I too would have preferred it.'

Yorda now knew that Shirrin had a sense of humour. He detected great intelligence in this animal, more so than the other elven horses. She stood proud and erect, her ears twitching, taking in all the sounds around her but her eyes never leaving Yorda for an instant.

'Why?' asked Yorda aloud, not even trying to send a message by thoughts alone.

'You would have died,' was the simple answer that was transferred back to Yorda.

'How did you know I was in trouble with Marosham?' Yorda added the name of the Black Elf to see what reaction he would get from the mare.

'I still feel him when he is around and I still sense his thoughts. I will never lose that, Yorda.'

'Are you still bonded with him, Shirrin?'

'In a way, yes. Until the death of either of us we are linked, but not as other bonded pairs are. I severed the links as far as was possible.'

Yorda was intrigued. It seemed that he was not the only anomaly in the elven kingdom. This horse had actively broken the bonding link between herself and her partner.

'Why?' Yorda repeated aloud the question he had asked before, but this time it was in reference to the severing of the bond between horse and master.

'Marosham does not have a stable mind. He has other attachments and priorities. His bond was not only to me.'

'I don't understand,' said Yorda. 'Was he bonded to another horse as well?'

'No. An elf and his horse are only bonded to each other. There was another involved. Another who was more important to Marosham than me.'

Yorda made a mental note to ask Mertok and Thalién about this. His teaching with his mysterious schoolteacher had not included anything about bonding with more than one animal.

Yorda could not get any extra information from Shirrin about this 'other' that was attached to Marosham. He gently probed the animal to check for any mental scars from her experience the other day and found that his healing had been effective and she carried no injuries from their encounter with Marosham.

'Come,' said Shirrin, dropping down as low as she could so that Yorda could mount her 'You are tired. I will take you back to the others. You still need rest to recover.'

Yorda was surprised at her perception but he had to admit that she was right. In fact he was feeling very tired and his leg was starting to throb. He graciously accepted her offer and climbed on, whereupon she lifted herself and walked towards the Great Hall.

Yorda was asleep on Shirrin by the time the horse walked into the heart of the Eternal City. Many elves had stopped what they were doing and watched Shirrin carrying the young healer. Horses were seldom seen this close to the quarters of the King and Queen except for the Royal Guard. Word was passed quickly and by the time Shirrin trotted into the area immediately underneath the Great Hall there was quite a welcoming committee. Shirrin walked forward and stopped in front of Thalién, who was standing with some other elves. Thalién stepped forward and placed a hand on Yorda's leg, whereupon the young healer awoke with a start.

Surprise was evident on the young man's face when he saw that he was surrounded by at least fifty elves. He could hear some muttering quietly, but loud enough for his enhanced hearing to pick up. 'What is she doing here?' and 'Why is he riding her?' seemed to be the type of comments he was hearing.

He got down gingerly from Shirrin, accepting a helping hand from Thalién and another elf who came forward when he saw the young man struggling.

'Why the welcoming committee?' asked Yorda when he dismounted, looking around at the large number of elves who had stopped what they were doing and gathered to see horse and rider arrive.

'It is forbidden for any unannounced riders to enter this section of the city,' answered Thalién. 'Shirrin knows well that she should not have come here.'

Yorda turned to see some ostlers approaching Shirrin. The horse reared up and, showing her teeth, kicked at the air in front of them. They backed away a little and then took some thin coiled ropes out of their belts.

'What are they doing?' asked Yorda.

'She must be removed and taken back to the paddock where she belongs. She is unbonded and cannot stay in the stables.'

Yorda stopped and turned back towards the group of ostlers, who were now circling around the animal, getting ready to throw their ropes around her neck.

'Wait!' shouted Yorda in a voice that was a lot louder then he had intended.

The gathered crowd became silent and the ostlers stopped and turned towards the booming voice that had issued the command.

Shirrin stopped her kicking but kept a wary eye on the ropes that were still being held at the ready.

Yorda moved back to the horse. 'You cannot stay here, Shirrin. You know it is not allowed.'

'I am here to take care of you, Yorda. You are weak and need me.'

'Do not worry; I will be fine. Go back to the paddock. I will come to you tomorrow, do not fear.'

Shirrin looked around at the elves, shook her head, turned and galloped off back towards the paddock. As she left, Yorda could feel her telling him that if he needed her, all he had to do was whisper and she would come.

Mertok had joined the edge of the group of elves and saw Shirrin leave. He walked over to Thalién. 'This does not look good, my brother,' he said.

Thalién nodded without comment and walked over to Yorda.

The two brothers needed to talk to Yorda. They realised that as a guest and a newcomer to the elven world he had limited experience of customs and laws. As such he was not to blame for bringing Shirrin into this area. What was worrying them was that Shirrin knew the laws and had deliberately broken them, a trait that had marked Marosham's time with them. An elven horse picked up a lot of its characteristics from its bonded partner. Marosham had had a habit of deliberately questioning laws and ignoring them if he saw no reason for them to be in place. It was partly for this that he was exiled.

Thalién approached Yorda and asked him to accompany him and Mertok to supper. Mertok realised what was happening and joined the two of them. Yorda was obviously tired and in a little pain so they asked one of the waiting elves to send a healer to Yorda's room to change his dressing and sent another elf off to get some food prepared and sent to the room.

While they ate, Yorda told them what had happened during his time in the paddock that day. Mertok suggested tactfully that Yorda should be careful of Shirrin. If she was not truly broken of the bonding with Marosham, he perhaps still had some control over her. Yorda disagreed.

'I can feel her thoughts, Mertok. She can sense him, but no more than that.' Yorda repeated what Shirrin had said about 'another' having some form of bonding with Marosham. Someone who took priority over his horse. Both Mertok and Thalién were worried by this but neither knew exactly what this meant or whom the other bonding was with.

Yorda said that Shirrin only wanted to protect him, even to the extent that all he had to do was whisper for her to come to him. Both Thalién and Mertok sat upright at this.

'Do you not realise what has happened, Yorda?' said Mertok.

Yorda looked at his friends and shook his head.

Thalién finished what Mertok had started to say. 'She has bonded with you, Yorda. Only bonded horses react to the whisper call.'

Yorda remembered when Mertok had called Meryat before leaving Parkent. He had stood and whispered something and within seconds she had arrived.

'This cannot be,' said Yorda. 'I have felt nothing extra towards Shirrin than I would to any animal.'

'Nevertheless it appears that is what has happened,' said Thalién.

Yorda looked at their worried faces. 'Is this a bad thing?' he said.

It took a little while before either of the brothers answered. Finally Mertok sighed.

'We do not know, Yorda. Like a lot of things that have happened recently, it is something that has never before occurred in our lands. You, my young friend, are something of an enigma.'

Mertok smiled and laid his hand on Yorda's shoulder. 'There is one thing I must say, however,' he continued, 'and that is, be careful with Shirrin. You must not forget whom she was once with. A lot of him will have gone into that horse and a bonding between the two of you may cause some of what has been passed to her to be passed to you.'

Yorda nodded his head. 'I will be careful, Mertok, Thalién. If what you say is true, then I may also learn a little more of our foe from her. It may turn out to give me some advantage when finally we meet.'

Mertok could see that Yorda was getting very tired so he and Thalién left their friend. As they walked back to their rooms the brothers were deep in thought and spoke little, but both were worried at the events of the day.

Chapter Twenty-Four

The next morning Yorda was woken by the sound of elves running around noisily outside. He got out of bed, noticing that his leg gave him much less pain than before when his foot made contact with the floor. He still used his crutches as he wasn't fully awake yet and thought that perhaps any sudden moves might open his wound, but he was surprised at how good his leg felt. He decided that he would try a little walking on it without the crutches later on. When he got to the window he looked down from his little tree house and saw a group of four armed elves talking to Thalién and Mertok. They immediately signalled for another elf and, after a few short words, Yorda saw the elf head off in the direction of the royal quarters.

Yorda followed what was happening for a short while, then quickly got dressed and hobbled his way down to ground level. Just as he arrived he noticed a very solemn-faced Tramulan being escorted to his sons. Dawson reached Yorda at that moment and asked what was going on.

'I have no idea, but it must be something important. Look at the King's face: he is deeply troubled.'

Mertok noticed Dawson and Yorda at that moment and signalled them over to him.

'There is grave news at the city limits. Will you come with us? This concerns all of us but especially Yorda.'

Mertok motioned to another elf and told him to ready Bettine for Yorda and Ted for Dawson. When Dawson started to speak, Mertok held up a hand. 'I will tell you on the way. For now we must get to the city limits as soon as we can. For you both, and especially you, Yorda, the quickest way is by horseback.'

The horses arrived several seconds later, Dawson admiring the speed with which the elves worked. He stroked Ted's nose and noticed that he was in fantastic condition. The big smith had seen to his horse every moment he could since arriving in the Eternal

City but even his expertise with horses paled in comparison with the elven ostlers. Ted's coat was gleaming. His tail and mane had been braided, which seemed to please the animal, as he stood proud and erect when his master reached for him. Dawson knew from the time he had lived in the forest with the elves before, that their food was second to none and seemed to supply more energy than any other food he had ever tasted. This seemed to be true for the horses. He had never before seen the effects of elven food on non-elf horses but both Ted and Bettine seemed to have grown slightly in height, maybe half a hand or so; yet both animals were much leaner and more muscular than when they had arrived.

Dawson and Mertok helped Yorda onto his horse. Yorda noticed that one of the elven saddlers had strapped a pouch onto the side of his saddle to place his crutches. He admired the workmanship of the pouch. It was made of some material that he had seen a couple of times in the city, but he had no idea what it was. As the crutches were placed into the pouch the material almost enveloped them and took a firm grip so that they would not slip out. Yorda reached down and touched the strange material. It felt incredibly tough and yet it was supple and very thin. He made a note to ask someone about it later. He had learnt a lot about the elves from his mysterious teacher but many things were still unknown to him.

The horses set off at a trot. Yorda could feel his wound throb a little and rubbed it gently with his thumb. The skin had completely healed over the area and the scar seemed quite tough. He pushed a little harder and could feel the muscle underneath. It too was much thicker than it had been the day before. He estimated that in a couple of days he would be able to dispense completely with his crutches and start toughening-up exercises on his leg.

Mertok had leapt onto Meryat as soon as his friends had set off and had drawn alongside them after a few seconds. A few more armed elves had formed an escort around them.

It wasn't long before they reached the city limits, where Yorda noticed a strong contingent of armed elves facing away from the city. He could make out the King dismounting, obviously having just arrived. One of the armed elves, a captain of the Royal Guard, said something to the King, who turned and beckoned the three friends forward.

After dismounting slowly, but more confidently than he expected, Yorda joined with the King, Thalién, Dawson and Mertok. The captain looked at the King, who nodded for him to repeat what he had just said.

'A short while ago one of Marosham's elves came out of that band of trees over there.' He pointed in the direction the elf had come from. It wasn't lost on the group how the captain had said the word 'elves' when referring to one of Marosham's men.

'He came bearing a white flag and we let him approach. He said he had word from Marosham about our envoy we sent several days ago to the Solhantille. When we asked him to convey the message he said it was to be given in the King's presence. I have sent out scouts to search the area. He is alone.'

'Why was he not spotted before today?' asked Tramulan. The captain looked a little uneasy.

'Sire, one lone elf on a horse is not considered a threat. I suppose that he has been seen by our patrols but was ignored as we are looking for raiding parties, or at least numerous sightings of lone elves. He is the only one we have seen for many leagues around the city.'

Thalién stepped forward. 'Do not be too harsh on the captain, sire. It was I who gave the order. We cannot stop and detain every single elf we see. Our own people would become unhappy with that as they would be the ones stopped all the time.'

The King sighed. 'Yes, you are correct. It is just that I do not like the possibility of any of his agents getting through to the city.'

The captain stood tall. 'My liege, that would never happen. All who approach the city limits are detained until their purpose is known.'

'Very well,' said the King. 'Let's go and find out what he has to say.'

The captain barked an order to one of his men and four of them rode out to the stand of trees where Yorda could hear the leader of the group call to the messenger that the King was ready to hear his message.

The messenger left the trees and rode forward towards the

King. He reined in his horse several metres from him. He took a parchment from his belt, unrolled it and started to read aloud.

'Tramulan of the Lohadrille,' he announced. No mention of his title, just his name. This was obviously the contempt that Marosham showed for the king of the elves.

'I, Lord Marosham, leader of the exiled elves from the kingdom of elves, have met with your council that was sent to influence and poison the minds of my allies, the Solhantille. They have no wish to meet or talk with their weaker brothers and to that end I intercepted the delegation. After listening to their proposals I decided to dismiss them and they will be returning in a short while. They would probably like to tell you of my plans, which I discussed with them, but I am afraid that cannot be allowed. To that end I have forwarded this.'

The elf reached behind him and pulled a sack from his horse. He opened the top and upended the contents onto the ground. A gasp arose from the surrounding elves and the King paled as he looked upon the heads of the council members now lying on the earth in front of him. Yorda had moved towards the King and had not taken his eyes off the messenger from Marosham. As soon as the heads had hit the floor the elf had pulled a short dagger from the lining of the sack and had thrown it at the King. All eyes were on the heads rolling on the floor in front of the messenger. As the knife flew through the air, the slight hissing sound brought some of the downcast eyes upward towards the sound. The King never saw the blade as Yorda reached out and neatly caught it mere inches from the King's heart.

Before any command could be made, the messenger was riddled with arrows from the Guard. He fell silently to the floor. Yorda rushed over and touched a hand to the elf's head. He withdrew it almost instantly.

'Marosham was in his mind. He had no control over his actions.'

The King had moved forward and was bending down to see the disembodied heads on the floor. His trembling hand touched one of the heads.

'My dear, dear friend,' he said as his fingers met with the head of Marianth, the Speaker for the Council of the Elders.

'This will not be allowed to happen again.'

The King stood and raised his hands high. 'My subjects, listen to me and hear me well. What has happened here today cannot ever be allowed to happen again. The elders have always been considered as untouchable by our laws. Marosham no longer respects even the highest and most revered citizens in the kingdom. I decree that the Lohadrille will now take up arms to wage war such has never been seen in these lands. Marosham must be wiped from this land.'

So saying, the King turned and strode towards his horse, followed by the Royal Guard.

Mertok moved towards Yorda, who was still holding the knife.

'It is coated with poison,' said the young healer. 'I can smell it. It is one that is used by my people. It is slow but deadly. His trackers must have got some when they were in my lands. Why Marosham would use it I have no idea. A poison as slow-working as this would be easy for me to nullify. The knife, however, could have killed the King quite effectively without being poisoned.'

Mertok looked at his young friend. 'How did you know?'

'That he would strike when he did?' asked Yorda.

Mertok nodded.

'It was the only time that everybody's attention would be distracted from him, if only for a second. I have learnt while playing with lions and wolves as a child that you never take your eyes off a potential enemy, whether you are being stalked or whether you are doing the stalking. Marosham also wanted to find out about me, how I would react. Perhaps he hoped that I would take the knife to save my king. In that situation perhaps he hoped that, while your healers were trying to find a way to stem the poison in my blood, I would either die or be left in a permanently weak state. This poison would attack my nerves and leave me severely disabled even if a remedy was found. I believe the attack was meant for me, not the King, but he would have been content with either result. I have learnt a little more about my enemy from this but unfortunately he has learnt more about me.'

'The biggest thing he has learnt, Yorda,' said Mertok, 'is that both you and the King are still alive and unhurt. That will be a big blow to his plans. I wish to thank you for saving my father's life.'

Yorda nodded, then turned and left for the city. His friends did likewise.

When they got back to the centre, there was furious activity. The King had already issued orders for an army to be made ready to meet Marosham and word was being sent to other villages and minor cities throughout the land to muster as many elves as possible to combat Marosham's army. A certain amount of preparation had been done already. A small army was in place to combat the raids that Marosham's elves had been making. This had been effective to a certain extent, but, no matter how large the army, the King realised that they could not stop every raid. The patrols were mainly to stop any large force from entering the land and also to act as a deterrent. This army had been well drilled and organised and would be an elite force in any larger group that was to be sent against the enemy.

The elven smiths got to work to produce armour and weapons for the new recruits who entered the city each day. Dawson, although a smith himself, found the elves made the finest steel he had ever seen. One of the smiths told him that elven metal, once honed to perfection, would never lose its sharpness. The big smith put his hand to his belt and touched the knife that had been given to him years before, when he had left the elven forest, and realised that the elf spoke the truth. His knife had been used on almost every surface he knew and the blade had never lost its sheen or the edge become dull.

He used the elven forges to make some shoes for Ted. Elven horses were much lighter on their feet than other horses and never needed the metal horseshoes that were common among horses in the human world. One of the elven smiths seemed interested in what Dawson was doing and showed him a way to make the shoes lighter and much stronger than conventional shoes.

The elven fletchers worked day and night to provide extra bows and arrows. Longbows were normally made only for battle, as the shorter version was much easier to carry and could be used in more confined spaces, though it was not as accurate as its larger cousin. Dawson came into his own in teaching the recruits the art of warfare. Having been a soldier all his life, his real skills were in the planning and consequent execution. He was aided by some of the captains of the Royal Guard, who added their knowledge of forest warfare, which Dawson saw merely as a way of hiding behind trees, keeping quiet until the enemy approached. Having said that, he realised that hiding and keeping quiet from elves was a lot more demanding of skill than it would be against humans.

Scouts were sent out to evacuate any villages that would be in the path of Marosham and the Solhantille. It would not be necessary to remove any crops in the fields, as a marching army of elves always carried enough food for their campaign. In any case, time now was too short. If the Solhantille made as much speed as they could they would arrive in no more than five to six days.

Yorda, meanwhile, spent most of his time either resting to get as much strength back in his leg as possible, or riding with Shirrin to various parts of the forest where raiding parties had struck and mysteriously disappeared.

After each raid by Marosham's men, his raiders would retreat into the forest where they would be pursued by either the King's patrol or by the elves that had by now organised themselves after the surprise of the initial attack. The story was always the same. The tracks of the raiders would be followed. Despite the scrutiny of the best elven trackers the trail would always lead in a roughly circular pattern. No tracks were ever seen to deviate from this pattern. Yorda too had noticed the marks left by the fleeing raiders. He could tell that the raiders, when discovered, would leave quickly, but after a while their tracks showed that they slowed to a walking pace. After following the tracks he would return to the area where the attack had taken place. Yorda just couldn't understand this. One set of tracks forming a circle; no beginning and no end. And yet no matter how many times these tracks were followed, and irrespective of the direction they were followed, no raiders were ever encountered. It really was as if they had disappeared.

At every site where a raiding party had been, Yorda could feel a lot more tingling in his feet than normal. He traced each trail that had not been covered by time and at the point of approximately the furthest distance from the attack he could feel the tingling almost become a burning on his soles. His assumption that there was some unnatural energy here could not be denied. Even in the forest of the Elänthoi, Yorda had not felt this sort of energy before. With the Elänthoi, and to a lesser extent in the elven forest, Yorda could accept the tingling as some form of contact between himself and the earth. He could even tap into this energy and use it, as he had done while healing Shirrin and causing grass and plants to grow where he had placed his hands. Here, this energy seemed much, much stronger, but he could not tap into it. This was a different energy that had been shed on the land by something, not an energy that was intrinsically part of the land. It seemed to Yorda that yet another unexplainable event had been introduced into the timeless land of the elves where nothing would change for thousands of years.

Yorda wondered how much of an accident and coincidence these 'new' events were. In fact he was even starting to wonder if his being here now had been planned by some unknown power. The prophecy seemed more and more to be a manipulation of forces pulled together by some power over which the beings on this planet had no control.

His mind went back to the meetings with Rimanathon and his mysterious teacher in the schoolroom. Were they the same entity? Did they have different agendas for Yorda? Rimanathon, or The Third as he said he was also called, admitted that his people, the Spellweavers, had the ability to nudge events so that they would happen in the way they wished. Could they be the creatures that had created the prophecy? If he were to be believed, then the Spellweavers were just the creatures that recorded events for their masters, the gods, when they returned.

Yorda's brain swam. There were just too many possibilities, and without any leads he could force himself to assume and believe anything he wished. He was sure that all would be made plain when the time was right. When this was all over he decided he would visit Rimanathon again. His friends seemed to have a very limited memory of what had happened there and Yorda had to admit to himself that his memory was a little clouded. Rimanathon was obviously a creature of great power, who could hide himself from the Elänthoi in their own domain.

Yorda racked his brain to try to remember everything that had gone on back in the forest of the Elänthoi while he was with Rimanathon. He could remember everything that Rimanathon had said but could remember little else. It was of no matter now, but Yorda, who normally had perfect recall, was not happy with the limited memory he had of his time with this Spellweaver.

At the last site he visited, Yorda felt the tingling even stronger than before. This was the latest raid by Marosham and his followers. Where the tingling was strongest, Yorda bent down and touched the ground. He could feel the prickling of energy all around him. He sat cross-legged on the earth, closed his eyes and breathed deeply. He tried to visualise exactly what had happened here. Some of the elves who lived in the village close by had tried to explain to him exactly what they had seen when the marauders had left. There were six of them, dressed in dark colours to camouflage themselves against the trees and shrubs of the forest. The usual tactics of these elves were to move in quickly to a lightly populated area and pick off some of the villagers with their bows. The poison in their arrow tips would work quickly, not giving any healers the opportunity to counter its effects. It was usual that four or five villagers would be hit and killed this way with each raid.

This time, however, the villagers had just received a visit from one of the patrols that were out looking for raiders, and the Dark Elves were forced to flee when the alarm brought the patrol back. An arrow had hit one of the raiders from the King's patrol and Yorda had spotted blood in several areas. The spaces between the injured elf's blood were constant, which showed that they were leaving the area at a steady pace. This was at odds with what he expected. Normally when pursued by a trained army patrol, raiders would flee quickly, stopping briefly to judge where their pursuers were, but this group had calmly retreated all together at no great speed. They knew that they would not be captured and furthermore knew that they had a safe area somewhere near.

There was something different about this site by comparison with the others. The blood from the injured elf had been dripping constantly up to this point where the tingling was strongest, but had apparently stopped as Yorda followed the tracks. Yorda reached out and touched the dried blood on the ground at the point where the drops ended abruptly. He felt a shudder go through his body and found himself suddenly running, but in pain. He had an arrow sticking in his leg. He was laughing and someone was replying in the elven tongue that the King's patrols were too soft, only firing untouched arrows. Yorda realised that somehow he was reliving what had happened through the spilled blood of the Dark Elf who had been shot.

He relaxed once more and breathed deeply. He could see five other elves running at not much more of a jog around him. They were all joking and laughing quietly. He recognised the area of forest around him as the one in which he was now sitting. There were two elves in front of him, running at an easy pace. Suddenly the first elf disappeared, followed almost instantly by the second. Yorda felt a stab of pain from his arrow wound and then he reached the point where the two lead elves had vanished, and without slowing and without surprise at the disappearance of his fellow elves he continued at the same pace straight on.

Yorda was no longer part of the earlier action. As the elf had run through the point which was directly in front of where Yorda was sitting, all memories of the event ceased. Yorda moved slowly forward and with his hand traced a line on the ground where the elves had disappeared. He found that at exactly this point the tingling was at the strongest.

He closed his eyes once again. What was it that had happened in the forest with Rimanathon? They had followed this strange being through some sort of doorway and on the other side he had been in his home, which could not have been possible. He concentrated even further. Trying to use some of the same techniques Marosham had used when luring him into the deepest parts of his brain, Yorda delved deeper into his own mind. There! He could see it. Some blocks had been raised in his mind. He moved forward towards them and could see that some of them had already broken down, but there were some that still looked firm. Yorda imagined himself pulling at these blocks and slowly but surely they started to move.

As each block fell, Yorda remembered more of what had

happened with Rimanathon. He could see a few more large, strong-looking blocks further ahead of him. He moved forward towards them but suddenly he was hurled back away from them and he heard the voice that had been with him since he was a young man saying 'They are not for you at this moment.'

Yorda opened his eyes. He had no recollection of the past few seconds and could remember only up to the point where he had pulled the last block down and released all of the memories of his time with The Third.

He looked once more at the spot where the elves had disappeared and suddenly could understand what had happened. Marosham must be using a portal. It made sense now. Yorda pieced together what must be happening at the raids. The raiders would enter this part of the forest through a portal that Marosham had somehow opened. From the tracks on the floor they must have entered at a run and then slowed to a jog and then a walk when they arrived at their destination. Once they had finished their raid they would leave and gather speed before entering the portal on the opposite side, but at the same pace at which they had left it. This would explain the circular tracks. Rimanathon had said that the portals were breaking down, but had made no mention of the fact that Marosham was already using them.

Yorda tried to absorb every sensation he had from this area where the portal must have formed and disappeared. The energy residue that he could feel in his feet at this point was very strong and Yorda tried to tap into it as he had done to the raider's blood. All he could feel was power and energy. It was a living energy but not one that he could connect with. He sighed and stood up. At least he felt he had discovered how the attacks were made, but at this point he had no idea how to stop them. He turned and leapt aboard Shirrin, not realising that he no longer had any pain or stiffness from the injury to his leg. His task now was to return to the city and give this information to the King and his friends.

Chapter Twenty-Five

There was a lot of activity in the centre of the city when Yorda rode in. He dismounted from Shirrin and she left. Yorda watched her trot off. He could definitely feel a stronger bond between himself and Shirrin. She would wander off into the forest and come whenever Yorda called her, or sometimes she would wait at the edge of the paddock if she fancied something a little tastier than the grass she munched normally. Yorda turned back and headed towards the Great Hall where he could see a large number of elves gathering.

Dawson was standing at the edge of the gradually increasing group. Yorda went up to him.

'Marosham's army is about two days' march from 'ere,' the big smith said, seeing the questioning look on Yorda's face. 'The King is going to make the news public any minute now,' he continued.

'Has Marosham been seen with his army?' asked Yorda.

Dawson looked with interest at his young friend.

'Now that is an interesting question, laddie. Do you not think 'e will be with them?'

Before he could answer he saw the King climb up onto the platform where he made all his announcements to the people. The crowd became silent and King Tramulan started to speak.

'My people. All of you here know what is going to befall us in the very near future. I must announce to you all that that future is only two days away. The army of Marosham has gathered west of here about two days' march. Our scouts have informed me that he has nearly 500 renegade elves fighting in the colours of the Black Elf. The army of the Solhantille are but one day's march away from them and they have over 2,000 elves in their number. We are armed and prepared to do battle against this enemy, but many elves will die. We of the Lohadrille will have many deaths alongside the deaths of our enemy. It will be a sad day for the kingdom.

'We have done as much as we can to prepare for this war and there is no turning back. Marosham has made his intentions plain and so we must counter his threat with force. We must repel these invaders even if it means fighting to the last elf. We will never surrender to his evil ways. Those of you who are to fight should return to your homes to get some rest, for when the battle starts it will be fierce and relentless. I will talk to my warriors once more before the battle begins.'

The King turned, descended the steps and made his way back to the palace.

Yorda sought out Mertok. He found him in the palace gardens talking to two of the captains of the King's Guard. He waited until Mertok had finished talking and then joined him. Mertok managed a smile for his friend, even though he was obviously under stress.

'How goes the preparation, my friend?' asked Yorda.

'The enemy outnumber us greatly, I am afraid,' answered Mertok. 'Our advantage lies only in the fact that we know the forest here and we have set up barriers around the perimeter of the city. I fear for our men, Yorda. The Solhantille have a very disciplined force. Our scouts have reported back that these men appear to be well trained and disciplined. Other than our Royal Guard we have no trained men.'

'Do not despair, my friend,' said Yorda. 'I have great faith in the training given by Dawson. He has more experience than any elf in this forest. It was his life before he came here. However, I do not think the combined army of Marosham and the Solhantille are the problem that faces us.'

Mertok looked at his friend with surprise. 'What then is the problem, Yorda?'

'The last few days I have spent examining the areas where Marosham has sent his small raiding parties. There is no real reason why he has been attacking the outlying villages other than to make our people frightened.'

Mertok nodded in agreement. 'Your point is, Yorda?'

'Today I found something very interesting.' Yorda recounted the events at the last site.

'Now that you have explained it, I seem to remember a little more of what happened in the forest with Rimanathon,' replied Mertok.

'It is not just that,' continued Yorda. 'I am sure that Marosham has been using portals to send his raiders through. This raises two questions. If he wanted to spread more fear and panic he could have sent a lot more people through the portal and caused serious damage and destruction, but the raiding parties always seem to consist of about five or six Dark Elves. This suggests to me that somehow the number of people coming through the portal is determined on the strength of the person opening it. Secondly, if he can open the portal near a village, then why does he not open the portal near the King's palace or even in it? He could do far more damage there and effectively finish the war without the bloodshed. Several attacks like that in the city would pretty much stop our resistance. How can we fight an enemy that strikes from out of thin air?'

Mertok sat down. 'I still don't see what point you are trying to make, Yorda.'

'I am not completely sure, but his use of the portals is not a coincidence. They form part of his battle plan. They must do, or why else would he be using them?'

'Because he can,' said Mertok.

'Perhaps, but having been in his head I have learnt a little of how he thinks. His real aim is to have me dead, which is why he sent his trackers for me. They came by foot and horseback, not by portal, so that means he cannot create a portal a great distance away from wherever he is. He knows where I am because of his annoying habit of getting into my head, but he doesn't send his raiders to the area where I am. So he cannot control where his portals go or he would open one up directly in front of me and kill me easily.'

Mertok interrupted. 'Yet he seems to be able to open his portals near to villages, so he must have some sort of control.'

'I just don't get it,' said Yorda. 'We are missing something here.'

The two friends sat in silence for a while; then Mertok rose.

'We do not have enough time to wonder at Marosham's plans. The enemy is closing on the city limits. I must go to meet with our captains of the guard. I will make mention of this to them. Maybe they have some idea of what is happening here. Perhaps Dawson could be of help also. He has much more experience of battle tactics. It is possible he may shed some light on this.'

The friends bade each other goodbye and Yorda made his way to the paddock. It was here among the horses that Yorda found he could think clearly. He was surprised to find Shirrin there, grazing among several other horses. Yorda smiled. Shirrin was at long last becoming more sociable with her own kind. When she saw Yorda she trotted over to him. He reached into the small pouch he carried on his left side and pulled out an apple. Shirrin munched it greedily, complaining that the food left for her and the other horses that day was not of the usual standard. Yorda chuckled but tried at the same time to impress upon her that war was imminent and most of the resources were being harnessed to repel Marosham. He leapt upon her back and spurred her forward.

'Let's ride, my friend. I have a lot of thinking to do and cannot do it surrounded by the war effort.'

Shirrin leapt forward and they galloped out of the paddock. A few of the other horses scattered to give Shirrin room to pass and she rushed straight into the forest.

It was good to escape the limits of the city. Yorda knew that this eastern side of the city was safe. The army would have several days' march if they wanted to invade on this front. Even so there were several manned posts to give an alert if any Dark Elves were seen. He waved as he passed some of the guards. He recognised a couple of them who returned his wave. The wind through his long hair made Yorda feel much better. His leg was now completely healed and he felt strong. If anything, he felt stronger than he had ever done. The magic of the elven forest, mixed with the new powers that had been given to him by his mysterious teacher, along with his already remarkable abilities, had made Yorda feel almost indestructible. The bite that Shirrin had taken out of his leg along with the mind battle he had had with Marosham had shown him that he was far from the indestructible being that he had felt he was, but nevertheless he had never felt better than at this moment.

Yorda's mind drifted and he thought about Ivaine, whom he had not seen for several months now. His parents too drifted through his thoughts. By now they would have realised that Yorda had returned to do battle with Marosham. What would they be doing now, he thought.

As his mind drifted he let Shirrin take him wherever she wished to go. She knew this forest as well as, and probably better than, most of the elves and animals that dwelled within it.

They had been galloping for nearly two hours when Yorda became aware of a very slight tingling sensation in the air around him. He slowed the forward rush of Shirrin and sniffed the air. There was nothing unusual that he could detect, but he could feel the tingling getting slightly stronger. 'A portal!' he gasped to himself. He recognised suddenly the same feeling he had received from the last raiding site he had visited.

He slowly pulled the short sword from its scabbard on his side. He had got into the habit of wearing a sword recently whenever he left the safety of the city limits, but he had never had the necessity to use it. Some of the Royal Guard had tried to teach Yorda how to use the sword but to no avail. He was so fast of arm that he required no formal teaching. No matter what attack any of his tutors had tried on him he would effortlessly block, move and thrust to take his opponent, or even, in fact, opponents, down as easily as if they were standing still.

Dawson had been watching him one day and soon was helpless with laughter. Yorda walked over to him quite peeved and asked him what was so funny. The big smith dried his eyes and, trying to keep a straight face, answered, 'Laddie, ye are the worst swordsman I 'ave ever seen. You 'ave no style, no grace, no finesse, no tactics, nothing; yet at the same time I am sure there is nobody in the whole land that could take your sword. Every movement you did out there on the practice ground would 'ave resulted in the death of any other fighter, but you dance around as if you 'ave a swarm of bees chasing you, swatting at anything that moves. I 'ope I don't 'ave to fight alongside you or I will be run through by my enemy because I won't be able to see 'im for the tears running down my cheeks from laughing.' At this, Dawson had burst out laughing again. His deep booming laugh soon got

Yorda to join in with him and even the well-disciplined Royal Guard on the practice ground had great difficulty keeping straight faces when they looked at the two friends doubled up and literally hanging on to each other for support.

Now, however, Yorda realised that if there were a portal open nearby then there would also be a raiding party, so any fighting here would not be the same as on the practice ground.

He edged Shirrin forward towards where the tingling was stronger. There were no tracks on the ground, so either the raiders had not passed this way yet or they were headed in a different direction. Yorda didn't recognise this part of the forest but even if he was parted from Shirrin he knew he could find his way back to the city without any problem. He had never been lost in his life. Even if he didn't know where he was, he always knew the way back to his starting point.

The tingling was getting a lot stronger now. He dismounted and moved forward, pinpointing the exact position of the portal. About twenty paces in front of him he could see some footprints leading away from the direction he was pointing. This was where the portal opened and the raiders had exited it from the other side, which meant that at sometime in the near future they would be coming back via the side that Yorda and Shirrin were now on.

He edged forward and knelt just in front of the strongest area of tingling. As far as Yorda could see there was nothing in front of him other than the forest, but he could feel the energy here. He picked up a stone and tossed it through what he considered would be the entrance to the portal. The stone flew through the air and gently landed on the ground on the other side. Perhaps only living things could go through the entrance, he thought. He didn't want to try to pass through it himself as he was unsure of what would be on the other side, although he was fairly certain it would be either Marosham or quite a lot of his troops. Yorda was sorely tempted just to push his hand through but wasn't sure of any safeguards that Marosham may have put on the portal's entrance. He didn't fancy having his hand neatly chopped off by some magical defence system, or possibly even being sucked through to the other side completely.

Yorda stood up and carefully made his way to the other side of the portal, carefully feeling where the tingling was at its strongest so that he could effectively measure its size. He had completely forgotten Shirrin and was made aware of her presence when she calmly walked through the entrance of the portal to join Yorda on the other side.

Perhaps animals cannot pass through, he thought, as Shirrin bent her neck and munched on some grass.

Just at that moment, Yorda heard some sound in the distance. He froze and listened. The noises were distant and getting further away. He could make out some voices but they were too quiet to hear what they were saying. He decided it must be the raiding party. Yorda jumped up onto Shirrin's back and edged the horse forward, telling her to be as quiet as possible in her movements.

'When I wish it there are none that are more quiet than me,' she said, rather indignantly.

Yorda chuckled slightly at her aggrieved tone but pushed her forward again. He had to admit that she was correct and made virtually no sound at all as they traced the tracks. A short while later Yorda could see a clearing in the trees appearing a little way ahead, and beyond that there were a few wooden huts. This small elven village was obviously the target for the raiding elves. Shirrin stood still as Yorda dismounted. He moved slowly forward, keeping his eyes and ears keen for any sounds or movements around him.

Then he saw them. There were six elves, the usual number in a raiding party. All six were gathered behind some bushes, taking in the layout of the village beyond. Yorda followed their gaze and saw a couple of elves working outside a small hut on the edge of the village. When he looked back he could see the raiders were spreading out slowly. One of them had removed the bow he was carrying on his back and was notching an arrow. Yorda moved forward and signalled for Shirrin to advance as well. Even if he shouted to warn the villagers, it would be too late to stop the arrow finding its mark and it would also alert the raiders to his presence. Six against one weren't very good odds, especially when you no longer have the element of surprise.

Chapter Twenty-Six

Dawson looked out in the direction from which the enemy army would surely attack. He marvelled at the work that had been done by the elves from the city. Great areas of forest had been cleared in front of the city limits so that any attacking army would have no cover in its final advance. The felled trees had been positioned so that some routes to the city were now impossible to pass. The elves had worked relentlessly to build the defences that Dawson had suggested and he now looked out over the almost completed work. There was still a lot of activity going on but most of it was cosmetic, mainly involving the covering of traps that had been built.

The open ground between the city's defences was about 200 paces, much too far for an arrow. This was the point of the gap. Tramulan's elves would be under cover while the attacking army had to cross open ground to meet with its foes. Dawson knew that many of the opposing elves would be killed in this charge so they would have to create some form of cover while they moved forward. If they built a large wooden wall and hid behind it while pushing forward, then the small trenches that had been dug out would be enough to block any forward movement. If the attackers used large shields and came forward en masse using their shields as cover – an attacking or defensive formation that he had used himself on several occasions – then the grid of thin trip wires that had been covered by light earth would be lifted using a series of pulleys. He had never been able to use this before but the elves made such incredibly strong but very thin cord that he was able to create this defence system.

His thoughts wandered back to the last big battle he had been involved in when his people had fought against the beast that had been unleashed upon them by General Balok. If Dawson's people had had these elves fighting with them then, he was sure that they could have held firm against the beast. What had happened to his people after his last desperate attempt to kill the beast? He had awoken in this very forest with no sign of the beast, his people or any familiar landmark around him. It still seemed as if it had happened yesterday, even though years had passed. He hoped that his people had somehow rallied to win the day, but deep in his heart he knew that the General was too strong. He could only hope that his people had died well and fought to the last man standing. If so, maybe the General could no longer maintain an army to continue his warlike ways.

A couple of scouts appeared at the far end of the clearing. They reined their horses in and waited for some elves to approach and guide them through the hidden maze of traps and pits. A couple of elves lagged behind and carefully cleared away the tracks that the horses had made. Dawson recognised the scouts. They were the last to return from charting the progress of the enemy and he knew that they could not be much more than a day's march from here. Tonight would be the last full night's sleep that he would get for a while.

He turned and followed the scouts to a small tent that had been erected within the defences. It was here that the captains of the Royal Guard waited and planned. He saw the two scouts enter the tent and he strode in behind them. Mertok was seated and had obviously been talking to the head captain, a strong and fierce-looking elf called Rellian. It was as he had thought. Marosham and his army had now joined with the Solhantille and were marching under one banner, the black-and-red flag emblazoned with golden flames.

After hearing the scouts' report, Dawson was more than certain that the attack would take place in this very spot. No enemy scouts had been seen but he was sure that they would be here before nightfall to give their captains some information on the lie of the land in front of the city defences. Let them come. There was nothing else that Dawson and his men could do now. It was better that all of the elves withdraw behind the defences and wait. Any attempt to catch the enemy scouts could give Marosham's men some information on the little traps and tricks that Dawson had laid down. The last thing they wanted was to have their own elves beating a retreat across this freshly cleared land, at the same time giving the enemy the best trap-free path to the city gates.

The captain, after hearing the scouts' report, ordered some of his sergeants to change the guard once more. He calculated that giving the men one more rest period each before the morning would refresh the elves. He ordered another sergeant to bring the bonded horses of his men near to the front lines. If they rested well this would help to recharge the batteries of the elves who were on watch and could not sleep. Another sergeant was sent to fetch the healers to the front lines. Now that it was almost certain that the attack would take place here tomorrow they needed extra support for the sick and wounded.

Dawson still found this city to be amazing. Although there were some fortifications around the city limits it seemed to him that a determined enemy could breach them with little effort. In many places there was little more than a wooden fence with a gate in it. Mertok had told him that when the Eternal City had been built, many thousands of years ago, some of the ancient elves had used the magic that they possessed to form a barrier that could not be broken down by invaders. The areas where these barriers were created coincided with the unmanned sections of the city's limits.

Dawson had been very dubious about the efficacy of these barriers. He believed that if elven magic had been used to create them, then elven magic could break them down. He had discussed this on several occasions with Mertok and Thalién but they both insisted that the magic used could only be undone by the elves that had created it.

As a seasoned soldier, Dawson was used to being told that things were impossible to do, only to see them being done in the heat of battle. Unassailable walls of castles were stormed and taken, indestructible gates were breached, and insurmountable odds were overcome. He realised that magic was a different matter, but he still felt less than completely confident of the unmanned areas. The thing that worried him most of all was that all of the magically protected areas could easily be crossed, and in fact frequently were, by normal elves going about their daily business. How a magic spell could distinguish between an invading force and a party of elven farmers returning home after a day's work could not be understood by the big man. His was not to reason why but to continue with the situation at hand.

After everybody else had left the tent, Dawson was left with Mertok.

'Are all of your little traps set and ready?' asked Mertok with a small smile.

'Aye, they are, Mertok. I wish I 'ad my soldiers behind the defences with your archers' accuracy and then I would feel a lot better about this. Even with my traps and your elves' ability to 'it anything that moves at fifty paces, I 'ave grave misgivings about our ability to defend the city.'

Mertok looked serious for a moment and then replied. 'We have no choice, my big friend. If we were to try to meet them in the forest they are too many for us. They have the same skills as do we when it comes to fighting and would surely overrun us quickly.'

'I know when two sides are equally matched in skill then surprise gives a big advantage. Because we are not expected to fight away from the city I am sure we could take their advantage down swiftly with a surprise attack.'

'This could be true, but because we are not expected to attack they may be prepared for the unexpected. This logic could continue, Dawson, until nothing could become a surprise. The real surprise we have on our side is your expertise plus the fact that they will probably expect us to make some form of attack before they reach us. No, my friend, I believe we have done all that we can for the moment.'

Dawson nodded, then turned and left the tent, muttering something about checking his defences once again. As he was leaving, Dawson passed Thalién, who entered the tent. The elf greeted the big man, who lifted a huge hand and patted Thalién on the shoulder, then left. Thalién sat in front of Mertok and listened as his brother told him of Dawson's concerns.

'Did you manage to put his worries to rest?' he asked.

'I don't think so, Thalién. He has more experience of warfare than any of us and he sees that we have little chance of stemming their attack for long. I have sent riders to the Merhantille and the Sharnadille to ask them one more time for help. I fear that they will keep the same counsel that they did before and not aid us. Even if they come it will be too late.' Mertok stood up and walked around the inside of the tent. 'Dare I say that if the Council of Elders had agreed to a war footing long ago we would be armed and prepared for this conflict?'

Thalién rubbed the back of his neck with his hand. 'I ask myself that question too, my brother. We have existed for millennia in this forest and have always trusted and acted upon the advice of the elders. Normally I could follow their decisions without question but there have been so many new and unexplainable happenings in the last few years that I am beginning to wonder if we are changing too slowly to live with them. Yorda said the very same thing to me the other day. Perhaps it takes the eyes of an outsider to tell us that we are standing still. Perhaps we need to change.'

Mertok looked at his brother and spoke softly. 'There was another elf who used to speak thus, my brother, and it is he who we are to face tomorrow.'

Thalién turned and smiled slightly at his brother. 'Do not fear, Mertok. Marosham wanted change as, I suppose, do many elves – you yourself I suspect. But the difference is that where we are quite prepared to lobby for any changes, we accept and support the decisions of our chosen elders. It does not mean we always have to agree with them. Tomorrow I will be killing my brethren outside this tent. I do not want to do it and I will feel the pain of every elf that falls by my sword, but it is something that needs to be done so I will do it. You too will gain no pleasure from killing, even if by some fortune we prevail, but you will stand side by side with our defenders until the last of us falls.'

Mertok lifted the tent flap and the two brothers looked out over the cleared ground. The sun was starting to drop below the trees and the light was fading. It made little difference to the night vision of the two brothers standing tall and strong, but both realised that perhaps this was the last sunset they would see on this world. Without comment they separated, each going to speak with the elves that were armed and ready behind the barriers.

Chapter Twenty-Seven

Yorda pulled a knife from his belt as he watched the drawstring of the bow being pulled back. He lifted the knife in his hand and took aim. The arrow and bow started to home in on their target.

Yorda released the knife before the Dark Elf could get a perfect aim. The blade buried deep in the neck of the elf, who collapsed, dying, not knowing who or what had taken him. The released arrow sped harmlessly past the two villagers who instantly sought cover when they realised that their village was being raided.

Of the remaining five elves, only the one next to the now-dead elf even saw what had happened. He turned in the direction from which the knife had been thrown. All that he was aware of was a pain in his chest as Yorda's remaining knife buried itself deep in his chest. He fell lifeless to the ground. The other elves had seen this and were now rushing in the direction of their foe.

Yorda drew his sword but before the remaining four elves got much closer Shirrin charged straight through the advancing elves. Flashing hooves and snapping teeth reminded Yorda of something that had happened to him not many days earlier and a part of him wanted to laugh at the irony of the situation. Two of the elves fell under Shirrin's savage attack and Yorda was sure that they would not rise again.

The remaining two elves closed on Yorda. This was the first time outside of the training ground that Yorda had used his sword. As the two elves closed they moved apart, trying to make sure that Yorda could only see one elf at a time, thus making it more difficult to defend against both. Shirrin could only look on as another charge could involve Yorda. If he were to be injured and either of the remaining elves was unhurt, her bonded mate could be killed with little effort.

Yorda confidently lowered his sword, almost inviting the elves to attack. As if from a signal they lunged forward at the same time but from opposite sides. A blur from Yorda's arm saw the first elf clutch at his stomach without really seeing what had happened to him. The second elf was still in mid-lunge when he felt a sting across his throat. His look of surprise stayed on his face as his head toppled neatly off his shoulders. Yorda immediately rushed over to the two elves that Shirrin had taken out. He knelt down carefully, in case they were pretending to be dead, but it was immediately obvious that they really were dead, one from a broken neck while the other's chest was caved in with his ribs puncturing his heart. It was a pity that they were all dead because Yorda would have liked to try to get some information out of them.

Yorda could feel his heart beating furiously. What surprised him more than the fact he had killed in battle was a strange feeling of excitement over the kill. He shook his head, then bent down to examine the corpses for any clues that they might have on their bodies. They were all dressed in the elven material that seemed to change colour depending on the surroundings. When they were standing you had the impression that they were blending in with the green background. Now that they were lying on the ground there was a lot more brown in the material. He heard a slight groan behind him. Turning round he saw the elf that had taken the cut to the stomach moving slightly. Yorda rushed over. He knew that the cut he had given his opponent was fatal and no healing power that Yorda possessed could reattach the intestines that had spilled onto the ground. As he looked at the mess before him he saw something moving in the blood and guts. One final groan escaped the elf as his eyes rolled up in his head and he breathed no more.

Yorda poked at the entrails on the ground and found a small, squirming creature that resembled a large slug. He reached forward to pick it up and was pushed violently back by Shirrin's nose.

'Do not touch that creature; it will infect you.'

Yorda kept a half-eye on the creature but turned towards his horse.

'What do you know of this squirming mess, Shirrin?'

'Only that Marosham gives these to the elves he captures from the forest and they then obey his every command.'

'Why have you not mentioned this before, Shirrin?'

'It has been a long time since I was with Marosham. I only remember seeing him do this on two occasions and until this moment it has never been one of my thoughts.'

Yorda realised that even though the elven horses were very intelligent, they still were quite primitive when compared with a human or elf mind. There was little else that Shirrin could recount about this little creature, other than it was placed on the lower back of its victim and burrowed in in a matter of seconds. Yorda wasn't quite sure what to do with the creature but he knew it must be important. He opened a small leather sack that was on his belt and carefully scooped the little creature up on his sword and dropped it into the open pouch. He placed the firmly closed sack into a second one he was carrying and fastened it to the hilt of his sword so that it dangled free from his body while he walked. He didn't want it to escape, and if it did the last thing he wanted was for it to be next to his skin when it got out.

Yorda recovered his two knives from the elves he had first killed and carefully cut the dead elves open one by one to see if they had the same parasite inside them. Each dead elf contained one of the creatures, but all of them were dead. Yorda concluded that if the creature was inside its host when it died, then it too would die. The living one in his pouch had been ejected from the body of its host when Yorda's sword had taken out most of the elf's insides.

By now the little village nearby had raised about a dozen brave elves who were approaching the position where Yorda was kneeling. One of them recognised Yorda and signalled for the other elves to put away their weapons. Yorda showed them the dead parasitic creatures that he had cut from the raiders. None of the elves had ever seen this type of creature. He would have to take it back to the city and ask the healers or even the elders if they had encountered anything like this before.

For now he had one more task to do. With the help of the villagers he took the bodies back to the portal's entrance. He had to find out how they were going to re-enter the portal.

First he took the head of the decapitated elf and threw it towards the entrance to the portal. It just passed through and landed on the other side. He then threw the rest of the body. It too landed on the other side. Yorda then tried throwing one of the dead creatures through, but it too landed on the ground on the far side of the portal. No matter what combinations of body and creature that were thrown at the portal, they all landed on the ground on the other side. The secret of how they got through would go with them to their graves.

Yorda asked the villagers if they could take the bodies back to the city for examination, then sat down in front of the portal entrance and waited. He had to try to get as much information as he could from the portal while it was still open.

Yorda reached forward and traced a line with his fingers across the ground where he could feel the tingling most. The opening was about five paces wide, enough to let four armed men or two horses through at a time. He assumed that it was a fixed size, although he had no evidence to back it up. He raised himself from the ground and tried to reach up to the highest point of the tingling but found it was too tall for him.

He called Shirrin over and jumped onto her back. Standing as high as he could on her back he could feel the limits of the portal. He estimated it to be about twice the height of a man. Again he could not be sure if the height could be changed but he reasoned that if six elves of normal height had been sent through and the portal's height could be changed, then why make it as high as this? No, he was sure that this entrance/exit was a fixed height.

He leapt back down off Shirrin's back and stood to the side of the portal. Placing one hand on the side of the entrance and another on the side of the exit he closed his eyes and concentrated. There was no distinguishable difference in the energy he could feel around his hands. He moved them closer together and when they were about three fingerwidths apart the tingling increased massively.

Yorda scratched his neck and felt the chain holding the amulet that had been given him by Rimanathon. He remembered the strange being telling him that he could use this amulet once to enter any portal but that it would take him to a place of no magic.

He lifted the chain from around his neck and looked at the strange object that must contain so much power. Just at that very moment Yorda felt a change in the energy field around the portal. He reached forward and could feel the energy subsiding. Placing his hands either side of the portal he again brought them together but this time there was no surge in the tingling as he had felt earlier. His hands moved closer and closer together until they touched. The portal had been closed.

It seemed to Yorda that this portal must have had some sort of timing mechanism linked to it. He calculated how long it would have taken for the raiders to return had they completed their sortie successfully, and by adding a few minutes extra he came to the conclusion that the portal was only meant to be open for a certain period of time. Could this be why no great raiding party with more serious intentions had ever been sent through the entrance? In that situation the gate would have closed before they could get back, thus stranding them here.

This seemed to make sense to Yorda. Whatever power Marosham possessed to enable him to create these portals seemed limited. Perhaps the height and width of the portal was also determined by the power needed. There were a lot of assumptions here but it started to make a little sense. It also, unfortunately, raised another question. If Yorda's assumptions were right then it also made sense that Marosham knew where the portal would be opening, otherwise the raiding parties would be too far away from any village to complete their mission before the portal closed. It still gave Yorda no sense of what Marosham was trying to do, other than cause inconvenience to the villages that were raided – no real damage or tactical advantage was being gained.

Yorda stood and motioned for Shirrin to follow him. The young man wanted to think, and he always thought best when he was running. A nice, long, steady run back to the city would give him plenty of thinking time. It was also a good opportunity to test his leg, which seemed to have completely healed. He set off at a fast jog with Shirrin following behind.

It was late when Yorda got back to the city, so he went immediately to find out what had been discovered from the bodies the villagers had brought back. After saying goodbye to

Shirrin, Yorda walked over to the healers' halls where he found Salurian talking with a few other healers. When she saw Yorda she called him over.

'What can you tell me about these bodies that you sent in ahead of you, Yorda?'

Yorda told her all that had happened that day, including his experience with the portal after the villagers had left. He then asked her what she had learnt from the bodies.

'Except for the fact that the four you killed were efficiently dispatched, likewise with the two that your horse attacked, nothing at all. The creatures that were within their bodies were withered to virtually nothing by the time they arrived.' She stopped talking as Yorda removed the pouch that was hanging from his sword. He lifted it up and Salurian could see it moving as if of its own accord.

'I wondered why there were only five of these creatures and six bodies. You managed to keep one alive?'

Yorda nodded and carefully opened the pouch, emptying the contents onto the table in front of the healers. The little grub-like creature was moving much more slowly than when it had left its host's body and its pinkish colour had faded to a grey. When Yorda had explained the change in its condition, Salurian replied, 'It must be dying, Yorda. I should imagine that it gets its sustenance from the elf who acts as its host.'

She leaned over to get a closer look and was surprised when the creature made a half-hearted attempt to jump at her. Salurian leapt back, shocked, and Yorda grabbed a clear-sided bowl and placed it over the little grub-like thing, which seemed to have lost more of its colour in its effort to make contact with Salurian.

As they were talking, Dawson entered the room and Yorda went over to talk with him.

'I 'eard that some dead raiders 'ad been brought in from the east. I couldn't sleep so I thought I would come down and look them over. Might give us some information.' Dawson could see the green splashes of blood on Yorda's shirt and gave a grim smile. 'Should 'ave known you were involved.'

'Not intentional, my big friend, I can assure you. I just happened to be in the wrong place at the wrong time.'

'Seems like your "training" paid off,' the big man said with more than a trace of sarcasm.

'I 'ad the best trainer, laddie,' said Yorda, giving a very passable impression of Dawson, who smiled broadly.

'Let's h-h-have a look at your h-h-handywork, then,' said Dawson, making Yorda laugh at the big man's attempt to pronounce his aitches.

They went over to some tables where the elves were laid out. The first table they came to contained an elf with a broken neck and another with a crushed ribcage.

'What in 'eaven's name did you do to these?'

Yorda looked at his friend. 'Remember when you tried to stop Shirrin from getting to me in the paddock?' Dawson nodded. 'Well, these poor creatures suffered the same fate that could have happened to you if you weren't the size that you were.'

'Shirrin?' asked Dawson.

Yorda nodded.

They moved on to the next table where the two elves that had taken Yorda's knives were lying. Dawson looked them over briefly and nodded approvingly at the accuracy of Yorda's throwing.

When they got to the last table, Dawson turned and put his hand on Yorda's shoulder. 'It is never easy killing a man but if you can do it quickly and cleanly that is as much as can be asked of a soldier. It doesn't get any easier, laddie, but when it really matters you know you can do it. It won't be any consolation for you, but it sure as 'ell will make the person whose back you are covering during battle feel a lot safer and more confident. I won't say congratulations but I will say well done.'

Dawson turned and saw the group of healers gathered around the bowl that was covering the parasite that had been removed from one of the raiders. 'What's going on over there?'

Yorda told him and Dawson moved quickly over to the table. When he got there he reached over and lifted up the bowl. Before anyone could stop him, with his other hand he brought it down quickly and crushed the grub flat.

'What are you doing?' demanded Salurian.

'If those wee creatures aren't killed immediately they can do no end of 'arm,' he answered, replacing the bowl over the crushed mess on the table.

'You know what it is?' asked the shocked healer.

Dawson looked around almost in amazement. 'You mean that you don't?'

Salurian explained that no one had ever seen anything like this before. Yorda added that outside of the elven forest he had never come across a creature like this either.

Dawson thought for a moment, then answered. 'Where I come from – or per'aps I should say where I came from – these little bugs were commonplace. They were normally found under the roots of trees. Whenever a tree was dug up there would be 'undreds of them swarming there. They can be killed easily enough but if any get onto your skin they will burrow underneath. Something inside them is secreted into the body which causes 'orrible pain and often paralyses the person. If they are cut out before they get deep into the body, then sometimes death can be avoided. I 'ave 'ad soldiers under my command who have begged for death when one 'as infected them before we can cut it out. It is not a pretty death.'

'It seems,' Salurian mused, 'that it doesn't affect elves in the same way. Both creature and elf seem to live quite happily in partnership. What effect it has on the elf is unknown, as we have no way of asking the host.' She shot a quick glance at Yorda, who didn't know whether he was being rebuked or not.

'What are they doing 'ere?' asked Dawson.

'Yet another mystery,' answered Yorda when no one else seemed able to comment.

Yorda sat down with Dawson when they got back to Yorda's quarters.

'I have been thinking quite a bit today, what with all that has been going on lately,' said Yorda. 'It may be,' he continued, 'that your appearance in this forest many years ago was as a result of one of these portals opening. I believe that you were brought here from I-don't-know-where through one of the gates opening. Who opened it and how it was done I don't know. I also don't know why it was done or where you came from. My mother also appeared mysteriously in this forest many years before you. Apparently her language was completely different from yours so she must have come from somewhere different than you did, but

I now believe that you were both brought here in the same fashion. If this is true there may be many others who are walking this earth that have been moved as you both were.

'Marosham seems to be able to control the portal that he is using to a certain extent. Whoever sent you could not. Or, if my guesswork involving Marosham is correct, your portal closed before you had time to return to your own land. Rimanathon spoke of the portals breaking down and it may also be that my mother and you were two of the first to use them. If they are breaking down it could also be that you stumbled on them accidentally. The little grub-like things may have just happened to be at the entrance of the portal when you passed through it and could possibly have crawled over the threshold and appeared here.'

Dawson lifted an eyebrow. 'There are an awful lot of ifs, buts, and maybes 'ere, laddie.'

'I know, I know, but what other reasons are there? We must look at all the possibilities. I have found over the last couple of months that impossibilities seem almost commonplace now. I cannot dismiss anything any more.'

The two friends talked for several hours without really coming to any conclusion. At about four in the morning, Dawson bade his friend farewell, saying he had better try to get some sleep before dawn. Yorda said goodbye but found that sleep would not come to him that night.

Chapter Twenty-Eight

The next morning Yorda dragged himself out of bed. Even with everything that had happened to him in the past couple of months he still enjoyed lying in bed and would have been quite happy doing the same thing today. He rubbed his eyes, almost hoping that he had been in a long, complicated dream and that he was actually at home in the forest outside Parkent. The sound of the elves going about their business below him on the ground and around him in the trees was evidence enough that it was no dream. He dressed and breakfasted quickly before going out to the city limits to catch up on the news.

The troops of the Lohadrille were gathered at their posts, waiting. Dawson was pacing back and forth talking to the troops, sometimes sharing a joke or giving a little encouragement. Yorda wondered at this man – so long a soldier and then a blacksmith and now back to his original profession. Nothing seemed to disturb the big man; he took everything as it came face-on.

A little way off he spied Mertok, who was just standing looking out over the recently cleared land. He made his way over to join his friend.

'I hear you had a little action yesterday,' Mertok said as Yorda came up to his side. 'I was briefed by Dawson,' he continued.

Yorda nodded. 'Not something I was actively looking for I can assure you.'

'Nevertheless, it is good that you came to no harm,' his friend said.

Yorda nodded towards the probable battlefield. 'Any news on the enemy?'

'They are expected today. Normally we would have heard something by now. Over 2,000 troops make enough noise to be felt many miles away. They stopped yesterday and no movement has been felt since. It is almost as if they were waiting for something before they make their final advance. Even Dawson doesn't understand what they are doing. Normally the enemy would camp out in front of the foe, if only to try to instil fear into them. It makes no sense to stop as far away as they have done. They must know by now that we do not intend to attack them in the forest.'

'Could they be waiting for more to join their ranks?' asked Yorda.

'That is a worrying thought,' replied Mertok, 'but if there was another sizeable force in the forest we would have known about it for some time.'

Yorda looked about him. On a tree just inside the defences was a pair of doves watching the proceedings below them. Yorda walked over to the tree and raised his right hand. At the same time he concentrated on one of the doves. Mertok followed what was going on and saw one of the doves gently swoop down to perch on Yorda's outstretched arm. He walked over slowly to where Yorda stood. After a minute or so Yorda lifted his arm and the bird took off and joined its mate.

'Birds have very scattered thoughts,' Yorda said without turning. 'It is difficult to get much information off them but he has no memory of seeing large amounts of people outside of this city and where the enemy are now waiting.'

Mertok looked upwards to where the doves were now nuzzling each other affectionately.

'Could you get the birds to look around for you and give us any more information?'

Yorda shook his head. 'No. The mind of a bird is too chaotic. I can retrieve a certain number of images from its brain and also implant images, but to get it to obey a command would not be possible. They have no real sense of time and their memories are too short. If you gave me a wolf or a big cat, even a small cat or dog, that would be different. They actually enjoy being given tasks to do.'

A noise at the edge of the clearing directly opposite them alerted the waiting troops. Into the clearing marched four elves dressed in battle armour. The lead elf, dressed in the colours of Marosham's army, held a white flag aloft. They had barely marched twenty paces when they stopped and the lead elf shouted, 'Army of the Lohadrille. I have a message for you.'

Mertok moved forward to the edge of the defences.

'What do you wish to say?' he calmly shouted back.

The messenger on the other side moved forward a few paces. He was still too far away from any of Dawson's traps to spot them, but Mertok didn't want to take the chance.

'Whom am I addressing?' shouted the messenger.

'I am Mertok of the Lohadrille, son of Tramulan, king of all the realm of the elves. Who wishes to know?'

The elf moved forward several more paces. Yorda could see him looking to his right and left as he advanced.

Yorda stepped forward. If the messenger came much closer he would realise that this ground between the enemy and the city was covered with various defences that could not be seen until you were upon them. Any advantage that the traps gave the Lohadrille would instantly be nullified and the attacking army would be quite happy to take a couple of extra days to find another place to attack the city. He lifted his hands to his head and tried to send out a strong thought to the messenger. *You do not wish to come any further. You will feel uncomfortable and vulnerable if you advance towards the enemy lines. It would be much better to stand and deliver your message where you are.*

Mertok saw the messenger falter in his forward movement. He seemed a little confused. The elf stopped and actually took two backward steps. His three companions who were behind him looked uncomfortable at this and one of them started to advance towards him. The messenger lifted an arm to stem his advance.

The answer to Mertok's challenge was slow coming but at last the messenger lifted his head and replied.

'I am Malien of the army of Marosham the Liberator. I have come to discuss the terms of your surrender. I am sure you have no wish to die, which you will surely do if you resist. To that end if you lay down your arms and your king gives himself up to us willingly, then no one will come to any harm. Lord Marosham also requests the company of the half-breed elf. Upon agreement of his requests we will enter and occupy the city and install the new government. You have three hours to deliberate. After this time we will advance and take your city, destroying any who stand in our way.'

Mertok listened impassively to the messenger. As he was about to answer, a hand was laid upon his shoulder. He turned and saw his father, King Tramulan, smiling at him. He bade his son gently to step back.

The King stepped forward.

'Thank you kindly for your offer, Malien. You are now speaking to King Tramulan of the Lohadrille. You know as well as does Marosham that your master's words are full of lies. If he thinks he can take the city he is welcome to try. His bones will be left for the carrion to feed on, along with yours and your army. We do not fear the words of a coward who hides behind his troops. Return to him and give him these words of mine. "You too may lay down your arms before it is too late." ' The King turned and walked back to his tent.

The messenger waited for the King to disappear; then he too turned and marched back to the cover of the trees, followed by his men.

Dawson joined Mertok and Yorda. 'Don't worry, lads, that is normal battle tactics. It is used just to try to cast some doubt in the minds of the opposition. Make them think that the attackers aren't really that bad. Our men won't fall for that.' He walked off to join his troops without waiting for a reply.

'Looks like the battle will start soon, then, Yorda,' said Mertok before he too left and followed his father into the tent.

A couple of hours later Yorda felt a very slight rumble begin under his feet. The enemy was on the march and was advancing on the city. Even though he didn't want the battle to start, he had the very disturbing feeling of eager anticipation at the possibility of killing the enemy. The young man felt deeply uneasy about this but put the thought from his mind.

The next morning the armies of Marosham and the Solhantille arrived at the edge of the clearing between the city and the forest. Tents were put up at the edge of the clearing, well out of reach of bowshot but near enough to show the defenders of the city that they were outnumbered and outarmed. The sound of trees being felled could clearly be heard by all who manned the city's defences. The enemy were at work creating their own methods of assault. Dawson had warned that they would try to create some barriers so that they could cross the cleared ground without losing too many of their men.

Tramulan came to watch the enemy from time to time, without saying anything. The look on his face was enough, a mixture of grim determination and sadness for what was to come. Thalién or Mertok were never far from the front and Dawson continually walked up and down the ranks of elves giving them advice and uttering some words occasionally to give them confidence. Yorda spent all morning just staring out at the enemy, wondering where Marosham was and what he was doing. Something still didn't seem right about all this. Why didn't he appear? Wasn't he with his troops? And if not, why not?

It was at noon that the first attack was launched. Three large, wheeled platforms emerged from the trees. Dawson smiled. His experience had proved him correct. The enemy was hoping to push these barriers forward using them as cover to hide behind. Once close enough they would emerge and engage the city's troops in battle while many more followed behind.

Mertok and his captains watched as the enemy grouped behind the barriers. Slowly they advanced on to the cleared ground. Dawson was amazed at how quickly the enemy had cut their trees and formed their barriers, but they could not advance far. The heavy wheels turned slowly as the elves pushed them forward. They reached the point where their messenger had stopped the day before and carried on. Soon they would be close enough to loose their arrows and start the attack in earnest.

A loud crunch was heard and one of the barriers tilted to the side. A spirited cheer went up from the elves on the city walls. The enemy had reached the covered trenches where the wheels had sunk in. No amount of pulling or pushing could shift the heavy wooden barriers now. The other two barriers suffered the same fate within several paces of the first. The elves behind the barriers made no effort to retreat but instead started attaching ropes to the fronts of the barriers.

A short while later Yorda and the others felt a rumbling beneath their feet, almost as if a stampede of horses was nearby. Suddenly from out of the trees came a dozen huge beasts, plated in armour and hauling chains behind them. Elephants. Mertok stepped forward instinctively, although the action of moving forward made no difference to his view of what was happening. Each elephant had an elf sitting on its neck. The animals were manoeuvred into position in front of the barriers and the chains were attached to the ropes. As one they started to pull. Almost immediately the barriers were dragged clear of the shallow ditches and started to roll forward.

Dawson rushed over to Mertok.

'This is not good. If the beasts pull their barriers any further they will trample straight over our wires and then in no time they will be on this side of the clearing. You must get the archers to bring the elephants down before they reach the wires or they will tear them up as they pass.'

Mertok looked around him. 'There is no way we can stop a creature that size clad in full elven armour.' He turned to his captains at his side. 'Tell our men to get ready for close-quarter fighting. They will soon be upon us.'

'Sir,' said one of the captains, pointing out to the field in front. 'What is Yorda doing?'

Mertok looked to where the captain was pointing and saw Yorda striding forward towards the elephants. He stopped about fifty paces from them.

'Get some archers out to him with some shields to cover him in case of enemy fire!' shouted Thalién from down the line. Instantly about thirty elves left their cover and dashed forward, forming a cover around the young healer.

'What the 'ell is 'e doing?' yelled Dawson as he joined Mertok.

'Your guess is as good as mine,' the elf replied.

Yorda had moved forward the moment he saw the elephants. He realised that if they were allowed to advance this battle would be over very quickly. He knew that he had to be as close as possible if what he planned to do was to work. As he advanced he pushed his thoughts forward, trying to make a connection with the big beasts. He had never seen an elephant before but he had heard stories of them being intelligent animals. He hoped that was the case. The more intelligent the animal the easier it was to make contact. Distance was the problem. For what he intended to do he would normally need to make physical contact with the animal.

He stopped as close as he safely could. Being shot by an arrow would not help the defence of the city and, he thought with a wry grin, it would certainly not help the prophecy come to fruition. As he pushed his thoughts even further forward he was dimly aware of elves springing up all around him and shields being lifted to cover as much of his body as possible.

A slight jolt told him that he had made contact with the lead animal. Yorda was amazed at the strength of mind that was inside this huge beast.

'You must stop. You cannot come any further.'

'We must; it is our way. We move forward until our riders wish otherwise.'

Yorda kept his mind focused. These creatures were strong-willed. They had no surprise at the fact that Yorda could 'talk' with them. He concentrated once more. The elephants were getting closer to the trip wires.

'There are bad things here. If you come any further you will meet them.'

Yorda pushed some images of hundreds of snakes crawling towards the big beasts. The images he received back were of the elephants crushing the snakes as they passed them. This was no good and still the elephants advanced, dragging the barriers with the enemy elves ensconced behind them.

An elf stepped out from behind one of the barriers and took aim with his bow. The arrow fell short by only a few paces. They were just about in range now.

Mertok could see several more of the enemy archers notching arrows and stepping out from behind the barriers. 'Covering fire!' he shouted. 'We must protect Yorda at all costs,' he said, more to himself than anyone else.

Yorda tried to get into the lead animal's mind. He was still much further away than he would like. What would turn the creatures? Did they have any natural predators? He wondered at the stupidity of such a question. These huge animals would be frightened of nothing.

Three more elves broke ranks and shot arrows. One of the

arrows clattered off a shield that was being held in front of Yorda. Two of the three elves were dropped by return shots from the archers with Yorda.

Yorda now had a good link with the lead animal. 'I've got it,' he suddenly said to himself. Once more he set up an image for the elephants to see. This time he had an immediate response. The front elephant stopped instantly in its tracks and started a loud trumpeting, followed almost immediately by the others. The riders tried to spur them forward and jabbed pointed sticks into the elephants' hides. Within seconds the elephants started to bolt away from the city, dragging the barriers with them. The elves behind were too surprised to move at first and many of them were either trampled by the now charging elephants or crushed by the barriers. In terms of the defence of the city it was almost too much to hope for. The elephants, in their rush to escape, managed to trample most of the tents and crush a lot of the stockpiled weapons for the battle ahead. The last that Yorda saw of them, they were charging through the woods back towards their homelands.

When he returned with his armed guard he was exhausted with the effort.

'What on earth happened out there?' asked Thalién, who was the first to reach him when he arrived back at the defences.

'They are strong creatures. I had a lot of trouble finding something that could scare them enough to send them back the way they came. I never expected it to be as successful as that.'

Mertok and Dawson had joined them by now and had overheard the conversation.

'What could scare a big beast like that?' asked Dawson.

Yorda smiled. 'I did think about sending images of loads of Dawsons charging at them, but I only wanted to turn them around and not frighten them to death.'

'Ha bloody ha,' said the big man.

'Seriously though,' said Yorda, 'what frightened them like that was an image of lots of mice chasing them.'

'*Mice?*' said Mertok.

'I don't understand it either, but it appears these animals are frightened of mice.'

Mertok looked back out over the field. On the other side there was much confusion.

'Well, whatever the reason, it seems to have given us a little more of a breather and also diminished their ranks by about fifty or so.'

The first dead of the war lay on the battlefield. So far it was only the enemy. It was only a matter of time before defenders lay among them.

Chapter Twenty-Nine

There was very little activity from the enemy camp for the rest of the day. A messenger walked out under a white flag asking for permission to collect the dead and dying. King Tramulan agreed on condition that no one was to advance further than the last injured or dead on the battlefield; if they did they would be considered as an aggressor and as such would be fired upon. The messenger agreed and hurried back behind his lines.

The defenders of the city watched as a small party of elves advanced on to the cleared ground, searching first for the injured, which they quickly took back. A second group of elves entered the clearing soon after. They were all dressed in black cloaks. In front and to the sides of these elves were several others, also cloaked in black, but each elf carried a long pole on the end of which was a small lantern with a lit candle inside. As each dead elf was recovered the candle would be extinguished by the elf carrying the lantern. This candle was removed and placed on the ground where the elf had died and another took its place in the lantern.

As the elves removed the dead they started to sing quietly. Mertok and Thalién took up the song and joined in. Soon the song could be heard floating across the field from both sides. Attacker and defender sang softly, praising the valiant efforts of the slain and wounded and wishing them a safe passage to the Halls of the Dead where they would join in the Endless Song.

Yorda and Dawson moved forward. Yorda could see some tears forming in the eyes of the big smith and he moved towards him. 'I never believed that death could be like this, so sad and yet at the same time so beautiful.'

Dawson turned to Yorda. 'Aye, laddie. I 'ave seen many a person die in battle but never 'ave I seen both sides sing the praises of the dead together. Now that I see the candles I understand why lives are so precious. A bright light being snuffed out is exactly what 'as 'appened to those elves. It is such a waste, and tomorrow there will be many more candles out on that field.' He turned back to watch the enemy retreat with their dead. 'I wonder if there will be anybody left to put out candles for us, Yorda.'

The evening was spent with both sides singing gently. It was an eerie experience. Now that the battle had started in earnest, Dawson noticed that all the songs were directed at the opposition, praising them for their prowess and wishing them courage for the coming day. The culture of the elves was amazing. He had often grudgingly praised an enemy during the heat of battle but it was never said so that the enemy could hear.

As the sun slowly rose behind the Eternal City, the fires were extinguished and the singing stopped. Mertok walked over to Yorda, who had spent the whole night standing and listening to the song and watching the enemy firelight.

'You should get some rest. Once the singing has stopped it means they are preparing to attack. The sun has to rise a little before they come at us. At the moment it would be right in their eyes, which makes it difficult for them to spot our archers in their positions.'

Yorda said he was quite all right but agreed that some food would help, and he retired to the food area a little way inside the city limits. He passed Dawson, who was asleep on the ground with a small blanket over him. His snores were so loud that Yorda half chuckled thinking that another fifty like him making that sound would scare off any enemy. Once he had broken his fast, he gathered up some bread and cheese and some of the elven wafers that he had become so fond of. At the end of one of the tables he lifted a wineskin and carried the food and drink over to his friend. Dawson was still snoring so Yorda sat down on the ground cross-legged by the big man and gently wafted the cheese under his nose. Dawson stopped mid-snore and his nose twitched. Yorda moved the cheese closer to him and noticed one eye opening.

'Good morning, Dawson. I thought you would like something to eat.'

Dawson sat up, grunting with the effort. The first thing he did was look out towards the enemy.

'They 'ave stopped singing. They will soon come at us again.' He grabbed the food and wine and ate hungrily.

'Mertok thinks we have about two hours before they leave their lines. You have time to take a leak before we start.'

' 'ave you noticed 'ow the elves fight, Yorda?' enquired Dawson.

'I'm not with you,' he answered.

'What I mean is, of all the battles I 'ave been in, I 'ave never seen an enemy that tells you when they are going to attack. It is eerie, laddie, 'ow everybody sits around singing and when the singing stops they come at you. It seems a bit too civilised for war, don't you think?'

'We have strong traditions regarding many things. War is one of them.'

Dawson noticed that Yorda said 'we'. It was the first time that he had considered himself one of the elves. Up until now he had recognised the fact that he was half elf but had always spoken of himself as human.

'I 'ave noticed that Marosham's men keep themselves apart from the other elves and they seem to take no part in the singing or in the courtesies of the battle.'

'No, I have noticed that also, my friend. They left the life of the elves some time ago because they could not fit in with the way of life here. It seems to me that they want no part of our traditions and practices except where they benefit them. I know you can never trust the enemy, but Marosham's men...' Yorda let the sentence trail off. Dawson knew exactly what he meant.

'Yes, laddie, I wouldn't want them on my side. If I 'ad to 'ave my throat cut I would prefer it done by the enemy in a clean fight. A warrior's death is a fitting end to a soldier, not the death meted out by some scum-sucking weasel.'

Dawson had finished his food by now so he rose and walked over to a large jug of water and a bowl that he had requested be brought to him. He lifted the jug and poured a little water into the bowl and then gave himself a quick once-over to clean most of the grime that always seemed to accumulate on the big man regardless of what he did.

Yorda smiled slightly. Elves seldom sweated and even then

gave off no smell. Dawson was another matter. He had, or so Yorda imagined, the smell of a soldier. Someone who would be on the field of battle for many hours. He had taken to washing himself frequently in deference to the elves, whose sense of smell was quite acute, but even so he could not seem to erase his body odour completely. His smell was much less noticeable than it had been, mainly because one of the children in the city had run up to the big man a few days earlier and handed him a small stone. She said it would help him with his problems if when he washed he rubbed the stone over his skin after he was dry. The look on his face had been a picture, Yorda recalled, but Dawson had taken the stone and thanked the girl and in fairness had been using it regularly since.

Dawson returned and Yorda noticed, quite appreciatively, that the big man had actually got rid of most of his odour. He saw him trying to hide the stone as he put it away. Yorda thought it best not to comment. If he wasn't open about using it, then he was probably a little self-conscious.

'Well,' said Dawson. 'Let's go see what the Solhantille will throw at us today. My bet is their first attack will be a tortoise movement.' Yorda looked blank and Dawson chuckled. 'Normally if the big walls, like they tried yesterday, fail, then besieging armies will send a large mass of men forward under cover of their shields. They can't see where they are going so they 'ave to move slowly. Once they encounter the enemy in 'and-to-'and fighting then the rest of the army follow in quickly be'ind them.'

'Well, hopefully your little tricks will cause that to fail,' said Yorda. 'So what will they do after that?'

'Well, unless they 'ave some more little tricks themselves, like their attempt with the elephants yesterday, then normally the next form of attack would depend on 'ow large the enemy force is. With the amount of men available and the relatively short distance they 'ave to go to encounter our men, I would expect a direct charge. They would suffer 'eavy losses crossing the clearing, but I suspect their men are much more used to battle than ours and, unless we 'ave superior numbers by the time we clash, then I think we 'ave got problems.'

Yorda shouted to one of the elves who was making sure the

defensive positions were fully equipped with bows, arrows, water and food. He asked him to fetch the weapons he had had made for him. Dawson looked puzzled, but when he asked what Yorda was doing the reply was, 'We, my friend, are going to cause the enemy to retreat.'

Dawson had no idea what his friend was intending to do but he waited patiently until the elf returned carrying two bows and a large quiver of arrows.

'How are you with a bow?' asked Yorda.

'I 'ave used them from time to time but I am no great archer,' answered Dawson.

'You don't need to be for this. Follow me.'

Yorda moved to the edge of the clearing and then, pointing a finger said, 'You see the big tent over there, just directly in front of us?' Dawson nodded. 'Just send a few arrows in that direction.'

'They are too far away, laddie. Even our best archers can't reach that.'

'That is very true, my friend, but unfortunately our best archers would not be able to draw these bows, whereas you and I can.'

Yorda tossed one of the bows in the direction of Dawson, who lifted it up and tested the draw.

'What the...? When did you get these made? This must be twice as 'ard to draw back than the normal bows.'

'When I listened to you talking about the possible enemy tactics, I thought about any advantage that we may have over Marosham and his men. One thing that came to mind was the fact that you are by far the strongest man I have ever seen and I am sure,' he said with a smile, 'that I am probably the strongest person that you have ever seen.'

Dawson had to admit that among the amazing abilities Yorda had demonstrated, strength was indeed one of them.

'Therefore,' continued Yorda, 'I got one of our fletchers to make a couple of bows with a much higher draw strength, which, if I am correct, only you and I could use. If we can toss a few arrows into that tent, even if we don't manage to bag us a couple of their commanders, I think we may cause enough panic to at least force the whole army to retreat a little. At the least we may have a little fun.'

A wicked smile played across Dawson's face.

'You know, laddie, I may make a soldier out of you yet. You are starting to think like one.'

The two friends spread some arrows out on the ground in front of them. Mertok wandered over to see what was going on and Dawson turned and winked at the elf. Mertok turned away, shaking his head but smiling.

Some of the enemy camp had noticed this strange behaviour from two of their enemy and quite of few of them had gathered to see what was going to happen.

'Are you ready, my big friend?' asked Yorda.

'I am at that, my strong young man,' laughed Dawson in reply.

They notched their first arrows and pulled the strings back.

Some of the enemy were starting to jeer at the two friends. They could see these lone archers trying to shoot at them when they were quite a way out of range.

The first two arrows were sent on their way, arcing high over the clearing. As the distance between archer and target started to narrow, the enemy jeering abated. It was quite plain to see that the arc of the arrows was taking them over their heads. Many turned to try to work out where they might land. Both the arrows started to descend. Faster and faster they dropped. Raised voices from the enemy told Yorda that their arrows were going to be on target. They ripped through the material of the tents. Almost everyone of the flaps opened and three elves ran out shouting. Yorda and Dawson notched another two arrows and let them fly. By now some of the enemy archers were returning shots but their arrows were falling woefully short of the mark. Cheers from the elves manning the city defences had replaced the jeers from the enemy. These two arrows hit the mark as well, although this time no one else exited the tent.

'OK,' said Yorda, 'shoot at anything that moves.'

'I don't like the look of that bunch over there,' said Dawson, letting fly another arrow.

Yorda now accelerated his shooting. His arms were almost a blur as he notched, released and notched again. Dawson stopped for a few seconds to watch his friend. He was almost a blur of speed.

The two friends continued their barrage and Mertok brought out some more arrows that had been prepared by the fletcher especially for Yorda.

'This will knock their attack plans back a little,' laughed the elf as he laid the arrows out on the floor for his two friends.

Dawson laughed aloud. 'I 'aven't 'ad this much fun for years.'

The enemy were running around like crazy, trying first to get out of the way of the dropping arrows and, second, gathering everything up before making a retreat out of range. Soon the arrows had run out and both Dawson and Yorda were gasping from the effort. They returned to a huge cheer from their own elves. King Tramulan was there to greet them.

'Well done, well done. They will think twice before advancing so close again.'

Dawson looked at Yorda and then at the King. 'I am afraid, sire, that it is only a temporary measure. If the enemy 'ave any sense they will construct foot-operated bows that are far less accurate but can cover the same distance. If we try the same thing again then they will use those against us. Even though they will 'ave very little chance of finding their mark, they know we won't risk our lives taking pot shots at them. Still, they are in disarray for a little time. If nothing else it 'as raised the morale of our troops.'

A couple of hours later, Yorda walked with Dawson to the perimeter defences and looked out at the enemy. They were assembling slowly but surely on the other side of the clearing. Yorda could see quite clearly that many shields were being gathered together. Dawson appeared to be correct. It seemed that the tortoise attack would be the next assault.

Yorda turned his head to take in the full extent of the enemy and could see the troops of Marosham to the right of the Solhantille. They were still engaged in eating their breakfast and almost seemed as if they had no intention of taking part in this battle. Marosham obviously had other plans for his men. Perhaps the Black Elf intended his men to take over the running of the Lohadrille when the battle was over. He suspected that this part of the kingdom would just become a large slave labour camp. This could not be allowed to happen. Again Yorda scanned the enemy lines. Where was Marosham? Even if he were to take no part in the battle it was worrying that he was not actually here to see his army attack.

It wasn't too long to wait before five distinct groups formed at the edge of the battlefield. Each group contained about fifty or so elves and each man was heavily armoured and carried a large shield. Dawson grunted when he saw what was happening and went off to make a final check on the pulley system that was being used to spring the hidden wires on the battlefield.

The five groups of elves formed themselves into an almost-square pattern. The front line of elves held their shields in front of their bodies, covering from the chest down almost to the ground. The second line held their shields high at an angle over the heads of the soldiers in the front line. This left a small space between the two shields for the front line of elves to see where they were going. Each successive line of elves held their shields over their heads forming an almost impenetrable barrier from above. On the sides of the tortoises, the elves held their shields at an angle to their bodies, giving protection from arrows fired from the sides.

Mertok came over to Yorda and asked, 'Why are they coming in five groups and not in just one long line?'

'I asked Dawson earlier how they would attack. He said that one long line would be more difficult to cover if some gaps formed in it through arrows breaching their defences. A square like this gives the opportunity for a fallen attacker to be replaced without compromising the overall shape and form of the tortoise.'

They watched as the tortoises formed exactly as Dawson had guessed. In a short period of time they were ready. The elves left behind the tortoises commenced a soft humming sound, which rose in volume as their comrades took the field. Then, from a signal given by some unseen commander, they started to beat their swords upon their shields. Dawson had returned to watch the spectacle.

'The noise would strike fear in the 'earts of many a man, but I see not one of your elves flinching, Mertok. They will make you proud of their efforts today.'

'I hope it will be more than just today. I hope that we will one day talk of our victory here.' He moved off to join his captains to issue more orders.

The tortoises continued their ponderous advance. Dawson was pleased that all five were roughly level with each other. They soon reached the spot where their men had been crushed by their own elephants the day before. Without pausing they continued. Once they reached bow range the elven archers were ordered to shoot. Hundreds of arrows arced through the air. They descended almost vertically and clattered onto the shields at the head of the tortoises. Yorda was impressed with the accuracy of the bowmen. There were virtually no stray arrows. They all found their mark but he could see no one falling from the line of advancing elves.

The barrage of arrows kept finding their mark as the tortoises advanced fully into firing range. One or two managed to penetrate the defensive shield and another replaced the fallen elf almost instantly. Imperceptibly the tortoises shrunk as elves dropped from enemy arrows.

When they were advanced enough, Dawson gave the order and some oxen that were tethered nearby, hidden from enemy sight, were urged forward. The ropes that were attached to them connected to long wires trailing out to the battlefield, all buried just under the earth. The wires linked up to hinged poles several inches long, which lifted out of the ground. Once these poles were erect the wires that connected them to each other, forming a grid-like pattern across the field, were pulled taut.

The advancing tortoises couldn't hear the slight noise as the poles lifted because of the sound of their own men beating their shields, but they were aware of very fine wires lifting between their legs and wrapping around their feet. As one man stumbled he would cause the next to fall. Within seconds the tortoises were breaking open as men fell, pulling their neighbours with them. The arrows from the defensive position continued to fill the air. The beating of the shields ceased as the enemy saw their comrades falling under the barrage of enemy arrows. The only sounds that could be heard were the twang of bowstrings and the cries of the dying men.

Dawson saw many of his poles snapping and the web of wires on the field breaking under the strain, but it didn't matter. They had worked better than he had hoped. He made a mental note that if he were ever to emerge alive from this war then he would get as much of this fine elven cord to use as he could carry.

As before, a request was made by the enemy to collect their dead and wounded. Before Mertok answered he called Dawson and asked him if the wire grids were still functional. The big man shook his head, saying that too many wires had been broken and also with the hinged poles being snapped there was no way to lift the grid above ground level. Mertok turned back to the messenger and gave his permission. If the grid had still been operational he couldn't risk the chance that the wires would have been cut by the enemy while they were rescuing their injured. Much as it would have hurt him he would have denied their request.

The same procession as had occurred the day before started again. The black-clad elves accompanied by the lantern bearers took the field. This time there were many more candles left on the battlefield, but King Tramulan noticed, as did all of his men, that this time the candles were a lot closer to his lines. Tomorrow, he was sure, would see candles from both sides strewn over the field.

Chapter Thirty

Early the next morning Thalién called Mertok and the other captains to the front line. On the other side of the field they could see a sizeable group of Marosham's army leaving the area and heading back into the forest. The rest stayed where they were but made no communication with the Solhantille who, it seemed, also had no warning as to why their comrades were apparently retreating. A scuffle broke out on the edge of the two camps, which had to be broken up by their respective commanders.

'Discontent among the troops?' said one of Mertok's captains.

'It seems so,' answered Thalién, 'but why, and more to the point, where, are those Dark Elves going and what do they intend to do?'

Yorda had seen the commotion among the troops of the Solhantille and Marosham's army and was deep in thought when Mertok spoke to him. He looked up at his friend and then stood.

'I'm sorry, Mertok, did you say something?'

'I was just wondering if you have any thoughts on why Marosham has started to pull some of his troops away from the front line.'

Yorda walked forward a few steps and scanned the enemy ranks.

'We are missing something here, Mertok. With the number of skilled warriors they have with them they could have stormed our position the first day. Sure, they would have suffered heavy losses, but they have enough men to breach our position. Dawson's experience and his traps would have stopped many of them but even he cannot believe that they haven't even tried to use force to crush us. Marosham would be quite happy, I am sure, if both armies were destroyed, for his men could take control not only of the Lohadrille but the Solhantille as well. And why is he not at the front with his armies? That is the question that worries me more than anything else.

Mertok shook his head. 'I too cannot understand his tactics. Their sending only small sorties towards us gives me the impression that they are only practising for the final assault.'

'But why practise when you can—' Yorda left his sentence unfinished and his eyes went wide. 'Oh no! I pray that I am wrong.'

Mertok looked baffled. 'What is it, Yorda?'

'Don't you see?' he said, 'Marosham *has* been practising, but not here on the battlefield – with his portals and the raids on the villages! Each time he launched a raid it was just to make his positioning of the portals more accurate, and his raiding squads were practising for their real target. The whole war is a ploy. He wants as many elves killed on both sides as possible, true, but his main aim is to get all our defences aligned on the city walls so that he can strike deep inside our own territory.

'But what could he strike at?' asked Mertok, looking more worried by the second.

Yorda held his head. 'How could I have been so stupid? What would cause the King to lay down his arms almost instantly?'

Shock appeared on Mertok's face. 'For all that we hold dear. Our Queen.'

Yorda was already starting to run to the city centre and the royal palace. Mertok called for a squad of elves to mount up and get to the palace as fast as possible. Dawson could hear what was going on and called Ted. Although his horse was nowhere near as fast as the others he managed a little head start and was soon chasing after Yorda, who was running faster than he ever had done before, leaving Shirrin, who was trying to keep up with her bonded partner, trailing behind him.

As Yorda neared the grounds of the palace he could feel a tingle in the air, a tingle he recognised as that of a portal. He slowed a little, realising that he would be no use to his grandmother if he ran straight into a trap. Drawing his sword he stopped and let his senses take in the direction of the portal. If it was still open, then Marosham had not yet captured the Queen. He decided that waiting at the portal would be the best idea.

He moved towards where the tingling got stronger and found himself heading to the small garden that the Queen visited and where she sat regularly. It was here that she had spent much time talking to Yorda when he was recuperating from his mental battle with Marosham. She would tell him stories of his parents, especially his father, and he in turn would tell her of his life growing up near Parkent.

He was no more than a hundred paces from the section of the royal palace where the Queen's quarters were when he heard the sounds of shouting and steel clashing against steel. He rushed forward with less regard for his own safety when he heard the voice of the Queen. She sounded frightened but was issuing orders to her servants.

As he broke into the garden he could see the tail end of a group of elves disappearing into the trees on the other side of the garden. There were about another twenty of the raiders forming an effective barrier against what little opposition was being put up by the Queen's personal staff. Male and female elves alike were trying in vain to get to their queen. Yorda could see the bodies of some of the Queen's servants lying in the garden. A couple of them were twitching, but at least four appeared dead.

Just as Yorda was about to enter the fray, Mertok, Dawson and the squad of soldiers turned up. Yorda turned once more to the raiders, who had seen the appearance of the soldiers. As a man they stood their ground and Yorda realised what was happening. These raiders were here to give up their lives if necessary so that their comrades could escape with the Queen.

He shouted to Mertok to engage the enemy. He knew that Marosham's men could hold out only for a short while, maybe five or ten minutes, before the Queen's defenders broke through, but that would be ample time for the Queen to be spirited away and through the portal. He had to give pursuit and hopefully slow the raiders down enough so that Mertok and Dawson could reach him.

Yorda barked out an order just before he gave chase.

'Keep at least one of them alive! It is imperative that they do not all die.'

With that he started to run at full speed towards the defensive line.

Another five tortoises started to leave the enemy positions and edge towards the city limits. King Tramulan and Thalién watched as their archers let loose barrage after barrage of arrows. The enemy advanced relentlessly. Occasionally one of the tortoises slowed for a while when some arrows penetrated its defensive shields, striking and either killing or injuring one of the elves within. As the defensive formation adjusted to cover the gap formed by the fallen comrade, the soldiers would start forward again. They were less than fifty paces from the waiting elves and still advancing.

Thalién looked out towards the enemy on the other side of the battlefield. Many were mounting armoured horses. He knew that once hand-to-hand fighting broke out then the remainder of the Solhantille would pour across the space. They outnumbered the forces of the Lohadrille and it was now made more difficult by the fact that the elite soldiers had gone back to the royal palace to counter whatever threat Yorda had discovered was taking place there.

Shirrin appeared in front of Yorda, about ten paces from the waiting line of raiders. His mental command to his horse had positioned her in precisely the correct spot for what he had in mind. He was still quite a way in front of Mertok and Dawson, but instead of slowing and waiting for his comrades, which was exactly what the enemy was expecting, Yorda accelerated straight towards them. He could see the eyes of each of the raiders. They had no fear in them at all. They knew that it was their job to die if need be and probably they were expecting it.

Yorda was about thirty paces away and moving fast. The enemy swords were raised; some had the green blood of the elven royal household still dripping from them. Yorda had no wish for his red blood to join it. He accelerated even faster, then leapt.

Because there had never been need to reinforce the perimeter limits of the city, there was no real defence against an attack by an army. The city walls were actually quite flimsy fences put up more as a boundary limit than as a defensive barrier. Any small raiding parties could be repelled without difficulty, but a large group of men acting together could quite easily push the fences over. They had been reinforced to a certain extent, more to provide a slowing down of the enemy than to stop them, but once the bulk of the Solhantille joined the field then it would only be a matter of minutes before they broke through.

Thalién and his captains had been well drilled by Dawson and they still had one or two little tricks left yet. The barrage of arrows continued until they were only a few paces from the as-yet unbreached defensive position. Then as one, from a command by Thalién, the defending elves retreated to a secondary barrier of felled tree logs about fifty paces back inside their own lines.

The enemy tortoises linked up as one and then the shields were lowered as they pushed against the fence. It toppled slightly but did not collapse completely, as rocks had been piled up behind it so that the enemy had to clamber over to get into the city.

Thalién could hear the rumble of horses' hoofs and the yell of the footsoldiers crossing the field. Some of the elven archers were able to install themselves into positions behind the new defences where they could loose off some arrows, but their targets were much more limited now that the overhanging branches covered their flight path to the enemy.

The first of the enemy clambered over the wall and charged the short distance to Tramulan's men. As soon as the first three lines of the enemy had crossed the first defence, Thalién shouted out an order. From high in the trees some elves cut the ropes that had been holding suspended tree trunks. They arced down, slowly at first but accelerating rapidly. The heavy logs were designed to swing just a little higher than the tumbled walls, giving the advancing army no chance to duck under the huge weights that they now saw falling towards them. A few who had already scaled the walls managed to duck but those that didn't were killed instantly as the falling trees arrived at head height.

The attackers who were on the broken wall were struck at about knee height. Legs were torn from the bodies of those who were upright when hit. The soldiers behind, who were still scaling the broken walls, probably didn't even see their death arriving. The swinging logs effectively sealed the path of retreat for the attackers that had encroached far enough into the city's defences, while at the same time holding off the advancing Solhantille.

Dawson's drilling came into its own now as the captains of the Royal Guard called on their men to close on the Solhantille who had been left parted from the rest of their men. The fighting was intense and the well-trained soldiers of the enemy killed nearly two defenders for each life lost of their own. Fortunately this battle was swift, and the defending elves managed to retreat behind their defences before the logs had stopped swinging and the horses of the enemy poured over the broken walls.

Yorda gained height as he jumped. His timing was perfect. Landing neatly on Shirrin's back he used his horse almost as a stepping stone to jump even higher. He could see the look of surprise on the raiders' faces as he floated well over the reaching swords. He had judged the distance well, managing to miss any overlapping branches that might have impeded his jump. Several of the raiders turned, just in case Yorda doubled back to attack from their rear, but made no attempt to follow him as he continued. He was even more certain that this was a suicide squad.

Once again he shouted behind him to his following comrades that they had to take at least one of the raiders alive. He accelerated until the passing bushes and trees were a blur. Behind him he could hear the clash of steel as Mertok and his men engaged the solid line of raiders. There were about thirty or so soldiers of the Royal Guard with Mertok so they would certainly triumph, but at what delay?

Up ahead, Yorda could hear some movement. He could see something glinting just to his right. Suddenly a raider leapt out of the bushes, his sword drawn. Yorda had no time for this. If he had stopped he could easily disarm the elf and keep him alive but the time taken to render him senseless might be too much in his pursuit of the Queen. He was certain, after seeing the line of raiders he had just left, that if he only injured the raider before continuing after the Queen, upon his return the elf would have killed himself rather than take the risk of being interrogated and giving out information to the enemy. Yorda swung his sword in an arc, neatly taking first the arm and second the head of the advancing elf.

He had hardly broken step as he continued forward. Then ahead of him he could see the group of elves that had left the garden a short while ago. His blood froze. The Queen was being half carried, half dragged forward. She was fighting all the way but even as he closed the distance he saw the Queen and the two elves who were constraining her disappear into thin air as they passed through the portal.

The four elves who were following turned when they heard Yorda and lifted their swords. A fifth elf lifted a short bow and notched an arrow. Everything now seemed to happen in slow motion from Yorda's point of view. The arrow flew towards him, straight for his chest. Yorda lifted his hand and swatted it away as it approached. It seemed to him that the enemy stopped moving and were frozen in time. All five elves were virtually unaware of the blurred sword that took their lives.

Yorda hurled himself at the entrance to the portal, praying that he could get through before it closed. He leapt forward and felt the intense tingle that he knew was the gateway between the royal gardens and wherever the Queen had been taken.

Dawson lifted his battleaxe. His enormous size and ferocity of attack would have frightened most soldiers, but these men stared impassively at him as he drove into them. Mertok was immediately to the right of Dawson and deflected a sword thrust aimed at his friend's midriff. The raiders were well drilled and held fast as the Royal Guard pressed forward. Slowly they were forced backwards under the onslaught but they kept a firm line between themselves and their retreating comrades.

Dawson's big axe descended, cleaving through the breastplate of one of the raiders. Green blood spurted out, hitting the big man in the face, making him momentarily lose vision. He stepped back quickly while his vision cleared. He knew that Mertok and the guard would cover him for the scant seconds he needed to re-engage the enemy. One of the Royal Guards fell to a sword thrust to the thigh but the defender had overextended himself and in turn took a blade under his ribcage.

One by one the raiders fell, but all were dead or nearly dead by the time they hit the ground. Mertok and his men pressed forward. They had lost five men, which was far fewer than he had feared, but he also realised that the raiders were only trying to delay the enemy and not kill as many as possible.

Dawson could see the same thing. He knew it was much easier to hold an enemy at bay if you were only trying to gain time, even if it meant you did not inflict many casualties on them. He gambled on this strategy and feinted a swing with his axe at one of the defenders. As the raider defended the swing, Dawson neatly twisted inside the defender's position and put his shoulder into the elf's chest. A huge grunt escaped the much smaller elf as the air escaped his body. Dawson shouted, 'Cover me, Mertok!' as he dropped to the floor on his opponent and with one large fist clubbed down on the elf's head. The raider's jaw dropped open as he lay unconscious on the floor.

Mertok and one of the Royal Guard stepped over Dawson and held off any attacks to their man. In fact the only attack towards their position seemed more with the intention of killing their own man. The battle became more intense as the raiders made one last determined effort to get to their fallen comrade, but the more experienced Royal Guards held them off, dispatching them one by one until none were left alive except for the one that Dawson had taken out. Mertok ordered three of the Royal Guard to stay with the fallen elf and rushed forward with the rest of his men in the direction Yorda had taken.

The mounted lancers of the Solhantille swept into the defensive positions of Thalién and his men. Archers stationed in the trees managed to pick off some of the first over the wall, but as soon as they closed on their opponents this became impossible, with the risk of hitting their own men too high. Dawson had suggested a small group of archers should station themselves well inside the defensive lines in case the mounted soldiers of the enemy broke through and headed for the city centre. It soon became obvious that they had no wish to do this. When Thalién realised that the sole purpose of the attack was to destroy all resistance, he called these men into forward positions and they took up swords.

Most of Thalién's men were engaged in battle against the horsemen who had vaulted the last defensive barrier and were causing havoc. The large, armour-clad steeds were difficult to bring down and the ground troops had to contend with a heavy beast charging at them, along with an attack with a longsword from above.

Dawson had instructed the making of nets with small boulders attached at the four corners, which were thrown over the attacking horses. This was effective in a number of cases, slowing the animals enough so that their riders could be dismounted and then quickly incapacitated. But it was taking too many men to work this tactic and the horses and men that were not snared this way proved more than a match for the ground troops.

Thalién was in a group of elves, the elite force of the Royal Guard that was covering the King. These soldiers were holding their ground very effectively but he could see some of the other defenders being forced to break ranks under the onslaught. The battle was turning to the advantage of the Solhantille.

At that moment one of the captains let out a shout. Thalién turned and his captain shouted, 'Look to the walls!'

Thalién, along with many of the elves, turned and saw that the footsoldiers had reached the edge of their front defensive line. Hundreds upon hundreds of the enemy were pouring like ants over the collapsed walls into the city.

Yorda hit the ground and rolled. He came up into a crouched position with his sword in one hand and his belt knife in the other. He turned quickly to scan the position. He was devastated, as he was still in the palace grounds. Either the portal had closed or for some reason he was unable to pass through it.

'My queen,' he said quietly to himself, 'I am so sorry. We have failed you.'

He turned back and moved to the area where the portal had been. Sure enough he could feel the tingling getting weaker. The portal had been closed when the last raider had passed through. Marosham must have been on the other side, waiting, and had closed the gate when the last raider had leapt through and told him that the Royal Guard was in pursuit. The only thing Yorda could do now was to go back to help his comrades. He had gone a short distance when Mertok and the other elves came into view. Yorda quickly told them what had happened. Mertok cursed softly under his breath while Dawson cursed out loud. Mertok told Yorda that they had managed to capture one of the raiders without killing him.

'What now, laddie?' the big man said.

'There are two things we must do immediately. Firstly I want to talk to the raider you captured, and secondly we must get back to the front. Marosham has got what he wanted; there is no reason for him to make another attack here. All our energies must be used to stop the advance of the Solhantille.'

The three elves of the Royal Guard were alert, with weapons at the ready, and the raider was still unconscious when Mertok and Yorda arrived. Yorda bent down and turned the elf onto his stomach. He pulled the rear of his tunic up, revealing his back. Placing both hands on his back he concentrated. 'Whoever you are, don't fail me now,' he said.

After several seconds, sure enough, he could hear the mysterious voice that always seemed to come to him when healing a patient. The words that came into his mind were just as alien as they had always been, but this time they were words he had not heard before. Yorda repeated them quietly at first and then, getting no reaction from the prone form of the raider, he said them louder. Mertok and his men watched without understanding what their comrade was doing. After what seemed an age one of the soldiers said, 'What on earth is that?'

The other elves had seen the same thing. At the bottom of the spine of the raider there was an unmistakable swelling appearing. The skin was moving as if bubbles of water were under the surface. Suddenly the skin split open and a grub-like creature emerged, writhing around. It gave the impression of being angry that it had been ripped from its warm host.

'Deal with it, Dawson,' said Yorda as he turned his prisoner over.

Dawson deftly flicked the grub onto the ground with his

sword and placed a big boot over it and twisted down hard. A mushy pulp remained of the parasite.

Yorda put one hand on the forehead of the still-unconscious raider and set his face in grim determination. Several seconds later the raider started to stir and woke up. At the sight of Yorda and the Royal Guard all gathered around him he tried to crawl away. Dawson reached down and with one huge hand grabbed the tunic of the prisoner.

'No, please don't kill me!' he cried.

'That is a bit of a change in character from a few minutes ago,' one of the captains of the guard noted aloud.

Yorda answered the captain without taking his gaze off the prisoner. 'He had no choice. That little creature was being used to control or at the very least condition the reaction of this elf.'

He looked straight into the eyes of the now-terrified elf.

'Tell me where the Queen has been taken. If you lie I will know and, believe me, it will not go well for you should that should happen.'

The elf looked around wildly and saw all of his fallen comrades.

'I do not know. Everything is so blurred. I am telling the truth. Please do not kill me.'

'Let me 'ave 'im, laddie', said Dawson. 'I will soon get the truth out of 'im.'

Yorda lifted his hand to stay the big man. 'No, Dawson. He is telling the truth. That grub that you just crushed had given Marosham total control over this helpless creature. He was helpless to resist the commands given him, as were the others who died here today.' He turned back towards the elf. 'Do not be afraid; this will not hurt,' and to himself he muttered, 'I hope.' Then he placed both hands on the head of the terrified elf.

Yorda used the mind techniques that Élonel had instructed him in before his encounter with Marosham. Reaching forward gently he entered the mind of the elf. He could see a lot of scarring caused by commands given to him by Marosham that were contrary to the wishes of the elf. He probed deeper and found the blocks that he knew would be there. These had been set by Marosham to hide any information from his raider should he be caught. Taking a deep breath, Yorda started to pull and tear at the blocks. They were strong but he was determined.

Mertok and the others stepped back as they saw the ground around the joined pair start to blacken. Grass that had been deep green turned to brown and withered.

Yorda tore down the first block and then the second behind it and finally the third. All of the elf's memories came flooding back into his conscious mind and Yorda saw where Marosham had opened the portal. He pulled out of the elf's mind as gently as he could.

'I am so sorry, so very, very sorry,' said the elf, and he started to cry, realising the enormity of what he had been a part of.

Yorda placed his hand once more over the forehead of the elf. 'It is not your fault. You had no control over what was asked of you. Sleep now. I will try to ease your pain.'

Yorda uttered another few strange words and then asked one of the soldiers to go and fetch some of the royal staff to collect and care for the prisoner. 'I know where Marosham is. He is not too far from here. If we go now we may be able to catch him unawares before he issues his ultimatum. Perhaps we may have the element of surprise on our side for the first time. Marosham believes he has won the day now that he has the Queen. Our only chance is to strike at the core of his defences now.'

'What about the attack on the city?' said one of the guard.

'Unfortunately we cannot help them now. We must go straight to Marosham. If he falls, then his army and the army of the Solhantille will fall also.'

Yorda got up and called Shirrin. He placed his hand on the animal's forehead and passed some information over to her. Immediately she pulled away and galloped off, making the loudest neighing sound any of the gathered company had ever heard from a horse.

'Come,' said Yorda, heading off in the direction of the continuing battle. 'Follow me and do not stop until we get to the Black Elf himself.'

The blood-spattered soldiers turned wearily and headed back to their horses with Yorda leading the way.

Hand-to-hand fighting had broken out between the defenders and the onrushing Solhantille. Thalién could see that even though his men were battling valiantly, slowly but surely they were losing ground and with every inch of ground lost they were losing elves. The initial charge by the mounted lancers had finally been repelled, but at a great cost to the forces of King Tramulan.

Once again Dawson's training was paying dividends. If not for his tactics and practices they would have been overrun just by the horsemen of the Solhantille. As it was they had suffered heavy losses but still had enough elves left to fight a regimented battle. This had obviously surprised the enemy on foot, who had expected to be charging down on just the remnants of the King's army. Their first attack had been repelled very effectively, giving the defence a little time to regroup. The Solhantille had retreated to just behind the fallen walls, using them as cover while they themselves regrouped. The next attack was a different matter. They now knew approximately how many elves they were facing and realised that they still greatly outnumbered the defenders of the city.

Thalién ordered his men back to their last defensive position. Again they took shelter behind some felled trees. When the footsoldiers of the enemy advanced, the last traps were sprung. Dawson, once again taking advantage of the fine elven ropes, had fashioned some nets which were hidden under some light earth. These were arranged in such a way that they could be sprung when the enemy walked on them. Thus they would lift up around the enemy troops, raising them high off the ground. Thalién knew as well as Dawson that the soldiers within would soon be able to cut their way out but, as in any battle, thinning down the enemy even for a short while makes it easier to dispatch the ones still fighting. This tactic had again slowed the retreat, and the archers had killed many of the suspended soldiers before they had freed themselves. The most recent assault by the enemy seemed to Thalién potentially the last. The army of the Solhantille were better swordsmen than the Lohadrille and the only way the defenders could stave off a rapid defeat was to retreat slowly against the pressing army.

One of the captains asked Thalién in passing what had

happened to Mertok and the men who had gone back to the city. Thalién had fended off an attack and cut down the enemy elf while at the same time replying that he had no idea but was sure that it must have been more important than what was happening here. The captain grunted that he hoped that their odds were better than the ones he and his men were facing now.

Thalién looked to his left and saw that the enemy were starting to break through and would soon circle around behind them. If that happened then all was lost. He looked around to see if they had any men who could cover the left flank, but saw that the right and centre were at full stretch as well.

At that moment a rumbling could be felt underfoot which rapidly grew in intensity. Both the Solhantille and the Lohadrille slowed in their efforts, trying to see what was happening. Thalién turned his head for an instant and listened. A roaring sound seemed to be coming from behind them in the direction of the city. Within seconds a herd of horses erupted from the trees behind the King and his remaining elves. Leading the horses was Shirrin, neighing loudly. Thalién recognised some of the horses behind. They were the mounts that had lost their bonded partners. At that precise moment he apologised to the grey mare for having doubts about her returning to the city while Marosham was alive.

Thalién called to his men above the roar to retreat quickly and give the horses space. Like a howling gale the animals tore straight through the enemy lines, mowing down many of the footsoldiers and scattering many others. Almost as soon as they had passed, another rumble followed, not as loud but from the same direction. Out of the trees appeared Yorda, running like the wind, followed by Mertok, Dawson and the elves of the Royal Guard who had left the battle earlier. A huge cheer went up as they followed the path opened up for them by the stampeding horses. As they passed, Mertok spotted his brother and smiled a grim smile: keep fighting, my brother; we will return when we can.

Although surprised and knowing that their help was sorely needed, Thalién knew that they must have an errand of extreme importance. He took the chance of the respite in the battle to gather his men and regain the first defensive barrier. Most of the enemy army had retreated behind the fallen walls, losing many of their number in the process. Thalién reckoned that the odds were not much greater than two to one against them now. With that number he should be able to hold out for a while.

Chapter Thirty-One

Yorda kept his pace down so that he wouldn't lose the rest of the party. While he ran he kept his eyes peeled and his ears open for any signs of enemy traps or hidden elves on the route. It soon seemed obvious to him that Marosham had no idea that he was going to receive some uninvited guests very soon.

Dawson and the following elves, although riding hard, welcomed the respite in the fighting and the chance to regain a little of their energy. They had no idea of the number of elves that would be awaiting them when they entered Marosham's camp. The element of surprise at least was on their side.

Yorda shouted over his shoulder to the following horses. 'When we reach the camp I will lift my arm and we enter at full gallop. You must take down anything that moves. I will find Marosham. It is certain that the Queen will be with him.'

Mertok was still amazed at his friend. Even running as fast as their horses, he was able to talk as if he were standing still. He prayed that he would still be strong when the final battle took place.

They had travelled about ten minutes or so when Yorda could hear the sound of many elves up ahead. He lifted his arm and accelerated.

The elves in the small camp had heard the sound of horses coming towards them and even, though they were a little surprised, not one of them thought that it could be anything but the horsemen of the Solhantille. Either they were retreating or they were coming to give an urgent message to Marosham. Most of the elves were actually facing the trees when Yorda broke through, but surprisingly few had their weapons ready.

Yorda emerged from the trees and headed straight into the centre of the group of elves standing around a fire. Yorda could see that none of these elves had had any intention of joining in the battle that was raging a short distance away. They were

Marosham's chosen few, who were probably going to be given the prime positions when the city was taken. Yorda's blurred sword killed the first three he came to before the rest of the party came into the small clearing. There were probably a hundred elves camped here as against the twenty or so with Yorda. After the initial surprise, where the enemy lost most of the elves standing, the attackers dismounted to face the rest of Marosham's men, who were now armed. Towards the rear of the camp was a large tent, which was heavily guarded. These elves made no advance towards the battle scene ahead of them but drew their weapons and waited. Yorda knew that the Queen was here and he could also feel the presence of Marosham.

Before he had a chance to throw himself at the defending guards, the tent flap opened and Marosham appeared. He looked at Yorda and smiled.

'My brother, my friend, you have come to visit me.'

As he said this Yorda felt a searing pain in his head and slowed to walking pace. His sword almost fell from his hand, as it seemed to gain weight many times heavier than it should have been. His legs had the feeling of dragging through mud.

He looked at Marosham, who laughed aloud. 'You dare to think you could attack me with impunity! How little about me you have learnt since that little game we played inside my head. You have grown stronger in your mental powers but when you are in my presence you are nothing more than a helpless puppy.'

Marosham drew his sword and his guards moved apart for him to advance. Marosham turned to what must have been one of his captains and said, 'I am going to have a little sport here. Make sure that no one disturbs us.'

Yorda could see that Mertok and the others were encountering strong resistance after their initial attack but were holding their own. Many of the enemy were lying slain on the ground and a few of Mertok's men had joined them. Dawson had received a gash on his shoulder from someone but Yorda knew from the way he was swinging his axe that whoever had done it was no longer on this earth.

'Defend yourself.'

Yorda turned and saw Marosham standing in front of him.

The first attack by Marosham was a tentative lunge with his sword. Normally Yorda would have been able to walk around such a slow, measured movement but his legs hardly moved and he felt the pain of the blade slice into his side. He let loose a gasp and his knees buckled.

'Get up, Yorda. I haven't started to have fun with you yet. Don't disappoint me. I expected more from you than this.'

Yorda looked up and focused his attention on Marosham's head. With one very quick thought he imagined an arrow being pushed into his tormentor's face. Marosham recoiled as if struck. Yorda had managed to send a bolt of pain into his enemy's head fast enough so that Marosham could not trap him in his mind again. As soon as he had done it he felt some strength returning into his body. He lifted his sword and lunged at Marosham. Even though Marosham had lost some of his concentration he still managed to slow Yorda's assault and defended against the slashing sword of his adversary.

One of the guards forming a ring around them stepped in and gave Yorda a thrust with his sword into the back of his left leg. Yorda buckled again and fell. Marosham turned to the man who had issued the injury and screamed at him.

'You fool! I told you to make sure that *no one* disturbs us. That includes you.' With that he plunged his sword into the man's chest.

Yorda stood once more. The pain running down the back of his leg was almost unbearable. He made another dash towards Marosham, hoping to catch him unawares while he dispensed with the soldier who had interrupted his sport. Marosham saw him coming and turned neatly, brushing him aside. As Yorda stumbled past, he felt a pain in his right shoulder and looking down saw a dagger protruding from just above the collarbone. He felt his right arm go numb so he transferred his sword to his left hand.

'I hope you are ambidextrous, Yorda. It would be such a shame for this to finish too quickly.'

Marosham lunged forward, knocking Yorda down into a kneeling position. He reached forward and pulled the knife out of Yorda's shoulder, giving it a vicious twist as he did so.

Stars passed in front of Yorda's eyes as the pain got more and more intense. He looked up at the gloating face of his enemy and heard a voice speaking to him. He continued to look at Marosham's face but saw it wasn't his voice that was talking. He tried to concentrate on the voice. It was familiar to him. He recognised it as the voice that came to him whenever he was healing. He listened to the words and repeated them quietly.

'What's that you are saying, my friend? Are you asking for mercy yet?' Marosham continued to gloat. 'Whatever language you are using, my answer is still the same. No mercy from the soon-to-be king of all elfland.'

Yorda felt strength pouring back into his body. He was still in agony but could feel power entering his arms and legs. He stood and smiled, motioning Marosham forward. 'I ask no mercy. I was merely giving you one last chance to surrender,' he lied.

Marosham howled. 'You dare to mock me! For that you will die now!'

He hurled himself forward towards Yorda. Even though a lot of Yorda's strength had come back, he was still much slower than he should be.

Marosham lifted his sword high and brought it down in a curving arc towards Yorda's head. Had it been but two minutes earlier Yorda could have offered no defence. This time, however, he deflected it with his own sword and counter-attacked. He drove forward with as much energy as he could gather, driving Marosham backwards, defending frantically. Marosham stepped back briskly as a slicing movement from Yorda saw his sword brush the Black Elf's chest. Marosham placed a hand to his chest and pulled it away, covered in green blood.

'It appears I underestimated you,' said Marosham. 'Luckily for me it is just a flesh wound. I will play with you no longer.'

Marosham now launched an attack, pushing Yorda back. The young man could feel the extra strength given to him starting to fade away. Each time the blade from Marosham's sword descended it seemed to Yorda that it had more and more force behind it. Finally one of his attacks got through. Yorda lifted his sword to stop another high swing but only succeeded in slowing the blade. He felt it dig deep into his neck as it descended. Yorda fell backwards onto the ground. He lowered his head and saw that he had been cut from the right hand side of his neck down his chest and across his stomach. He knew he would not stand again to face his enemy.

Marosham advanced and grinned down at the form on the ground in front of him.

'You have entertained me long enough. It was fun as long as it lasted.'

Yorda was dimly aware of the battle still going on around him. He could hear the sound of steel upon steel and was at least comforted by the fact that his friends were still alive. He had let them down and for that he was sorry. He wished that he had been more interested in the lessons given by Dawson with the sword. Maybe that could have turned the battle in his favour. He would never know now. His last thoughts were of Ivaine. He would never know if this beautiful woman would have become his wife. Would Marosham expand his power into the lands of the humans? It was no longer any problem of his.

Marosham knelt down by Yorda and took his sword from his hand. Yorda's fingers were getting cold to the touch. He was aware that the pain screaming through his body only moments before was starting to ebb.

Marosham took the knife that he had earlier plunged into Yorda's shoulder and held it above his chest.

'There comes a time in every creature's life when they must see an end to their existence. You are lucky because you know it will happen to you. Many animals have no conception of death. They just carry on doing their everyday things and then one day they just cease to exist. You do realise, my brother, that I must take your still-beating heart from your body. By holding your heart in my hand as it gives it last few beats I will truly know that your life was mine. Goodbye, Yorda. Time to die.'

Marosham placed the knife on Yorda's chest and started to push. Yorda felt no pain but was aware of his face becoming very warm and sticky and a heaviness descending on his body. He looked up once more at Marosham and noticed that the Black Elf no longer had a head. Blood was pouring over Yorda from the open neck of his adversary. His eyes moved a little and saw Dawson standing over the body of Marosham.

Mertok and the others had fought well, pushing the enemy slowly back. Dawson had been aware of Yorda struggling against Marosham and had attracted Mertok's attention.

The two friends had launched a concerted attack to get to their friend. Mertok had taken a sword to his chest covering the big man so that he could get to Marosham. He arrived just as Marosham was about to drive the knife into Yorda's chest. He had no chance to do anything other than swing his axe. He had stopped the Black Elf from carving Yorda's heart out of his chest but he could see that it was too late to save Yorda – or Mertok, who was lying critically wounded a short distance away.

Dawson dropped to the floor. He was bleeding heavily himself, but he paid no regard to his own wounds. He took Yorda's hand. Tears started to flow as he saw the condition of his friend.

'I am sorry, laddie. I didn't get to you in time.'

Yorda looked up at Dawson and smiled. He coughed a couple of times and large gobs of blood came from his mouth.

'You did get to me in time, my big friend. He never got the satisfaction of seeing me die. I saw him go, thanks to you.'

Queen Miælla had left the tent where she had been held captive and came and knelt by Yorda. She placed her hand on his forehead.

'Thank you, Yorda, for coming to my rescue, but I fear that the price you have paid to save the life of an old elf has been too great.' She lifted his hand and placed it in her own.

'You will not be forgotten, my grandson. Should the Lohadrille survive the war, then we shall sing great songs of your heroism. I pray that you join in the Endless Song when you join your ancestors and walk the Halls of the Dead.'

Yorda smiled once more, then closed his eyes. Queen Miælla could feel Yorda's fingers loosen their grip on hers and his hand went limp. Dawson saw his breathing get shallower. Through his tears it seemed as if the sky were getting brighter and his friend was covered in a glow. He blinked back the tears and realised that a white light was actually starting to emanate from Yorda. Dawson stepped back to watch. All the fighting that had gone on behind him ceased as the others saw what was happening. Mertok managed to prop himself up.

The body of Marosham was emitting the same glow. Slowly but surely the two glows expanded towards one another until the two mighty adversaries were bathed in the white light. A loud whining noise pierced the air, and all who were able lifted their hands to protect their ears. A wind sprang up out of nowhere and blew the branches of the trees every which way.

Dawson struggled to see into the white glow. Too many bits of leaves and dirt were driving into his eyes. He turned his head away and a short while later the wind started to decrease in force.

When he could see clearly again he looked over at Yorda. The white glow had gone and his friend was lying peacefully on the floor. He moved over to Yorda once more and reached out to touch his hand. It was not as cold as before and it was getting warmer.

He looked at Yorda's face and saw his friend's mouth quivering as he started to breath. The wound on his neck was starting to close, as was the gash moving down his chest.

He turned almost in panic to look at Marosham, half believing that the same thing was happening to him. The body of the Black Elf lay motionless on the floor, his head still lying a little distance away from the body. When he looked back, Yorda was opening his eyes and colour was flooding back to his face.

'Dawson,' the young healer croaked, 'did we win?'

'Yes, we won this battle but at great cost. Mertok will not recover from 'is injuries and I don't know 'ow the battle goes back at the city. Not well, I think.'

Yorda propped himself up on one elbow and Dawson could see that the wound in his shoulder caused by Marosham's knife had completely healed. The young man looked over at Mertok, who was bleeding heavily but still conscious.

'I must go to him, Dawson,' said Yorda.

Yorda stood up, a little shakily but under his own power. Dawson could not believe his eyes. Just seconds ago his friend was as close to death as anyone could be without actually being dead, and now he was walking with no apparent injuries.

He walked over groggily to where Mertok lay. The elf was breathing shallowly but he turned his head and smiled at Yorda. Yorda reached down and placed his hand on his friend. Almost instantly the same thing started to happen to Mertok as had happened to Yorda moments before. His wounds started healing and his breathing started getting deeper and more regular.

Yorda turned and left Mertok, then went round the camp doing the same to all the injured. He then called all the enemy left standing to him. For each of them he placed his hand on their backs and pulled out the grub-like creature, tossing it on the floor and crushing it under his feet. All of the soldiers seemed to waken from a deep sleep and instantly dropped to their knees to beg forgiveness for what they had done. Yorda said it was the King who would determine if they were to be forgiven or not. He turned back towards Dawson and it was then that he realised his big friend was injured and losing blood. He went towards him, but Dawson stopped him.

'Yorda, all I want you to do is to tell me if the injuries I 'ave can be healed naturally. If not, then I welcome your 'elp. But if they can, then as a soldier I prefer to keep the scars of my battles.'

Yorda quickly examined his friend.

'You are a tough man, very hard to kill. The wounds you have are losing blood but you will live. Come, we must all go back to the city. I must stop the war.'

There were six elves from the Royal Guard still alive and about double that of the enemy. It was plain to see that now Marosham was dead they had no wish to fight against their brethren, so they joined the six Lohadrille and rode back to the battlefield, leaving the Queen with two of the Royal Guard to circle around the fighting and make their way back to the royal palace by a safer but longer route. Yorda took a horse, as he was still a little shaken by all that had happened. Dawson noticed that his friend seemed very preoccupied with something and could get no reply from him when he talked, but he was sure after all that had happened it was no surprise.

When they got back to the clearing in front of the city walls Mertok and the others saw that things were going badly for their comrades. There were barely fifty left. They had formed a tight circle protecting their king, and the Solhantille army was pressing forward. It would be only a matter of minutes before all resistance was extinguished.

Yorda galloped forward and dismounted a short distance from the battle. The rest of his party did the same and rushed towards their comrades. Yorda lifted his hand to hold them back.

'No. Go no further. I will finish this.'

He advanced and was spotted by one of the enemy captains. An order was issued and about twenty of the attackers turned and ran towards Yorda. As they advanced, Yorda lifted his arm and a slight ripple of air moved outwards towards the attackers. As it reached them, one by one they were thrown backwards to land stunned on the floor. Yorda advanced towards the last of the fighting. Once more he lifted his arm and now all of the Solhantille collapsed to the floor, gasping for breath.

As the noise of the battle ceased, Yorda shouted, 'The war is over! Marosham is no more. You of the Solhantille have no more need to fight your brethren. I call to you now to bring me your injured. If they breath then they must be brought to me.'

He dropped his arm and the soldiers who were gasping for breath on the floor started to rise. A couple tried to take up arms once again but a movement of Yorda's hand saw their weapons pulled from their grasp.

In a matter of minutes, injured were being brought to the young healer. As with Mertok he took them one by one and healed their wounds. For those who had lost a limb he could do no more than seal their wounds and take away their pain, but they would all live.

As each injured elf recovered, they in turn went out to the battlefield to bring in more of their injured comrades. It took several hours to get to everyone, but more than 700 elves from both camps were returned to health by Yorda.

When he had administered to all the injured, Yorda went over to the King, who was in discussion with Thalién and several of the captains of the Royal Guard. Dawson was sitting on the floor having bandages wound around several of his wounds. He looked up at his friend as he approached. Yorda nodded but had a grim expression on his face as he walked past.

King Tramulan turned and saw Yorda as he covered the last few paces. 'My child. It is over at last. The war is ended.'

Yorda looked over at the troops of the Solhantille who had

been stripped of their weapons and were at that very moment being bound as prisoners of war. The King raised his voice so that the prisoners could hear.

'Great destruction has been caused here today,' the King said. 'We must now mourn our dead and rebuild. Many lives have been lost here, lives that will never be replaced. We have lost thousands of years of life on this battlefield. It must never happen again. Without Marosham we can move forward and once more live in peace with our brethren. You will be allowed to leave soon and I hope that you will return to your people and tell them what has happened here today and convince them of the futility of war, of the needless death and destruction caused by it. You will be brought to the city where you will be clothed and fed and given time to recover from what has happened here. When you wish to leave you may go in peace with an invitation to return as friends whenever you wish.'

He turned to Yorda once again. 'It seems that the prophecy was not fulfilled after all. Mertok tells me that it was Dawson who finally took Marosham's life. Perhaps we elves too should question our beliefs a little more.'

Yorda looked at his grandfather.

'No, my king, the prophecy was completely fulfilled. Dawson was the champion of which the prophecy spoke. He is the champion who returned. I now believe that he does not come from our world. He had passed through a portal to our world when he battled the Vortak. After he was healed he left the kingdom. He returned with me and dealt the final blow, which saved not only my life but also all the lives of our people.'

'And the rest of the prophecy?' asked the King.

'It does appear that I have received extra knowledge and power. I can feel something very different inside me, something which, I do not understand why, frightens me greatly. I must take some time to think about this and try to make sense of it all. I have the knowledge that Marosham possessed before he died. I can feel his evil within me now, but what worries me most of all is that what has taken place here today was not completely of his own doing. There are other forces at play. Forces that I cannot as yet connect with.'

Mertok had been listening nearby, and he interrupted. 'Do you think it wise to try and connect with this force, whatever it is?'

'I have no choice. Whatever was Marosham is now part of me. I am no longer just Yorda; I have become something different. I am now the sum of the parts that were Yorda and Marosham.'

Yorda turned and, without waiting to be dismissed by the King, left the camp in deep concentration. He headed towards the city.

Chapter Thirty-Two

The soldiers of Marosham's army, now that they had been released from the influence of the parasitic grubs, were desperate to do anything they could to help their brethren and were the first to request permission to help collect all the bodies off the battlefield. King Tramulan stood and watched until every elf had been removed from Marosham's camp and from the city's limits and then returned with the funeral procession, grieving deeply. When they got back to the city centre, the King called an immediate meeting of the Council of Elders and to that end requested that his sons, his queen, Yorda and Dawson be present, along with the Solhantille captains that were still alive, and finally the senior-ranked elves from the remnants of Marosham's army.

Yorda had requested that he not be disturbed after returning from the city's walls and had refused to see anyone except his grandmother. When she returned to the city she had gone immediately to Yorda and found him sitting in the corner of his room with his knees dragged up close to his chest, rocking gently from side to side.

'May I come in, Yorda?' she asked softly from the doorway.

Yorda seemed not to notice her for a moment. Then his eyes cleared and he nodded. Queen Miǽlla sat cross-legged next to her grandson and stared deep into his blue eyes.

'What is it, my child? Can it be that the shock of the battle has caused you to be like this?'

Yorda continued to rock slowly. It was several seconds before he answered.

'My queen, yesterday I was Yorda; today I do not know who I am. The prophecy said that the survivor would claim the power of the other. I can feel the power that has been transferred to me. But it is more than that. I am Marosham as well as Yorda today. I have his memories within me. Now that the heat of battle is over and my mind is no longer focused on stopping the war and saving the injured, I can feel his thoughts within me.'

Yorda looked at his queen with a desperate look.

'I remember every deed that he did. I can see the look on the faces of the elves that I killed.' The Queen noticed that Yorda had said 'I' and not 'he'. Yorda continued. 'I see all the evils that have been visited on this land by Marosham over the last 200 years. I can even see the time that he was in the schoolroom with our mysterious tutor. The page of the Book that he was given to read is now in my mind. It showed him how to create and use a portal. But none of this was designed to make him do what he has done. Another was controlling him. Shirrin spoke of this to me when she said that he was bonded to another. I can hear this being trying to contact Marosham. It is a being of immense power and I dare not reply for I fear he may control me also.'

The Queen reached out to take Yorda's hand, but he pulled back from her.

'Grandmother, this is not as it was meant to be. Some great force of which we know nothing designed the prophecy. Perhaps it was the gods themselves that were testing us, good against evil. The joining of the two powers was to be the result and I am being tested as to whether I can control the constant war between the two powers. But something else has joined in this battle, something that should not be there. Something so great and so powerful that Marosham could not resist it, and I am having trouble myself stopping it from seizing my mind and controlling us.'

Once more the Queen noticed that Yorda had not said 'me'. She said nothing but made a mental note to mention it to Mertok and Thalién later.

'Yorda,' she said softly, 'you are in the best place you can be at this time. You are surrounded by the magic of the kingdom. Your family is here; you have friends here. We will not let anything happen to you.'

Yorda looked at her and smiled. 'I do not believe you could stop it, but thank you anyway.'

The Queen stood and moved back to the doorway. 'Your grandfather the king has called a meeting of the council to discuss what should be done now that the war is over. We must rebuild not only the city walls but also our bonds with our brethren the Solhantille. He has requested your presence in the Great Hall. Do you wish me to send you anything before you descend?'

Yorda stood slowly and smiled at his grandmother. 'No. I have everything I need, thank you.'

The Queen looked at her grandson for a moment, thinking that his answer was a little strange, and then turned and left the room.

Yorda went over to a small table and sat down at it. Taking a sheet of paper he placed it before him on the table. He reached over and picked up a quill. Dipping it into a small pot of ink on the table he started to write.

Dawson limped painfully along next to Mertok. The tall elf looked down at the big man's bandaged leg.

'How goes it, my big friend?'

Dawson laughed.

'I've 'ad worse. It is just another scar to add to my collection. I will be fine in a week or two.'

He stopped walking and Mertok halted as well.

'Mertok? You took a sword for me back there. Normally that would 'ave meant your death if it wasn't for our young friend. I am indebted to you for that.'

Mertok started to walk again and Dawson hobbled along beside him.

'Someone had to get to Yorda to help him. You seemed to be in the best position to do so. I am sure you would have done the same for me.'

'Aye, that is true, but it doesn't alter the fact that you did it. Thank you, my friend. *Arhnôs dir ŭrshial*.'

Mertok extended his hand and grasped the already outstretched arm of Dawson.

'You are welcome.'

The two friends carried on towards the council meeting.

King Tramulan entered the Great Hall and everybody stood. He walked slowly to his seat. In the past two days he had aged greatly, which was understandable. He sat and motioned for everybody else to sit also. When all were seated he rose once again. Silence fell on all who were gathered there.

'My friends,' he started, 'and I mean friends.' He looked in the direction of the selected Solhantille and exiled elves that had made up Marosham's army. 'We here are the survivors of a terrible mistake. Elves have fought against elves for no other reason than that Marosham wished to rule these lands. Many of our brethren have died this day. Too many. I call to our forefathers to take their souls into the Halls of the Dead and let them join in the Endless Song.'

A murmur of agreement from all who were seated passed around the room.

'Many more would be lying slain on the battlefield this very minute had it not been for Yorda.'

The King looked around the room but could not find his grandson seated anywhere. He turned to Mertok, who was seated on the left of the King, and asked where Yorda was. Mertok replied that he had not seen him since he had left the battlefield. Queen Miælla gently touched the robe that the King was wearing and when he turned towards her told him that she had just left him and that he should have got here by now. The King called for one of the elves waiting by the door and asked him to fetch Yorda.

He turned once more to the gathered elves in the room. 'I would ask everyone here to be patient for just a little longer. We will continue when Yorda arrives.'

He sat back down and started talking quietly to his queen while the rest of the elves and Dawson gathered in the hall sat silently.

Only a few minutes had passed when the elf who had been sent to summon Yorda returned at a run, holding a sheet of paper. He rushed up to the King and passed it over to him. Without asking where Yorda was, King Tramulan read the note. He reread it and then stood once again.

'It appears that Yorda will not be coming to the council meeting after all. His letter says that he believes he is too much of a threat to all of us at this moment and he has gone to find Rimanathon in the lands of the Elänthoi. He believes that he is the only person who can help him come to terms with what has happened since the prophecy was fulfilled.'

The King placed the letter on the table and the Queen picked it up and read it. Her eyes filled with tears as she pushed it over to Mertok.

The King spoke again. 'We shall continue the meeting.'

He took in all who were present and carried on speaking.

Yorda left his room silently and descended the steps to ground level. He sent out a mental command. Out in the paddock Shirrin lifted her head and, turning, trotted towards the rear of the gardens at the royal palace. When she got there Yorda was waiting. He was wearing the clothes that he had had on him when he had first entered the forest of the elves. Shirrin snickered and Yorda stroked her nose. He leapt onto her back and they trotted off towards the east. After a few minutes Yorda stopped Shirrin and lifted his hand. Sweeping it around in a large arc he felt the now familiar tingle in the air. He spurred Shirrin forward and the two of them disappeared as they entered the portal.

Epilogue

Once again the Spellweavers joined minds and created the special bond that only they could have.

THE FIRST: Where is The Third?

THE SECOND: He has not made contact.

THE FOURTH: We cannot concern ourselves with him at this moment.

THE SECOND: Now the boy has become whole we can do nothing.

THE FIRST: We can only continue to watch and record.

Printed in the United Kingdom
by Lightning Source UK Ltd.
134028UK00001B/454-468/P